PENGUIN BOOKS

GROWING UP ETHNIC IN AMERICA

Maria Mazziotti Gillan is the founder and director of the Poetry Center at Passaic County Community College in Paterson, New Jersey, and editor of the *Paterson Literary Review*. With her daughter Jennifer Gillan, she coedited the acclaimed 1994 anthology *Unsettling America: An Anthology of Contemporary Multicultural Poetry* and *Identity Lessons: Contemporary Writing About Leaning to Be American*, published by Penguin in 1999. She is also the author of seven books of poetry, including *Where I Come From: Selected and New Poems* (Guernica), *The Weather of Old Seasons* (Cross Cultural Communications), and *Winter Light*, an American Literary Translator's Award winner. She has had several poems published in *The New York Times*, *The Christian Science Monitor*, and *Poetry Ireland*, as well as in numerous other journals. Awards for her work include the 1998 May Sarton Award, two New Jersey State Council on the Arts fellowships, and a Chester H. Jones Foundation Award. In addition, she was a finalist in the PEN Syndicated Fiction competition. She has appeared on National Public Radio's *All Things Considered*, Leonard Lopate's *Books and Co.*, and Garrison Keillor's *Writer's Almanac*. Her latest book, *Things My Mother Told Me*, was published by Guernica in 1999. Currently, she is at work on a memoir entitled *My Mother's Stoop*.

Jennifer Gillan is an assistant professor in American literature and culture at Bentley College in the Boston area. With Maria Mazziotti Gillan, she coedited the acclaimed anthology *Unsettling America: An Anthology of Contemporary Multicultural Poetry* and *Identity Lessons: Contemporary Writing About Learning to Be American*. She has authored several articles that have appeared in journals including *American Literature*, *American Book Review*, *Arizona Quarterly*, and the Modern Language Association's *Approaches to Teaching* series. She is currently at work on a book, *Ambivalent Ancestries: Critical Perspectives on Chivalry, Rescue, and the Wild West*, a study of the ways in which the concept of chivalric rescue is constructed and contested in narratives of national and literary history.

GROWING UP ETHNIC
IN AMERICA

Contemporary Fiction
About Learning to Be American

EDITED BY MARIA MAZZIOTTI GILLAN
AND JENNIFER GILLAN

Penguin Books

PENGUIN BOOKS
Published by the Penguin Group
Penguin Group (USA) Inc., 375 Hudson Street, New York, New York 10014, U.S.A.
Penguin Books Ltd, 80 Strand, London WC2R 0RL, England
Penguin Books Australia Ltd, 250 Camberwell Road, Camberwell, Victoria 3124, Australia
Penguin Books Canada Ltd, 10 Alcorn Avenue, Toronto, Ontario, Canada M4V 3B2
Penguin Books India (P) Ltd, 11 Community Centre, Panchsheel Park, New Delhi – 110 017, India
Penguin Books (N.Z.) Ltd, Cnr Rosedale and Airborne Roads, Albany, Auckland, New Zealand
Penguin Books (South Africa) (Pty) Ltd, 24 Sturdee Avenue,
Rosebank, Johannesburg 2196, South Africa

Penguin Books Ltd, Registered Offices: 80 Strand, London WC2R 0RL, England

First published in Penguin Books 1999

9 10 8

Copyright © Maria Mazziotti Gillan and Jennifer Gillan, 1999
All rights reserved

Pages 377–379 constitute an extension of this copyright page.

PUBLISHER'S NOTE
These selections are works of fiction. Names, characters, places, and
incidents either are the product of the authors' imagination or are used
fictitiously, and any resemblance to actual persons, living or dead, business
establishments, events, or locales is entirely coincidental.

LIBRARY OF CONGRESS CATALOGING IN PUBLICATION DATA
Growing up ethnic in America : contemporary fiction about learning to
be American / edited by Maria Mazziotti Gillan and Jennifer Gillan.
p. cm.
ISBN 0 14 02.8063 4
1. American fiction—Minority authors. 2. Minority youth—United
States Fiction. 3. Ethnic groups—United States Fiction.
4. Acculturation—United States Fiction. 5. Immigrants—United
States Fiction. 6. Minorities—United States Fiction. 7. American
fiction—20th century. I. Gillan, Maria M. II. Gillan, Jennifer.
PS647.E85G76   1999
813'.54080920693—dc21   99–25762

Printed in the United States of America
Set in Granjon
Designed by Betty Lew

In Loving Memory

Arturo Mazziotti

1906–1998

Contents ❧

NEGOTIATING

BRIDGING

Introduction ∾

Growing up on the Spokane reservation, Sherman Alexie learned to measure himself by the boundaries of a thirteen-inch television screen, proclaiming himself to be a *"Brady Bunch* Indian"; for Sandra Cisneros it was a three-foot Barbie doll that loomed menacingly behind her in every mirror, the doll's hourglass figure and shimmering whiteness helping to shape Cisneros's own brown face into an unacceptable distortion; for Gary Soto it was TV's Cleaver family with their two-story house and finely manicured lawn that haunted his daydreams and reminded him of just how unusual it was in the 1960s to eat burritos for dinner. What Alexie, Cisneros, and Soto have in common is the dislocation and distortion that can accompany growing up ethnic in America. What they also share is a determination to write stories that challenge those images so that the next generation of children can grow up secure in the knowledge that there are many shades and shapes of American faces, many ways to be American.

We have tried to capture this variety of American experience in our selections. We hope that the stories included in *Growing Up Ethnic in America* chronicle how the definitions of what it means to be American are changing. While several of the authors featured in the anthology write about their complicated, and often failed, attempts at assimilation, others tell of gaining strength from the preservation of their ethnic communities. Some recall the alienation they felt growing up; others look back on their childhoods and realize that it was their difference from the norm that helped them to succeed. Most of all, the works in this collection testify to the profound effect ethnic differences have on personal and communal understandings of America and the diversity that is the source of the nation's great discord and its infinite promise.

Our attempt to chronicle this diversity continues the project we began with *Unsettling America: An Anthology of Contemporary Multicultural American Poetry*. Those readers who enjoyed *Unsettling America* and those who shared it with their students have asked often for a companion volume of prose selections. As in our first anthology, we chose writing that deals directly and unflinchingly with the complicated terrain of race and ethnicity in the United States, hoping to suggest that what constitutes American identity is far from settled. In order to open a new space for cross-cultural conversations, we organized the stories so that they spoke to each other across ethnic differences and community conflicts.

The sections into which the book is divided are intended to encourage, rather than stifle, dialogue. Obviously, many of the pieces could easily have been placed elsewhere. Yet through our section groupings we have tried to suggest the stages involved in claiming one's American identity: the attempts to imitate and embody American types under the heading "Performing"; the various border crossings one undertakes in "Crossing"; the sacrifices and exchanges made in order to balance one's multiple cultural allegiances in "Negotiating"; and the attempts to reestablish connections with communities from which one may have withdrawn in "Bridging."

While the selections in *Growing Up Ethnic in America* all are concerned in some way with reenvisioning American identity, many of the writers also chronicle their personal confrontations with American stereotypes and recall how their childhood years were shaped by particular media images and icons. Humorously and poignantly, the contributors to this collection describe how they have performed and imitated these American identities. As a nation of immigrants, Americans have always had to invent an identity and a common past for themselves. This search for the essence of "Americanness" continues even though the actual diversity of our national population prohibits such uniformity. Unfortunately, instead of accepting this diversity as healthy and the lack of static cultural definitions as enabling, Americans have often fought bitter battles over what it means to be American and who exactly gets to qualify under the umbrella term.

The "average American," depicted in the media as blandly middle-class, has been represented by such TV families as the Cleavers and the Bradys. Certainly, most Americans, even those who fit the assumed "average American" racial and class profile—middle-class, white, Anglo-Saxon Protestants—have measured themselves against these kinds of families and found their own wanting. Clearly, apart from media fiction, the perfectly well-adjusted mainstream American does not exist. Yet the Americanness of immigrants, African Americans, and Native American Indians is often assessed in terms of the degree to which they resemble the fictional composite. Of course, embodying that figure is impossible, but that hasn't stopped people from trying. The irony is that while generations of Americans have been frustrated at their failure to resemble icons such as John Wayne and Marilyn Monroe, even Marion Morrison and Norma Jean Baker, the real-life counterparts to those public personas, could not measure up to their screen images.

Not aware of such ironies, the narrator of Gary Soto's humorous story "Looking for Work" sincerely believes that TV families such as the Andersons of *Father Knows Best* fame are the norm. He is frustrated that his family won't even try to be like the families on TV. He pleads with them to at least wear shoes to dinner. His brother responds by donning swim trunks and his sister by swearing during their next family meal. His family's inability to see the important relation between looking like Americans and "being liked" by Americans baffles the boy. Commenting on this correlation between appearance and success, Bebe Moore Campbell explores the impact such a mythology has on poor children. The narrator in her story "The Best Deal in America" develops an "uncontrollable urge to decorate her life with shiny new things." When she test-drives a new sports car, she even imagines herself to be playing the Diana Ross part in the film *Mahogany*.

In E. L. Doctorow's "The Writer in the Family," such role-playing is forced on Jonathan, the story's narrator. When his father dies suddenly, Jonathan is asked by his aunt to compose fictional letters to his ailing grandmother in which he pretends not only that he is his father, but that the whole family has moved to Arizona for health and business reasons. These fictional letters convince Jonathan's grandmother that her son, who was in actuality just a salesman who never even left New York City, has finally "made it" in the business world. After writing several letters, Jonathan also sees his father from a different perspective; gradually, he understands his father's frustrations about his lack of success and how that disappointment was connected to the icons against which he measured himself.

On another level, Doctorow's story is about the way becoming a writer often places one outside the community. In the New York Jewish community out of which he writes, kin groups are valued over self, and family secrecy above all. As a writer who wants to capture the truth of his father's experience, Jonathan is berated by his aunt because he seems to have betrayed the family secrets. To some extent, all of the contributors in this anthology have experienced a similar alienation as writers, usually compounded by the outsider status bestowed upon them by their ethnicity.

Indeed, the narrator of Nash Candelaria's "The Day the Cisco Kid Shot John Wayne" perceives himself as an alien in his own community when he is finally able to see his own actions and culture critically. In the story, Candelaria describes how a group of Chicanos attend Saturday matinees and form a club called "Los Indios" that celebrates the Indian and Mexican characters in Hollywood Westerns by shouting insults at the cowboys and pioneer heroes. As an adult, however, the narrator realizes that even John Wayne defied the scripted stereotypes he so effectively established. With that realization, the narrator recognizes how many transformations he has undergone and how much more complicated is the American border culture in which he lives than the one represented on the screen.

As Candelaria's story demonstrates, American performances often require a movement between identities and cultures. His story acknowledges the way we all must "cross over" cultural, linguistic, and actual bridges in our attempts to embody an American identity. Such crossings can be physical—leaving one's community and entering another—or biological—maturing from child to adolescent to adult. These physical transitions of growing up can be confusing and painful enough for the average adolescent without the added burden of a cultural transition.

Such cultural transitions may be dealt with differently by writers from the same community. To this end, we placed Lynne Sharon Schwartz's "Killing the Bees," Liz Rosenberg's "Magic," and Daniel Asa Rose's "The Cossacks of Connecticut" in the same section because all three confront, albeit in very different ways, the difficulties of growing up Jewish in a Christian suburb. While each of these writers also touches on the complexities of friendships that cross racial and ethnic lines, this issue is more fully explored in Judith Ortiz Cofer's "American History." As several other selections, including those by Mary Bucci Bush, Bruce A. Jacobs, and Simon J. Ortiz, also probe the complexities of such relationships, any two can be usefully compared. Through this emphasis on inter- and intracultural dialogue among writers on similar topics, we have tried to show that conversations about race and ethnicity are not only possible, but also necessary.

Often, the cultural crossings many adolescents undertake are so confusing that they cannot articulate their feelings about the transition. As the children in Sandra Cisneros's "Mericans" feel themselves becoming more Americanized, they feel less able to communicate their feelings to their families. They recognize that once they cross over to mainstream culture, they have to decide how often to go back or whether such a return is even possible. Caught between cultures, they have to sacrifice some of one in order to gain part of the other. The stories that deal with such cultural negotiations are some of the most poignant in the book as they reveal the price one must pay for "switching sides." Afaa Michael Weaver tells the story in "Honey Boy" of a group of boys who decide to abandon the African American swimming pool in their neighborhood and venture to the white pool on the other side of town. Forced to negotiate the turbulent waters of racial integration, they pay a dear price for transgressing these boundaries.

As schools are more often the place in which racial integration occurs, it is not surprising that there is an abundance of writing on the topic. We have collected a separate anthology of school experiences entitled *Identity Lessons* (Penguin, 1999), but have included a few pieces here that deal with the issues as well. Nash Candelaria, Gish Jen, and Laura Boss examine the degree to which children feel the pressure to assimilate most intensely in the school system. Because of how

American these children become, a rift often develops between them and their parents. This rift is described in Maria Mazziotti Gillan's story about a mother who listens to talk radio in order to bridge the ever-widening gap between her Americanized children and herself. Beena Kamlani also explores this tension in "Brandy Cake," a story about an Indian American girl's attempt to negotiate divergent social and sexual standards. This story unflinchingly explores the repressive features of both the Indian and American communities. Kamlani, like other writers in this collection, does not slip into a simplistic idealization of ethnicity and is willing to represent the unflattering aspects of her communities.

Despite all the dislocation that growing up ethnic in America may cause, many writers look back fondly on their childhoods. As adults, they often want to construct bridges back to those communities they once desired to leave behind. Writers who reclaim their own difference unsettle standard notions of what constitutes American culture. In Fred L. Gardaphé's "Grandpa's 'Chicaudies,' " for example, the main character moves from a feeling of shame that his grandfather picks "weeds" to cook for dinner to wonder at his grandfather's tenacity for holding on to his own cultural practices despite the ever-encroaching assembly-line culture of frozen dinners and TV sitcoms. Gardaphé's story indicates that in the rush to embrace America, people often fail to appreciate their own cultural riches. Like Gardaphé, many other writers wonder how much of their own cultural difference they sacrificed as they plunged headfirst into murky American cultural waters. Because ethnic enclaves can provide safe havens in which the language and value system are comfortably familiar, those neighborhoods can become even more cherished, even the places for which one nostalgically yearns, especially after one is forced to leave them behind to attend school and engage in social activities outside the community.

We hoped to avoid this nostalgia by including stories such as Sherman Alexie's "This Is What It Means to Say Phoenix, Arizona" that offer believable and inspiring balances between the old identities and the new.

Part of this balance involves a special kind of vision afforded to those on the outskirts of society. From the vantage point of the outsider, it may be easier to see beyond limited cultural assumptions and analyze American culture more critically. This ability to travel between two worlds affords one the kind of perspective that is necessary for both personal growth and empathy for others. Indeed, learning to see others from their points of view is necessary to foster understanding across and among cultures and generations. To capture this spirit, *Growing Up Ethnic in America* concludes with Helena María Viramontes's "The Moths" and Sylvia A. Watanabe's "Talking to the Dead," both accounts of young people who become more connected with their ancestry by caring for a dying relative. These final stories provide a bridge to those in the book's first section since they are concerned with the difficult cultural negotiations one must undergo to become an American individual while still retaining one's cultural heritage.

Throughout this anthology, we have tried to weave a dialogue through the way the stories are arranged, choosing those that seem provocative and inspiring as well as complementary to each other. We hope this organization helps the reader to consider the implications of multiple perspectives on each issue. The juxtaposition of the stories often produces a conversation that reflects the enormous gulf existing among those who often share the same public space. Our hope is that the tension that this conversation generates is productive. Where dialogue is most needed in America—across subway aisles, across stereotypes, across cultural antagonisms—these stories respond.

In the end, it is Martin Luther King Jr.'s philosophy of bringing hidden tension to the surface, out "into the open where it can be seen and dealt with," that is the impetus for this anthology. We challenge and encourage its readers to value the experience of ethnic America, to confront the significance of the history of racial conflict and ethnic diversity in the United States, and to understand the ways that race and ethnicity have shaped the identity of our nation.

Jennifer Gillan
Cambridge, Massachusetts

Performing

The Writer in the Family

E. L. DOCTOROW

In 1955 my father died with his ancient mother still alive in a nursing home. The old lady was ninety and hadn't even known he was ill. Thinking the shock might kill her, my aunts told her that he had moved to Arizona for his bronchitis. To the immigrant generation of my grandmother, Arizona was the American equivalent of the Alps, it was where you went for your health. More accurately, it was where you went if you had the money. Since my father had failed in all the business enterprises of his life, this was the aspect of the news my grandmother dwelled on, that he had finally had some success. And so it came about that as we mourned him at home in our stocking feet, my grandmother was bragging to her cronies about her son's new life in the dry air of the desert.

My aunts had decided on their course of action without consulting us. It meant neither my mother nor my brother nor I could visit Grandma because we were supposed to have moved west too, a family, after all. My brother Harold and I didn't mind—it was always a nightmare at the old people's home, where they all sat around staring at us while we tried to make conversation with Grandma. She looked terrible, had numbers of ailments, and her mind wandered. Not seeing her was no disappointment either for my mother, who had never gotten along with the old woman and did not visit when she could have. But what was disturbing was that my aunts had acted in the manner of that side of the family of

making government on everyone's behalf, the true citizens by
blood and the lesser citizens by marriage. It was exactly this
attitude that had tormented my mother all her married life.
She claimed Jack's family had never accepted her. She had
battled them for twenty-five years as an outsider.

A few weeks after the end of our ritual mourning my
Aunt Frances phoned us from her home in Larchmont. Aunt
Frances was the wealthier of my father's sisters. Her husband was a lawyer, and both her sons were at Amherst. She
had called to say that Grandma was asking why she
didn't hear from Jack. I had answered the phone. "You're the
writer in the family," my aunt said. "Your father had so
much faith in you. Would you mind making up something?
Send it to me and I'll read it to her. She won't know the difference."

That evening, at the kitchen table, I pushed my homework
aside and composed a letter. I tried to imagine my father's response to his new life. He had never been west. He had never
traveled anywhere. In his generation the great journey was
from the working class to the professional class. He hadn't
managed that either. But he loved New York, where he had
been born and lived his life, and he was always discovering
new things about it. He especially loved the old parts of the
city below Canal Street, where he would find ships' chandlers
or firms that wholesaled in spices and teas. He was a salesman for an appliance jobber with accounts all over the city.
He liked to bring home rare cheeses or exotic foreign vegetables that were sold only in certain neighborhoods. Once he
brought home a barometer, another time an antique ship's
telescope in a wooden case with a brass snap.

"Dear Mama," I wrote. "Arizona is beautiful. The sun
shines all day and the air is warm and I feel better than I have
in years. The desert is not as barren as you would expect, but
filled with wildflowers and cactus plants and peculiar

crooked trees that look like men holding their arms out. You can see great distances in whatever direction you turn and to the west is a range of mountains maybe fifty miles from here, but in the morning with the sun on them you can see the snow on their crests."

My aunt called some days later and told me it was when she read this letter aloud to the old lady that the full effect of Jack's death came over her. She had to excuse herself and went out in the parking lot to cry. "I wept so," she said. "I felt such terrible longing for him. You're so right, he loved to go places, he loved life, he loved everything."

We began trying to organize our lives. My father had borrowed money against his insurance and there was very little left. Some commissions were still due but it didn't look as if his firm would honor them. There was a couple of thousand dollars in a savings bank that had to be maintained there until the estate was settled. The lawyer involved was Aunt Frances's husband and he was very proper. "The estate!" my mother muttered, gesturing as if to pull out her hair. "The estate!" She applied for a job part-time in the admissions office of the hospital where my father's terminal illness had been diagnosed, and where he had spent some months until they had sent him home to die. She knew a lot of the doctors and staff and she had learned "from bitter experience," as she told them, about the hospital routine. She was hired.

I hated that hospital, it was dark and grim and full of tortured people. I thought it was masochistic of my mother to seek out a job there, but did not tell her so.

We lived in an apartment on the corner of 175th Street and the Grand Concourse, one flight up. Three rooms. I shared the bedroom with my brother. It was jammed with furniture because when my father had required a hospital bed in the last weeks of his illness we had moved some of the living-room pieces into the bedroom and made over the living room for him. We had to navigate bookcases, beds, a gateleg table, bureaus, a record player and radio console, stacks of 78 albums, my brother's trombone and music stand, and so on. My mother continued to sleep on the convertible sofa in the living room that had been their bed before his illness. The two rooms were connected by a narrow hall made even narrower by bookcases along the wall. Off the hall were a small kitchen and dinette and a bathroom. There were lots of appliances in the kitchen—broiler, toaster, pressure cooker, countertop dishwasher, blender—that my father had gotten through his job, at cost. A treasured phrase in our house: *at cost.* But most of these fixtures went unused because my mother did not care for them. Chromium devices with timers or gauges that required the reading of elaborate instructions were not for her. They were in part responsible for the awful clutter of our lives and now she wanted to get rid of them. "We're being buried," she said. "Who needs them!"

So we agreed to throw out or sell anything inessential. While I found boxes for the appliances and my brother tied the boxes with twine, my mother opened my father's closet and took out his clothes. He had several suits because as a salesman he needed to look his best. My mother wanted us to try on his suits to see which of them could be altered and used. My brother refused to try them on. I tried on one jacket which was too large for me. The lining inside the sleeves chilled my arms and the vaguest scent of my father's being came to me.

"This is way too big," I said.

"Don't worry," my mother said. "I had it cleaned. Would I let you wear it if I hadn't?"

It was the evening, the end of winter, and snow was coming down on the windowsill and melting as it settled. The ceiling bulb glared on a pile of my father's suits and trousers on hangers flung across the bed in the shape of a dead man. We refused to try on anything more, and my mother began to cry.

"What are you crying for?" my brother shouted. "You wanted to get rid of things, didn't you?"

A few weeks later my aunt phoned again and said she thought it would be necessary to have another letter from Jack. Grandma had fallen out of her chair and bruised herself and was very depressed.

"How long does this go on?" my mother said.

"It's not so terrible," my aunt said, "for the little time left to make things easier for her."

My mother slammed down the phone. "He can't even die when he wants to!" she cried. "Even death comes second to Mama! What are they afraid of, the shock will kill her? Nothing can kill her. She's indestructible! A stake through the heart couldn't kill her!"

When I sat down in the kitchen to write the letter I found it more difficult than the first one. "Don't watch me," I said to my brother. "It's hard enough."

"You don't have to do something just because someone wants you to," Harold said. He was two years older than me and had started at City College; but when my father became ill he had switched to night school and gotten a job in a record store.

"Dear Mama," I wrote. "I hope you're feeling well. We're all fit as a fiddle. The life here is good and the people are very friendly and informal. Nobody wears suits and ties here. Just a pair of slacks and a short-sleeved shirt. Perhaps a sweater in the evening. I have bought into a very successful radio and record business and I'm doing very well. You remember

Jack's Electric, my old place on Forty-third Street? Well, now it's Jack's Arizona Electric and we have a line of television sets as well."

I sent that letter off to my Aunt Frances, and as we all knew she would, she phoned soon after. My brother held his hand over the mouthpiece. "It's Frances with her latest review," he said.

"Jonathan? You're a very talented young man. I just wanted to tell you what a blessing your letter was. Her whole face lit up when I read the part about Jack's store. That would be an excellent way to continue."

"Well, I hope I don't have to do this anymore, Aunt Frances. It's not very honest."

Her tone changed. "Is your mother there? Let me talk to her."

"She's not here," I said.

"Tell her not to worry," my aunt said. "A poor old lady who has never wished anything but the best for her will soon die."

I did not repeat this to my mother, for whom it would have been one more in the family anthology of unforgivable remarks. But then I had to suffer it myself for the possible truth it might embody. Each side defended its position with rhetoric, but I, who wanted peace, rationalized the snubs and rebuffs each inflicted on the other, taking no stands, like my father himself.

Years ago his life had fallen into a pattern of business failures and missed opportunities. The great debate between his family on one side, and my mother Ruth on the other, was this: who was responsible for the fact that he had not lived up to anyone's expectations?

As to the prophecies, when spring came my mother's prevailed. Grandma was still alive.

One balmy Sunday my mother and brother and I took the

PERFORMING | 9

bus to the Beth El cemetery in New Jersey to visit my father's grave. It was situated on a slight rise. We stood looking over rolling fields embedded with monuments. Here and there processions of black cars wound their way through the lanes, or clusters of people stood at open graves. My father's grave was planted with tiny shoots of evergreen but it lacked a headstone. We had chosen one and paid for it and then the stonecutters had gone on strike. Without a headstone my father did not seem to be honorably dead. He didn't seem to me properly buried.

My mother gazed at the plot beside his, reserved for her coffin. "They were always too fine for other people," she said. "Even in the old days on Stanton Street. They put on airs. Nobody was ever good enough for them. Finally Jack himself was not good enough for them. Except to get them things wholesale. Then he was good enough for them."

"Mom, please," my brother said.

"If I had known. Before I ever met him he was tied to his mama's apron strings. And Essie's apron strings were like chains, let me tell you. We had to live where we could be near them for the Sunday visits. Every Sunday, that was my life, a visit to mamaleh. Whatever she knew I wanted, a better apartment, a stick of furniture, a summer camp for the boys, she spoke against it. You know your father, every decision had to be considered and reconsidered. And nothing changed. Nothing ever changed."

She began to cry. We sat her down on a nearby bench. My brother walked off and read the names on stones. I looked at my mother, who was crying, and I went off after my brother.

"Mom's still crying," I said. "Shouldn't we do something?"

"It's all right," he said. "It's what she came here for."

"Yes," I said, and then a sob escaped from my throat. "But I feel like crying too."

My brother Harold put his arm around me. "Look at this old black stone here," he said. "The way it's carved. You can see the changing fashion in monuments—just like everything else."

Somewhere in this time I began dreaming of my father. Not the robust father of my childhood, the handsome man with healthy pink skin and brown eyes and a mustache and the thinning hair parted in the middle. My dead father. We were taking him home from the hospital. It was understood that he had come back from death. This was amazing and joyous. On the other hand, he was terribly mysteriously damaged, or, more accurately, spoiled and unclean. He was very yellowed and debilitated by his death, and there were no guarantees that he wouldn't soon die again. He seemed aware of this and his entire personality was changed. He was angry and impatient with all of us. We were trying to help him in some way, struggling to get him home, but something prevented us, something we had to fix, a tattered suitcase that had sprung open, some mechanical thing: he had a car but it wouldn't start; or the car was made of wood; or his clothes, which had become too large for him, had caught in the door. In one version he was all bandaged and as we tried to lift him from his wheelchair into a taxi the bandage began to unroll and catch in the spokes of the wheelchair. This seemed to be some unreasonableness on his part. My mother looked on sadly and tried to get him to cooperate.

That was the dream. I shared it with no one. Once when I woke, crying out, my brother turned on the light. He wanted to know what I'd been dreaming but I pretended I didn't remember. The dream made me feel guilty. I felt guilty *in* the dream too because my enraged father knew we didn't want to live with him. The dream represented us taking him home, or trying to, but it was nevertheless understood by all of us that he was to live alone. He was this derelict back from death, but what we were doing was taking him to some place where he would live by himself without help from anyone until he died again.

At one point I became so fearful of this dream that I tried not to go to sleep. I tried to think of good things about my father and to remember him before his illness. He used to call me "matey." "Hello, matey," he would say when he came home from work. He always wanted us to go someplace—to the store, to the park, to a ball game. He loved to walk. When I went walking with him he would say: "Hold your shoulders back, don't slump. Hold your head up and look at the world. Walk as if you meant it!" As he strode down the street his shoulders moved from side to side, as if he was hearing some kind of cakewalk. He moved with a bounce. He was always eager to see what was around the corner.

The next request for a letter coincided with a special occasion in the house. My brother Harold had met a girl he liked and had gone out with her several times. Now she was coming to our house for dinner.

We had prepared for this for days, cleaning everything in sight, giving the house a going-over, washing the dust of disuse from the glasses and good dishes. My mother came home early from work to get the dinner going. We opened the gateleg table in the living room and brought in the kitchen chairs. My mother spread the table with a laundered white cloth and put out her silver. It was the first family occasion since my father's illness.

I liked my brother's girlfriend a lot. She was a thin girl with very straight hair and she had a terrific smile. Her presence seemed to excite the air. It was amazing to have a living breathing girl in our house. She looked around and what she said was: "Oh, I've never seen so many books!" While she and my brother sat at the table my mother was in the kitchen putting the food into serving bowls and I was going from the kitchen to the living room, kidding around like a waiter, with a white cloth over my arm and a high style of service, placing the serving dish of green beans on the table with a flourish. In the kitchen my mother's eyes were sparkling. She looked at me and nodded and mimed the words: "She's adorable!"

My brother suffered himself to be waited on. He was wary of what we might say. He kept glancing at the girl—her name was Susan—to see if we met with her approval. She worked in an insurance office and was taking courses in accounting at City College. Harold was under a terrible strain but he was excited and happy too. He had bought a bottle of Concord grape wine to go with the roast chicken. He held up his glass and proposed a toast. My mother said: "To good health and happiness," and we all drank, even I. At that moment the phone rang and I went into the bedroom to get it.

"Jonathan? This is your Aunt Frances. How is everyone?"

"Fine, thank you."

"I want to ask one last favor of you. I need a letter from Jack. Your grandma's very ill. Do you think you can?"

"Who is it?" my mother called from the living room.

"OK, Aunt Frances," I said quickly. "I have to go now, we're eating dinner." And I hung up the phone.

"It was my friend Louie," I said, sitting back down. "He didn't know the math pages to review."

The dinner was very fine. Harold and Susan washed the dishes and by the time they were done my mother and I had folded up the gateleg table and put it back against the wall and I had swept the crumbs up with the carpet sweeper. We all sat and talked and listened to records for a while and then my brother took Susan home. The evening had gone very well.

Once when my mother wasn't home my brother had pointed out something: the letters from Jack weren't really necessary. "What is this ritual?" he said, holding his palms up. "Grandma is almost totally blind, she's half deaf and crippled. Does the situation really call for a literary composition? Does it need verisimilitude? Would the old lady know the difference if she was read the phone book?"

"Then why did Aunt Frances ask me?"

"That is the question, Jonathan. Why did she? After all, she could write the letter herself—what difference would it make? And if not Frances, why not Frances's sons, the Amherst students? They should have learned by now to write."

"But they're not Jack's sons," I said.

"That's exactly the point," my brother said. "The idea is *service*. Dad used to bust his balls getting them things wholesale, getting them deals on things. Frances of Westchester really needed things at cost. And Aunt Molly. And Aunt Molly's husband, and Aunt Molly's ex-husband. Grandma, if she needed an errand done. He was always on the hook for something. They never thought his time was important. They never thought every favor he got was one he had to pay back. Appliances, records, watches, china, opera tickets, any goddamn thing. Call Jack."

"It was a matter of pride to him to be able to do things for them," I said. "To have connections."

"Yeah, I wonder why," my brother said. He looked out the window.

Then suddenly it dawned on me that I was being implicated.

"You should use your head more," my brother said.

ϾϪϿ

Yet I had agreed once again to write a letter from the desert and so I did. I mailed it off to Aunt Frances. A few days later, when I came home from school, I thought I saw her sitting in her car in front of our house. She drove a black Buick Roadmaster, a very large clean car with whitewall tires. It was Aunt Frances all right. She blew the horn when she saw me. I went over and leaned in at the window.

"Hello, Jonathan," she said. "I haven't long. Can you get in the car?"

"Mom's not home," I said. "She's working."

"I know that. I came to talk to you."

"Would you like to come upstairs?"

"I can't, I have to get back to Larchmont. Can you get in for a moment, please?"

I got in the car. My Aunt Frances was a very pretty white-haired woman, very elegant, and she wore tasteful clothes. I had always liked her and from the time I was a child she had enjoyed pointing out to everyone that I looked more like her son than Jack's. She wore white gloves and held the steering wheel and looked straight ahead as she talked, as if the car was in traffic and not sitting at the curb.

"Jonathan," she said, "there is your letter on the seat. Needless to say I didn't read it to Grandma. I'm giving it back to you and I won't ever say a word to anyone. This is just between us. I never expected cruelty from you. I never thought you were capable of doing something so deliberately cruel and perverse."

I said nothing.

"Your mother has very bitter feelings and now I see she has poisoned you with them. She has always resented the family. She is a very strong-willed, selfish person."

"No she isn't," I said.

"I wouldn't expect you to agree. She drove poor Jack crazy

with her demands. She always had the highest aspirations and he could never fulfill them to her satisfaction. When he still had his store he kept your mother's brother, who drank, on salary. After the war when he began to make a little money he had to buy Ruth a mink jacket because she was so desperate to have one. He had debts to pay but she wanted a mink. He was a very special person, my brother, he should have accomplished something special, but he loved your mother and devoted his life to her. And all she ever thought about was keeping up with the Joneses."

I watched the traffic going up the Grand Concourse. A bunch of kids were waiting at the bus stop at the corner. They had put their books on the ground and were horsing around.

"I'm sorry I have to descend to this," Aunt Frances said. "I don't like talking about people this way. If I have nothing good to say about someone, I'd rather not say anything. How is Harold?"

"Fine."

"Did he help you write this marvelous letter?"

"No."

After a moment she said more softly: "How are you all getting along?"

"Fine."

"I would invite you up for Passover if I thought your mother would accept."

I didn't answer.

She turned on the engine. "I'll say good-bye now, Jonathan. Take your letter. I hope you give some time to thinking about what you've done."

That evening when my mother came home from work I saw that she wasn't as pretty as my Aunt Frances. I usually thought my mother was a good-looking woman, but I saw now that she was too heavy and that her hair was undistinguished.

"Why are you looking at me?" she said.

"I'm not."

"I learned something interesting today," my mother said. "We may be eligible for a VA pension because of the time your father spent in the Navy."

That took me by surprise. Nobody had ever told me my father was in the Navy.

"In World War I," she said, "he went to Webb's Naval Academy on the Harlem River. He was training to be an ensign. But the war ended and he never got his commission."

After dinner the three of us went through the closets looking for my father's papers, hoping to find some proof that could be filed with the Veterans Administration. We came up with two things, a Victory medal, which my brother said everyone got for being in the service during the Great War, and an astounding sepia photograph of my father and his shipmates on the deck of a ship. They were dressed in bell-bottoms and T-shirts and armed with mops and pails, brooms and brushes.

"I never knew this," I found myself saying. "I never knew this."

"You just don't remember," my brother said.

I was able to pick out my father. He stood at the end of the row, a thin, handsome boy with a full head of hair, a mustache, and an intelligent smiling countenance.

"He had a joke," my mother said. "They called their training ship the S.S. *Constipation* because it never moved."

Neither the picture nor the medal was proof of anything, but my brother thought a duplicate of my father's service record had to be in Washington somewhere and that it was just a matter of learning how to go about finding it.

"The pension wouldn't amount to much," my mother said. "Twenty or thirty dollars. But it would certainly help."

I took the picture of my father and his shipmates and

propped it against the lamp at my bedside. I looked into his youthful face and tried to relate it to the Father I knew. I looked at the picture a long time. Only gradually did my eye connect it to the set of Great Sea Novels in the bottom shelf of the bookcase a few feet away. My father had given that set to me: it was uniformly bound in green with gilt lettering and it included works by Melville, Conrad, Victor Hugo, and Captain Marryat. And lying across the top of the books, jammed in under the sagging shelf above, was his old ship's telescope in its wooden case with the brass snap.

I thought how stupid, and imperceptive, and self-centered I had been never to have understood while he was alive what my father's dream for his life had been.

On the other hand, I had written in my last letter from Arizona—the one that had so angered Aunt Frances—something that might allow me, the writer in the family, to soften my judgment of myself. I will conclude by giving the letter here in its entirety.

Dear Mama,

This will be my final letter to you since I have been told by the doctors that I am dying.

I have sold my store at a very fine profit and am sending Frances a check for five thousand dollars to be deposited in your account. My present to you, Mamaleh. Let Frances show you the passbook.

As for the nature of my ailment, the doctors haven't told me what it is, but I know that I am simply dying of the wrong life. I should never have come to the desert. It wasn't the place for me.

I have asked Ruth and the boys to have my body cremated and the ashes scattered in the ocean.

Your loving son,
Jack

Rules of the Game

AMY TAN

I was six when my mother taught me the art of invisible strength. It was a strategy for winning arguments, respect from others, and eventually, though neither of us knew it at the time, chess games.

"Bite back your tongue," scolded my mother when I cried loudly, yanking her hand toward the store that sold bags of salted plums. At home, she said, "Wise guy, he not go against wind. In Chinese we say, Come from South, blow with wind—poom!—North will follow. Strongest wind cannot be seen."

The next week I bit back my tongue as we entered the store with the forbidden candies. When my mother finished her shopping, she quietly plucked a small bag of plums from the rack and put it on the counter with the rest of the items.

My mother imparted her daily truths so she could help my older brothers and me rise above our circumstances. We lived in San Francisco's Chinatown. Like most of the other Chinese children who played in the back alleys of restaurants and curio shops, I didn't think we were poor. My bowl was always full, three five-course meals every day, beginning with a soup full of mysterious things I didn't want to know the names of.

We lived on Waverly Place, in a warm, clean, two-bedroom flat that sat above a small Chinese bakery specializing in steamed pastries and dim sum. In the early morning, when the alley was still quiet, I could smell fragrant red beans as they were cooked down to a pasty sweetness. By daybreak, our flat was heavy with the odor of fried sesame balls and sweet curried chicken crescents. From my bed, I would listen as my father got ready for work, then locked the door behind him, one-two-three clicks.

At the end of our two-block alley was a small sandlot playground with swings and slides well-shined down the middle with use. The play area was bordered by wood-slat benches where old-country people sat cracking roasted watermelon seeds with their golden teeth and scattering the husks to an impatient gathering of gurgling pigeons. The best playground, however, was the dark alley itself. It was crammed with daily mysteries and adventures. My brothers and I would peer into the medicinal herb shop, watching old Li dole out onto a stiff sheet of white paper the right amount of insect shells, saffron-colored seeds, and pungent leaves for his ailing customers. It was said that he once cured a woman dying of an ancestral curse that had eluded the best of American doctors. Next to the pharmacy was a printer who specialized in gold-embossed wedding invitations and festive red banners.

Farther down the street was Ping Yuen Fish Market. The front window displayed a tank crowded with doomed fish and turtles struggling to gain footing on the slimy green-tiled sides. A handwritten sign informed tourists, "Within this store, is all for food, not for pet." Inside, the butchers with their bloodstained white smocks deftly gutted the fish while customers cried out their orders and shouted, "Give me your freshest," to which the butchers always protested, "All are freshest." On less crowded market days, we would inspect the crates of live frogs and crabs which we were warned not to poke, boxes of dried cuttlefish, and row upon row of iced prawns, squid, and slippery fish. The sand dabs made me shiver each time; their eyes lay on one flattened side and reminded me of my mother's story of a careless girl who ran into a crowded street and was crushed by a cab. "Was smash flat," reported my mother.

At the corner of the alley was Hong Sing's, a four-table café with a recessed stairwell in front that led to a door marked "Tradesmen." My brothers and I believed the bad people emerged from this door at night. Tourists never went to Hong Sing's, since the menu was printed only in Chinese. A Caucasian man with a big camera once posed me and my playmates in front of the restaurant. He had us move to the side of the picture window so the photo would capture the roasted duck with its head dangling from a juice-covered rope. After he took the picture, I told him he should go into Hong Sing's and eat dinner. When he smiled and asked me what they served, I shouted, "Guts and duck's feet and octopus gizzards!" Then I ran off with my friends, shrieking with laughter as we scampered across the alley and hid in the entryway grotto of the China Gem Company, my heart pounding with hope that he would chase us.

My mother named me after the street that we lived on: Waverly Place Jong, my official name for important American documents. But my family called me Meimei, "Little Sister." I was the youngest, the only daughter. Each morning before school, my mother would twist and yank on my thick black hair until she had formed two tightly wound pigtails. One day, as she struggled to weave a hard-toothed comb through my disobedient hair, I had a sly thought.

I asked her, "Ma, what is Chinese torture?" My mother shook her head. A bobby pin was wedged between her lips. She wetted her palm and smoothed the hair above my ear, then pushed the pin in so that it nicked sharply against my scalp.

"Who say this word?" she asked without a trace of knowing how wicked I was being. I shrugged my shoulders and said, "Some boy in my class said Chinese people do Chinese torture."

"Chinese people do many things," she said simply. "Chinese people do business, do medicine, do painting. Not lazy like American people. We do torture. Best torture."

My older brother Vincent was the one who actually got the chess set. We had gone to the annual Christmas party held at the First Chinese Baptist Church at the end of the alley. The missionary ladies had put together a Santa bag of gifts donated by members of another church. None of the gifts had names on them. There were separate sacks for boys and girls of different ages.

One of the Chinese parishioners had donned a Santa Claus costume and a stiff paper beard with cotton balls glued to it. I think the only children who thought he was the real thing were too young to know that Santa Claus was not Chinese. When my turn came up, the Santa man asked me how old I was. I thought it was a trick question; I was seven according to the American formula and eight by the Chinese calendar. I said I was born on March 17, 1951. That seemed to satisfy him. He then solemnly asked if I had been a very, very good girl this year and did I believe in Jesus Christ and obey my parents. I knew the only answer to that. I nodded back with equal solemnity.

Having watched the other children opening their gifts, I already knew that the big gifts were not necessarily the nicest ones. One girl my age got a large coloring book of biblical characters, while a less greedy girl who selected a smaller box received a glass vial of lavender toilet water. The sound of the box was also important. A ten-year-old boy had chosen a box that jangled when he shook it. It was a tin globe of the world with a slit for inserting money. He must have thought it was full of dimes and nickels, because when he saw that it had just ten pennies, his face fell with such undisguised disappointment that his mother slapped the side of his head and led him out of the church hall, apologizing to the crowd for her son who had such bad manners he couldn't appreciate such a fine gift.

As I peered into the sack, I quickly fingered the remaining presents, testing their weight, imagining what they contained. I chose a heavy, compact one that was wrapped in shiny silver foil and red satin ribbon. It was a twelve-pack of Life Savers and I spent the rest of the party arranging and rearranging the candy tubes in the order of my favorites. My brother Winston chose wisely as well. His present turned out to be a box of intricate plastic parts; the instructions on the box proclaimed that when they were properly assembled he would have an authentic miniature replica of a World War II submarine.

Vincent got the chess set, which would have been a very decent present to get at a church Christmas party, except it was obviously used and, as we discovered later, it was missing a black pawn and a white knight. My mother graciously thanked the unknown benefactor, saying, "Too good. Cost too much." At which point, an old lady with fine white, wispy hair nodded toward our family and said with a whistling whisper, "Merry, merry Christmas."

When we got home, my mother told Vincent to throw the chess set away. "She not want it. We not want it," she said, tossing her head stiffly to the side with a tight, proud smile. My brothers had deaf ears. They were already lining up the chess pieces and reading from the dog-eared instruction book.

I watched Vincent and Winston play during Christmas week. The chessboard seemed to hold elaborate secrets waiting to be untangled. The chessmen were more powerful than old Li's magic herbs that cured ancestral curses. And my brothers wore such serious faces that I was sure something was at stake that was greater than avoiding the tradesmen's door to Hong Sing's.

"Let me! Let me!" I begged between games when one brother or the other would sit back with a deep sigh of relief and victory, the other annoyed, unable to let go of the outcome. Vincent at first refused to let me play, but when I offered my Life Savers as replacements for the buttons that filled in for the missing pieces, he relented. He chose the flavors: wild cherry for the black pawn and peppermint for the white knight. Winner could eat both.

As our mother sprinkled flour and rolled out small doughy circles for the steamed dumplings that would be our dinner that night, Vincent explained the rules, pointing to each piece. "You have sixteen pieces and so do I. One king and queen, two bishops, two knights, two castles, and eight pawns. The pawns can only move forward one step, except on the first move. Then they can move two. But they can only take men by moving crossways like this, except in the beginning, when you can move ahead and take another pawn."

"Why?" I asked as I moved my pawn. "Why can't they move more steps?"

"Because they're pawns," he said.

"But why do they go crossways to take other men? Why aren't there any women and children?"

"Why is the sky blue? Why must you always ask stupid questions?" asked Vincent. "This is a game. These are the rules. I didn't make them up. See. Here. In the book." He jabbed a page with a pawn in his hand. "Pawn. P-A-W-N. Pawn. Read it yourself."

My mother patted the flour off her hands. "Let me see book," she said quietly. She scanned the pages quickly, not reading the foreign English symbols, seeming to search deliberately for nothing in particular.

"This American rules," she concluded at last. "Every time people come out from foreign country, must know rules. You not know, judge say, Too bad, go back. They not telling you why so you can use their way go forward. They say, Don't know why, you find out yourself. But they knowing all the time. Better you take it, find out why yourself." She tossed her head back with a satisfied smile.

I found out about all the whys later. I read the rules and looked up all the big words in a dictionary. I borrowed books from the Chinatown library. I studied each chess piece, trying to absorb the power each contained.

I learned about opening moves and why it's important to control the center early on; the shortest distance between two points is straight down the middle. I learned about the middle game and why tactics between two adversaries are like clashing ideas; the one who plays better has the clearest plans for both attacking and getting out of traps. I learned why it is essential in the endgame to have foresight, a mathematical understanding of all possible moves, and patience; all weaknesses and advantages become evident to a strong adversary and are obscured to a tiring opponent. I discovered that for the whole game one must gather invisible strengths and see the endgame before the game begins.

I also found out why I should never reveal "why" to others. A little knowledge withheld is a great advantage one should store for future use. That is the power of chess. It is a game of secrets in which one must show and never tell.

I loved the secrets I found within the sixty-four black and white squares. I carefully drew a handmade chessboard and pinned it to the wall next to my bed, where at night I would stare for hours at imaginary battles. Soon I no longer lost any games or Life Savers, but I lost my adversaries. Winston and

Vincent decided they were more interested in roaming the streets after school in their Hopalong Cassidy cowboy hats.

On a cold spring afternoon, while walking home from school, I detoured through the playground at the end of our alley. I saw a group of old men, two seated across a folding table playing a game of chess, others smoking pipes, eating peanuts, and watching. I ran home and grabbed Vincent's chess set, which was bound in a cardboard box with rubber bands. I also carefully selected two prized rolls of Life Savers. I came back to the park and approached a man who was observing the game.

"Want to play?" I asked him. His face widened with surprise and he grinned as he looked at the box under my arm.

"Little sister, been a long time since I play with dolls," he said, smiling benevolently. I quickly put the box down next to him on the bench and displayed my retort.

Lau Po, as he allowed me to call him, turned out to be a much better player than my brothers. I lost many games and many Life Savers. But over the weeks, with each diminishing roll of candies, I added new secrets. Lau Po gave me the names. The Double Attack from the East and West Shores. Throwing Stones on the Drowning Man. The Sudden Meeting of the Clan. The Surprise from the Sleeping Guard. The Humble Servant Who Kills the King. Sand in the Eyes of Advancing Forces. A Double Killing Without Blood.

There were also the fine points of chess etiquette. Keep captured men in neat rows, as well-tended prisoners. Never announce "Check" with vanity, lest someone with an unseen sword slit your throat. Never hurl pieces into the sandbox after you have lost a game, because then you must find them again, by yourself, after apologizing to all around you. By the end of the summer, Lau Po had taught me all he knew, and I had become a better chess player.

A small weekend crowd of Chinese people and tourists would gather as I played and defeated my opponents one by one. My mother would join the crowds during these outdoor exhibition games. She sat proudly on the bench, telling my admirers with proper Chinese humility, "Is luck."

A man who watched me play in the park suggested that my mother allow me to play in local chess tournaments. My mother smiled graciously, an answer that meant nothing. I desperately wanted to go, but I bit back my tongue. I knew she would not let me play among strangers. So as we walked home I said in a small voice that I didn't want to play in the local tournament. They would have American rules. If I lost, I would bring shame on my family.

"Is shame you fall down nobody push you," said my mother.

During my first tournament, my mother sat with me in the front row as I waited for my turn. I frequently bounced my legs to unstick them from the cold metal seat of the folding chair. When my name was called, I leapt up. My mother unwrapped something in her lap. It was her *chang,* a small tablet of red jade which held the sun's fire. "Is luck," she whispered, and tucked it into my dress pocket. I turned to my opponent, a fifteen-year-old boy from Oakland. He looked at me, wrinkling his nose.

As I began to play, the boy disappeared, the color ran out of the room, and I saw only my white pieces and his black ones waiting on the other side. A light wind began blowing past my ears. It whispered secrets only I could hear.

"Blow from the South," it murmured. "The wind leaves no trail." I saw a clear path, the traps to avoid. The crowd rustled. "Shhh! Shhh!" said the corners of the room. The wind blew stronger. "Throw sand from the East to distract him." The knight came forward ready for the sacrifice. The wind hissed, louder and louder. "Blow, blow, blow. He cannot see. He is blind now. Make him lean away from the wind so he is easier to knock down."

"Check," I said, as the wind roared with laughter. The wind died down to little puffs, my own breath.

My mother placed my first trophy next to a new plastic chess set that the neighborhood Tao society had given to me. As she wiped each piece with a soft cloth, she said, "Next time win more, lose less."

"Ma, it's not how many pieces you lose," I said. "Sometimes you need to lose pieces to get ahead."

"Better to lose less, see if you really need."

At the next tournament, I won again, but it was my mother who wore the triumphant grin.

"Lost eight piece this time. Last time was eleven. What I tell you? Better off lose less!" I was annoyed, but I couldn't say anything.

I attended more tournaments, each one farther away from home. I won all games, in all divisions. The Chinese bakery downstairs from our flat displayed my growing collection of trophies in its window, amidst the dust-covered cakes that were never picked up. The day after I won an important regional tournament, the window encased a fresh sheet cake with whipped-cream frosting and red script saying "Congratulations, Waverly Jong, Chinatown Chess Champion." Soon after that, a flower shop, headstone engraver, and funeral parlor offered to sponsor me in national tournaments. That's when my mother decided I no longer had to do the dishes. Winston and Vincent had to do my chores.

"Why does she get to play and we do all the work," complained Vincent.

"Is new American rules," said my mother. "Meimei play, squeeze all her brains out for win chess. You play, worth squeeze towel."

By my ninth birthday, I was a national chess champion. I was still some 429 points away from grand-master status, but I was touted as the Great American Hope, a child prodigy and a girl to boot. They ran a photo of me in *Life* magazine next to a quote in which Bobby Fischer said, "There will never be a woman grand master." "Your move, Bobby," said the caption.

The day they took the magazine picture I wore neatly plaited braids clipped with plastic barrettes trimmed with rhinestones. I was playing in a large high school auditorium that echoed with phlegmy coughs and the squeaky rubber knobs of chair legs sliding across freshly waxed wooden floors. Seated across from me was an American man, about the same age as Lau Po, maybe fifty. I remember that his sweaty brow seemed to weep at my every move. He wore a dark, malodorous suit. One of his pockets was stuffed with a great white kerchief on which he wiped his palm before sweeping his hand over the chosen chess piece with great flourish.

In my crisp pink-and-white dress with scratchy lace at the neck, one of two my mother had sewn for these special occasions, I would clasp my hands under my chin, the delicate points of my elbows poised lightly on the table in the manner my mother had shown me for posing for the press. I would swing my patent leather shoes back and forth like an impatient child riding on a school bus. Then I would pause, suck in my lips, twirl my chosen piece in midair as if undecided, and then firmly plant it in its new threatening place, with a triumphant smile thrown back at my opponent for good measure.

☙❦

I no longer played in the alley of Waverly Place. I never visited the playground where the pigeons and old men gathered. I went to school, then directly home to learn new chess secrets, cleverly concealed advantages, more escape routes.

But I found it difficult to concentrate at home. My mother had a habit of standing over me while I plotted out my games. I think she thought of herself as my protective ally. Her lips would be sealed tight, and after each move I made, a soft "Hmmmmph" would escape from her nose.

"Ma, I can't practice when you stand there like that," I said one day. She retreated to the kitchen and made loud noises with the pots and pans. When the crashing stopped, I could see out of the corner of my eye that she was standing in the doorway. "Hmmmmph!" Only this one came out of her tight throat.

My parents made many concessions to allow me to practice. One time I complained that the bedroom I shared was so noisy that I couldn't think. Thereafter, my brothers slept in a bed in the living room facing the street. I said I couldn't finish my rice; my head didn't work right when my stomach was too full. I left the table with half-finished bowls and nobody complained. But there was one duty I couldn't avoid. I had to accompany my mother on Saturday market days when I had no tournament to play. My mother would proudly walk with me, visiting many shops, buying very little. "This my daughter Wave-ly Jong," she said to whoever looked her way.

One day after we left a shop I said under my breath, "I wish you wouldn't do that, telling everybody I'm your daughter." My mother stopped walking. Crowds of people with heavy bags pushed past us on the sidewalk, bumping into first one shoulder, then another.

"Aiii-ya. So shame be with mother?" She grasped my hand even tighter as she glared at me.

I looked down. "It's not that, it's just so obvious. It's just so embarrassing."

"Embarrass you be my daughter?" Her voice was cracking with anger.

"That's not what I meant. That's not what I said."

"What you say?"

I knew it was a mistake to say anything more, but I heard my voice speaking, "Why do you have to use me to show off? If you want to show off, then why don't you learn to play chess?"

My mother's eyes turned into dangerous black slits. She had no words for me, just sharp silence.

I felt the wind rushing around my hot ears. I jerked my hand out of my mother's tight grasp and spun around, knocking into an old woman. Her bag of groceries spilled to the ground.

"Aii-ya! Stupid girl!" my mother and the woman cried. Oranges and tin cans careened down the sidewalk. As my mother stooped to help the old woman pick up the escaping food, I took off.

I raced down the street, dashing between people, not looking back as my mother screamed shrilly, "Meimei! Meimei!" I fled down an alley, past dark, curtained shops and merchants washing the grime of their windows. I sped into the sunlight, into a large street crowded with tourists examining trinkets and souvenirs. I ducked into another dark alley, down another street, up another alley. I ran until it hurt and I realized I had nowhere to go, that I was not running from anything. The alleys contained no escape routes.

My breath came out like angry smoke. It was cold. I sat down on an upturned plastic pail next to a stack of empty boxes, cupping my chin with my hands, thinking hard. I imagined my mother, first walking briskly down one street or another looking for me, then giving up and returning home to await my arrival. After two hours, I stood up on creaking legs and slowly walked home.

The alley was quiet and I could see the yellow lights shining from our flat like two tiger's eyes in the night. I climbed the sixteen steps to the door, advancing quietly up each so as not to make any warning sounds. I turned the knob; the door was locked. I heard a chair moving, quick steps, the locks turning—click! click! click!—and then the door opened.

"About time you got home," said Vincent. "Boy, are you in trouble."

He slid back to the dinner table. On a platter were the remains of a large fish, its fleshy head still connected to bones swimming upstream in vain escape. Standing there waiting for my punishment, I heard my mother speak in a dry voice.

"We not concerning this girl. This girl not have concerning for us."

Nobody looked at me. Bone chopsticks clinked against the inside of bowls being emptied into hungry mouths.

I walked into my room, closed the door, and lay down on my bed. The room was dark, the ceiling filled with shadows from the dinnertime lights of neighboring flats.

In my head, I saw a chessboard with sixty-four black and white squares. Opposite me was my opponent, two angry black slits. She wore a triumphant smile. "Strongest wind cannot be seen," she said.

Her black men advanced across the plane, slowly marching to each successive level as a single unit. My white pieces screamed as they scurried and fell off the board one by one. As her men drew closer to my edge, I felt myself growing light. I rose up into the air and flew out the window. Higher and higher, above the alley, over the tops of tiled roofs, where I was gathered up by the wind and pushed up toward the night sky until everything below me disappeared and I was alone.

I closed my eyes and pondered my next move.

Looking for Work

GARY SOTO

One July, while killing ants on the kitchen sink with a rolled newspaper, I had a nine-year-old's vision of wealth that would save us from ourselves. For weeks I had drunk Kool-Aid and watched morning reruns of *Father Knows Best,* whose family was so uncomplicated in its routine that I very much wanted to imitate it. The first step was to get my brother and sister to wear shoes at dinner.

"Come on, Rick—come on, Deb," I whined. But Rick mimicked me and the same day that I asked him to wear shoes he came to the dinner table in only his swim trunks. My mother didn't notice, nor did my sister, as we sat to eat our beans and tortillas in the stifling heat of our kitchen. We all gleamed like cellophane, wiping the sweat from our brows with the backs of our hands as we talked about the day: Frankie our neighbor was beat up by Faustino; the swimming pool at the playground would be closed for a day because the pump was broken.

Such was our life. So that morning, while doing in the train of ants which arrived each day, I decided to become wealthy, and right away! After downing a bowl of cereal, I took a rake from the garage and started up the block to look for work.

We lived on an ordinary block of mostly working-class people: warehousemen, egg candlers, welders, mechanics, and a union plumber. And there were many retired people who kept their lawns green and the gutters uncluttered of the chewing gum wrappers we dropped as we rode by on our bikes. They bent down to gather our litter, muttering at our evilness.

At the corner house I rapped the screen door and a very large woman in a muu-muu answered. She sized me up and then asked what I could do.

"Rake leaves," I answered, smiling.

"It's summer, and there ain't no leaves," she countered. Her face was pinched with lines; fat jiggled under her chin. She pointed to the lawn, then the flower bed, and said: "You see any leaves there—or there?" I followed her pointing arm, stupidly. But she had a job for me and that was to get her a Coke at the liquor store. She gave me twenty cents, and after ditching my rake in a bush, off I ran. I returned with an unbagged Pepsi, for which she thanked me and gave me a nickel from her apron.

I skipped off her porch, fetched my rake, and crossed the street to the next block where Mrs. Moore, mother of Earl the retarded man, let me weed a flower bed. She handed me a trowel and for a good part of the morning my fingers dipped into the moist dirt, ripping up runners of Bermuda grass. Worms surfaced in my search for deep roots, and I cut them in halves, tossing them to Mrs. Moore's cat who pawed them playfully as they dried in the sun. I made out Earl whose face was pressed to the back window of the house, and although he was calling to me I couldn't understand what he was trying to say. Embarrassed, I worked without looking up, but I imagined his contorted mouth and the ring of keys attached to his belt—keys that jingled with each palsied step. He scared me and I worked quickly to finish the flower bed. When I did finish Mrs. Moore gave me a quarter and two peaches from her tree, which I washed there but ate in the alley behind my house.

I was sucking on the second one, a bit of juice staining the front of my T-shirt, when Little John, my best friend, came walking down the alley with a baseball bat over his shoulder, knocking over trash cans as he made his way toward me.

Little John and I went to St. John's Catholic School, where we sat among the "stupids." Miss Marino, our teacher, alternated the rows of good students with the bad, hoping that by sitting side-by-side with the bright students the stupids might become more intelligent, as though intelligence were contagious. But we didn't progress as she had hoped. She grew frustrated when one day, while dismissing class for recess, Little John couldn't get up because his arms were stuck in the slats of the chair's backrest. She scolded us with a shaking finger when we knocked over the globe, denting the already troubled Africa. She muttered curses when Leroy White, a real stupid but a great softball player with the gift to hit to all fields, openly chewed his host when he made his First Communion; his hands swung at his sides as he returned to the pew looking around with a big smile.

Little John asked what I was doing, and I told him that I was taking a break from work, as I sat comfortably among high weeds. He wanted to join me, but I reminded him that the last time he'd gone door-to-door asking for work his mother had whipped him. I was with him when his mother, a New Jersey Italian who could rise up in anger one moment and love the next, told me in a polite but matter-of-fact voice that I had to leave because she was going to beat her son. She gave me a homemade popsicle, ushered me to the door, and said that I could see Little John the next day. But it was sooner than that. I went around to his bedroom window to suck my popsicle and watch Little John dodge his mother's blows, a few hitting their mark but many whirring air.

It was midday when Little John and I converged in the alley, the sun blazing in the high nineties, and he suggested that we go to Roosevelt High School to swim. He needed five

cents to make fifteen, the cost of admission, and I lent him a
nickel. We ran home for my bike and when my sister found
out that we were going swimming, she started to cry because
she didn't have the fifteen cents but only an empty Coke bottle. I waved for her to come and three of us mounted the
bike—Debra on the crossbar, Little John on the handlebars
and holding the Coke bottle which we would cash for a
nickel and make up the difference that would allow all of us
to get in, and me pumping up the crooked streets, dodging
cars and pot holes. We spent the day swimming under the afternoon sun, so that when we got home our mom asked us
what was darker, the floor or us? She feigned a stern posture,
her hands on her hips and her mouth puckered. We played
along. Looking down, Debbie and I said in unison, "Us."

That evening at dinner we all sat down in our bathing
suits to eat our beans, laughing and chewing loudly. Our
mom was in a good mood, so I took a risk and asked her if
sometime we could have turtle soup. A few days before I had
watched a television program in which a Polynesian tribe
killed a large turtle, gutted it, and then stewed it over an
open fire. The turtle, basted in a sugary sauce, looked delicious as I ate an afternoon bowl of cereal, but my sister, who
was watching the program with a glass of Kool-Aid between
her knees, said, "Caca."

My mother looked at me in bewilderment. "Boy, are you a
crazy Mexican. Where did you get the idea that people eat
turtles?"

"On television," I said, explaining the program. Then I
took it a step further. "Mom, do you think we could get
dressed up for dinner one of these days? David King does."

"*Ay, Dios,*" my mother laughed. She started collecting the
dinner plates, but my brother wouldn't let go of his. He was
still drawing a picture in the bean sauce. Giggling, he said it
was me, but I didn't want to listen because I wanted an an-

swer from Mom. This was the summer when I spent the mornings in front of the television that showed the comfortable lives of white kids. There were no beatings, no rifts in the family. They wore bright clothes; toys tumbled from their closets. They hopped into bed with kisses and woke to glasses of fresh orange juice, and to a father sitting before his morning coffee while the mother buttered his toast. They hurried through the day making friends and gobs of money, returning home to a warmly lit living room, and then dinner. *Leave It to Beaver* was the program I replayed in my mind:

"May I have the mashed potatoes?" asks Beaver with a smile.

"Sure, Beav," replies Wally as he taps the corners of his mouth with a starched napkin.

The father looks on in his suit. The mother, decked out in earrings and a pearl necklace, cuts into her steak and blushes. Their conversation is politely clipped.

"Swell," says Beaver, his cheeks puffed with food.

Our own talk at dinner was loud with belly laughs and marked by our pointing forks at one another. The subjects were commonplace.

"Gary, let's go to the ditch tomorrow," my brother suggests. He explains that he has made a life preserver out of four empty detergent bottles strung together with twine and that he will make me one if I can find more bottles. "No way are we going to drown."

"Yeah, then we could have a dirt clod fight," I reply, so happy to be alive.

Whereas the Beaver's family enjoyed dessert in dishes at the table, our mom sent us outside, and more often than not I went into the alley to peek over the neighbor's fences and spy out fruit, apricot or peaches.

I had asked my mom and again she laughed that I was a crazy *chavalo* as she stood in front of the sink, her arms rising and falling with suds, face glistening from the heat. She sent me outside where my brother and sister were sitting in the shade that the fence threw out like a blanket. They were talking about me when I plopped down next to them. They looked at one another and then Debbie, my eight-year-old sister, started in.

"What's this crap about getting dressed up?"

She had entered her profanity stage. A year later she would give up such words and slip into her Catholic uniform, and into squealing on my brother and me when we "cussed this" and "cussed that."

I tried to convince them that if we improved the way we looked we might get along better in life. White people would like us more. They might invite us to places, like their homes or front yards. They might not hate us so much.

My sister called me a "craphead," and got up to leave with a stalk of grass dangling from her mouth. "They'll never like us."

My brother's mood lightened as he talked about the ditch—the white water, the broken pieces of glass, and the rusted car fenders that awaited our knees. There would be toads, and rocks to smash them.

David King, the only person we knew who resembled the middle class, called from over the fence. David was Catholic, of Armenian and French descent, and his closet was filled with toys. A bear-shaped cookie jar, like the ones on television, sat on the kitchen counter. His mother was remarkably kind while she put up with the racket we made on the street. Evenings, she often watered the front yard and it must have upset her to see us—my brother and I and others—jump from trees laughing, the unkillable kids of the very poor, who got up unshaken, brushed off, and climbed into another one to try again.

David called again. Rick got up and slapped grass from his

pants. When I asked if I could come along he said no. David said no. They were two years older so their affairs were different from mine. They greeted one another with foul names and took off down the alley to look for trouble.

I went inside the house, turned on the television, and was about to sit down with a glass of Kool-Aid when Mom shooed me outside.

"It's still light," she said. "Later you'll bug me to let you stay out longer. So go on."

I downed my Kool-Aid and went outside to the front yard. No one was around. The day had cooled and a breeze rustled the trees. Mr. Jackson, the plumber, was watering his lawn and when he saw me he turned away to wash off his front steps. There was more an hour of light left, so I took advantage of it and decided to look for work. I felt suddenly alive as I skipped down the block in search of an overgrown flower bed and the dime that would end the day right.

The Best Deal in America

BEBE MOORE CAMPBELL

The money is yours until you give it away. The credo was Maxine's mama's, honed over half a century of parsimonious dealings and painstakingly passed on to her youngest daughter during the formative years of her improverished childhood. Neither the potency of the lesson nor the uncontrollable yearning to decorate her life with shiny new things had diminished over the years.

As Maxine waited at the counter of World of Linens, she "read" the saleslady, just the way her mama had taught her to: the emotional type. Her slim fingers inched the sheets toward the woman, like a blind beggar extending her cup. "See?" she said, pointing to a small mark. "There's a stain right here."

"Well, Miss, did you try to find another set?" the saleslady asked.

"This is the last one." Maxine made her lips tremble.

"Well, gee, I'm really sorry." The saleslady watched as the young black woman lowered her glance, then heard the deep sigh and saw the spasms shuddering through her body. "Is there anything I can do, Honey?" she asked, putting her hand on top of her customer's. Maxine counted to three in her head, then lifted her eyes just slightly. "I really need them, I've got guests coming. Do you think I could get a little discount?" she asked.

"What did you have in mind?" The woman still held her hand.

"Oh, 15 percent." Ten. Ten. Ten.

"We're only allowed to give 10."

"Ten will be fine," Maxine said, swallowing her smile.

Maxine was the Bargain Queen. She knew where she could haggle for Giorgio, Poison and Obsession—not knock-offs, the real stuff—and pay $10 a bottle. At a little shop in Chinatown, when the owner wasn't around, she could get a full set of silk-wrapped fingernails for just $9. Jewelry? That would be Virgilio's on Los Angeles Street: the best gold for the lowest prices. The man to ask for was Salvador; Maxine knew his shift.

"The discount diva strikes again," Denise, her roommate, said when she brought home the sheets. Sitting at the kitchen table, she looked up from the California bar review book she was poring over. Denise was a wiry girl, with skin the color of Kentucky bourbon. "How much did you save this time?"

"Four eighty-seven," Maxine said, ignoring Denise's sarcasm.

Denise rolled her eyes. Why anyone would grovel—and she'd seen Maxine do just that—over a few bucks was beyond her. She thought of the hardball the lawyers played at the firm where she worked. *That* was deal-making. "You need to expand your vision," she said, turning back to her workbook.

Maxine climbed the stairs and threw the sheets into the linen closet, slammed the door, then pressed her forehead against the cool wood for a moment and waited for yet another fit of inexplicable rage to subside. Lately, when she finished shopping, anger crept around her neck like a pearl choker, and she'd remember the times her mama begged the neighborhood grocer to sell her peaches for 10 cents a pound, all of them rotten. When she turned around, Denise was standing in front of her. "Listen," she said. "I didn't mean to hurt your feelings, but you don't even use half the stuff you buy. You waste so much money."

"You didn't come up like I did," Maxine said in a low voice.

Denise looked into her friend's face, saw the tense jaw, the anger in her dark eyes, and stepped back. "I know you used to be poor," she said, remembering the time she visited Maxine's mother's house in Louisiana. Clean, but Lord . . .

"No. You just think you know."

But all her scrimping would soon be worthwhile, Maxine thought a week later as she stared through the plate-glass window of the new-car showroom. Her gaze settled on the gleaming blue convertible parked in the center of the floor. No one in her family had ever owned a car, let alone a new one. She'd been saving for a car for three years and finally had enough money, if she could strike the right deal. Oblivious to the people walking past her on the street, she closed her eyes and saw herself tooling around L.A., her head thrown back in raucous laughter, the summer breeze blowing through her hair, the sun kissing her chocolate skin, the music on the radio loud and vibrant. She opened her eyes, and what she saw was a party on four wheels.

But looming just ahead of her windblown future, plastered to the car window, was the sticker price: $17,500. Maxine studied the numbers for a moment, rolling them around in her mind like a pair of dice. She'd pay $16,800 and not a cent more.

The showroom felt frigid after the heat of the summer day. Maxine stepped over to the convertible, opened the door, and sat down. Then she looked out the window, studying the faces of the three men and one woman on the floor. They were all white and somber-looking, except for one smiling young man she judged to be the flirtatious type.

Ted took her for a test-drive and described the many wonderful features the car possessed. As she whipped around corner after corner, Maxine told cute little jokes in a Diana Ross voice, *Mahogany* vintage, setting him up for the kill.

"You sure look great in that car, Maxine," Ted said with a grin when she was seated across from him in his office. "I can write up the papers now." He leaned forward eagerly, giving off a light scent of Drakkar Noir, then picked up a pen. "Let's see, $17,500 at . . ."

Maxine cleared her throat. Ted looked up. "I was hoping you could give me a little better deal than that."

The small man leaned back in his chair. His polished nails gleamed. "What did you have in mind?"

Careful. Careful. "I was thinking of $16,650," she said. It was a good place to start, according to the books she'd read.

Ted dropped his pen. "No way."

She'd never seen eyes turn so hard so fast. Diana Ross and the Supremes couldn't help her out. "What's your best offer?" she asked, her voice businesslike.

He took out a form from his desk drawer and wrote quickly, then slid the paper toward her. She read $17,300 with dismay.

"What about . . ." Maxine began.

Ted said evenly, "That's my final offer." His eyes wandered to the plate-glass partition, then became suddenly alert; he stood up. "Would you excuse me for a second?" he asked, grabbing papers on his desk, leaving yellow copies behind. "I have to see a customer."

Through the partition, Maxine watched as Ted shook hands with a lanky blond man and handed him the papers. Without hesitating, Maxine picked up the copies on the desk and examined them. She held in her hand a bill of sale for the convertible. Scanning to the bottom line, she almost dropped the papers. $16,700. She looked again and saw the men grinning at each other. Heat flared up in her chest, just enough to make her sway. Maxine folded her offer and slid it in her purse. As she passed Ted in the showroom, she said, "I'll get back to you."

Denise was sitting on her bed when Maxine came in, the

stock market pages of the paper spread all around her. On television, black South Africans waited to vote in lines that stretched for miles. Their raised fists seemed to cut through the air.

"I don't know whether this is a race thing or a gender thing," Maxine said quietly after she explained to Denise what had happened. Her roommate didn't respond, but the crease between her eyebrows kept getting deeper.

"The kids in my neighborhood used to laugh because my mother always gave us rotten peaches to eat. She'd try to cut away the bad spots, but . . ." Maxine lifted up her hands, and when they dropped back into her lap, she was crying. Each sob seemed to send up a ray of light, illuminating her for Denise.

"You're not a poor little girl anymore," Denise said, putting one arm around her friend and picking up the telephone with her other hand. "You need a lawyer."

Two days later, at 1 o'clock in the afternoon, Maxine was sitting in the parking lot behind the car dealership when she heard a tap on her window.

"Denise explained your problem to me," Bill said after she got out of the car and they shook hands. His thin brown hair was tied up in a wispy ponytail. He wore earrings and Earth shoes. "Peace Corps," was written all over him. "To think that in 1994 in the United States this kind of discrimination goes on—It's just . . . just appalling," he said, his voice rising. He balled up his right fist and punched it into his other palm. "And yours isn't an isolated case. Just wait here. As soon as the guy gives me an offer in writing, I'll come out and get you."

Nearly an hour later, Maxine was sitting in the office of the manager of the dealership; he and Ted had the same twisted lips and ghostly pallor. Bill turned to the men. "I believe you have something to say to my client," he said.

Paul, the manager, eyed Bill with the caution of a man

fearing a hidden weapon. Semiautomatic. "Yes, Miss Cranston, on behalf of the company, we would like to extend our sincere apologies for this . . . uh . . . unfortunate misunderstanding. And to underscore our sincerity, we'd like to offer you the convertible, at no cost to you, with our . . ."—only death could have been paler than Paul's face—". . . our compliments."

Looking at the two men, Maxine wanted to scream until all the anger and helplessness that Ted had stirred up within her—all the terrible memories—had subsided. "It's not enough!" she wanted to yell. But she didn't. She was her mama's child.

Denise noticed later that the convertible sat untouched at first, like a fresh peach too pretty to be eaten. "Sometimes I feel like it's too good for me," Maxine admitted. But gradually she began to drive the car regularly, to put the top down and feel the wind in her hair, to let the sun kiss her face. Denise saw a promise there that she knew would take time to be fulfilled. But she was hopeful. An expanded vision is not something that tends to recede.

The Day the Cisco Kid Shot John Wayne

NASH CANDELARIA

Just before I started the first grade we moved from Los Rafas into town. It created a family uproar that left hard feelings for a long time.

"You think you're too good for us," Uncle Luis shouted at Papa in Spanish, "just because you finished high school and have a job in town! My God! We grew up in the country. Our parents and grandparents grew up in the country. If New Mexico country was good enough for them—"

Papa stood with his cup and saucer held tightly in his hands, his knuckles bleached by the vicious grip as if all the blood had been squeezed up to his bright red face. But even when angry, he was polite to his older brother.

"I'll be much closer to work, and Josie can have the car to shop once in a while. We'll still come out on weekends. It's only five miles."

Uncle Luis looked around in disbelief. My aunt tried not to look at either him or Papa, while Grandma sat on her rocking chair smoking a hand-rolled cigarette. She was blind and couldn't see the anger on the men's faces, but she wasn't deaf. Her chair started to rock faster, and I knew that in a moment she was going to scream at them both.

"It's much closer to work," Papa repeated.

Before Uncle Luis could shout again, Grandma blew out a puff of cigarette smoke in exasperation. "He's a grown man, Luis. With a wife and children. He can live anywhere he wants."

"But what about the—"

He was going to say orchard next to Grandma's house. It belonged to Papa and everyone expected him to build a house there someday. Grandma cut Uncle short: "Enough!"

As we bumped along the dirt of Rafas Road toward home in the slightly used Ford we were all so proud of, Papa and Mama talked some more. It wasn't just being nearer to work, Papa said, but he couldn't tell the family because they wouldn't understand. It was time for Junior—that was me—to use English as his main language. He would get much better schooling in town than in the little country school where all the grades were in just two rooms.

"Times have changed," Papa said. "He'll have to live in the English-speaking world."

It surprised me. I was, it turned out, the real reason we were moving into town, and I felt a little unworthy. I also felt apprehensive about a new house, a new neighborhood, and my first year in school. Nevertheless, the third week in August we moved into the small house on Fruit Avenue, not far from Immaculate Heart Parochial School.

I barely had time to acquaint myself with the neighborhood before school began. It was just as well. It was not like the country. Sidewalks were new to me, and I vowed to ask Santa Claus for roller skates at Christmas like those that city kids had. All of the streets were paved, not just the main highway like in the country. At night streetlights blazed into life so you could see what was happening outside. It wasn't much. And the lights bothered me. I missed the secret warm darkness with its silence punctuated only by the night sounds of owls and crickets and frogs and distant dogs barking. Somehow the country dark had always been a friend, like a warm bed and being tucked in and being hugged and kissed good night.

There were no neighbors my age. The most interesting

parts of the neighborhood were the vacant house next door and the vacant lot across the street. But then the rush to school left me no time to think or worry about neighbors.

I suppose I was a little smug, a little superior, marching off that first day. My little sister and brother stood beside Aunt Tillie and watched anxiously through the front window, blocking their wide-eyed views with their steaming hot breaths. I shook off Mama's hand and shifted my new metal lunchbox to that side so she wouldn't try again.

Mama wanted to walk me into the classroom, but I wouldn't let her, even though I was frightened. On the steps in front of the old brick school building a melee of high voices said goodbye to mothers, interrupted by the occasional tearful face or clinging hand that refused to let go. At the corner of the entrance, leaning jauntily against the bricks, leered a brown-faced tough whose half-closed eyes singled me out. Even his wet, combed hair, scrubbed face, and neatly patched clothes did not disguise his true nature.

He stuck out a foot to trip me as I walked past. Like with my boy cousins in the country, I stepped on it good and hard without giving him even so much as a glance.

Sister Mary Margaret welcomed us to class. "You are here," she said, "as good Catholic children to learn your lessons well so you can better worship and glorify God." Ominous words in Anglo that I understood too well. I knew that cleanliness was next to godliness, but I never knew that learning your school lessons was—until then.

The students stirred restlessly, and during the turmoil I took a quick look around. It reminded me of a chocolate sundae. All the pale-faced Anglos were the vanilla ice cream, while we brown Hispanos were the sauce. The nun, with her starched white headdress under her cowl, could have been the whipped cream except that I figured she was too sour for that.

I had never been among so many Anglo children before; they outnumbered us two to one. In the country church on Sundays it was rare to see an Anglo. The only time I saw many of these foreigners—except for a few friends of my father's—was when my parents took me into town shopping.

"One thing more," Sister Mary Margaret said. She stiffened, and her face turned to granite. It was the look that I later learned meant the ruler for some sinner's outstretched hands. Her hard eyes focused directly on me. "The language of this classroom is English. This is America. We will only speak English in class and on the school grounds." The warning hung ominously in the silent, crackling air. She didn't need to say what we brownfaces knew: If I hear Spanish, you're in trouble.

As we burst from the confines of the room for our first recess, I searched for that tough whose foot I had stomped on the way in. But surprise! He was not in our class. This puzzled me, because I had thought there was only one first grade.

I found him out on the school grounds, though. Or rather, he found me. When he saw me, he swaggered across the playground tailed by a ragtag bunch of boys like odds and ends of torn cloth tied to a kite. One of the boys from my class whispered to me in English with an accent that sounded normal—only Anglos really had accents. "Oh, oh! Chango, the third-grader. Don't let his size fool you. He can beat up guys twice as big." With which my classmate suddenly remembered something he had to do across the way by the water fountain.

"*¡Ojos largos!*" Chango shouted at me. I looked up in surprise. Not so much for the meaning of the words, which was "big eyes," but for his audacity in not only speaking Spanish against the nun's orders, but shouting it in complete disregard of our jailers in black robes.

"Yes?" I said in English like an obedient student. I was afraid he would see my pounding heart bumping the cloth of my shirt.

Chango and his friends formed a semicircle in front of me. He placed his hands on his hips and thrust his challenging face at me, his words in the forbidden language. "Let's see you do that again."

"What?" I said in English, even though I knew what.

"And talk in Spanish," he hissed at me. "None of your highfalutin Anglo."

Warily I looked around to see if any of the nuns were nearby. "*¿Qué?*" I repeated when I saw that the coast was clear.

"You stepped on my foot, big eyes. And your big eyes are going to get it for that."

I shook my head urgently. "Not me," I said in all innocence. "It must have been somebody else."

But he knew better. In answer, he thrust a foot out and flicked his head at it in invitation. I stood my ground as if I didn't understand, and one of his orderlies laughed and hissed, "*¡Gallina!*"

The accusation angered me. I didn't like being called chicken but a glance at the five of them waiting for me to do something did wonders for my self-restraint.

Then Chango swaggered forward, his arms out low like a wrestler's. He figured I was going to be easy, but I hadn't grown up with older cousins for nothing. When he feinted an arm at me, I stood my ground. At the next feint, I grabbed him with both hands, one on his wrist, the other at his elbow, and tripped him over my leg that snapped out like a jack-knife. He landed flat on his behind, his face changing from surprise to anger and then to caution, all in an instant.

His cronies looked down at him for the order to jump me, but he ignored them. He bounced up immediately to show that it hadn't hurt or perhaps had been an accident and snarled, "Do that again."

I did. This time his look of surprise shaded into one of respect. His subordinates looked at each other in wonder and bewilderment. "He's only a first-grader," one of them said. "Just think how tough he's going to be when he's older."

Meanwhile I was praying that Chango wouldn't ask me to do it a third time. I had a premonition that I had used up all of my luck. Somebody heard my prayer, because Chango looked up from the dirt and extended a hand. Was it an offer of friendship, or did he just want me to pull him to his feet?

To show that I was a good sport, I reached down. Instead of a shake or a tug up, he pulled me down so I sprawled alongside him. Everybody laughed.

"That's showing him, Chango," somebody said.

Then Chango grinned, and I could see why the nickname. With his brown face, small size, and simian smile there could be no other. "You wanna join our gang?" he asked. "I think you'll do." What if I say no? I thought. But the bell saved me, because they started to amble back to class. "Meet us on the steps after school," Chango shouted. I nodded, brushing the dust from my cords as I hurried off.

That was how I became one of Los Indios, which was what we called ourselves. It was all pretty innocent, not at all what people think of when they see brown faces, hear Spanish words, and are told about gangs. It was a club really, like any kid club. It made us more than nonentities. It was a recognition, like the medal for bravery given to the Cowardly Lion in *The Wizard of Oz*.

What we mostly did was walk home together through enemy territory. Since we were Los Indios, it was the cowboys and the settlers we had to watch out for. The Anglo ones. *Vaqueros y paisanos* were okay. Also, it was a relief to slip into Spanish again after guarding my tongue all day so it wouldn't incite Sister Mary Margaret. It got so I even began to dream in English and that made me feel very uncomfortable, as if I were betraying something very deep and ancient and basic.

Some of the times, too, there were fights. As I said before, we were outnumbered two to one, and the sound of words in another language sometimes outraged other students, although they didn't seem to think about that when we all prayed in Latin. In our parish it was a twist on the old cliché; the students that pray together fight together—against each other.

But there was more to Los Indios than that. Most important were the movies. I forget the name of the theater. I think it was the Rio. But no matter. We called it the Rat House. When it was very quiet during the scary part of the movie, just before the villain was going to pounce on the heroine, you could hear the scamper of little feet across the floor. We sat with our smelly tennis shoes up on the torn seats—we couldn't have done any more harm to those uncomfortable lumps. And one day someone swore he saw a large, gray furry something slither through the cold, stale popcorn in the machine in the lobby. None of us would ever have bought popcorn after that, even if we'd had the money.

For a dime, though, you still couldn't beat the Rat House. Saturday matinees were their specialty, although at night during the week they showed Spanish-language movies that parents and aunts and uncles went to see. Saturdays, though, were for American Westerns, monster movies, and serials.

Since I was one of the few who ever had money, I was initiated into a special assignment that first Saturday. I was the front man, paying hard cash for a ticket that allowed me to hurry past the candy counter—no point in being tempted by what you couldn't get. I slipped down the left aisle near the screen, where behind a half-drawn curtain was a door on which was painted "Exit." No one could see the sign because the light bulb was burned out, and they never replaced it in all the years we went there. I guess they figured if the lights were too strong, the patrons would see what a terrible wreck the theater was and not come back.

The owner was a short, round, excitable man with the wrinkles and quavering voice of a person in his seventies but with black, black hair. We kept trying to figure out whether it was a toupee or not, and if it was, how we could snatch it off.

For all his wrinkles, though, he could rush up and down the aisles and grab an unruly kid by the collar and march him out like nothing you ever saw. So fast that we nicknamed him Flash Gordo. We would explode into fits of laughter when one of us saw him zoom down the aisle and whispered "Flash Gordo" to the rest of us. He gave us almost as many laughs as Chris-Pin Martin of the movies.

I counted out my money that first Saturday. I was nervous, knowing what I had to do, and the pennies kept sticking to my sweaty fingers. Finally, in exasperation, Flash Gordo's long-nosed wife counted them herself, watching me like a hawk so I wouldn't try to sneak in until she got to ten, and then she growled, "All right!"

Zoom! Past the candy counter and down the aisle like I said, looking for Flash. I didn't see him until I got right up front, my heart pounding, and started to move toward the door. That's when this circular shadow loomed in the semi-dark, and I looked up in fright to see him standing at the edge of the stage looking at the screen. Then he turned abruptly and scowled at me as if he could read my mind. I slipped into an aisle seat and pretended I was testing it by bouncing up and down a couple of times and then sliding over to try the next one.

I thought Flash was going to say something as he walked

in my direction. But he suddenly bobbed down and picked something off the floor—a dead rat?—when a yell came from the back of the theater. "Lupe and Carlos are doing it again! Back in the last row!"

Flash bolted upright so quickly my mouth fell open. Before I could close it, he rushed up the aisle out of sight, toward those sex maniacs in the last row. Of all the things Flash Gordo could not tolerate, this was the worst. And every Saturday some clown would tattle on Lupe and Carlos, and Flash would rush across the theater. Only later did I learn that there never was any Lupe or Carlos. If there had been, I'm sure Los Indios would have kept very quiet and watched whatever it was they were doing back there.

"Oh, Carlos!" someone yelled in a falsetto. "Stop that this minute!"

I jumped out of my seat and rushed to the door to let Los Indios in. By the time Flash Gordo had shined his flashlight over and under the seats in the back, we were all across the theater at the edge of the crowd where we wouldn't be conspicuous. Later we moved to our favorite spot in the front row, where we craned our necks to look up at the giant figures acting out their adventures.

While the movies were fantastic—the highlight of our week—sometimes I think we had almost as much fun talking about them afterwards and acting them out. It was like much later when I went to high school; rehashing the Saturday night dance or party was sometimes better than the actual event.

We all had our favorites and our definite point of view about Hollywood movies. We barely tolerated those cowboy movies with actors like Johnny Mack Brown and Wild Bill Elliot and Gene Autry and even Hopalong Cassidy. Gringos! we'd sniff with disdain. But we'd watch them in preference to roaming the streets, and we'd cheer for the Indians and sometimes for the bad guys if they were swarthy and Mexican.

They showed the Zorro movies several times each, including the serials, with one chapter each Saturday. Zorro drew mixed reviews and was the subject of endless argument. "Spanish dandy!" one would scoff. *"¿Dónde están los mejicanos?"* Over in the background hanging on to their straw sombreros and smiling fearfully as they bowed to the tax collector, I remember.

"But at least Zorro speaks the right language."

Then somebody would hoot, "Yeah, Hollywood *inglés*. Look at the actors who play Zorro, Gringos every one. John Carroll. Reed Handley. Tyrone Power. *¡Mierda!*"

That was what Zorro did to us. Better than Gene Autry but still a phony Spaniard, while all the *indios y mestizos* were bit players.

That was no doubt the reason why our favorite was the Cisco Kid. Even the one gringo who played the role, Warner Baxter, could have passed for a Mexican. More than one kid said he looked like my old man, so I was one of those who accepted Warner Baxter. Somebody even thought that he was Mexican but had changed his name so he could get parts in Hollywood—you know how Hollywood is. But we conveniently leaped from that to cheering for the "real" Cisco Kids without wondering how *they* ever got parts in that Hollywood: Gilbert Roland, César Romero, Duncan Renaldo. With the arch-sidekick of all time, Chris-Pin Martin, who was better any day than Fuzzy Knight, Smiley Burnette, or Gabby Hayes.

"*Sí,* Ceesco," we'd lisp to each other and laugh, trying to sound like Chris-Pin.

We'd leave the theater laughing and chattering, bumping and elbowing each other past the lobby. There Flash Gordo would stare at us as if trying to remember whether or not we had bought tickets, thoughtfully clicking his false teeth like castanets. We'd quiet down as we filed past, looking at that toupee of his that was, on closer inspection, old hair blackened with shoe polish that looked like dyed rat fur. *Hasta la vista*, Flash, I'd think. See you again next week.

One Saturday afternoon when I returned home there was a beat-up old truck parked in front of the empty house next door and a slow parade in and out. In the distance I saw the curious stare of a towhead about my age.

When I rushed into the house, my three-year-old brother ran up to me and excitedly told me in baby talk, *"La huera. La huera, huera."*

"Hush," Mama said.

Uncle Tito, who was Mama's unmarried younger brother, winked at me. "Blondie's wearing a halter top and shorts," he said. "In the backyard next door."

"Hush," Mama said to him, scowling, and he winked at me again.

That night when I was supposed to be sleeping, I heard Mama and Papa arguing. "Well," Mama said, "what do you think about that? They swept up the gutters of Oklahoma City. What was too lightweight to settle got blown across the panhandle to New Mexico. Right next door."

"Now, Josefa," Papa said, "you have to give people a chance."

"Halter top and shorts," Mama snipped. "What will the children think?"

"The only child who's going to notice is Tito, and he's old enough, although sometimes he doesn't act it."

But then my eyelids started to get heavy, and the words turned into a fuzzy murmur.

One day after school that next week, Chango decided that we needed some new adventures. We took the long way home all the way past Fourth Street Elementary School, where all the pagan Protestants went. "Only Catholics go to heaven," Sister Mary Margaret warned us. "Good Catholics." While her cold eye sought out a few of us and chilled our hearts with her stare.

But after school the thaw set in. We wanted to see what those candidates for hell looked like—those condemned souls who attended public school. And I wondered: if God had only one spot left in heaven, and He had to choose between a bad Catholic who spoke Spanish and a good Protestant who spoke English, which one He would let in. A fearful possibility crossed my mind, but I quickly dismissed it.

We rambled along, picking up rocks and throwing them at tree trunks, looking for lizards or maybe even a lost coin dulled by weather and dirt but still very spendable. What we found was nothing. The schoolyard was empty, so we turned back toward home. It was then, in the large empty field across from the Rio Valley Creamery, that we saw this laggard, my new neighbor, the undesirable Okie.

Chango gave a shout of joy. There he was. The enemy. Let's go get him! We saddled our imaginary horses and galloped into the sunset. Meanwhile, John Wayne, which was the name I called him then, turned his flour-white face and blinked his watery pale eyes at us in fear. Then he took off across the field in a dead run, which only increased our excitement, as if it were an admission that he truly was the enemy and deserved thrashing.

He escaped that day, but not before he got a good look at us. I forgot what we called him besides Okie *gabacho gringo cabrón*. In my memory he was John Wayne to our Cisco Kid, maybe because of the movie about the Alamo.

That then became our favorite after-school pastime. We'd make our way toward the Fourth Street Elementary School looking for our enemy, John Wayne. As cunning as enemies usually are, we figured that he'd be on the lookout, so we stalked him Indian-style. We missed him the next day, but the day after that when we were still a long block away, he suddenly stopped and lifted his head like a wild deer and seemed to feel or scent alien vibrations in the air, because he set off at a dogtrot toward home.

"Head him off at the pass!" Chango Cisco shouted, and we headed across toward Fifth Street. But John Wayne ran too fast, so we finally stopped and cut across to Lomas Park to work out a better plan.

We ambushed him the next day. Four of us came around the way he'd expect us to, while the other two of us sneaked the back way to intercept him between home and the elementary school. At the first sight of the stalkers he ran through the open field that was too big to be called a city lot. Chango and I waited for him behind the tamaracks. When he came near, breathing so heavily we could hear his wheeze, and casting quick glances over his shoulder, we stepped out from behind the trees.

He stopped dead. I couldn't believe anyone could stop that fast. No slow down, no gradual transition. One instant he was running full speed; the next instant he was absolutely immobile, staring at us with fright.

"You!" he said breathlessly, staring straight into my eyes.

"You!" I answered.

"*¿Que hablas español?*" Chango asked.

His look of fear deepened, swept now with perplexity like a ripple across the surface of water. When he didn't answer, Chango whooped out a laugh of joy and charged with clenched fists. It wasn't much of a fight. A couple of punches and a bloody nose and John Wayne was down. When we heard the shouts from the others, Chango turned and yelled to them. That was when John Wayne made his escape. We didn't follow this time. It wasn't worth it. There was no fight in him, and we didn't beat up on sissies or girls.

On the way home it suddenly struck me that since he lived next door, he would tell his mother, who might tell my mother, who would unquestionably tell my father. I entered the house with apprehension. Whether it was fear or conscience didn't matter.

But luck was with me. That night, although I watched my father's piercing looks across the dinner table with foreboding (or was it my conscience that saw his looks as piercing?), nothing came of it. Not a word. Only questions about school. What were they teaching us to read and write in English? Were we already preparing for our First Communion? Wouldn't Grandma be proud when we went to the country next Sunday. I could read for her from my schoolbook, *Bible Stories for Children.* Only my overambitious father forgot that *Bible Stories for Children* was a third-grade book that he had bought for me at a church rummage sale. I was barely at the reading level of "Run, Spot. Run." Hardly exciting fare even for my blind grandmother, who spoke no English and read nothing at all.

Before Sunday, though, there was Saturday. In order to do my share of the family chores and "earn" movie money instead of accepting charity, my father had me pick up in the backyard. I gathered toys that belonged to my little sister and brother, carried a bag of garbage to the heavy galvanized can out back by the shed, even helped pull a few weeds in the vegetable garden. This last was the "country" that my father carried with him to every house we lived in until I grew up and left home. You can take the boy out of the country, as the old saying goes. And in his case it was true.

I dragged my feet reluctantly out to the tiny patch of yard behind the doll's house in which we lived, ignoring my mother's scolding about not wearing out the toes of my shoes.

I must have been staring at the rubber tips of my tennis shoes to watch them wear down, so I didn't see my archenemy across the low fence. I heard him first. A kind of cowardly snivel that jolted me like an electric shock. Without looking I knew who it was.

"You!" he said as I looked across the fence.

"You!" I answered back with hostility.

Then his eyes watered up and his lips twitched in readiness for the blubbering that, in disgust, I anticipated.

"You hate me," he accused. I squatted down to pick up a rock, not taking my eyes off him. "Because I don't speak Spanish and I have yellow hair."

No, I thought, I don't like you because you're a sniveler. I wanted to leap the fence and punch him on those twitching lips, but I sensed my father behind me watching. Or was it my conscience again? I didn't dare turn and look.

"I hate Okies," I said. To my delight it was as if my itching fist had connected. He all but yelped in pain, though what I heard was a sharp expulsion of air.

"Denver?" The soft, feminine voice startled me, and I looked toward the back stoop of their house. I didn't see what Tito had made such a fuss about. She was blond and pale as her son and kind of lumpy, I thought, even in the everyday housedress she wore. She tried to smile—a weak, sniveling motion of her mouth that told me how Denver had come by that same expression. Then she stepped into the yard where we boys stared at each other like tomcats at bay.

"Howdy," she said in a soft funny accent that I figured must be Oklahoma. "I was telling your mother that you boys ought to get together, being neighbors and all. Denver's in the second grade at the public school."

Denver backed away from the fence and nestled against his mother's side. Before I could answer that Immaculate Heart boys didn't play with sniveling heathens, I heard our back door squeak open, then slam shut.

"I understand there's a nice movie in town where the boys

go Saturday afternoons," she went on. But she was looking over my head toward whoever had come out of the house.

I looked back and saw Mama. Through the window over the kitchen sink I saw Papa. He's making sure she and I behave, I thought.

"It would be nice for the boys to go together," Mama said. She came down the steps and across the yard.

You didn't ask me! my silent angry self screamed. It's not fair! You didn't ask me! But Mama didn't even look at me; she addressed herself to Mrs. Oklahoma as if Snivel Nose and I weren't even there.

Then an unbelievable thought occurred to me. For some reason Denver had not told his mama about being chased home from school. Or if he did, he hadn't mentioned me. He was too afraid, I decided. He knew what would happen if he squealed. But even that left me with an uneasy feeling. I looked at him to see if the answer was on his face. All I got was a weak twitch of a smile and a blink of his pleading eyes.

I was struck dumb by the entire negotiation. It was settled without my comment or consent, like watching someone bargain away my life. When I went back into the house, all of my pent-up anger exploded. I screamed and kicked my heels and even cried—but to no avail.

"You have two choices, young man," my father warned. "Go to the matinee with Denver or stay in your room." But his ominous tone of voice told me that there was another choice: a good belting on the rear end.

Of course, this Saturday the Rat House was showing a movie about one of our favorite subjects where the *mejicanos* whipped the gringos: the Alamo. I had to go. Los Indios were counting on me to let them in.

I walked the few blocks to town, a boy torn apart. One of me hurried eagerly toward the Saturday afternoon adventure. The other dragged his feet, scuffing the toes of his shoes to spite his parents, all the while conscious of this hated stranger walking silently beside him.

When we came within sight of the theater, I felt Denver tense and slow his pace even more than mine. "Your gang is waiting," he said, and I swear he started to tremble.

What a chicken, I thought. "You're with me," I said. But then he had reminded me. What would I tell Chango and the rest of Los Indios?

They came at us with a rush. "What's he doing here?" Chango snarled.

I tried to explain. They deflected my words and listened instead to the silent fear they heard as they scrutinized Denver. My explanation did not wash, so I tried something in desperation.

"He's not what you think," I said. Skepticism and disbelief. "Just because he doesn't understand Spanish doesn't mean he can't be one of us." Show me! Chango's expression said. "He's—he's—" My voice was so loud that a passerby turned and stared. "He's an Indian from Oklahoma," I lied.

"A blond Indian?" They all laughed.

My capacity for lying ballooned in proportion to their disbelief. I grew indignant, angry, self-righteous. "Yes!" I shouted. "An albino Indian!"

The laughs froze in their throats, and they looked at each other, seeing their own doubts mirrored in their friends' eyes. "Honest to God?" Chango asked.

"Honest to God!"

"Does he have money?"

Denver unfolded a sweaty fist to show the dime in his palm. Chango took it quickly, like a rooster pecking a kernel of corn. "Run to the dime store," he commanded the fastest of his lackeys. "Get that hard candy that lasts a long time. And hurry. We'll meet you in the back."

Denver's mouth fell open but not a sound emerged.

"When we see him running back," Chango said to me, "you buy the ticket and let us in." Then he riveted his suspicious eyes on Denver and said, "Talk Indian."

I don't remember what kind of gibberish Denver faked. It didn't have to be much, because our runner had dashed across the street and down the block and was already sprinting back.

Our seven-for-the-price-of-one worked as always. When the theater was dark, we moved to our favorite seats. In the meantime, I had drawn Denver aside and maliciously told him he had better learn some Spanish. When we came to the crucial part of the movie, he had to shout what I told him.

It was a memorable Saturday. The hard sugar candy lasted through two cartoons and half of the first feature. We relived the story of the Alamo again—we had seen this movie at least twice before, and we had seen other versions more times than I can remember. When the crucial, climactic attack began, we started our chant. I elbowed Denver to shout what I had taught him.

"*¡Maten los gringos!*" Kill the gringos! Then others in the audience took up the chant, while Flash Gordo ran around in circles trying to shush us up.

I sat in secret pleasure, a conqueror of two worlds. To my left was this blond Indian shouting heresies he little dreamed of, while I was already at least as proficient in English as he. On my right were my fellow tribesmen, who had accepted my audacious lie and welcomed this albino redskin into our group.

But memory plays its little tricks. Years later, when I couldn't think of Denver's name, I would always remember the Alamo—and John Wayne. There were probably three or four movies about that infamous mission, but John Wayne's was the one that stuck in my mind. Imagine my shock when I learned that his movie had not been made until 1960, by which time I was already through high school, had two years of college, and had gone to work. There was no way we could have seen the John Wayne version when I was in the first grade.

Looking back, I realized that Wayne, as America's gringo hero, was forever to me the bigoted Indian hater of *The Searchers* fused with the deserving victim of the attacking Mexican forces at the Alamo—the natural enemy of the Cisco Kid.

Another of my illusions shattered hard when I later learned that in real life Wayne had married a woman named Pilar or Chata or maybe both. That separated the man, the actor, from the characters he portrayed and left me in total confusion.

But then life was never guaranteed to be simple. For I saw the beak of the chick I was at six years old pecking through the hard shell of my own preconceptions. Moving into an alien land. First hating, then becoming friends with aliens like my blond Indian Okie friend, Denver, and finally becoming almost an alien myself.

The New Negro

DARRYL PINCKNEY

No one sat me down and told me I was a Negro. That was something I figured out on the sly, late in my childhood career as a snoop, like discovering that babies didn't come from an exchange of spinach during a kiss. The great thing about finding out I was a Negro was that I could look forward to going places in the by and by that I would not have been asked to as a white boy.

There was nothing to be afraid of as long as we were polite and made good grades. After all, the future, back then, assembled as we were on the glossy edge of the New Frontier, belonged to us, the Also Chosen. The future was something my parents were either earning or keeping for my two sisters and me, like the token checks that came on birthdays from grandparents, great-uncles, great-aunts.

The future was put away for us, the way dark-blue blazers were put away until we could grow into them, the way meatloaf was wrapped up for the next nervous quiz meal and answers to our stormy looks were stored up for that tremendous tomorrow. Every scrap of the future mattered, but I didn't have to worry my breezy head about it because someone was seeing to things and had been ever since my great-grandfather's grandmother stepped on the auction block.

All men were created equal, but even so, lots of mixed messages with sharp teeth waited under my Roy Rogers pillow. You were just as good as anyone else out there, but they—whoever "they" were—had rigged things so that you had to be close to perfect just to break even. You had nothing to fear, though every time you left the house for a Spelling Bee or a Music Memory Contest the future of the future hung in the balance. You were not an immigrant, there were no foreign accents, weird holidays, or funny foods to live down, but still you did not belong to the great beyond out there; yet though you did not belong it was your duty as the Also Chosen to get up and act as though you belonged, especially when no one wanted you to.

You had nothing to be ashamed of, though some of the Also Chosen talked in public at the top of their lungs, said "Can I get" instead of "May I have," and didn't say "please" ever. United we stood, which did not include everyone on the block. It wasn't right to think you were better than your neighbor, but it also wasn't smart to want to be like the kids who ran up and down the alley all day and were going to end up on a bad corner in front of a record shop dancing under the phonograph speaker strapped above the door.

Forgiveness was divine, but people who moved away from you at the movies, tried to short-change you at the new shopping mall, or didn't want you to have a table at the Indianapolis Airport restaurant would get what was coming to them, though they acted that way because they didn't know any better. All you had to do was ignore them, pretend you hadn't heard. Those who dwelled in the great beyond out there could not stop His truth from marching on, but until His truth made it as far as restricted Broadripple Park, you did not go swimming, because even the wading pool at Douglas Park had something floating in it that put your mother off. Douglas Park was not much fun. There were no train engines to climb over, no hand-carved carousels. The YMCA that met there let its beginning swimmers splash naked. Your father could step around whatever turned up in the water as often as he liked, but if you and your sisters got sick from swallowing something other than chlorine your mother was going to go back to her mother in Atlanta and never speak to your father again.

To know where you were going, you had to know where you'd come from, though the claims that the past had on you were like cold hands in the dark. Those elderly relatives, old-timers in charcoal-gray suits and spinsters in musty foxtails, who went out of their way to come to Indianapolis to have a look at you, those wizards licking gold fillings and widows coughing on their bifocals whom you didn't want to travel miles and miles or eat ice cream with—they were among the many pearly reasons you had to hold your Vaselined head high, though you were never to mention in company your father's Uncle Ralph Waldo, who had lived the blues so well that he wound up in a nuthouse without the sense he was born with because of a disease. Grandfather Eustace spelled its name so fast not even your sisters were able to catch the letters.

Above all, you had to remember that no one not family was ever going to love you really. The Also Chosen were one big happy family, though the elderly relatives who hung over holidays like giant helium balloons couldn't stand the sight of one another, which gave fuel to the blue flame of confidences and bitter fine points that burned until the stars folded up. Sometimes the old-timers seemed to be all there was. They far outnumbered their younger relatives. The family tapered off, depopulated itself from shelf to shelf, but the ranks of the old-timers promised never to thin. They enlisted the departed in their number, on their side, which added to their collective power to dominate those of you who would never know what they knew.

The old-timers boasted of their ability to bug you from the grave, saying one day you'd want to talk to them and they wouldn't be there anymore. They'd hint that they'd be watching you closely from wherever they went when they passed on. Your dearest reminded you every morning of the problem that you would never, never get away from. However, escape I did, the burden of consciousness was lifted from my round little shoulders, and for a while there I was gorgeously out of it.

A Half-Breed's Dream Vacation

TIFFANY MIDGE

Day 1

There are no travel brochures for the reservation vacation.
No glossy posters and prints depicting pairs of Indian lovers
intertwined along the concrete shores of the Fort Peck
Dam. There's no 1-800 number to call ahead and secure
reservations. Consider yourself already booked. The only
travel agency you'll want to call is the tribal one at the edge
of town. They'll ensure that you belong, that your stay
is comfortable, that you'll return home refreshed. If you
want, they'll even offer to enroll you—issue you a photo ID.
If you don't fully qualify as a member of the tribe, they'll
refer you to other bands that are advertising—maybe you
could roadie.

Day 2

It's July the 4th. Poplar is celebrating its Centennial. I can't
remember if the old saying goes *Good luck comes in threes* or if
it's *Bad luck goes in threes*. Either way, this town has opened
every window, shaken out the rugs, and hung out every piece
of laundry on the line. Downtown is a regular three-ring circus. Crepe-paper floats are sailing through Main Street carrying 500 years of forgiveness, 216 years of red-blooded
American pride, and 100 years of a prospector's wet dream.
Smokie the Bear is lumbering behind a Dodge Dakota four-
by-four filled with buffalo robes and Indian princesses waving sparklers. The Poplar Junior High marching band is

creeping behind the pioneer's horse-drawn covered wagon to the tune of the motion-picture theme song "Eye of the Tiger." The Fort Peck troop of Vietnam war vets are dodging the missives of Bozo the Clown's Tootsie Pop ambush. The Poplar High School pep squad is passing out their high-kick rendition of spirit to a crowd of Japanese tourists wearing *Northern Exposure* T-shirts. The troop members of Desert Storm are being pursued by the ghosts from the Seventh Cavalry who are topped with nondairy Dream Whip. A John Deere tractor is pulling a tinfoil-wrapped Santa Maria filled with evangelist missionaries treading behind a tragic clown's trail of tears. BIA agents in ten-gallon hats are dishing out miniature flags to a congregation of undercover AIM activists posing as nuns and cheerleaders. This evening I write a postcard to my coworkers.

Hey guys! Today I witnessed 500 years crammed into a mini-segment of *60 Minutes*. Andy Rooney would love this! After today, I know for sure that the melting pot is definitely melting. Perhaps we should recycle it and repair the Liberty Bell. Having a wonderful time. Wish you were here.

Day 3
Blue reservation mornings . . .

I am recovered by sobbing explosions, whiny country chords of Garth Brooks which Cousin Cookie has detonated in the living room. She keeps the volume at maximum while she pieces together star quilts, or restores rodeo-dud fabric in her yellow sewing room down the hall. An expert seamstress, she handiworks the prom gowns for the female student body at Poplar High. She draws her own patterns, designs her own rhythms. You could give her any page from the formal section in the Sears Catalogue and she'd sew it by sight. Her mind's eye is a charmed needle, her slim fingers remnants of stained satin or silk.

Blue reservation nights . . .

Alice Brought Plenty arrives at the house delivering years of regret. Her shoulders sag from balancing buckets of accumulated tears. Her mother's tears, her grandmother's tears, her sister's tears, her own tears. Her broken heart is a country-and-western ballad ripped, mangled, and torn beyond recognition. She throws the shards at Cookie's feet. Cookie gathers the fragments patiently, tenderly, as if she's collecting fragile and valuable pieces of glass. Alice stands waiting at the door while Cookie repairs her damaged heart. With surgical grace, Cookie bastes the brittle splinters using her own regretful years as a guide. She stitches Alice's heart with strands of her grandmother's hair. The needles she uses are slivers of her children's bones. She knots the ends of the threads with mercy, with blood. The vessels are secure, the chambers sealed.

Pain cannot arrive if it hasn't a place to sleep.

Day 4
Poplar is devoid of grand casinos and gambling parlors. No golden palaces of chance to lay down your stakes and wager an accumulated lifetime of credit. But today, to commemorate the town's 100 years, the officials have designated a white rancher's field to compete with the riches and splendor of Las

Vegas and the American Dream. The wide-open throat of this acreage is painted with numbers, sectioned five feet by five feet, until a government handout purchased by a jolly rancher adopts the appearance of a casino's roulette board. Passenger-filled planes jetting over this crude design mistake eastern Montana as a holy shrine. The television newscasts preempt *Days of Our Lives* to inform the American public that the Fort Peck Indian Reservation is now the center of miracles. TV evangelists and talk-show hosts begin speculating as to the significance of the sacred site. The *National Enquirer* wants to know God's motivation behind the divine conception. Cranks fill the circuits on syndicated radio waves. Eyewitnesses of the account sell their stories to *The New York Times* and the *National Examiner.* There is a rumor that the Pope is coming. An AP bulletin is issued to the Defense Department. The President assures the public that he is taking the matter under the advisement of the Congress and that in the meantime, there is no need for alarm. Busloads of tourists come to the reservation to snap Polaroids and interview tribal elders. Somebody spotted Elvis eating Indian tacos. The government organized negotiations to trade the Black Hills for this newly discovered sacred shrine. Jane Fonda donates millions to the American Indian Fund. Oliver Stone makes a movie, casts John Trudell in the lead. Mother Teresa abandons the leper colonies and commits her life's service to the North American Indians. Years later, the truth is finally revealed. The Holy Shrine is demoted to the Big Joke. "Indin" humor rocks and shakes the bellies of every human being on the planet. During an interview with Phil Donahue, the rancher who once owned the plot of land is quoted as saying, "It weren't no shrine; we was having us a cow-chip lottery." When asked what's a cow-chip lottery, the rancher replied, "Everybody bets their lives on one square patch of land, the cattle are unloaded, then everybody waits for nature to call. From the looks of things, I'd say everybody went home a winner." The world explodes in laughter.

Day 5

The rodeo got cancelled. None of the Indians want to be cowboys this year. Somebody suggests a buffalo hunt, but then we remember all the buffalo are gone. Cookie invites everyone over to her digs to watch videos, but nobody wants to on account of we already know the end of the movie. Silas Tail Spins says, "We could get drunk." But Thunderbird has lost its power. Gladys Everybody Talks About advocates the entertainment value in a good round of gossip. But everyone already knows everyone else's business. Alice Brought Plenty suggests we have a powwow, but everyone says. "Been there, done that." Victoria Walking Child says, "I could do everyone's tarot reading." But everyone can already guess at their futures. Cain Long Bow says, "We could interview the elders and learn about our heritage." But all the elders have retired to Florida. Ennui covers the most hopeful of days with a blanket of apathy. Nobody knows what to do. So we all go home and sleep for a good long time. Nobody dreams.

Day 6

We drive out to South Dakota to view a national monument, a symbol of America's pride. I think of baseball, hot dogs, apple pie, and Chevrolets, and a conquered people's dream that perished so violently to accommodate this uncertain present. A once magnificent past is reduced to Hallmark cards postmarked galaxies away. When we finally arrive, a band of Hell's Angels are attempting to make a monetary treaty with the motel desk clerk. But the desk clerk won't take their money. They offer him booze, firearms, women, gold. At first glance you can tell the desk clerk is no stranger to bribery; you can tell he's a subscriber to Pat Robertson and

Jimmy Swaggart; you can tell that he is a man shrouded in a heavy coat of fear. Fear of spiders, fear of dust, fear of public restrooms, fear of his mother, fear of his children, fear of his own mortality. But especially fear of bikers, gypsies, Indians. Fear of anything that defies confinement. We turn around just in time to hear the echo of breaking glass. We know it isn't Armageddon, but centuries of accumulated fear. We drive to the "shrine." Gutzon Borglum is captured in the rock immediately below Lincoln's heavy brows, as if to say *Justice is just, but revenge is sweet.* Winnebago and Apache land cruisers are positioned randomly throughout the parking area as if to say *One man's shrine is another man's cemetery.* A bright ribbon of red paint is smeared across Washington's classic nose, as if to say *Goddamn, this elevation has given me a nosebleed.* Trapped within another mountain, several miles away, a warrior's arm is pointed toward the men's room, as if to say *America is going to the toilet.* On our way out of Keystone, we stop at a souvenir shop. I can't resist buying the Indian bow, arrow, and knife set, wrapped up in a slick package of artificial African leopard skin.

Day 7
We arrive at Bullhead just in time to watch Evel Knievel make his infamous jump over the Snake River Canyon. I don't have the heart to tell my cousins that he failed this leap years ago and that the TV broadcast has only just now reached their antennas. Cousin Alfred bets everyone that Evel Knievel is really Elvis Presley staking out the territory of a new career. I hold back from informing him that Elvis is dead. There's nothing to eat in the house except inedible commodity food, so Alfred, Penny, Trudi, Johnny, Liza, and her friend all pile into my half-sister's Dodge Dakota four-by-four and we drive to the Mercantile. Halfway out of the yard, Johnny screams savagely, *"You're dragging a dog, you're*

dragging a dog!" My sister slams on her brakes; everybody is thrust forward. Johnny is laughing. *"Just fooling . . . aaay!"* At the Mercantile, we pile up our purchases on the counter: two loaves of Wonder Bread, a case of Vienna Sausages, catsup, mustard, sweet rolls, milk, Kool-Aid, bacon, two dozen eggs, six cartons of cigarettes, and an apple. When we arrive back at the house, we're surrounded by Indians. Auntie Mugs has spread the word that we are in town and will pay cash for commodity cheese. When we finally leave, she pulls my mother aside and asks if she could please mail her any extra VCRs.

Day 8

Returning to Poplar in time for the Oil Celebration Pow-wow, we meet up with my mother's childhood friend Patsy who is visiting from Vegas. Pulling up to the powwow grounds, we're stopped by a young tribal officer. He searches the inside of our car with his flashlight. *"Are you carrying any alcohol?"* Patsy grins, leans out the window, and shoots back, *"No . . . you got any?"* Everybody cracks up. Patsy reloads. *"Officer, I'm clean but I don't know about my friend here; you should give her a strip-search, aaay!"* At the arena we buy Cokes and fry bread and claim a length of bleachers. The men's traditionals are wearing Ray•Bans. The grass dancers are adorned in acres of yarn. The fancy dancers are kicking up their Adidas sneakers. The jingle dancers are chiming and clanging years of accumulated Copenhagen-chew top lids. The shawl dancers are dancing circles around the hoop dancers. Somebody drops an eagle feather. All the whirling, buzzing, singing, swirling, bustling, drumming, and frenzy abruptly stops to a dead calm. A solemn ceremony is presented. A tall Indian man with elk teeth dangling around his neck and deer antlers crowning his head slowly marches to the center of the arena. Everyone watches, waits, listens to him offer a prayer to the spirits that preside. He shakes a tortoise rattle over his head to each of the four directions. He sings a holy song in a barely audible whisper. He leans down toward his moccasinned feet and tentatively, slow, slow, slowly plucks the fallen feather from the sawdust as if he's recovering sharp glass amid water and graciously turns to return it to its owner. The dancing resumes.

Americanism

KATHRYN NOCERINO

Say whatever you like about the 1950s; from where I stood, smack in the center of our living room in Flushing, they stank! Five times a week, I'd drag myself home from a hard day slaving over my desk at PS 214. All I wanted to do at the close of such a day was to collapse in an unsightly heap on our genuine imitation Oriental rug and watch my favorite TV program. My favorite program went under a lot of different names but always contained the following non-negotiable elements: guys in cowboy hats, on horses. The guys fell into two basic categories: good guys and bad guys. The good guys were boring and wore white hats; the bad guys wore black and had interesting character defects, but you had to watch out for them. When you were really lucky an American Indian would show up—bold, doomed, and romantic, and then everyone on your TV screen would participate in a ruckus. One of my favorite programs was this same show with a Mexican accent. Two guys would begin and end each episode: the tall, handsome one, who was a good guy even though he dressed totally in black like Roy Orbison, would say, "Hey, Pancho!" His pal, this short, ridiculous fat guy, would yell, "Hey, *Ceesco!!!*" I'd suffer through the entire half-hour no matter how tedious, just to hear this; it was like that number on the *Andy Devine Show* with the talking cat. Andy would lean over this cat and squeal, "Hey, Midnight, say 'nice.' " And Midnight would say "nice" in the most insincere falsetto voice in show biz.

But more and more often, by the time I got home, at around three in the afternoon, my mother, her hair in curlers, would already be in the front-row seat on our Castro Convertible, absolutely hypnotized. I didn't have to ask; I already knew what she was watching: there was this big huge table which went on for miles, lots of microphones on it, and all these people, guys mostly, facing each other on either side. None of these people were in costume. There was no music at all. Nobody fired off any revolvers. There was an audience in the room, but hardly any of them ever laughed, and, in fact, looked distinctly embarrassed for even doing so. For some reason, my parents insisted on watching this stuff; in point of fact, it fascinated them.

"Is it almost over?" I'd ask my mother (the same question I always asked my father during the baseball games). She told me to go into the kitchen and make myself some chocolate milk. Chocolate milk, I thought; if I drink much more of that I'm going to become a perfect sphere, like that buffoon in the sombrero . . .

When I got back to the living room, she was still watching. Some fellow in the middle of the table, on the side facing the audience, balding, with exceptionally heavy eyebrows, Caveman eyebrows, was holding up a piece of paper and yelling, "I have here in my hand a list with the names of 205 Communists in the State Department!"

"What's a Communist?" I said.

My mother didn't even look up; what was going on was much too interesting. She said, still fixated on the shouting man, "Did you find the oatmeal cookies? They're in the bread box."

"Communist." That word was all over the place. Related terms, equally mysterious to me, also came up a lot in conversation. Instead of "communist," someone could be, say, a "Russia Firster," a "pinko," a "fellow traveler," a "Red Pepper." The man who was currently the Vice President had originally run against a woman who, he claimed, was "pink right down to her underwear." You'd open up a newspaper or a magazine, and they'd be in there too: "Your Child Could Become a Communist" by Herbert Hoover. Hoover ran the FBI, which was always on TV in a baggy suit, firing off revolvers.

The man on the TV screen in our living room went on, seeming to get more and more excited: "Fifth Amendment Communists . . . pinkos everywhere you look . . ."

If the weather was bad, I'd just go into my room and do the homework. On good days, I'd go outside and look for adventures. Parts of Flushing still existed that had not been covered over for the Invaders (ourselves) with bricks, mortar, concrete, and/or those squares of manufactured turf which always went brown at the tips in late July. That week, I remember, the word was out in school that a bunch of guys were building a raft and were going to sail it into the center of the swamp across from PS 214. The Loch Ness monster supposedly lived there, in the deepest portion, and would come up if you fed it something out of your lunch box, preferably a bologna sandwich. It would not eat tuna fish; that would be Cannibalism. Now, I didn't really believe this; maybe some of the younger kids did, the kindergarten weenies, but not me. Then again, I hadn't believed the story about the snapping turtles either, and Janet Kozlowski, one of the kids who lived in the 1920s row houses south of the basketball field, pointed one out to me; it was a full fourteen inches in diameter.

So, I went looking for the Expedition. Sure enough, there they were, the usual crowd: Eddie, Dickie, Frank, Robbie; and, off to one side, Allen, the school defective. Each of them was a distinct type, but all shared one important characteristic: like every seven-year-old boy in the known universe, they hated girls.

"Hi," I said, "can I help?" I was hoping that if I hammered a few nails or something, they'd let me onto the raft.

Dickie looked up. I felt sorry for Dickie because he was the only kid in school with glasses thicker than my own, and mine were practically as thick as the bottom of a Coke bottle. "Yeah," he said, "what we need is elbow grease."

I was game: "Where do I pick this stuff up?"

Dickie didn't even blink: "Why don't you try the hardware store?"

I walked the three blocks, past the one-room storefront which served as the Mitchell Gardens public library, past the Hebrew National Delicatessen, past the supermarket which was always going out of business, past the row of little old ladies on the benches, and then I finally came to the hardware store. I went up to the counter and asked Mr. Schneider if he had any elbow grease in stock.

Schneider gave me what I considered a funny look. "Hey, Jack," he yelled to his son-in-law who always worked the back, "you got any elbow grease? It should be right there on the top shelf."

"Oh, hee hee ho ho ha ha," the other guy went.

I stomped back home, fuming; the boys had pulled one of their delightful practical jokes on me again! In my mind's eye, I could see them laughing their heads off on their ship in the middle of Dismal Swamp, throwing cold cuts at the Loch Ness monster without me.

That night, both of my parents insisted on watching their favorite incomprehensible program, *The Table Show*. "How dare you talk to me like that, you pinko?" the man in the center was howling; "I'm a war hero."

"War hero my ass," my father said.

"Teddy . . .," went my mother.

"Some war hero. 'Tail Gunner Joe.' The way he drinks, I bet he couldn't hit a palm tree if he used a cannon!"

My father knew what he was talking about. During World

War II he was in ROTC and they trained him to be a marksman. He could shoot as well as Buffalo Bill. Or even Geronimo!

The man on the set was continuing: "Do you know what a 'pixie' is, sir?"

The man on the other side of the table answered, "Yes, I believe I do."

Mr. Eyebrows said, "Is this statement true or false: is a 'pixie' closely related to a 'fairy'?"

I didn't know why they watched this nonsense. I was especially disappointed that night since I was counting on *Abbott and Costello Meet Frankenstein* or at the very least, Walt Disney, to help me forget the rotten afternoon I had.

Naturally, I was still ticked the following day when I showed up for Assembly. Nothing much to look forward to, here. Assembly, which used to be more fun than a barrel of monkeys, had become as routine as the *Andy Devine Show*. We'd sing "The Star-Spangled Banner," followed by "America the Beautiful"; then, if Miss Stanforth was feeling particularly energetic, "The Street I Live On." Then we'd all stand up, clap our right arm over our chest diagonally, and recite the Pledge of Allegiance.

I enjoyed doing all this the first few times, but eventually, I could sing the songs and do the Pledge in my sleep. I started thinking, involuntarily, about the Elbow Grease incident. Now, assuming—just for the sake of conjecture, you understand—that there *was* a monster in the swamp, what color would it be? Would it be a murky pea-green like the dinosaurs which were starting to appear, in absolutely hair-raising artist's renditions, in the pages of *Life* magazine, or would it be a dusty gray like the elephants in the Central Park Zoo? Would it make noises? Could you teach it to say things like the kitten on the *Andy Devine Show* who I was actually sure was a ventriloquist who taught Andy to do his unvarying assortment of dim-bulb routines?

Next thing I knew, a very loud voice was calling my name: "*Miss* Nocerino, you shall come up on stage. Immediately. And you too, Allen!"

I looked around me. Everyone else was in his or her seat. And they were all looking straight at me. I was still upright, my hand diagonally over my chest.

Miss Stanforth took each of us by the collar. "Look at these students, children!" she said. "They, by their reprehensible behavior, have shown deliberate disrespect for the flag of our country!"

"But Miss Stanforth" I squeaked, "I was only thinking!"

"I know what you were thinking," she said. "You were thinking this is all a big joke. Well, it's not a joke. Senator McCarthy, one of our greatest war heroes, is putting himself on the line to fight for our basic freedoms . . ."

"He's no war hero," I piped up. "My father said he couldn't hit a palm tree if he used a cannon!"

Miss Stanforth changed colors under her makeup: "*Your father is a Communist!*"

Wow, I thought, so that's what a Communist is; no wonder he won't let me have a Captain Video Club Ring . . .

Miss Stanforth continued, gasping for breath, "You are going home right now and you will not come back until your parents, both of them, have spoken to the Principal. You will learn what it means to be an American!"

Allen, she merely gave a light cuff upside his head. He'd been shooting pellets again out of a straw. Allen would just go out the front door and maybe visit the Five-and-Dime to shoplift something. His mother, one of the two divorced women in our community, was away in Manhattan, Land of Mystery and Danger, at work.

Allen and I walked out the front door of PS 214. "Hey, Allen," I said, "you want my lunch? I'm not hungry." I took it out of its Minnie Mouse lunch box, a cream cheese and jelly sangwidge on Wonder Bread.

"Sure," he said, and immediately began wolfing it down. "Hey, wanna throw rocks?" he asked, between bites.

I waved goodbye to him and trudged home. Oh, boy, I'm in for it now, I thought, anticipating the look that would be on my mother's face as I showed up from school five hours too early.

The apartment was very quiet for a while. When my father came home, the two of them went into a back room and talked. Then my father patted me on the head. "You're my daughter," he said. "No child of ours is un-American!"

I smiled. My father was the smartest person in the world. He'd prove I was an American: he'd walk into PS 214 the next day with my birth certificate. I'd seen it once. It said, right there in black and white, that I was born in St. Raymond's Hospital in the South Bronx . . .

"Let's put the damn TV on," he said.

After he adjusted the rabbit ears and whacked the set once or twice for good measure, the image flickered into place. Oh, no, I thought, it's all those people at the table again. The man with the eyebrows that met in the center of his forehead was jogging up and down in his seat and bellowing, "There are 6,791 Communists in *your toilet bowl*. America, wake up!"

My father said something under his breath and, for the first time in months, changed the channel.

Railroad Standard Time

FRANK CHIN

"This was your grandfather's," Ma said. I was twelve, maybe fourteen years old when Grandma died. Ma put it on the table. The big railroad watch, Elgin. Nineteen-jewel movement. American made. Lever set. Stem wound. Glass face cover. Railroad standard all the way. It ticked on the table between stacks of dirty dishes and cold food. She brought me in here to the kitchen, always to the kitchen to loose her thrills and secrets, as if the sound of running water and breathing the warm soggy ghosts of stale food, floating grease, old spices, ever comforted her, as if the kitchen was a paradise for conspiracy, sanctuary for us *juk sing* Chinamen from the royalty of pure-talking China-born Chinese, old, mourning, and belching in the other rooms of my dead grandmother's last house. Here, private, to say in Chinese, "This was your grandfather's," as if now that her mother had died and she'd been up all night long, not weeping, tough and lank, making coffee and tea and little foods for the brokenhearted family in her mother's kitchen, Chinese would be easier for me to understand. As if my mother would say all the important things of the soul and blood to her son, me, only in Chinese from now on. Very few people spoke the language at me the way she did. She chanted a spell up over me that conjured the meaning of what she was saying in the shape of old memories come to call. Words I'd never heard before set me at play in familiar scenes new to me, and ancient.

She laid the watch on the table, eased it slowly off her fingertips down to the tabletop without a sound. She didn't touch me, but put it down and held her hands in front of her like a bridesmaid holding an invisible bouquet and stared at the watch. As if it were talking to her, she looked hard at it, made faces at it, and did not move or answer the voices of the old, calling her from other rooms, until I picked it up.

A two-driver, high-stepping locomotive ahead of a coal tender and baggage car, on a double track between two semaphores showing a stop signal, was engraved on the back.

"Your grandfather collected railroad watches," Ma said. "This one is the best." I held it in one hand and then the other, hefted it, felt out the meaning of "the best," words that rang of meat and vegetables, oils, things we touched, smelled, squeezed, washed, and ate, and I turned the big cased thing over several times. "Grandma gives it to you now," she said. It was big in my hand. Gold. A little greasy. Warm.

I asked her what her father's name had been, and the manic heat of her all-night burnout seemed to go cold and congeal. "Oh," she finally said, "it's one of those Chinese names I . . ." in English, faintly from another world, woozy and her throat and nostrils full of bubbly sniffles, the solemnity of the moment gone, the watch in my hand turned to cheap with the mumbling of a few awful English words. She giggled herself down to nothing but breath and moving lips. She shuffled backward, one step at a time, fox-trotting dreamily backward, one hand dragging on the edge of the table, wobbling the table, rattling the dishes, spilling cold soup. Back down one side of the table, she dropped her butt a little with each step then muscled it back up. There were no chairs in the kitchen tonight. She knew, but still she looked. So this dance and groggy mumbling about the watch being no good, in strange English, like an Indian medicine man in a movie.

I wouldn't give it back or trade it for another out of the

collection. This one was mine. No other. It had belonged to my grandfather. I wore it braking on the Southern Pacific, though it was two jewels short of new railroad standard and an outlaw watch that could get me fired. I kept it on me, arrived at my day-off courthouse wedding to its time, wore it as a railroad relic/family heirloom/grin-bringing affectation when I was writing background news in Seattle, reporting from the shadows of race riots, grabbing snaps for the 11:00 P.M., timing today's happenings with a nineteenth-century escapement. (Ride with me, Grandmother.) I was wearing it on my twenty-seventh birthday, the Saturday I came home to see my son asleep in the back of a strange station wagon, and Sarah inside, waving, shouting through an open window, "Goodbye, Daddy," over and over.

I stood it. Still and expressionless as some good Chink, I watched Barbara drive off, leave me, like some blond white goddess going home from the jungle with her leather patches and briar pipe sweetheart writer and my kids. I'll learn to be a sore loser. I'll learn to hit people in the face. I'll learn to cry when I'm hurt and go for the throat instead of being polite and worrying about being obnoxious to people walking out of my house with my things, taking my kids away. I'll be more than quiet, embarrassed. I won't be likable anymore.

I hate my novel about a Chinatown mother like mine dying, now that Ma's dead. But I'll keep it. I hated after reading *Father and Glorious Descendant, Fifth Chinese Daughter, The House That Tai Ming Built.* Books scribbled up by a sad legion of snobby autobiographical Chinatown saps all on their own. Christians who never heard of each other, hardworking people who sweat out the exact same Chinatown book, the same cunning "Confucius says" joke, just like me. I kept it then and I'll still keep it. Part cookbook, memories of Mother in the kitchen slicing meat paper-thin with a cleaver. Mumbo jumbo about spices and steaming. The secret of Chinatown rice. The hands come down toward the food. The food crawls with culture. The thousand-year-old living Chinese meat makes dinner a safari into the unknown, a blood ritual. Food pornography. Black magic. Between the lines, I read a madman's detailed description of the preparation of shrunken heads. I never wrote to mean anything more than word fun with the food Grandma cooked at home. Chinese food. I read a list of what I remembered eating at my grandmother's table and knew I'd always be known by what I ate, that we come from a hungry tradition. Slop eaters following the wars on all fours. Weed cuisine and mud gravy in the shadow of corpses. We plundered the dust for fungus. Buried things. Seeds, plucked out of the wind to feed a race of lace-boned skinnies, in high school English, become transcendental Oriental art to make the dykeish spinster teacher cry. We always come to fake art and write the Chinatown book like bugs come to fly in the light. I hate my book now that Ma's dead, but I'll keep it. I know she's not the woman I wrote up like my mother, and dead, in a book that was like everybody else's Chinatown book. Part word map of Chinatown San Francisco, shop to shop down Grant Avenue. Food again. The wind sucks the shops out and you breathe warm roast ducks dripping fat, hooks into the neck, through the head, out an eye. Stacks of iced fish, blue and fluorescent pink in the neon. The air is thin soup, sharp up the nostrils.

All mention escape from Chinatown into the movies. But we all forgot to mention how stepping off the streets into a face full of Charlie Chaplin or a Western on a ripped and stained screen that became caught in the grip of winos breathing in unison in their sleep and billowed in and out, that shuddered when cars went by . . . we all of us Chinamans watched our own Movie About Me! I learned how to box watching movies shot by James Wong Howe. Cartoons were our nursery rhymes. Summers inside those neon-and-stucco downtown hole-in-the-wall Market Street Frisco movie houses blowing three solid hours of full-color seven-minute cartoons was school, was rows and rows of China-mans learning English in a hurry from Daffy Duck.

When we ate in the dark and recited the dialogue of cartoon mice and cats out loud in various tones of voice with our mouths full, we looked like people singing hymns in church. We learned to talk like everybody in America. Learned to need to be afraid to stay alive, keeping moving. We learned to run, to be cheerful losers, to take a sudden pie in the face, talk American with a lot of giggles. To us a cartoon is a desperate situation. Of the movies, cartoons were the high art of our claustrophobia. They understood us living too close to each other. How, when you're living too close to too many people, you can't wait for one thing more without losing your mind. Cartoons were a fine way out of waiting in Chinatown around the rooms. Those of our Chinamans who every now and then break a reverie with "Thank you, Mighty Mouse," mean it. Other folks thank Porky Pig, Snuffy Smith, Woody Woodpecker.

The day my mother told me I was to stay home from Chinese school one day a week starting today, to read to my father and teach him English while he was captured in total paralysis from a vertebra in the neck on down, I stayed away from cartoons. I went to a matinee in a white neighborhood looking for the Movie About Me and was the only Chinaman in the house. I liked the way Peter Lorre ran along nonstop routine hysterical. I came back home with Peter Lorre. I turned out the lights in Pa's room. I put a candle on the dresser and wheeled Pa around in his chair to see me in front of the dresser mirror, reading Edgar Allan Poe out loud to him in the voice of Peter Lorre by candlelight.

The old men in the Chinatown books are all fixtures for Chinese ceremonies. All the same. Loyal filial children kow-tow to the old and whiff food laid out for the dead. The dead eat the same as the living but without the sauces. White food.

Steamed chicken. Rice we all remember as children scrambling down to the ground, to all fours and bonking our heads on the floor, kowtowing to a dead chicken.

My mother and aunts said nothing about the men of the family except they were weak. I like to think my grandfather was a good man. Even the kiss-ass steward service, I like to think he was tough, had a few laughs, and ran off with his pockets full of engraved watches. Because I never knew him, not his name, nor anything about him, except a photograph of him as a young man with something of my mother's face in his face, and a watch chain across his vest. I kept his watch in good repair and told everyone it would pass to my son someday, until the day the boy was gone. Then I kept it like something of his he'd loved and had left behind, saving it for him maybe, to give to him when he was a man. But I haven't felt that in a long time.

The watch ticked against my heart and pounded my chest as I went too fast over bumps in the night and the radio on, on an all-night run downcoast, down country, down old Highway 99, Interstate 5. I ran my grandfather's time down past road signs that caught a gleam in my headlights and came at me out of the night with the names of forgotten high school girlfriends—Bellevue Kirkland, Roberta Gerber, Aurora Caney—and sang with the radio to Jonah and Sarah in Berkeley, my Chinatown in Oakland and Frisco, to raise the dead. Ride with me, Grandfather, this is your grandson the ragmouth, called Tampax, the burned scarred boy, called Barbecue, going to San Francisco to bury my mother, your daughter, and spend Chinese New Year's at home. When we were sitting down and into our dinner after Grandma's funeral, and ate in front of the table set with white food for the dead, Ma said she wanted no white food and money burning after her funeral. Her sisters were there. Her sisters took charge of her funeral and the dinner afterwards. The dinner would most likely be in a Chinese restaurant in Frisco. Nobody had these dinners at home anymore. I wouldn't mind people having dinner at my place after my funeral, but no white food.

The whiz goes out of the tires as their roll bites into the steel grating of the Carquinez Bridge. The noise of the engine groans and echoes like a bomber in flight through the steel roadway. Light from the water far below shines through the grate, and I'm driving high, above a glow. The voice of the tires hums a shrill rubber screechy mosquito hum that vibrates through the chassis and frame of the car into my meatless butt, into my tender asshole, my pelvic bones, the roots of my teeth. Over the Carquinez Bridge to Crockett Martinez closer to home, roll the tires of Ma's Chevy, my car now, carrying me up over the water southwest toward rolls of fog. The fat man's coming home on a sneaky breeze. Dusk comes a drooly mess of sunlight, a slobber of cheap pawnshop gold, a slow building heat across the water, all through the milky air through the glass of the window into the closed atmosphere of a driven car, into one side of my bomber's face. A bomber, flying my mother's car into the unknown charted by the stars and the radio, feels the coming of some old night song climbing hand over hand, bass notes plunking as steady and shady as reminiscence to get on my nerves one stupid beat after the other crossing the high rhythm six-step of the engine. I drive through the shadows of the bridge's steel structure all over the road. Fine day. I've been on the road for sixteen hours straight down the music of Seattle, Spokane, Salt Lake, Sacramento, Los Angeles, and Wolfman Jack lurking in odd hours of darkness, at peculiar altitudes of darkness, favoring the depths of certain Oregon valleys and heat and moonlight of my miles. And I'm still alive. Country 'n' western music for the night road. It's pure white music. Like "The Star-Spangled Banner," it was the first official American music out of school into my jingling earbones sung by sighing white big tits in front of the climbing promise of Face and Every Good Boy Does Fine chalked on the blackboard.

She stood up singing, one hand cupped in the other as if to catch drool slipping off her lower lip. Our eyes scouted through her blouse to elastic straps, lacy stuff, circular stitching, buckles, and in the distance, finally some skin. The color of her skin spread through the stuff of her blouse like melted butter through bread nicely to our tongues and was warm there. She sat flopping them on the keyboard as she breathed, singing "Home on the Range" over her shoulder, and pounded the tune out with her palms. The lonesome prairie was nothing but her voice, some hearsay country she stood up to sing a capella out of her. Simple music you can count. You can hear the words clear. The music's run through Clorox and Simonized, beating so insistently right and regular that you feel to sing it will deodorize you, make you clean. The hardhat hit parade. I listen to it a lot on the road. It's that get-outta-town beat and tune that makes me go.

Mrs. Morales was her name. Aurora Morales. The music teacher us boys liked to con into singing for us. Come-on opera, we wanted from her, not them Shirley Temple tunes the girls wanted to learn, but big notes, high long ones up from the navel that drilled through plaster and steel and skin and meat for bone marrow and electric wires on one long tit-popping breath.

This is how I come home, riding a mass of spasms and death throes, warm and screechy inside, itchy, full of ghost-piss, as I drive right past what's left of Oakland's dark wooden Chinatown and dark streets full of dead lettuce and trampled carrot tops, parallel all the time in line with the tracks of the Western Pacific and Southern Pacific railroads.

Crossing

American History

JUDITH ORTIZ COFER

I once read in a *Ripley's Believe It or Not* column that Paterson, New Jersey, is the place where the Straight and Narrow (streets) intersect. The Puerto Rican tenement known as El Building was one block up from Straight. It was, in fact, the corner of Straight and Market; not "at" the corner, but *the* corner. At almost any hour of the day, El Building was like a monstrous jukebox, blasting out *salsas* from open windows as the residents, mostly new immigrants just up from the Island, tried to drown out whatever they were currently enduring with loud music. But the day President Kennedy was shot, there was a profound silence in El Building; even the abusive tongues of viragoes, the cursing of the unemployed, and the screeching of small children had been somehow muted. President Kennedy was a saint to these people. In fact, soon his photograph would be hung alongside the Sacred Heart and over the spiritist altars that many women kept in their apartments. He would become part of the hierarchy of martyrs they prayed to for favors that only one who had died for a cause would understand.

On the day that President Kennedy was shot, my ninth grade class had been out in the fenced playground of Public School Number 13. We had been given "free" exercise time and had been ordered by our P.E. teacher, Mr. DePalma, to "keep moving." That meant that the girls should jump rope and the boys toss basketballs through a hoop at the far end of the yard. He in the meantime would "keep an eye" on us from just inside the building.

It was a cold gray day in Paterson. The kind that warns of early snow. I was miserable, since I had forgotten my gloves and my knuckles were turning red and raw from the jump rope. I was also taking a lot of abuse from the black girls for not turning the rope hard and fast enough for them.

"Hey, Skinny Bones, pump it, girl. Ain't you got no energy today?" Gail, the biggest of the black girls who had the other end of the rope, yelled, "Didn't you eat your rice and beans and pork chops for breakfast today?"

The other girls picked up the "pork chop" and made it into a refrain: "Pork chop, pork chop, did you eat your pork chop?" They entered the double ropes in pairs and exited without tripping or missing a beat. I felt a burning on my cheeks, and then my glasses fogged up so that I could not manage to coordinate the jump rope with Gail. The chill was doing to me what it always did, entering my bones, making me cry, humiliating me. I hated the city, especially in winter. I hated Public School Number 13. I hated my skinny flat-chested body, and I envied the black girls who could jump rope so fast that their legs became a blur. They always seemed to be warm while I froze.

There was only one source of beauty and light for me that school year. The only thing I had anticipated at the start of the semester. That was seeing Eugene. In August, Eugene and his family had moved into the only house on the block that had a yard and trees. I could see his place from my window in El Building. In fact, if I sat on the fire escape I was literally suspended above Eugene's backyard. It was my favorite spot to read my library books in the summer. Until that August the house had been occupied by an old Jewish couple. Over the years I had become part of their family, without their knowing it, of course. I had a view of their kitchen and their backyard, and though I could not hear what they said, I knew when they were arguing, when one of them was sick, and many other things. I knew all this by watching them at mealtimes. I could see their kitchen table, the sink, and the stove. During good times, he sat at the table and read his newspapers while she fixed the meals. If they argued, he would leave and the old woman would sit and stare at nothing for a long time. When one of them was sick, the other would come and get things from the kitchen and carry them out on a tray. The old man had died in June. The last week of school I had not seen him at the table at all. Then one day I saw that there was a crowd in the kitchen. The old woman had finally emerged from the house on the arm of a stocky middle-aged woman whom I had seen there a few times before, maybe her daughter. Then a man had carried out suitcases. The house had stood empty for weeks. I had had to resist the temptation to climb down into the yard and water the flowers the old lady had taken such good care of.

By the time Eugene's family moved in, the yard was a tangled mass of weeds. The father had spent several days mowing, and when he finished, I didn't see the red, yellow, and purple clusters that meant flowers to me from where I sat. I didn't see this family sit down at the kitchen table together. It was just the mother, a red-headed tall woman who wore a white uniform—a nurse's, I guessed it was; the father was gone before I got up in the morning and was never there at dinner time. I only saw him on weekends when they sometimes sat on lawn chairs under the oak tree, each hidden behind a section of the newspaper; and there was Eugene. He was tall and blond, and he wore glasses. I liked him right away because he sat at the kitchen table and read books for hours. That summer, before we had even spoken one word to each other, I kept him company on my fire escape.

Once school started I looked for him in all my classes, but P.S. 13 was a huge, overpopulated place and it took me days and many discreet questions to discover that Eugene was in honors classes for all his subjects; classes that were not open to me because English was not my first language, though I was a straight A student. After much maneuvering I managed "to run into him" in the hallway where his locker was— on the other side of the building from mine—and in study hall at the library, where he first seemed to notice me but did not speak; and finally, on the way home after school one day when I decided to approach him directly, though my stomach was doing somersaults.

I was ready for rejection, snobbery, the worst. But when I came up to him, practically panting in my nervousness, and blurted out: "You're Eugene. Right?" He smiled, pushed his glasses up on his nose, and nodded. I saw then that he was blushing deeply. Eugene liked me, but he was shy. I did most of the talking that day. He nodded and smiled a lot. In the weeks that followed, we walked home together. He would linger at the corner of El Building for a few minutes then walk down to his two-story house. It was not until Eugene moved into that house that I noticed that El Building blocked most of the sun and that the only spot that got a little sunlight during the day was the tiny square of earth the old woman had planted with flowers.

I did not tell Eugene that I could see inside his kitchen from my bedroom. I felt dishonest, but I liked my secret sharing of his evenings, especially now that I knew what he was reading, since we chose our books together at the school library.

One day my mother came into my room as I was sitting on the windowsill staring out. In her abrupt way she said: "Elena, you are acting 'moony.'" *Enamorada* was what she really said—that is, like a girl stupidly infatuated. Since I had turned fourteen and started menstruating my mother had been more vigilant than ever. She acted as if I was going to go crazy or explode or something if she didn't watch me and nag me all the time about being a señorita now. She kept talking about virtue, morality, and other subjects that did not interest me in the least. My mother was unhappy in Paterson, but my father had a good job at the blue jeans factory in Passaic, and soon, he kept assuring us, we would be moving to our own house there. Every Sunday we drove out to the suburbs of Paterson, Clifton, and Passaic, out to where people mowed grass on Sundays in the summer and where children made snowmen in the winter from pure white snow, not like the gray slush of Paterson, which seemed to fall from the sky in that hue. I had learned to listen to my parents' dreams, which were spoken in Spanish, as fairy tales, like the stories about life in the island paradise of Puerto Rico before I was born. I had been to the Island once as a little girl, to Grandmother's funeral, and all I remembered was wailing women in black, my mother becoming hysterical and being given a pill that made her sleep two days, and me feeling lost in a crowd of strangers all claiming to be my aunts, uncles, and cousins. I had actually been glad to return to the city. We had not been back there since then, though my parents talked constantly about buying a house on the beach someday, retiring on the Island—that was a common topic among the residents of El Building. As for me, I was going to go to college and become a teacher.

But after meeting Eugene I began to think of the present more than of the future. What I wanted now was to enter that house I had watched for so many years. I wanted to see the other rooms where the old people had lived and where the boy I liked spent his time. Most of all, I wanted to sit at the kitchen table with Eugene like two adults, like the old man and his wife had done, maybe drink some coffee and talk about books. I had started reading *Gone With the Wind*. I was enthralled by it, with the daring and the passion of the beautiful girl living in a mansion, and with her devoted parents and the slaves who did everything for them. I didn't believe such a world had ever really existed, and I wanted to ask Eugene some questions, since he and his parents, he had told me, had come up from Georgia, the same place where the novel was set. His father worked for a company that had transferred him to Paterson. His mother was very unhappy, Eugene said, in his beautiful voice that rose and fell over words in a strange, lilting way. The kids at school called him the Hick and made fun of the way he talked. I knew I was his only friend so far, and I liked that, though I felt sad for him sometimes. Skinny Bones and the Hick, was what they called us at school when we were seen together.

The day Mr. DePalma came out into the cold and asked us to line up in front of him was the day that President Kennedy was shot. Mr. DePalma, a short, muscular man with slicked-down black hair, was the science teacher, P.E. coach, and disciplinarian at P.S. 13. He was the teacher to whose homeroom you got assigned if you were a troublemaker, and the man called out to break up playground fights, and to escort violently angry teenagers to the office. And Mr. DePalma was the man who called your parents in for "a conference."

That day, he stood in front of two rows of mostly black and Puerto Rican kids, brittle from their efforts to "keep moving" on a November day that was turning bitter cold. Mr. DePalma, to our complete shock, was crying. Not just silent adult tears, but really sobbing. There were a few titters from the back of the line where I stood, shivering.

"Listen." Mr. DePalma raised his arms over his head as if he were about to conduct an orchestra. His voice broke, and he covered his face with his hands. His barrel chest was heaving. Someone giggled behind me.

"Listen," he repeated, "something awful has happened." A strange gurgling came from his throat, and he turned around and spit on the cement behind him.

"Gross," someone said, and there was a lot of laughter.

"The president is dead, you idiots. I should have known that wouldn't mean anything to a bunch of losers like you kids. Go home." He was shrieking now. No one moved for a minute or two, but then a big girl let out a "yeah!" and ran to get her books piled up with the others against the brick wall of the school building. The others followed in a mad scramble to get their things before somebody caught on. It was still an hour to the dismissal bell.

A little scared, I headed for El Building. There was an eerie feeling on the streets. I looked into Mario's drugstore, a favorite hangout for the high school crowd, but there were only a couple of old Jewish men at the soda bar, talking with the short order cook in tones that sounded almost angry, but they were keeping their voices low. Even the traffic on one of the busiest intersections in Paterson—Straight Street and Park Avenue—seemed to be moving slower. There were no horns blasting that day. At El Building, the usual little group of unemployed men were not hanging out on the front stoop, making it difficult for women to enter the front door. No music spilled out from open doors in the hallway. When I walked into our apartment, I found my mother sitting in front of the grainy picture of the television set.

She looked up at me with a tear-streaked face and just said: *"Dios mio,"* turning back to the set as if it were pulling at her eyes. I went into my room.

Though I wanted to feel the right thing about President Kennedy's death, I could not fight the feeling of elation that stirred in my chest. Today was the day I was to visit Eugene in his house. He had asked me to come over after school to study for an American history test with him. We had also planned to walk to the public library together. I looked down into his yard. The oak tree was bare of leaves, and the ground looked gray with ice. The light through the large kitchen window of his house told me that El Building blocked the sun to such an extent that they had to turn lights on in the middle of the day. I felt ashamed about it. But the white kitchen table with the lamp hanging just above it looked cozy and inviting. I would soon sit there, across from Eugene, and I would tell him about my perch just above his house. Maybe I would.

In the next thirty minutes I changed clothes, put on a little pink lipstick, and got my books together. Then I went in to tell my mother that I was going to a friend's house to study. I did not expect her reaction.

"You are going out *today?*" The way she said "today" sounded as if a storm warning had been issued. It was said in utter disbelief. Before I could answer, she came toward me and held my elbows as I clutched my books.

"*Hija,* the president has been killed. We must show respect. He was a great man. Come to church with me tonight."

She tried to embrace me, but my books were in the way. My first impulse was to comfort her, she seemed so distraught, but I had to meet Eugene in fifteen minutes.

"I have a test to study for, Mama. I will be home by eight."

"You are forgetting who you are, *Niña.* I have seen you staring down at that boy's house. You are heading for humiliation and pain." My mother said this in Spanish and in a resigned tone that surprised me, as if she had no intention of stopping me from "heading for humiliation and pain." I started for the door. She sat in front of the TV, holding a white handkerchief to her face.

I walked out to the street and around the chain-link fence that separated El Building from Eugene's house. The yard was neatly edged around the little walk that led to the door. It always amazed me how Paterson, the inner core of the city, had no apparent logic to its architecture. Small, neat, single

residences like this one could be found right next to huge, di-
lapidated apartment buildings like El Building. My guess
was that the little houses had been there first, then the immigrants had come in droves, and the monstrosities had been
raised for them—the Italians, the Irish, the Jews, and now us,
the Puerto Ricans, and the blacks. The door was painted a
deep green: *verde,* the color of hope. I had heard my mother
say it: *Verde-Esperanza.*

I knocked softly. A few suspenseful moments later the
door opened just a crack. The red, swollen face of a woman
appeared. She had a halo of red hair floating over a delicate
ivory face—the face of a doll—with freckles on the nose. Her
smudged eye makeup made her look unreal to me, like a
mannequin seen through a warped store window.

"What do you want?" Her voice was tiny and sweet-
sounding, like a little girl's, but her tone was not friendly.

"I'm Eugene's friend. He asked me over. To study." I
thrust out my books, a silly gesture that embarrassed me almost immediately.

"You live there?" She pointed up to El Building, which
looked particularly ugly, like a gray prison with its many
dirty windows and rusty fire escapes. The woman had
stepped halfway out, and I could see that she wore a white
nurse's uniform with "St. Joseph's Hospital" on the name tag.

"Yes. I do."

She looked intently at me for a couple of heartbeats, then
said as if to herself, "I don't know how you people do it."
Then directly to me. "Listen, Honey, Eugene doesn't want to
study with you. He is a smart boy. Doesn't need help. You
understand me. I am truly sorry if he told you you could
come over. He cannot study with you. It's nothing personal.
You understand? We won't be in this place much longer, no
need for him to get close to people—it'll just make it harder
for him later. Run back home now."

I couldn't move. I just stood there in shock at hearing these things said to me in such a honey-drenched voice. I had never heard an accent like hers except for Eugene's softer version. It was as if she were singing me a little song.

"What's wrong? Didn't you hear what I said?" She seemed very angry, and I finally snapped out of my trance. I turned away from the green door and heard her close it gently.

Our apartment was empty when I got home. My mother was in someone else's kitchen, seeking the solace she needed. Father would come in from his late shift at midnight. I would hear them talking softly in the kitchen for hours that night. They would not discuss their dreams for the future, or life in Puerto Rico, as they often did; that night they would talk sadly about the young widow and her two children, as if they were family. For the next few days, we would observe *luto* in our apartment; that is, we would practice restraint and silence—no loud music or laughter. Some of the women of El Building would wear black for weeks.

That night, I lay in my bed, trying to feel the right thing for our dead president. But the tears that came up from a deep source inside me were strictly for me. When my mother came to the door, I pretended to be sleeping. Sometime during the night, I saw from my bed the streetlight come on. It had a pink halo around it. I went to my window and pressed my face to the cool glass. Looking up at the light I could see the white snow falling like a lace veil over its face. I did not look down to see it turning gray as it touched the ground below.

The Red Convertible

LOUISE ERDRICH

I was the first one to drive a convertible on my reservation. And of course it was red, a red Olds. I owned that car along with my brother Henry Junior. We owned it together until his boots filled with water on a windy night and he bought out my share. Now Henry owns the whole car, and his younger brother Lyman (that's myself), Lyman walks everywhere he goes.

How did I earn enough money to buy my share in the first place? My one talent was I could always make money. I had a touch for it, unusual in a Chippewa. From the first I was different that way, and everyone recognized it. I was the only kid they let in the American Legion Hall to shine shoes, for example, and one Christmas I sold spiritual bouquets for the mission door to door. The nuns let me keep a percentage. Once I started, it seemed the more money I made the easier the money came. Everyone encouraged it. When I was fifteen I got a job washing dishes at the Joliet Café, and that was where my first big break happened.

It wasn't long before I was promoted to busing tables, and then the short-order cook quit and I was hired to take her place. No sooner than you know it I was managing the Joliet. The rest is history. I went on managing. I soon became part owner, and of course there was no stopping me then. It wasn't long before the whole thing was mine.

After I'd owned the Joliet for one year, it blew over in the worst tornado ever seen around here. The whole operation was smashed to bits. A total loss. The fryalator was up in a tree, the grill torn in half like it was paper. I was only sixteen. I had it all in my mother's name, and I lost it quick, but before I lost it I had every one of my relatives, and their relatives, to dinner, and I also bought that red Olds I mentioned, along with Henry.

The first time we saw it! I'll tell you when we first saw it. We had gotten a ride up to Winnipeg, and both of us had money. Don't ask me why, because we never mentioned a car or anything, we just had all our money. Mine was cash, a big bankroll from the Joliet's insurance. Henry had two checks— a week's extra pay for being laid off, and his regular check from the Jewel Bearing Plant.

We were walking down Portage anyway, seeing the sights, when we saw it. There it was, parked, large as life. Really as *if* it was alive. I thought of the word *repose,* because the car wasn't simply stopped, parked, or whatever. That car reposed, calm and gleaming, a FOR SALE sign in its left front window. Then, before we had thought it over at all, the car belonged to us and our pockets were empty. We had just enough money for gas back home.

We went places in that car, me and Henry. We took off driving all one whole summer. We started off toward the Little Knife River and Mandaree in Fort Berthold and then we found ourselves down in Wakpala somehow, and then suddenly we were over in Montana on the Rocky Boy, and yet the summer was not even half over. Some people hang on to details when they travel, but we didn't let them bother us and just lived our everyday lives here to there.

I do remember this one place with willows. I remember I lay under those trees and it was comfortable. So comfortable. The branches bent down all around me like a tent or a stable.

And quiet, it was quiet, even though there was a powwow close enough so I could see it going on. The air was not too still, not too windy either. When the dust rises up and hangs in the air around the dancers like that, I feel good. Henry was asleep with his arms thrown wide. Later on, he woke up and we started driving again. We were somewhere in Montana, or maybe on the Blood Reserve—it could have been anywhere. Anyway it was where we met the girl.

All her hair was in buns around her ears, that's the first thing I noticed about her. She was posed alongside the road with her arm out, so we stopped. That girl was short, so short her lumber shirt looked comical on her, like a nightgown. She had jeans on and fancy moccasins and she carried a little suitcase.

"Hop on in," says Henry. So she climbs in between us.

"We'll take you home," I says. "Where do you live?"

"Chicken," she says.

"Where the hell's that?" I ask her.

"Alaska."

"Okay," says Henry, and we drive.

We got up there and never wanted to leave. The sun doesn't truly set there in summer, and the night is more a soft dusk. You might doze off, sometimes, but before you know it you're up again, like an animal in nature. You never feel like you have to sleep hard or put away the world. And things would grow up there. One day just dirt or moss, the next day flowers and long grass. The girl's name was Susy. Her family really took to us. They fed us and put us up. We had our own tent to live in by their house, and the kids would be in and out of there all day and night. They couldn't get over me and Henry being brothers, we looked so different. We told them we knew we had the same mother, anyway.

One night Susy came in to visit us. We sat around in the tent talking of this and that. The season was changing. It was getting darker by that time, and the cold was even getting just a little mean. I told her it was time for us to go. She stood up on a chair.

"You never seen my hair," Susy said.

That was true. She was standing on a chair, but still, when she unclipped her buns the hair reached all the way to the ground. Our eyes opened. You couldn't tell how much hair she had when it was rolled up so neatly. Then my brother Henry did something funny. He went up to the chair and said, "Jump on my shoulders." So she did that, and her hair reached down past his waist, and he started twirling, this way and that, so her hair was flung out from side to side.

"I always wondered what it was like to have long pretty hair," Henry says. Well we laughed. It was a funny sight, the way he did it. The next morning we got up and took leave of those people.

On to greener pastures, as they say. It was down through Spokane and across Idaho then Montana and very soon we were racing the weather right along under the Canadian border through Columbus, Des Lacs, and then we were in Bottineau County and soon home. We'd made most of the trip, that summer, without putting up the car hood at all. We got home just in time, it turned out, for the army to remember Henry had signed up to join it.

I don't wonder that the army was so glad to get my brother that they turned him into a Marine. He was built like a brick outhouse anyway. We liked to tease him that they really wanted him for his Indian nose. He had a nose big and sharp as a hatchet, like the nose on Red Tomahawk, the Indian who killed Sitting Bull, whose profile is on signs all along the

North Dakota highways. Henry went off to training camp, came home once during Christmas, then the next thing you know we got an overseas letter from him. It was 1970, and he said he was stationed up in the northern hill country. Whereabouts I did not know. He wasn't such a hot letter writer, and only got off two before the enemy caught him. I could never keep it straight, which direction those good Vietnam soldiers were from.

I wrote him back several times, even though I didn't know if those letters would get through. I kept him informed all about the car. Most of the time I had it up on blocks in the yard or half taken apart, because that long trip did a hard job on it under the hood.

I always had good luck with numbers, and never worried about the draft myself. I never even had to think about what my number was. But Henry was never lucky in the same way as me. It was at least three years before Henry came home. By then I guess the whole war was solved in the government's mind, but for him it would keep on going. In those years I'd put his car into almost perfect shape. I always thought of it as his car while he was gone, even though when he left he said, "Now it's yours," and threw me his key.

"Thanks for the extra key," I'd said. "I'll put it up in your drawer just in case I need it." He laughed.

When he came home, though, Henry was very different, and I'll say this: the change was no good. You could hardly expect him to change for the better, I know. But he was quiet, so quiet, and never comfortable sitting still anywhere but always up and moving around. I thought back to times we'd sat still for whole afternoons, never moving a muscle, just shifting our weight along the ground, talking to whoever sat with us, watching things. He'd always had a joke, then, too, and now you couldn't get him to laugh, or when he did it was more the sound of a man choking, a sound that stopped up the throats of other people around him. They got to leaving him alone most of the time, and I didn't blame them. It was a fact: Henry was jumpy and mean.

I'd bought a color TV set for my mom and the rest of us while Henry was away. Money still came very easy. I was sorry I'd ever bought it though, because of Henry. I was also sorry I'd bought color, because with black-and-white the pictures seem older and farther away. But what are you going to do? He sat in front of it, watching it, and that was the only time he was completely still. But it was the kind of stillness that you see in a rabbit when it freezes and before it will bolt. He was not easy. He sat in his chair gripping the armrests with all his might, as if the chair itself was moving at a high speed and if he let go at all he would rocket forward and maybe crash right through the set.

Once I was in the room watching TV with Henry and I heard his teeth click at something. I looked over, and he'd bitten through his lip. Blood was going down his chin. I tell you right then I wanted to smash that tube to pieces. I went over to it but Henry must have known what I was up to. He rushed from his chair and shoved me out of the way, against the wall. I told myself he didn't know what he was doing.

My mom came in, turned the set off real quiet, and told us she had made something for supper. So we went and sat down. There was still blood going down Henry's chin, but he didn't notice it and no one said anything even though every time he took a bite of his bread his blood fell onto it until he was eating his own blood mixed in with the food.

While Henry was not around we talked about what was going to happen to him. There were no Indian doctors on the reservation, and my mom couldn't come around to trusting the old man, Moses Pillager, because he courted her long ago and was jealous of her husbands. He might take revenge through her son. We were afraid that if we brought Henry to a regular hospital they would keep him.

"They don't fix them in those places," Mom said; "they just give them drugs."

"We wouldn't get him there in the first place," I agreed, "so let's just forget about it."

Then I thought about the car.

Henry had not even looked at the car since he'd gotten home, though like I said, it was in tip-top condition and ready to drive. I thought the car might bring the old Henry back somehow. So I bided my time and waited for my chance to interest him in the vehicle.

One night Henry was off somewhere. I took myself a hammer. I went out to that car and I did a number on its underside. Whacked it up. Bent the tail pipe double. Ripped the muffler loose. By the time I was done with the car it looked worse than any typical Indian car that has been driven all its life on reservation roads, which they always say are like government promises—full of holes. It just about hurt me, I'll tell you that! I threw dirt in the carburetor and I ripped all the electric tape off the seats. I made it look just as beat up as I could. Then I sat back and waited for Henry to find it.

Still, it took him over a month. That was all right, because it was just getting warm enough, not melting, but warm enough to work outside.

"Lyman," he says, walking in one day, "that red car looks like shit."

"Well it's old," I says. "You got to expect that."

"No way!" says Henry. "That car's a classic! But you went and ran the piss right out of it, Lyman, and you know it don't deserve that. I kept that car in A-one shape. You don't remember. You're too young. But when I left, that car was running like a watch. Now I don't even know if I can get it to start again, let alone get it anywhere near its old condition."

"Well you try," I said, like I was getting mad, "but I say it's a piece of junk."

Then I walked out before he could realize I knew he'd strung together more than six words at once.

After that I thought he'd freeze himself to death working on that car. He was out there all day, and at night he rigged up a little lamp, ran a cord out the window, and had himself some light to see by while he worked. He was better than he had been before, but that's still not saying much. It was easier for him to do the things the rest of us did. He ate more slowly and didn't jump up and down during the meal to get this or that or look out the window. I put my hand in the back of the TV set, I admit, and fiddled around with it good, so that it was almost impossible now to get a clear picture. He didn't look at it very often anyway. He was always out with that car or going off to get parts for it. By the time it was really melting outside, he had it fixed.

I had been feeling down in the dumps about Henry around this time. We had always been together before. Henry and Lyman. But he was such a loner now that I didn't know how to take it. So I jumped at the chance one day when Henry seemed friendly. It's not that he smiled or anything. He just said, "Let's take that old shitbox for a spin." Just the way he said it made me think he could be coming around.

We went out to the car. It was spring. The sun was shining very bright. My only sister, Bonita, who was just eleven years old, came out and made us stand together for a picture.

Henry leaned his elbow on the red car's windshield, and he took his other arm and put it over my shoulder, very carefully, as though it was heavy for him to lift and he didn't want to bring the weight down all at once.

"Smile," Bonita said, and he did.

That picture. I never look at it anymore. A few months ago, I don't know why, I got his picture out and tacked it on the wall. I felt good about Henry at the time, close to him. I felt good having his picture on the wall, until one night when I was looking at television. I was a little drunk and stoned. I looked up at the wall and Henry was staring at me. I don't know what it was, but his smile had changed, or maybe it was gone. All I know is I couldn't stay in the same room with that picture. I was shaking. I got up, closed the door, and went into the kitchen. A little later my friend Ray came over and we both went back into that room. We put the picture in a brown bag, folded the bag over and over tightly, then put it way back in a closet.

I still see that picture now, as if it tugs at me, whenever I pass that closet door. The picture is very clear in my mind. It was so sunny that day Henry had to squint against the glare. Or maybe the camera Bonita held flashed like a mirror, blinding him, before she snapped the picture. My face is right out in the sun, big and round. But he might have drawn back, because the shadows on his face are deep as holes. There are two shadows curved like little hooks around the ends of his smile, as if to frame it and try to keep it there— that one, first smile that looked like it might have hurt his face. He has his field jacket on and the worn-in clothes he'd come back in and kept wearing ever since. After Bonita took the picture, she went into the house and we got into the car. There was a full cooler in the trunk. We started off, east, toward Pembina and the Red River because Henry said he wanted to see the high water.

The trip over there was beautiful. When everything starts changing, drying up, clearing off, you feel like your whole life is starting. Henry felt it, too. The top was down and the car hummed like a top. He'd really put it back in shape, even the tape on the seats was very carefully put down and glued back in layers. It's not that he smiled again or even joked, but his face looked to me as if it was clear, more peaceful. It looked as though he wasn't thinking of anything in particular except the bare fields and windbreaks and houses we were passing.

The river was high and full of winter trash when we got there. The sun was still out, but it was colder by the river. There were still little clumps of dirty snow here and there on the banks. The water hadn't gone over the banks yet, but it would, you could tell. It was just at its limit, hard swollen, glossy like an old gray scar. We made ourselves a fire, and we sat down and watched the current go. As I watched it I felt something squeezing inside me and tightening and trying to let go all at the same time. I knew I was not just feeling it myself; I knew I was feeling what Henry was going through at that moment. Except that I couldn't stand it, the closing and opening. I jumped to my feet. I took Henry by the shoulders and I started shaking him. "Wake up," I says, "wake up, wake up, wake up!" I didn't know what had come over me. I sat down beside him again.

His face was totally white and hard. Then it broke, like stones break all of a sudden when water boils up inside them. "I know it," he says. "I know it. I can't help it. It's no use."

We start talking. He said he knew what I'd done with the car. It was obvious it had been whacked out of shape and not just neglected. He said he wanted to give the car to me for good now, it was no use. He said he'd fixed it just to give it back and I should take it.

"No way," I says, "I don't want it."

"That's okay," he says, "you take it."

"I don't want it, though," I says back to him, and then to emphasize, just to emphasize, you understand, I touch his shoulder. He slaps my hand off.

"Take that car," he says.

"No," I say. "Make me," I say, and then he grabs my jacket and rips the arm loose. That jacket is a class act, suede with tags and zippers. I push Henry backwards, off the log. He jumps up and bowls me over. We go down in a clinch and come up swinging hard, for all we're worth, with our fists. He socks my jaw so hard I feel like it swings loose. Then I'm at his rib cage and land a good one under his chin so his head snaps back. He's dazzled. He looks at me and I look at him and then his eyes are full of tears and blood and at first I think he's crying. But no, he's laughing. "Ha! Ha!" he says. "Ha! Ha! Take good care of it."

"Okay," I says. "Okay, no problem. Ha! Ha!"

I can't help it, and I start laughing, too. My face feels fat and strange, and after a while I get a beer from the cooler in the trunk, and when I hand it to Henry he takes his shirt and wipes my germs off. "Hoof-and-mouth disease," he says. For some reason this cracks me up, and so we're really laughing for a while, and then we drink all the rest of the beers one by one and throw them in the river and see how far, how fast, the current takes them before they fill up and sink.

"You want to go on back?" I ask after a while. "Maybe we could snag a couple nice Kashpaw girls."

He says nothing. But I can tell his mood is turning again.

"They're all crazy, the girls up here, every damn one of them."

"You're crazy too," I say, to jolly him up. "Crazy Lamartine boys!"

He looks as though he will take this wrong at first. His face twists, then clears, and he jumps up on his feet. "That's right!" he says. "Crazier 'n hell. Crazy Indians!"

I think it's the old Henry again. He throws off his jacket and starts springing his legs up from the knees like a fancy dancer. He's down doing something between a grass dance and a bunny hop, no kind of dance I ever saw before, but neither has anyone else on all this green growing earth. He's wild. He wants to pitch whoopee! He's up and at me and all over. All this time I'm laughing so hard, so hard my belly is getting tied up in a knot.

"Got to cool me off!" he shouts all of a sudden. Then he runs over to the river and jumps in.

There's boards and other things in the current. It's so high. No sound comes from the river after the splash he makes, so I run right over. I look around. It's getting dark. I see he's halfway across the water already, and I know he didn't swim there but the current took him. It's far. I hear his voice, though, very clearly across it.

"My boots are filling," he says.

He says this in a normal voice, like he just noticed and he doesn't know what to think of it. Then he's gone. A branch comes by. Another branch. And I go in.

By the time I get out of the river, off the snag I pulled myself onto, the sun is down. I walk back to the car, turn on the high beams, and drive it up the bank. I put it in first gear and then I take my foot off the clutch. I get out, close the door, and watch it plow softly into the water. The headlights reach in as they go down, searching, still lighted even after the water swirls over the back end. I wait. The wires short out. It is all finally dark. And then there is only the water, the sound of it going and running and going and running and running.

from *The Bluest Eye*

TONI MORRISON

She slept in the bed with us. Frieda on the outside because she is brave—it never occurs to her that if in her sleep her hand hangs over the edge of the bed "something" will crawl out from under it and bite her fingers off. I sleep near the wall because that thought *has* occurred to me. Pecola, therefore, had to sleep in the middle.

Mama had told us two days earlier that a "case" was coming—a girl who had no place to go. The county had placed her in our house for a few days until they could decide what to do, or, more precisely, until the family was reunited. We were to be nice to her and not fight. Mama didn't know "what got into people," but that old Dog Breedlove had burned up his house, gone upside his wife's head, and everybody, as a result, was outdoors.

Outdoors, we knew, was the real terror of life. The threat of being outdoors surfaced frequently in those days. Every possibility of excess was curtailed with it. If somebody ate too much, he could end up outdoors. If somebody used too much coal, he could end up outdoors. People could gamble themselves outdoors, drink themselves outdoors. Sometimes mothers put their sons outdoors, and when that happened, regardless of what the son had done, all sympathy was with him. He was outdoors, and his own flesh had done it. To be put outdoors by a landlord was one thing—unfortunate, but an aspect of life over which you had no control, since you could not control your income. But to be slack enough to put oneself outdoors, or heartless enough to put one's own kin outdoors—that was criminal.

There is a difference between being put *out* and being put out*doors*. If you are put out, you go somewhere else; if you are outdoors, there is no place to go. The distinction was subtle but final. Outdoors was the end of something, an irrevocable, physical fact, defining and complementing our metaphysical condition. Being a minority in both caste and class, we moved about anyway on the hem of life, struggling to consolidate our weaknesses and hang on, or to creep singly up into the major folds of the garment. Our peripheral existence, how- ever, was something we had learned to deal with—probably because it was abstract. But the concreteness of being out- doors was another matter—like the difference between the concept of death and being, in fact, dead. Dead doesn't change, and outdoors is here to stay.

Knowing that there was such a thing as outdoors bred in us a hunger for property, for ownership. The firm possession of a yard, a porch, a grape arbor. Propertied black people spent all their energies, all their love, on their nests. Like frenzied, desperate birds, they overdecorated everything; fussed and fidgeted over their hard-won homes; canned, jellied, and preserved all summer to fill the cupboards and shelves; they painted, picked, and poked at every corner of their houses. And these houses loomed like hothouse sunflowers among the rows of weeds that were the rented houses. Renting blacks cast furtive glances at these owned yards and porches, and made firmer com- mitments to buy themselves, "some nice little old place." In the meantime, they saved, and scratched, and piled away what they could in the rented hovels, looking forward to the day of property.

Cholly Breedlove, then, a renting black, having put his family outdoors, had catapulted himself beyond the reaches of human consideration. He had joined the animals; was, indeed, an old dog, a snake, a ratty nigger. Mrs. Breedlove was staying with the woman she worked for; the boy, Sammy, was with some other family; and Pecola was to stay with us. Cholly was in jail.

She came with nothing. No little paper bag with the other dress, or a nightgown, or two pair of whitish cotton bloomers. She just appeared with a white woman and sat down.

We had fun in those few days Pecola was with us. Frieda and I stopped fighting each other and concentrated on our guest, trying hard to keep her from feeling outdoors.

When we discovered that she clearly did not want to dominate us, we liked her. She laughed when I clowned for her, and smiled and accepted gracefully the food gifts my sister gave her.

"Would you like some graham crackers?"

"I don't care."

Frieda brought her four graham crackers on a saucer and some milk in a blue-and-white Shirley Temple cup. She was a long time with the milk, and gazed fondly at the silhouette of Shirley Temple's dimpled face. Frieda and she had a loving conversation about how cu-ute Shirley Temple was. I couldn't join them in their adoration because I hated Shirley. Not because she was cute, but because she danced with Bojangles, who was *my* friend, *my* uncle, *my* daddy, and who ought to have been soft-shoeing it and chuckling with me. Instead he was enjoying, sharing, giving a lovely dance thing with one of those little white girls whose socks never slid down under their heels. So I said, "I like Jane Withers."

They gave me a puzzled look, decided I was incomprehensible, and continued their reminiscing about old squint-eyed Shirley.

Younger than both Frieda and Pecola, I had not yet arrived at the turning point in the development of my psyche which would allow me to love her. What I felt at that time was unsullied hatred. But before that I had felt a stranger, more frightening thing than hatred for all the Shirley Temples of the world.

It had begun with Christmas and the gift of dolls. The big, the special, the loving gift was always a big, blue-eyed Baby Doll. From the clucking sounds of adults I knew that the doll represented what they thought was my fondest wish. I was bemused with the thing itself, and the way it looked. What was I supposed to do with it? Pretend I was its mother? I had no interest in babies or the concept of motherhood. I was interested only in humans my own age and size, and could not generate any enthusiasm at the prospect of being a mother. Motherhood was old age, and other remote possibilities. I learned quickly, however, what I was expected to do with the doll: rock it, fabricate storied situations around it, even sleep with it. Picture books were full of little girls sleeping with their dolls. Raggedy Ann dolls usually, but, they were out of the question. I was physically revolted by and secretly frightened of those round moronic eyes, the pancake face, and orangeworms hair.

The other dolls, which were supposed to bring me great pleasure, succeeded in doing quite the opposite. When I took it to bed, its hard unyielding limbs resisted my flesh—the tapered fingertips on those dimpled hands scratched. If, in sleep, I turned, the bone-cold head collided with my own. It was a most uncomfortable, patently aggressive sleeping companion. To hold it was no more rewarding. The starched gauze or lace on the cotton dress irritated any embrace. I had only one desire: to dismember it. To see of what it was made, to discover the dearness, to find the beauty, the desirability that had escaped me, but apparently only me. Adults, older girls, shops, magazines, newspapers, window signs—all the world had agreed that a blue-eyed, yellow-haired, pink-skinned doll was what every girl child treasured. "Here," they said, "this is beautiful, and if you are on this day 'worthy' you may have it." I fingered the face, wondering at the single-stroke eyebrows; picked at the pearly teeth stuck like two piano keys between red bowline lips. Traced the turned-up nose, poked the glassy blue eyeballs, twisted the yellow hair. I could not love it. But I could examine it to see what it was that all the world said was lovable. Break off the tiny fingers, bend the flat feet, loosen the hair, twist the head around, and the thing made one sound—a sound they said was the sweet and plaintive cry "Mama," but which sounded to me like the bleat of a dying lamb, or, more precisely, our icebox door opening on rusty hinges in July. Remove the cold and stupid eyeball, it would bleat still, "Ahhhhhh," take off the head, shake out the sawdust, crack the back against the brass bed rail, it would bleat still. The gauze back would split, and I could see the disk with six holes, the secret of the sound. A mere metal roundness.

Grown people frowned and fussed: "You-don't-know-how-to-take-care-of-nothing. I-never-had-a-baby-doll-in-my-whole-life-and-used-to-cry-my-eyes-out-for-them. Now-you-got-one-a-beautiful-one-and-you-tear-it-up-what's-the-matter-with-you?"

How strong was their outrage. Tears threatened to erase the aloofness of their authority. The emotion of years of un-fulfilled longing preened in their voices. I did not know why I destroyed those dolls. But I did know that nobody ever asked me what I wanted for Christmas. Had any adult with the power to fulfill my desires taken me seriously and asked me what I wanted, they would have known that I did not want to have anything to own, or to possess any object. I wanted rather to feel something on Christmas day. The real question would have been, "Dear Claudia, what experience would you like on Christmas?" I could have spoken up, "I want to sit on the low stool in Big Mama's kitchen with my lap full of lilacs and listen to Big Papa play his violin for me alone." The lowness of the stool made for my body, the security and warmth of Big Mama's kitchen, the smell of the lilacs, the sound of the music, and, since it would be good to have all of my senses engaged, the taste of a peach, perhaps, afterward.

Instead I tasted and smelled the acridness of tin plates and cups designed for tea parties that bored me. Instead I looked with loathing on new dresses that required a hateful bath in a galvanized zinc tub before wearing. Slipping around on the zinc, no time to play or soak, for the water chilled too fast, no time to enjoy one's nakedness, only time to make curtains of soapy water careen down between the legs. Then the scratchy towels and the dreadful and humiliating absence of dirt. The irritable, unimaginative cleanliness. Gone the ink marks from legs and face, all my creations and accumulations of the day gone, and replaced by goose pimples.

I destroyed white baby dolls.

But the dismembering of dolls was not the true horror. The truly horrifying thing was the transference of the same impulses to little white girls. The indifference with which I could have axed them was shaken only by my desire to do so. To discover what eluded me: the secret of the magic they weaved on others. What made people look at them and say. "Awwwww," but not for me? The eye slide of black women as they approached them on the street, and the possessive gentleness of their touch as they handled them.

If I pinched them, their eyes—unlike the crazed glint of the baby doll's eyes—would fold in pain, and their cry would not be the sound of an icebox door, but a fascinating cry of pain. When I learned how repulsive this disinterested violence was, that it was repulsive because it was disinterested, my shame floundered about for refuge. The best hiding place was love. Thus the conversion from pristine sadism to fabricated hatred, to fraudulent love. It was a small step to Shirley Temple. I learned much later to worship her, just as I learned to delight in cleanliness, knowing, even as I learned, that the change was adjustment without improvement.

Killing the Bees

LYNNE SHARON SCHWARTZ

After Ilse and Mitch had both been stung twice, Mitch sprayed insecticide around the flower beds at the side of the house, where the bees seemed to congregate. But the very next day Cathy, their youngest child, got stung on the back of the neck. It was a bright May afternoon, the three of them out on the lawn with the Sunday papers, Cathy plugged into her Walkman. Quiet Ilse made a great fuss, jumped up and grabbed a handful of damp soil from the flower bed to slap on the bite, then crooned soothing words—as if, Cathy said with a brave patronizing smile, she were an infant and not almost fifteen.

"But doesn't it hurt a lot?"

"It hurts, Mom, but I'll live."

"What's the matter?" Mitch must have been dozing behind the travel section. He rearranged his body in the lawn chair and blinked, trying to look alert. He was a graying man of fifty-three, handsome in a ruddy, solid, ex-athlete's way, with strikingly pale blue eyes. He owned a chain of hardware stores. A safe man, Ilse thought each evening when he returned from work. And decent, competent, sexy: mornings, watching him dress—the ritual bending, reaching, zipping, and buttoning—she felt a reflexive pleasure, compounded with satisfaction, like the interest on capital, at how durable this pleasure had proved. If that was love, then she loved him well enough.

"It's those bees again. We really must do something about

them. Poor baby. Come, let me wash it and put on some oint-
ment."

"God, what would you do if I had rabies?"

Ilse knew why she was making a fuss: the one time she
herself had been stung as a child—at four years old—her
usually attentive mother hardly seemed to care. That baffling
lapse, the utter failure to respond properly, even more than
the throng at the airport or the loudspeaker barking, the
pinched, scared faces and the forest of gleaming tall
boots, told Ilse something portentous was happening. Her
father had already kissed them goodbye and disappeared,
leaving her mother teary, and she was close to tears again
five minutes later, showing some papers to a mustached,
uniformed man at a desk, who waved his clipboard in the
air and called them to a halt in a gritty voice. Soon, like a
little firecracker fizzling out, he spat a bad name at them
and sent them on. Her mother was tugging her by the hand,
rushing towards the stairs at the plane, when Ilse let out
a howl.

"Shh! Don't make noise. What is it?"

"Something is in my dress! In back!"

Her mother yanked at the dress and slapped her back
hard—to kill the bee, she said later—but that only made the
sting worse.

"Be still now, Ilse!" she ordered. "I'll take care of it afterwards."

But Ilse wailed running up the stairs, and as they entered
the plane people looked up disapprovingly. Her mother kept
her head bowed. Only when they were above the clouds did
she become herself again, rubbing spit on the sting till Ilse
calmed down.

"When we meet our cousins," she said, belatedly kissing
the sore spot, "can you say 'How do you do,' in English?
How do you do?" She exaggerated the shape of the words on

her lips and Ilse repeated. How do you do. But for long after, she felt betrayed in her moment of need.

In England, when she asked for her father, her mother said, "He's coming. He'll come as soon as he can." In time she understood there was a war going on: the children at school wouldn't let her play and made fun of the way she spoke. Her mother couldn't get a job and often they were hungry. Just as the hunger was becoming unbearable, food would appear, Ilse never knew how. If she complained, her mother said cryptically, "Still, we're lucky. Lucky." She stopped asking about her father and eventually the war was over. When they went looking for a flat in London she heard her mother tell the landladies he was killed in the war. Then her mother would murmur some words very low, as if she were embarrassed, and the landladies' granite faces would loosen a bit, and a Mrs. Soloway finally let them have a room.

In bed with Mitch that night, Ilse heard a humming noise, muffled, but rhythmic and relentless like the plangent moan of an infirmary.

"Listen. Do you hear anything?" she whispered.

"Only you breathing." Mitch lay with his head on her stomach, his arms locked around her hips. Always, after they made love, his voice was heavy and sweet with a childlike contentment. "You sound sensational, Ilse. Do it a little harder." He began kissing her belly again.

She smiled even though the noise agitated her. "Not that, silly. Listen. It sounds like something in the wall."

He groaned and sat up, businesslike, turning on the lamp as if that could make the noise clearer. They stared at each other, concentrating, and indeed enlightenment came. "I bet it's those bees. They've managed to get into the wall now. Jesus Christ!" He turned away to roll himself in the sheets.

"Hey, I didn't put them there," Ilse said softly. "Come on back."

"You know what I'll have to do now? Make a hole in the goddamn wall and spray inside. Just what we needed. A bee colony."

"My sweet baby," she said, stroking him. "My prince to the rescue. My Saint George killing the dragon."

"It's going to stink to high heaven," he said.

Mitch slept, but hours later Ilse was still trapped in wakefulness by the humming noise. She pictured a gigantic swarm of bees fluttering their wings together in the dark, a shuddering jellylike mass. It was an unbearable sound, ominous, droning. Of course, she thought. Drones.

The next two evenings Mitch forgot to bring the extra-strength spray home from the store. On the third day Ilse phoned to remind him. "Look, I hate to keep nagging, but I've hardly slept."

"They can't come out, Ilse."

"I know. I'm not afraid of bees anyway. It's the noise. Just bring it, will you please?"

After dinner he listened with his ear to the wall for the place where the noise was loudest, then chipped with a screwdriver until a tiny hole appeared. Quickly he shoved a small rectangle of shirt cardboard over the hole, and using that as a shield, made the hole bigger. When it was about a half inch in diameter, he told Ilse to go out of the room and close the door. She closed the door but stayed, standing back. It didn't seem fair to protect herself while he was in danger. Besides, she felt an eerie fascination. Mitch moved the cardboard aside and inserted the nozzle of the spray can. The smell was nasty and stinging, but not as bad as she had imagined. Then he covered the hole again and they fixed the cardboard to the wall with thumbtacks. Ilse heard a sharp crackling like the sound of damp twigs catching a flame.

"What's that?"

"It's them. That's what you wanted, isn't it? Let's just hope it gets them all."

A wave of nausea and dizziness assaulted her, and she lay down till it passed. That night she slept well, in blissful silence.

The following morning, one of her days off—she worked as a part-time secretary at a law firm in town—she was outside, kneeling to put in the marigolds, when she noticed a patch a few feet off that looked like speckled black velvet. She crawled closer. The corpses of bees, hundreds, thousands, the obscene remains of a massacre. She had never thought about where they would go, never thought further than getting rid of them. Why hadn't they simply rotted in the wall unseen? Peering up, she spied a dark mass the size of a cantaloupe, attached like a tumor to the outside wall not far from their bedroom window, and almost hidden by the thick leaves of the maple. Somehow they had never thought to look for a hive, but now it seemed obvious.

Ilse was not squeamish. She had disposed of dead ants and flies and even mice, but the sight of the slaughtered bees paralyzed her. She knelt in the garden for a long time, then dragged herself inside and phoned Mitch, but when he answered she found she couldn't tell him right away.

"This must be our lucky day," she said instead. "Both wanderers heard from." There had been a postcard from their son, Brian, who was working on a cattle ranch in Wyoming, and another from Melissa, who had just completed her second year of law school and, with three girlfriends, was recuperating for a week in Jamaica before starting her summer job.

"That's great." He sounded distracted.

Stammering a bit, Ilse mentioned the dead bees and the hive near the bedroom window.

"A hive, eh? I should have known. Well, just sweep them up, Ilse, okay? I'll have a look when I get home."

"Yes, well—you can't imagine how hideous . . . These are enormous bees. It's like a battlefield. . . . What should I do with them?"

"Do with them? Put them in the garbage, sweetheart. Unless you want to hold a mass funeral."

"I see I shouldn't have bothered you."

"Ilse, it's just that I've got a store full of customers. Leave it if you can't do it. Or have Cathy do it. It's not worth bickering over."

She tried sweeping them into a dustpan, but as she watched the bodies roll and tumble, the wings and feelers lacing and tangling, she felt faint. Finally she abandoned the task and left the marigolds, too, for another day. When Cathy came home from school she asked her to do it and Cathy obliged, with pungent expressions of disgust but no apparent difficulty.

Mitch got on a ladder and sprayed the hive. There was silence for several nights and they thought it was over. Then Ilse woke before dawn and heard the humming in the wall, fainter, but still insistent. She began to weep, very quietly, so as not to wake Mitch.

After the war her mother got a clerical job at the National Gallery in London, where she met an American tour guide and married him.

"We're going to have a new life, darling," she told Ilse excitedly. Mostly they spoke German when they were alone, but her mother said this in English. "We're going to America with Robbie. Denver. You'll love it, I know." Ilse nodded. She was a silent child, the kind who seems full of secrets. At school she had few friends, was politely enigmatic, and did her work adequately, but the teachers nonetheless accused her of dreaming. In America she changed. Robbie was all right; he looked like a cowboy and sounded like Gary Cooper, and Ilse treated him as a casual friend of the family. But she did love America. No one shunned her. They liked her British accent and were eager to hear stories of life in London. I can be a normal girl, she whispered to herself one morning in the mirror. From now on. And she behaved as she perceived other normal girls to behave, a tactic which worked so well that she adopted it for the rest of her life. Meanwhile, when she was old enough to understand, around Cathy's age, she went on a binge of reading books about the war, till she was satisfied that she comprehended what had happened to her father, what his final years or months had been like, and had lived them in her bones up to the point where his own bones lay in a ditch, indistinguishable from the millions of others.

"You never talk about him." She expected her mother would hedge and say, About who? but she was mistaken.

"What can I say? He died in the war."

"But I mean, about how."

"Do you know how?" her mother asked.

"Yes."

"Well, so do I. So . . ."

She was craving a significant scene, tears and embraces, or lies and shouting, culminating in cloak-and-dagger truths, secret horrors not included in any books, and above all in profundities vast enough to connect the past to the present, but her mother offered nothing.

"Did you cry?"

"What a question, Ilse. I cried plenty, yes."

But she was not about to cry anew for Ilse. They were lucky, her mother repeated with lips stiff and quaking. "Remember all your life what a lucky person you are."

Ilse fled from the room. Now she had long forgiven her

mother. At the time they boarded the plane for London, she realized, the day she got stung, her mother was twenty-four years old. A girl the age of Melissa, who was swimming and dancing in the Caribbean moonlight and about to earn extravagant sums of money. And at the time of their talk, her mother had known Robbie for as long as she had known Ilse's father. Her mother was truly lucky. In compassion, Ilse stopped pestering her and let her live her lucky life.

Twice more Mitch moved aside the cardboard and sprayed into the hole. Twice more the bees crackled, the room smelled, and the nights were silent, then the noise returned.

"It's no use. We need an exterminator." And he sighed a husbandly sigh of overwork.

"I'll take care of that." Ilse was expert at arranging for services and dealing with repairmen. In the yellow pages she found just what was needed: Ban-the-Bug, which promised to rid your home of pests for good. Ban-the-Bug's logo was a familiar black-bordered circle with a black line running diagonally through the center. Three times a week Ilse saw that same symbol, but in red, on the door of Ban-the-Bomb, a local group with a small office opposite her own. Except instead of the mushroom cloud in the center, Ban-the-Bug's circle displayed a repulsive insect suggesting a cross between a winged cockroach and a centipede. The black line was firm and categorical: it meant, Ilse knew, No More, Get Rid Of, *Verboten*.

On the telephone, she did not even have to supply details. Ban-the-Bug understood all about the problem and would send a man over late that afternoon.

"Don't worry, you'll never have to hear that sound again," a reassuring, motherly voice told Ilse.

Never again. She would sleep in peace. The soothing promise echoed as she shopped and chatted in the market and set out on the kitchen counter all the ingredients for a Chinese dinner. With another secretary from the law firm she was taking a course in Chinese cooking, and Mitch and Cathy had been teasing her for a demonstration. Cathy had brought a friend home from school, and both girls volunteered to help. As Ilse sautéed garlic and ginger, the kitchen filled with a luxurious, tangy odor. She chopped the pork and set the girls to work on the peppers and scallions and cabbage.

The smell made her hungry, and as usual, hunger made her think of being hungry in London, such a different kind of hunger, long-lasting and tedious, like a sickness, and panicky, with no hope of ever being fully eased.

That was far away now, though. Her present hunger is the good kind, the hunger of anticipation.

The girls are jabbering across the large kitchen. Having raised two children to adulthood, Ilse is not passionately interested in the jabbering of teenagers. But this conversation is special. It snares her. Evidently they are learning about World War II in history class, and Mary Beth, a thin, still flat-chested girl with straight blond hair, is a Quaker, Ilse gathers. She is explaining to Cathy the principles of nonviolence.

"But there must be limits," Cathy says. "Like supposing it was during the war and you saw Hitler lying in the road, half dead and begging for water. You wouldn't have to actually kill him, just . . . sort of leave him there."

"If a dying person asks me for water I would have to give it," says Mary Beth.

"Even Hitler?"

Mary Beth doesn't hesitate. "He's a human being." Ilse chops pork steadily with her cleaver. She rarely mixes in.

"But my God! Well, supposing he asks you to take him to a hospital?"

"I guess I would. If it was to save his life."

"You'd probably nurse him and help him get back to work, right?" Cathy is irate, Ilse notes with a keen stab of pleasure in her gut.

"No, you don't understand. I'd never help him make war. But see, if I let him die it would be basically the same as killing him, and then I would become like him, a killer."

"So big deal. You'd also be saving a lot of people."

"I'd rather try to save them by talking to him, explaining what—"

"Oh, come on, Mary Beth. What horseshit."

Ilse accidentally grazes her finger with the cleaver and bleeds onto the pork. She sucks, tasting the warm blood with surprising glee. It has just left her heart, which strains toward her daughter with a weight of love.

"Look, Cathy," replies Mary Beth, "the real issue is what do I want to be? Do I want to be a truly good person or do I want to spend the next fifty years knowing I could have saved a life and didn't? How could I face myself in the mirror? I'd be, like, tainted."

This Mary Beth is a lunatic, that much is clear, thinks Ilse. Get rid of her this instant. Out, out of the house! But of course she cannot do that. The girl is Cathy's blameless little friend, invited for a Chinese dinner.

"Who gives a damn about your one soul!" exclaims Cathy. "What about all the other souls who'll die?"

Enough already, please! moans Ilse silently, watching her blood ooze through a paper napkin. What kind of people could teach their children such purity? They should teach her instead about the generous concealments of mirrors. Taste every impurity, she would like to tell Mary Beth, swallow them and assimilate them and carry them inside. When you're starving you'll eat anything. Ilse has. And none of it shows in any mirror.

"I'm sorry for those people. I mean it. I'd try to help them too. But I can't become a killer for them."

"That's the most selfish, dumbest thing I ever heard."

It begins to appear the friends will have a real falling-out. Not worth it, in the scheme of things. "How're you girls doing with the chopping?" Ilse breaks in. "Oh, that looks fine. Mary Beth, do the cabbage a little bit smaller, okay? Cathy, would you get me a Band-Aid? I cut my finger."

As soon as she gets the Band-Aid on, she hears a van pull into the driveway. Ban-the-Bug. The symbol with the grotesque insect is painted on the van. In her torment she has forgotten the appointment. She greets the smiling young man at the kitchen door and takes him around to the side of the house where the hive is. Behind her she can hear the girls tittering over how good-looking he is. Well, fine, that will re-unite them. And indeed he is, a dazzling Hollywood specimen, tall, narrow-hipped, and rangy, with golden hair and tanned skin. Blue eyes, but duller than Mitch's. Wonderful golden-haired wrists and big hands. He is holding a clipboard with some papers, like a functionary, and *Ban-the-Bug* is written in red script just above the pocket of his sky blue shirt, whose sleeves are rolled up to the shoulders, revealing noteworthy muscles. Ilse points out the hive and he nods, unamazed.

"I would judge from the size," he says, "you've got about forty thousand bees in there."

Ilse gasps.

"Yup, that's right." His tone is cheerfully sympathetic. Really a charming young man. Perhaps attended the local community college for two years, like Brian, Ilse thinks, found he was not academically inclined, though bright enough, and looked for any old job till he could decide what he wanted. He would make a nice tennis instructor. "They're honeybees. There's most likely a lot of honey in the wall."

"Oh, can we get it out?" Ilse loves honey.

"Well, once we spray, it won't be good anymore." He sounds genuinely regretful. "You see, the bees take turns fanning the honey with their wings to keep it at sixty-five degrees. But now with the warm weather it'll melt pretty fast. You might even have to break though the wall and get rid of it. It could smell or stain, it's hard to say."

She envisions forty thousand bees frantically fanning, protecting their product and livelihood, their treasure and birthright. That is the terrifying demented noise she hears at night.

"Will you get them all?"

"Oh sure." He laughs. "No problem. We guarantee. Any that don't die just fly away—with the hive gone, you won't be seeing them around. Except if you have holes in the wall some might try to get back in and start all over."

"I don't think there are any holes."

"Could you just sign this paper, please?" He holds out the clipboard.

Ilse is always careful about what she signs. Robbie taught her that when she first came to America. "What is it?"

"Just routine. That we're not responsible for any damage to property, the terms of payment, the guarantee, and so on. Go ahead, read it. Take your time."

Feeling rather foolish, she scans the document. It is merely what he said, as far as she can see, and seems excessively formal for so simple a transaction. The undersigned is to pay half now and half on completion of the service, but since this case will probably require only one visit, the young man says, she can pay all at once. A hundred dollars for forty thousand bees. A quarter of a cent per bee, Ilse rapidly calculates, though it is a meaningless statistic. She signs and hands the document back.

"How long will it take?"

"Ten, fifteen minutes at the most."

"No, I mean before they're all gone."

"Oh," He chuckles at his little error. "The stuff works gradually, like, in stages. You might still hear something this evening, but then, during the night"—and he grins so ingenuously that she realizes he is just a boy, after all—"*baaad* things will happen to them."

He pauses, but Ilse has no ready response.

"Okay, I'll do the inside first." He fetches several cans and a small toolbox from the van and follows her up to the bedroom, where she shows him the makeshift cardboard patch. He nods as if he has seen it all before, and asks her to leave the room and close the door. Although she again has a secret hankering to stay and watch, Ilse obeys. So she never gets to see exactly what is done, but sits at the kitchen table, writes out a check, and waits. The girls have vanished for the moment, leaving their assigned vegetables ably chopped. In a few minutes the Ban-the-Bug man reappears and goes outside to do the hive. After she thanks him and watches him drive away, Ilse scrubs her hands at the sink before returning to the food—why, she does not know, for she has touched nothing alien except his pen and paper.

Mitch, when he comes home, is pleased at what she has accomplished, and listens respectfully as she relates all the pertinent facts. The dinner is excellent and lavishly praised, and the girls seem to be reconciled. Mary Beth is not such a thoroughgoing prig, as it turns out—she can be highly amusing on the subject of her family's foibles and idiosyncrasies. Later, in bed, Mitch wants to make love, but Ilse cannot summon the spirit to do it. He is disappointed, even a trifle irked, but it will pass. There will be other nights. She lies awake listening. The sound is feebler, and intermittent. She trusts it will stop for good very soon, as she was promised.

The next day, after work, she returns home and finds

Cathy stretched out on a lawn chair, Walkman on, eyes closed. She calls to get her attention and Cathy unplugs. Ilse asks her to gather up and dispose of the corpses, which are so numerous they look like a thick, lush black and gold carpet. Shaking her head morosely at her fate, Cathy fetches a broom and dustpan. Ilse remains there as if turned to a salt block, watching her daughter work.

"Do we really need to go to all this trouble?" Cathy grumbles. "I mean, maybe you could use them for fertilizer or something."

She darts two giant steps to Cathy, grabs her shoulder, and shakes her hard. "How dare you say such a thing!" Her other hand is lifted, in a fist, as if to deliver a killing blow. "How dare you!"

Cathy, pale, shrinks back from her mother. "What did I say? Just tell me, what on God's green earth did I say?"

Drowning

MARY BUCCI BUSH

After the week-long rain, it was too wet for working in the cotton fields, and there were too many snakes for clearing the swamp of stumps and branches. Isola's mother saw that look come onto her daughter's face. "Don't you go to the levee," she told her. "You stay here and fix the clothes with me."

The water came from everywhere. The river swelled and, once, came within inches of the top of the levee, powerful and deep and dangerous. Puddles formed in the woods, the *bosc'* her family called it, big puddles like ponds, and fish swam in the water, fish from nowhere. The land itself turned into a patchwork of streams and ponds and puddles. Even stepping on what looked like dry land became a risk: put your foot on a grassy spot and you might find yourself in water over your ankles.

"Where do you think you're going?" her mother said.

"Nowhere. I got to pee."

"You gotta work, that's what you gotta do." She took the dress from her daughter's hand and shook it out. "Look at this," she said. "What's gonna happen to you when you try to get a husband and he sees you do a mess like this with your sewing?"

"Mamma," she pleaded. "Maybe I'm not gonna get a husband."

Her mother made a sound like she was spitting coffee grounds from her mouth. Then she crossed herself. "I pray for you, dear God, what's gonna happen if you gotta be like this?"

Isola rubbed her foot back and forth along the floor, scratching the ball of her foot on a rough spot on the wood. Oswaldo was out hunting frogs with their father for their supper. Angelina was outside in the sun stringing tomatoes to dry. They had picked as many as they could before the rain came and ruined them. Everyone else was outside doing something, and here she was stuck in the house with her mother's prayers and a needle and thread.

Her mother stood and went for a candle and her statue of the Blessed Virgin Mary. Isola groaned to herself as she watched. Her mother placed the statue on the floor, then lit the candle in front of the statue. She pointed to the floor. "Get down there and pray before the devil takes you to go live with him for good," she said. Isola got down on her knees next to her mother and they prayed: Hail Mary, Our Father, Hail Holy Queen. Then they were quiet for a long time. Isola watched the flame flicker in front of Mary's chipped blue robe. Mary's face was like a little doll's face, and she looked like a girl, maybe a girl Isola's age, with an expression that made Isola think that Mary's mother must have yelled at her all the time, too.

The Italians worked like animals, her father said, scrounging for a penny every minute of the day. When they weren't working off their shares for Mr. Gracey they were hiring out to chop weeds for other farmers, or they were selling tomatoes or eggs house to house or patching people's clothes or washing them or fixing a wagon for them. A penny here, a penny there, and it all got saved. The black people didn't seem to be as crazy about working and making money as the Italians were, even though they got yelled at more for not working enough, and punished in other ways. Most of the time Isola wished she was a black girl so she could play with Birdie more, or sing with her while they worked in the fields.

Isola's mother reached over and snuffed out the candle with her fingers.

"Can I go pee now?" Isola said.

"Go pee. And then you stop and see why the chickens are so quiet, maybe they got drowned out there. Bring the eggs in."

Isola moved toward the door, relieved.

Everything was happening outside. The sun was already beginning to dry the land, and old Step Hall was bringing a mule and wagon down the road, going somewhere for the boss. He raised his hand to her and waved. She moved past Angelina with her strings of tomatoes, down near the road. Birdie was following behind her father on foot, trailing a branch in the dirt.

"Mornin', Miss Isola," Step said as he drove by. "Glad to see you out and about."

Birdie stopped alongside Isola, dragging the branch in the dirt. "Lookit the designs I'm making," she said.

Isola looked at the swirls in the muddy dirt. "My Papa's at the swamp catching frogs," she told Birdie.

Birdie shuddered, dropping the branch. "Frogs," she said. "I don't know how you can eat 'em."

"Just sometimes," Isola said.

Step was nearly down the road. He turned and called out to Birdie, "Don't you be dawdling here. Git back home."

Birdie watched her father ride away. Then she told Isola, "Daddy say a man drowned in the lake. Say his boat got turned over."

"Drowned?" Isola said. She stared at Birdie, wide-eyed.

Isola walked toward the back of the chicken shed so Angelina wouldn't be able to see or hear them.

"Daddy 'spec he was drunk," Birdie told her, "trying to cross the lake to see his gal. He goin' to see now."

"He's going to see a drowned man?" Isola said.

"Got to see who he is, bring him back to bury him if he from here. Nobody know yet. I'm mad he won't take me."

Isola tried to imagine a drowned man. She knew the river was dangerous: nobody ever went in the river, not even with a boat unless it was one of the big river boats. But the lake. Everybody went fishing in the lake, and swimming sometimes too, and they all crossed the lake on Primo's ferry, or in the priest's rowboat.

"If we was in the woods," Birdie said, "we could see when Daddy brung him back."

"My Mamma told me I have to stay away from the levee," Isola said. "She told me to check the chickens and get the eggs."

"Woods ain't no levee," Birdie said. "Your dumb chickens okay."

They listened to the quiet clucking coming from inside the shed.

"She told me to get the eggs. And I have to sew." But even as she said the words to Birdie she saw a big dark figure in her mind, the swollen shape of a man being pulled from the lake and then him lying on the ground, his wet clothes plastered to his bloated body while she moved closer and closer to get a look at his drowned face. But all she could see was a man sleeping, and she saw his puffy closed eyes and his puffy black cheeks and the diamonds of water glistening in his black hair.

They cut through the damp weeds and over across to where the road picked up again. The road was muddy and warm. Heat rose up, like heat from the stove when the fire was just starting to burn—warm, but not too hot.

Besides Birdie, the water was about the only good thing about living on the plantation. Back home they'd had the ocean, but it was different. Even though the tides made the water move, it always moved in the same way. Here, the water was wild. One day it was quiet and sweet and low; the next day it was pulling down houses and carrying mules away, or it was crashing from the sky in sudden, terrifying thunder and lightning storms, or it was seeping into everything through the ground that wasn't the solid ground it seemed to be; or like with the puddles in the *bosc'* a lake would form overnight where there'd only been dry land before. Even the air was full of water, humid, stifling in the summer. You could choke just breathing it, Isola's father said.

The girls slowed down when they reached the SanAngelo house. Nina was their friend. Her mother had the fever and her father had gone off with some other men to try to find work in a mill while Nina and the rest of the family ran the farm. Mr. Gracey's men from the store had gone after Mr. SanAngelo and the others to bring the men back. Everybody on the plantation was talking about it, wondering if they'd be shot, like the black ones who ran away, and wondering too what would happen to their families once the fathers were shot.

"You see her?" Isola whispered.

"I don't see nobody," Birdie told her. They walked slowly, craning their necks to see. The house was closed. The door was closed, and the window panes were closed, like you do when somebody dies. "I wonder if they're inside," Birdie said.

They stopped for a minute and peered at the house, listening. Maybe they were gone out in the fields working, since the land was starting to dry up, and they'd been working even harder than usual since the men from the store went looking for Mr. SanAngelo. Nobody had thought it was a bad idea to go away to look for work to pay off the bills. But once the boss sent his men out, it seemed like a terrible idea. Going away meant you were trying to cheat the boss.

The SanAngelo house was a little shack, like everybody else's, weathered boards built up on tree stumps in case of floods or snakes, not that it kept the snakes from getting in. Two windows and a door, no screens. A stove pipe jutted out of the roof, the stove inside used to cook on and to heat all three rooms in the winter. A tree stump served as a step.

Near the house, the SanAngelos' little vegetable garden lay flattened from the rain. Sticks that had held the tomato plants stood upright, twine still tied to them, while the plants lay on their sides in the sandy dirt. A few smashed red tomatoes lay in the heap.

They hadn't seen Nina in a few days now, and they missed her. But it would be strange to see her, Isola thought, knowing her father had run off and that he was being hunted like an animal and that maybe he would be shot, too.

"Stay away from her," Isola's mother and father had told her. "Maybe the Americans will make trouble for us, too, if they see you playing with her."

But her father wasn't staying away from the SanAngelos. He'd gone to the priest to try to get help for Mrs. SanAngelo and to keep Mr. SanAngelo from going to jail or getting in worse trouble. But so far the priest hadn't done anything. It was a secret. Isola wasn't supposed to tell anyone, or else maybe the men would do something bad to her father if they found out. She couldn't even tell Birdie.

"My Papa says we all have to watch out now," Isola told Birdie.

"What for?"

Isola looked around. She moved closer to Birdie and lowered her voice. "That if we play with Nina the Americans will shoot us. Or maybe burn down our house."

Birdie took a step back and looked at Isola. "Where you got such a crazy idea?"

"That's what the Gracey men do," Isola said. "That's what my Papa told me."

Birdie put her hands on her hips. "You dumb or something? White folks don't shoot white folks." She walked faster, so that Isola had to trot to catch up with her.

"But we're not white," Isola told her. "We're Italian."

They reached the corner field where, despite the recent rain, a few people were out working. It was the Titus land, Birdie's cousins. The black people waded through the tall green plants checking for damage and chopping weeds. The plants that had been broken or knocked down had to be pulled out. Lud Titus called out to Birdie to get home, her Mamma wanted her to work. Birdie waved back to Lud, and then the two of them started running, not down the road that went to Birdie's house but straight ahead toward the woods. They giggled as they ran, over the sight of fat Lud with hardly any hair on her head, and no teeth at all.

The woods was on the way to the lake. The road ran right past the woods, and if a wagon came, especially a wagon carrying a drowned man, they'd be able to run out to see. The water was up in the woods, and the ponds were back. A few fallen limbs, cracked from the storm, their white insides shining, dangled from the trees or lay strewn in the weeds and low grass. The girls ran to the big pond just inside the trees. The ground was spongy under their feet, and mud squished through their toes.

"I wonder if the fish is back this time," Birdie said. She splashed her feet at the edge of the pond. Isola followed her, stepping into the water. It was cool. She rubbed her feet along the grass under the water and watched the mud swirl up, both from the earth and from the dirt on her feet. They found sticks to poke into the water to test its depth. Isola held the hem of her dress bunched in her hands as she poked with her stick in the shallow water.

"See any?" Birdie said. She waded a little farther and bent over, letting her dress get wet.

"There's something," Isola said, pointing. She jumped, but then stood still again. She was afraid of snakes, ever since she'd felt in one of the chicken nests for eggs only to find a big snake slithering through her fingers.

Birdie slapped at the fish with her stick and the fish disappeared. They were small, only a few inches long. Isola's mother said the fish swam in the earth, in water underground, to get to the puddles in the *bosc'*. But her father said they came out of the river and walked across the land at night and jumped into whatever water they found. Isola wondered why she never saw fish walking, since she'd been outside at night lots of times. Or why they never found dead fish on land, the ones that couldn't make it to a piece of water. And how did they *walk,* since they didn't have any legs? The fish looked like ordinary fish: thin and silvery and covered with scales. *Pesce di bosc',* the old people called them, though they said there was nothing like them back home, they'd only seen such things here in this strange country.

"I'm gonna catch one," Birdie said. She was already walking through the water crouched forward, her dress dragging below the surface, plastered against her legs. She held her arms out, ready to grab the first thing that moved.

Birdie was probably the smartest person Isola knew. She had taught Isola and Nina, and some of the others too, a lot of English, even though Birdie couldn't read and wasn't allowed to go to the school. When Mr. Gracey wasn't around her father let her drive the mule. And once, when Birdie and Isola were at the Company store and were hungry for a tin of crackers, Birdie took the crackers up to the clerk and told him she was going to buy them on credit. The man snatched the tin away from her and told them to get out of the store, calling Birdie a "crazy nigger." To Isola, Birdie wasn't being crazy, she was being smart. And brave. Isola would never have dared ask the Americans for credit like the grown men and women did.

"You gonna git in trouble, Missy," Step Hall told his daughter. Sometimes he said it the way any father would, but sometimes, like when he heard about her asking for credit, he said it in an awful, quiet way, and his face went darker than normal, and you could tell he was worried and there was nothing he or anybody else could do.

Two fish swam by and Isola shot her arms into the water to catch them. The hem of her dress fell, and the water soaked her dress halfway up. The fish got away.

"You got to sneak up behind 'em," Birdie told her. "You git over here, stir 'em up, chase 'em my way."

"I'm going to get one myself," Isola told her, but she stirred the fish Birdie's way just the same. Birdie lunged for the fish, landing on her knees.

Isola knelt down in the cool water next to Birdie. They moved their arms through the water and watched the ripples travel slowly to the edge of the pond. She could feel the grass at the bottom of the pond swaying with the currents against her legs, and her dress lift and move with the currents too. Little silver fish swam around them.

"What they going to do with the man when your Papa brings him back?" Isola asked.

Birdie shrugged. "What else? Bury him."

"I wonder if he's somebody we know," Isola said.

"Probably," Birdie answered. "Listen to that. They be looking for me soon enough."

A woman had started singing, far off. That meant more people were back in the fields working. A lot of times they sang while they worked, or they repeated funny rhymes that didn't make any sense. Birdie and her people worked, but not like the Italians. Birdie could play, or "dawdle," as her Papa called it, and she wouldn't get whipped for it. Isola worried that she would get a whipping when she got home, or worse, that if her family went back in the fields to work and she wasn't with them her father would get in trouble, maybe get put in jail like they were going to do with Mr. SanAngelo.

"I better go," she told Birdie, and she stood up in the water. "My Papa will be coming back and we have to go work." Her dress felt heavy as she stood, and the water poured from the skirt. She looked down at it. The cloth unfolded and a long silver fish tumbled out. She grabbed it before it fell into the water. Birdie shrieked, then laughed.

The fish squirmed in Isola's hands. It was cool and slippery and it gave her goose bumps to be touching it, but she couldn't let it go. She had never held a fish that alive, fresh out of the water, before. She splashed out of the pond with Birdie following, and she threw the fish on the grass.

"Did you know it was in there?" Birdie cried. "Didn't you feel it?" And she patted her own dress, as if a fish might be hidden inside her clothes too, and be ready to drop out and scare her.

"I didn't feel it," Isola said. "I didn't even know there was no fish near me."

They bent over and watched the fish. Birdie laid her hand on the fish's side, then pulled back quickly. "Slimy," she said. "Let's make a puddle for it."

They dug clumps of dirt and grass with sticks and started building a levee around the fish. Then they scooped water with their hands and splashed it into the levee but most of the water seeped into the ground. The fish flipped around and moved its mouth and stared out at the sky with its shiny eye.

"Fish pie," Birdie said. "Like mud pie. Scoop faster."

A few inches of water filled the mound they had built, and the fish moved around in the water, on its side. Its gill opened and closed. Isola poked a blade of grass into the gill, then pulled it out again. They splashed more water on the fish.

"A fish drowns in air," Birdie told Isola.

Isola watched the fish, its mouth and gills opening and closing. She had never thought of it that way. She tried to imagine what it was like in the night for the black man whose boat had tipped over. Did he work his mouth in the water the way the fish worked its mouth in the air? She took a deep breath, wondering what it would be like to have water come in and fill your lungs when you breathed. She couldn't understand how breathing could kill a fish.

"A man drowns in water," Isola said. She laughed, then stopped.

Her Papa had told them about a man drowning once, when they lived in Senigallia and he worked on a fishing boat. They had to pull him in with a fishing net, and there were fish in the net with him. The fish they brought home and sold. The man they brought home and buried. They couldn't make money any more in Senigallia, that's why they'd left. Things were bad. The government was bad, her father said. But things were bad here, and Isola knew that all those pennies her father saved were to buy them passage back to Italy, not to buy his own farm here like he'd said in the beginning. "I'm not gonna die in this place," he told his family. "I'm gonna die back home."

They heard a noise just outside the woods, a man's voice, and a girl crying out. "It's your Papa," Isola said. "Must be they found out who the man is." They stood away from the fish and looked at each other. They hesitated, then moved near the edge of the woods, toward the road, so they could hide and watch the wagon go by. Before they reached the road the man shouted out, closer. He sounded angry, and the girl cried. They ducked behind some bushes and waited.

It was Mr. Horton, who worked for the Company. He was pulling a black girl into the woods, and one of his hands was over her mouth. They could see the pistol tucked into his pants, the way all the boss's men carried their pistols. Mr. Horton yelled at the girl, "Shut up," he told her. He was pulling at her clothes, and pulling at her.

She cried and slapped the air. She was a big girl, older than Angelina, and when she turned just so they saw who it was:

Lecie Titus, Birdie's cousin. Birdie rose up on her knees, as if she would stand up and go help her. But instead she put her hand on Isola's arm, and Isola looked at her, and there was nothing they could do.

Mr. Horton pulled his pistol out of his pants. He tossed his hat and pistol on the grass and the gun shone there, silver. And then he pushed Lecie onto the ground and climbed on top of her. When she cried out he slapped her face, and then he kept his hand on her neck.

Isola stared, horrified. She knew what was happening, though no one had ever told her about such things. She felt Birdie's fingers pressing into her arm. All she could think was if she had stayed home and done what her mother had told her maybe this wouldn't be happening to Lecie. She thought of sewing, how she hated it, but how she would learn to love it, and would help her mother take in sewing and they would make a lot of money and save it all and then go back to Italy like her father said.

Mr. Horton stood up and wiped his hand across his face. He picked up his hat and the pistol and pushed the pistol back into his pants. "Get to work," he told Lecie, "before your whole family catches hell." Lecie stood up, whimpering. She moved away from him, and then she turned and ran, the back of her ragged dress wet and covered with mud. Horton bent over and brushed at his knees. He put the hat back on his head and walked out of the woods.

Birdie and Isola stayed crouched behind the bushes, hardly daring to breathe. Finally they looked at each other. Birdie's eyes were bright with tears that hadn't fallen. The girls stood slowly, keeping their eyes on the spot where it had happened. The woods were so quiet. The birds sang, the woods smelled rich and muddy and green, and everything was so peaceful. The pond lay still and peaceful and white under the green branches. Everything was rich and beautiful. But as they moved closer to the pond, they saw the matted spot on the ground where Lecie had lain with Horton on top of her. And then near the pond there was the little levee they had built, with the silver fish still in it, but most of the water was gone. The fish's mouth moved slowly, with long rests in between.

Isola picked up the fish. It felt dry, and pieces of grass and twigs stuck to it. She threw it back into the pond and it floated. They ran out of the woods as fast as they could.

There was no one on the road or in the field across from the trees. The sun burned down on them, and the air was heavy with the humidity that seemed to rise right up out of the damp earth.

They headed back toward the Titus land, where people were working. They saw Lecie out there, her head just showing above the tall green cotton. She was leaning against a *zoppa*, standing still, not chopping the weeds. Others worked around her, nipping off broken branches, chopping at weeds, humming, calling to each other. But Lecie stood off by herself, looking at the ground.

Birdie broke away from Isola and ran down the road.

"Birdie Hall, ain't you got home yet?" old Lud Titus called to her. Isola tried to follow Birdie, but then stopped. She knew she had to get home herself or she would be in big trouble. "Wait, Birdie," she called.

Birdie turned and looked back at Isola. "Stupid," she called over her shoulder. "Stupid Dago." Then she ran home.

Magic

LIZ ROSENBERG

When I was a child, Christmas was a borrowed holiday. It wasn't for Jews. We couldn't live with it, and yet we couldn't seem to live without it. We drove in slow, loopy circles on December evenings to admire our Christian neighbors' lights. The green Buick dipped and swayed along the streets, like a boat skimming waves, while my father sang "Sweet Molly Malone," and "Mack the Knife" in his pleasant, fading monotone.

I sat in the back seat, my breath fogging the car window, and clung to a baggy pouch of green leather upholstery that had torn loose from the back of the seat, but which I believed had been placed there by some genius who understood about children and automobiles.

Each year we would undertake the pilgrimage to Oyster Bay, to visit the yard of the Christmas Man. His house and shrubbery were loaded down with blinking, flashing lights, as if he were signaling some catastrophe to the rest of the Milky Way. It was said he lived alone. A mannequin Santa, oversized and lit from within, leaned drunkenly against an upstairs window. Christmas carols blared through loud-speakers attached to the porch, and a battery-operated Santa waved from the middle of the front lawn. His red sled was filled to the brim with sourballs—there must have been thou-sands of them—each one wrapped separately in cellophane. A clumsily hand-lettered sign invited each child to take one. I'd choose a red candy, shout "Thank you!" toward the loud-speakers, and skid away on the soles of my galoshes to the safety of the warm car, where I would join in my father's refrain as we nosed toward home: "Alive, alive o-oh! Alive, alive-o-oh! Crying cockles and mussels, alive, alive-oh!"

On other, less thrilling evenings, riding home from my grandparents' apartment in Brooklyn, I would count all the lit houses we passed, like stars in a valley; windows framed in blue and red and green, each shrub with a spiral of lights; or, more rarely, a menorah with three or four of its orange electric candles lit, glowing behind a living room drape.

On Christmas Eve I was loaned out to help decorate the Piscatellis' tree. Marie Piscatelli was my best friend. She lived three houses down and four around the corner. Two hemlocks, encircled in greenish-blue lights, guarded either side of her front porch, where I would stand shifting my weight and stamping my feet like a small, embarrassed horse.

These were confusing evenings—irresistible, because the Christmas decorations were so delicate and baroque, so unlike anything at home. There were clear glass baubles with snowy religious scenes inside; gilt decorations as pointed as needles at both ends; silver ornaments dusted with white frosting like the sugared dates set out for us on the Christmas china. It was somehow humiliating, too, because none of these things were mine. I had to be careful around them.

This need for caution made me exquisitely clumsy. On Christmas Eve some devil in me emerged; I would fall into the fine-needled tree and knock things loose, my arms swinging like windmills. I remember one hand-blown ornament I dropped on the rug; it slipped down between my fingers, then exploded like falling snow.

Marie's mother tried to console me. She liked me because I was polite, and a good eater. I dismantled the stuffed artichokes she served before dinner, tasted the veal and peppers, lasagna, antipasti, hard cheeses, button mushrooms, and roasted chestnuts. I sipped wine like an adult and, when pressed, took seconds of the pastries she bought at the Italian bakery in Hempstead. Marie's father had ulcers. No magic for him. He lived on cottage cheese and canned pears, and spent his weekends cleaning the garage, whereas Marie picked at her food and swallowed her green peas whole, like bitter pills.

By the time my parents came for me I would be stretched out on the living room sofa with a cup of cocoa cooling in front of me, half asleep; stupefied by the bright, blinking Christmas lights indoors, the pyramid of gifts beneath the tree, the heavy dinner. In fact, I was a little tipsy.

My mother would tighten her hand around mine as we walked home, and we came as close as we ever did to a theological discussion.

"Remember, this is not our holiday," she would remind me.

"What's our holiday?"

"Hanukkah."

But Hanukkah was already a dim memory, a faint sweet odor of melting candle wax. "Why can't we have Christmas, too? Everybody else does."

"Christmas is for Christians. It's to celebrate the birth of Jesus Christ. Do you believe in Jesus Christ?"

"No," I said, "but neither does Mr. Piscatelli. And you don't even believe in God."

There was a heavy silence. We walked a little faster. "We celebrate people's birthdays all the time," I told her. "What's so bad about this one?"

"You'll understand when you're older," my mother said.

But Christmas was a child's holiday. That fact was inescapable. Adults gave things in such abundance it made you dizzy and sick for a month, like falling under a spell. If it was a holiday for children, wasn't it mine as well, by right? I tried to unravel these mysteries while I staggered down the block, swept along by my mother's strong hand, but always I was too sleepy to figure it out, asleep before I'd even had my bath.

Christmas morning, early—before my parents had had their first cup of coffee—Marie would call me up. It was time for the Listing of the Presents. Mine was a short list and I went first. After I had finished I waited in a long silence while Marie enumerated her gifts in lavish and scientific detail: pink coral earrings from her parents, and a glow-in-the-dark radio; from her aunt and uncle an angora sweater set; a silk petticoat from one grandmother and from the other a gilt-edged catechism; French chocolates sent by distant cousins; two stuffed bears; a chintz bedspread for her canopy bed; slippers made of rabbit's fur, and brand-new Barbie doll outfits, which she would elaborate down to each gold hem or tiny shoulder pad.

Most of these gifts were from Santa Claus, who was no acquaintance of mine; a sort of rich cousin to Jesus Christ. My parents divided things equally between the two holidays— eight tiny presents for Hanukkah, and one big, practical one for Christmas, despite my mother's reservations—a new winter coat or, one year, a bookshelf for my room. We weren't an extravagant family, and I was content with little luxuries and the few big necessities.

Then one year I fell in love with a red sled. This had for me the symptoms of a genuine infatuation. I had seen it gleaming, languishing against the brick face of the hardware store downtown, and had admired it from a distance, and studied it up close from every angle, like a chandelier. It was expensive. My father's pharmacy was going through hard times; he'd recently had to lay off two part-time employees. Still, the vehemence of my longing made the sled both realer than life and slightly unreal to me—like the shapes in the fireplace that leaped up green and blue when my father sprinkled on a special powder made of sulfur and hydrochloride. If I stared into the fire for a long time—till the top of my forehead grew hot to the touch—I would begin to see things in the flames, as I did in summertime, watching cloud formations swim overhead. When I nagged my mother about the sled she just looked grim and said, "We'll see" and "We'll see" till at last one day, riding by the store, I saw that it was gone for good.

Eight nights in a row the Hanukkah candles burned down to blackish nubs, nothing like the sanctified oil in the Bible. I nibbled at the burned edges of the potato latkes. No one was surprised when, a few days later, I dragged myself home from school with a sore throat and high fever.

I would have to miss Christmas Eve at the Piscatellis' that year. I overheard my mother talking with Marie's mother on the phone. In compensation came a platter of Mrs. Piscatelli's sugar-dusted dates and walnut-stuffed figs, which sat at the foot of my bed like disembodied things. My mother wheeled the TV set into my room and brought me tiny paper cups of ginger ale and a stack of comics on loan from my father's store. She even offered to play Go Fish with me—an invitation which stunned me so that I forgot my sickness for an hour or two, as I hid beneath the covers reading the new comic books. My mother was not a playful woman; we'd never played games together, and I wouldn't have known how to start, even if I had wanted to.

On Christmas Eve my fever climbed higher, and anxious phone calls went back and forth between my house and the doctor's office. I soon lost track of time. It seemed to me that I had lain in bed for weeks and was now better. I kept pleading to go to the Piscatellis', begging my parents to walk down the street with me. But even the tears were scalding on my face, and hurt me. The wallpaper by my bed was patterned all over with teakettles which began to issue clouds of steam and then to shriek. My mother kept coming to me in the gloomy half-light with aspirins and damp washcloths. She and my father would walk me, wobbly legged, to my small white vanity, on which the vaporizer percolated like a coffeepot. I sat drenched in sweat and Vicks VapoRub, surrounded by billowing clouds from the vaporizer, under the thick towel my mother held over my head, commanding me to breathe, breathe deeper.

I must have finally slept, for I woke suddenly with the collar of my plaid wool robe scratching my face and a sense of someone standing very near my bed. There were two of them. It was my mother and father, and they gazed at me tenderly, standing shoulder to shoulder. I noticed they looked shorter and squatter than normal, and insubstantial, like the reflections in a funhouse mirror. They stared at me and I stared back at them for a long time, as if each of us was looking at the other down a long dark tunnel. Then I knew that they were ghosts, not my parents at all. I was not afraid, but my mouth was dry. I hoped they had come to my bedside to bring me a glass of cool water. "I want—" I began. "I want—" I stopped talking.

They looked interested, but I had a sense that because they weren't alive they couldn't speak, or act. It made them seem pitiable and helpless. I noticed that their feet did not quite touch my rug, as sometimes my own feet did not touch the floor when I sat in a chair. After a few long, slow seconds— just when I had grown accustomed to the oddity of their being there at all—they grew wavier and wavier, like bad reception on a TV set, and vanished.

I woke in the cold, damp grayish light an hour or two before dawn. It was too early to be awake on Christmas morning—I had the guilty sense of having stolen something in advance, stolen time. The vaporizer hissed quietly now. It gurgled and sighed to itself in a corner of the room. I could see the puffs of steam it sent up, like clouds of breath on a cold day. And just there, leaning against the bed, against my wooden footboard, substantial in the cool bluish-gray light, so beautiful and radiant that it brought a pang to my heart, was the red sled.

The Cossacks of Connecticut

DANIEL ASA ROSE

I was raised an assimilated Jew in a WASP town on the Connecticut shore. Rowayton in the '50s was half lobstermen who
would finish their labors by noon every day and half advertising execs who would ride the 7:02 to Grand Central every
morning and the 7:14 back every night. There was also a
smattering of poets and painters who through luck or good
sense could afford to live by the water. These were my neighbors, and I felt much closer to the children of these lobstermen and admen and artists than I did to my elegant pale
cousins in New York, the Orthodox cousins who went to *shul*
on Saturdays while we were out fishing for horseshoe crabs
to kill with our bare feet.

It would be incorrect to call Rowayton a suburb. In the
'50s it was a small town not unlike a small rural town in Minnesota, say, or Winesburg, Ohio, where everyone knew
everyone else: You knew which girl had scallion breath at
dancing school, whose mother beat him with a clothes hanger
for hanging out at Hummiston's Drug Store, which family
had jellyfish coming out of their radiators during hurricane
season. The only difference from a town in Minnesota or
Ohio was that from Rowayton's beaches you could see the
spires of Manhattan twinkling in the blue haze forty miles
down the shore. The capital of the universe was one hour
away. And of course this made all the difference in the world.

Rowayton in those days had world-class WASP icons. The
Man in the Hathaway Shirt——that distinguished-looking

gent with the black eye patch—could frequently be spotted at the helm of his ketch puttering up the Five Mile River. The yacht club around the corner from my house fired off its cannon each day at sunset. At Miss Hunnibell's ballroom dancing school both girls *and* boys had to wear white gloves. Charles Lindbergh was forever flying overhead to his estate across the river, and when our grade school principal Mr. Cunningham rattled on at assembly about how much he appreciated the verse being published by Lucky Lindy's wife, he failed to mention the fact that Lindbergh was what was most charitably called an "isolationist" at the beginning of World War II—as if all Lindbergh did was advise us to stay out of the war, not revisit Germany numerous times and express admiration for their way of life.

And of course there were the lobstermen. If there were Cossacks in the Connecticut of the 1950s, they would have been the lobstermen—a nonmenacing version of those ruffian cavalrymen who had so terrified my antecedents under the tsars. Full of pomp and swagger, they were up and out on the river before dawn every day to boisterously set their traps, then spent the rest of the afternoon rather meekly playing checkers on a couple of weatherbeaten benches by the docks. The pomp and swagger that started out so fresh at dawn was, by lunchtime, more than a little faded, in the way that I imagined Cossacks would be faded by the middle of the day when they had to come home for lunch. The lobstermen of Rowayton were almost but not quite dashing in the way that the Cossacks of Russia were almost but not quite dashing, cutting a glamorous figure from a distance, standing tall and proud in their stirrups or the cockpits of their lobster boats, posting to the galloping plains or waves, but up close they both smelled pretty bad (booze and horse in the one case, booze and fish in the other). If any pogroms had taken place in Rowayton they would be the ones to conduct them, but they were totally devoid of malice; the rowdiest they ever got was to occasionally stray, drunk and harmless, through the halls of our elementary school, the squeak of their moist rubber boots on waxed linoleum making them sound not so much like fierce warriors as tardy schoolboys, lost and wet, and perpetually at a loss to find homeroom.

I never witnessed anything like an incident of out-and-out anti-Semitism in our town. I was liked by teachers and classmates both, so everyone took pains to protect me from the faintly distasteful secret that I was different. In my presence, the grade school teachers overprotectively referred to Moses as a "Hebrew." To spare me embarrassment, Mrs. Wallace in current events class once referred to Israel as being inhabited by "people of the Hebraic persuasion." My classmates, solicitously and with great concern, sometimes asked me if I celebrated Halloween. The fact that I was not Christian was tolerated, the way a mascot will be forgiven his limp so that it's almost not noticed anymore. All this of course had echoes far beyond our cosmopolitan hick town: Assimilated Poles in the 1800s used to say of themselves that they were "of Mosaic denomination." If there had been a grade school yearbook they might have called me "our Jew," the way some Czech or Rumanian villagers were said, in centuries past, to have grown fond of the few Jews in their midst.

Rarely did someone in Rowayton not know that I was Jewish, and on those occasions the information was received with benevolent surprise. "Really? A Jew?"

"Sure," I would reply, shyly. "What'd you think I was?"

"I didn't think you were anything!" came the reply. A backhanded compliment if ever there was one, for they were right: I wasn't.

My instinct was to wince and blush. I felt apologetic, for no reason I understood. In school there was sort of an unofficial don't ask, don't tell policy: Everyone knew, but it was unmannerly to talk about it. I wasn't trying to pass—that would have been shameful—but neither did I want to push anyone's face in it. We had a mezuzah on our house and I thought it proper to have one but I wished we could have had it on the back door where it wouldn't be so visible. It was proper that we did not celebrate Christmas but that didn't stop me from feeling self-conscious that the garbageman saw no boxes of discarded glittery wrapping paper down by our mailbox the morning after.

It's like what they say about sabras: hard on the outside, but on the inside, very hard. I was embarrassed on the outside, but on the inside, very embarrassed. Being Jewish was like having a shoe fetish. We were part of a special group, all right; I just wasn't sure it was anything to boast about.

For all appearances I looked perfectly assimilated, but there was a lot going on under the surface. My self-consciousness was as acute as Woody Allen's in *Annie Hall* imagining that strangers were calling him a Jew when in fact they were only saying *"Didju . . ."* Scanning a newspaper article, my eyes would be alert to words starting with J. I lowered my voice when I sang the chorus of the Beatles song "Hey Jude." I was mortified that the license plate on our family station wagon had the letters "YD" in it, thinking we were pegged. On those unlikely occasions when I happened to look up something Jewish in a library card catalogue, I would leave the file open to a different topic so the next person wouldn't suspect what I'd been perusing, in much the way an overweight person will push the weights back before stepping off a scale.

But I wasn't merely embarrassed. I was also aware that I was supposed to be proud. Even while blushing at photographs of Hasids, I was conscious that there was a sense of honor integral to being Jewish. I tried to do it both ways. At High Holiday services, conducted in a nearby borrowed

church, I would fantasize about how I would save "my people" by throwing myself on a grenade some anti-Semite
might toss in the window, but at the same time I wore an earphone that snaked down into my suit jacket pocket where I
had my hidden transistor radio tuned to Cousin Brucie on
WABC, so while the rest of the congregation was singing the
Kol Nidre, I was humming Herman's Hermits under my
breath.

In twelve years of growing up in Rowayton, whatever
anti-Semitism I encountered was of the most mild generic
sort—as benign as such a thing could ever be said to be. The
mother of a friend, a kindly watercolorist with bangs in her
eyes and an interest in books, asked me with genuine anthro-
pological curiosity if my family ate "bajels"—pronouncing
bagels with a soft G as in Jell-O. I never saw it firsthand, but
I heard of another neighborhood mother who routinely offered her family their choice of two kinds of bread: "white
bread or Jew bread" (rye). The only discourtesy I ever received at the hands of my classmates took place where most
American children learn their first hard lessons of life, at the
junior high school bus stop.

Our bus stop was made up of the same two knots of people
all American bus stops were: the girls, talking decorously
among themselves with round little puffs of white breath,
and the boys, standing in a circle, stamping their feet against
the cold and making valiant stabs at scatological conversation. And although the circle of boys always seemed to be
aligned against me every morning as I walked the long block
toward them toting my little clarinet case, I knew this was
just my imagination. They only *seemed* to be staring at me as
an outsider, and every morning after I walked up and took
my rightful place in the circle I acknowledged that staring
was just a condition of the waiting; whoever was in the circle
would always stare at the newest straggler who was walking

up the street just as self-consciously as I had. These were the locals I had grown up with since first grade, and though we now ran in different crowds at junior high—some of us in the drama club, some of us building up steam to drop out— there was a more or less mutual respect, a more or less genuine effort at trying to find things we still held in common and could agreeably talk about. We were polite, mostly, and our attempts at scatological humor fell generally short of the mark, that early in the morning. Though we thought ourselves rough and tumble, we were basically all good little suburban gentlemen and the idea of being overtly rude or cruel—of singling someone out because he was different, or even using the word for his difference in a disparaging way—was unthinkable. Which was why it was so odd when it did happen one morning.

It was prompted by a foreign boy, significantly, the only actual foreigner among us. Grady Vanderhausen had come over from Holland in third grade and made it his career since to disguise any group memory in us that he was not local. My mother, who was from the Low Countries herself (she had escaped Belgium in 1939), had been instrumental in getting his family out of Europe in the mid-'50s, and had even hired his mother for a few months to help clean our house. Maybe this was humiliating to the Vanderhausen household; maybe Grady had picked up talk around his dinner table about "those rich Roses." (We weren't really rich but just enough so to be different: My father was a doctor, our sandwiches were made of pumpernickel instead of Wonder Bread, we played marbles on Persian rugs, Pablo Casals could be heard blasting out of our windows on Sunday.) But Grady was the one who used the word at the bus stop that morning, the only time I ever heard it used in a negative way. Referring to the shop teacher, he said, "Oh, he's such a Jew." There was a general murmur of assent around the circle, then an almost audible intake of breath as they remembered; then a pause, followed by a torrent of apologies as they blinked and blushed at the one kid who stood there clutching his clarinet case. "Not you, Danny," they assured me, "you're a *good* Jew."

So this was a new thought. There were good Jews, apparently; what did that make all the others? I accepted their lavish apologies like the good sport I was and we all went back to stamping our feet and staring at the latest newcomer. But for the first time I thought: Ah ha.

Discomfort made me rash. I was rebellious and confused and ferocious. I was what my parents called me, "Piss 'n Vinegar," even though I melted in the company of people I sensed were truly kind. I was the picture of paradox: hot-blooded, thin-skinned, quick-tempered, strangulated by the world's injustices and full of get-even schemes, but ever ready to dissolve into a puddle of milk at the slightest word of warmheartedness from a stranger, which came not infrequently. My loyalty to that stranger would thereafter be iron.

Perhaps the most noticeable thing about me was my proclivity for recklessness. This made perfect sense, though I didn't grasp it for a couple of decades. It was this: that my specialty of hiding was intrinsically cowardly, so I compensated by exhibiting bravado in other areas. I dangled from high places with one hand, jumped across chasms, talked back to teachers, played pranks on policemen, rode ice floes around the harbor. I drove my bike blindfolded. I studied how close my sled could come to the back wheels of moving cars. I alarmed friends by how long I stayed underwater. I leapt from a cliffside rope swing into the water during lightning storms. Not that I was invulnerable. Far from it. The tree limb frequently snapped, the ladder tipped, the teacher flipped. I chipped my teeth, sprained my ankles, broke my leg and then broke the cast racing a friend on crutches and had to have the leg set again. By the time I was twelve, I had fallen through the ice of Long Island Sound four times. I remember calculating my odds, that if I continued in this fashion, I'd be falling through every third winter for the rest of my life. I was to get into a total of thirteen car accidents.

Actions like these and a dozen others convinced me and people around me that I was an intrepid fellow. I wasn't. I resorted to such foolishness because I couldn't do the one truly brave thing that is asked of any human being, and that is to be who he is.

To the limited extent that I defined myself as a Jew, therefore, it was not through positive associations but through negative. We did not go to church. We did not hang lights at Christmas. My mother the refugee hid in her bedroom when "Christian gangs"—otherwise known as carolers—stormed the snowy driveway. What were the positive associations I had? That we celebrated Hanukkah? But that was such a dinky event, compared to the onslaught of Christmas, that it was embarrassing: even at its grandest, on the final night, it was like holding eight pencil-thin candles up to a 50,000 megawatt Santa Claus on his neon reindeer. Ho ho ho! like a jolly green giant of the Arctic north, laughing at our paltry attempts at winter cheer. Instead of pride at my heritage I felt shame. Shame at a mother who beneath her gaiety was brittle as a piece of buttered matzo, shame at the little skullcaps that seemed like embroidered bald spots, shame at the phlegmy Eastern European accents that made me want to leap on a chair and shout, "For cripes' sake, clear your throats!"

In direct proportion to my shame, I was pleased to be assimilated. In our home we ate rice pilaf rather than noodle pudding. When we gathered round the piano it was more likely to sing "In the Good Old Summertime" than "Sunrise, Sunset." At school assemblies I soloed "Edelweiss" on my clarinet. I was known to be one of the fastest hunters at neighborhood Easter egg hunts. I did not care to know the difference between Purim and Sukkos, and only remembered that the year in Hebrew chronology was 57-something because Heinz had 57 varieties of ketchup. I could read a few lines of Hebrew but only with the vowels added, beginner style, not like real Jews who could skim through text without the aid of such training wheels. And though I was barmitzvahed and it meant something to me, my girlfriends were blond and blue-eyed as a matter of course. Jewish girls, though beautiful in a heartbreaking way, seemed too sisterly; the notion of kissing them raised in my mind the specter of incest.

I turned to the Christian world for the sex appeal I found lacking in Judaism. I found my parents' hard-drinking Christian friends glamorous, friends like the old *New York Times* Moscow bureau chief who would drive up from Manhattan in his convertible Spitfire and twirl his fiery Italian countess wife out of the passenger seat on the driveway——he was very light on his feet, in his faded seersucker suit and those pallid eyelashes of his——and the two of them would waltz to the back of the car and pop the trunk revealing a tumbler of martinis, nicely shaken by the drive up the Connecticut Turnpike upon which one in six drivers were said to be rip-roaringly smashed out of their gourds. To be a drinker was to proclaim one's non-Jewishness loud and clear, it seemed to me, and I was glad about the hard-drinking Rowayton social whirl that my parents were in the thick of, my mother so very gay, in the '50s sense of the word, at the loud jazz parties they would throw where I as bartender would serve fisherman's punch and Scotch-and-sodas. Rowayton was a series of fizzy fascinating cocktail parties where world-renowned psychoanalysts in Fijian shirts would stuff the bathroom floor to ceiling full of balloons so no one could squeeze in, and middle-aged heiresses would plunk down on the floor next to the Labrador retriever and teach the dumb mutt to beg, and famous TV news anchors would pass out on the Castro Convertible in my bedroom, which doubled as the guest room. They were giddy, racy, boisterous parties and my parents would let my sister and me have a glass or two and encourage us to mingle, to mingle, then afterward report how Mrs. McKissock declared us to be charming; and we were, we were charming in the Connecticut manner, despite or as a result of the fact that I wore that earphone, and the whole time I was mingling I was listening to Cousin Brucie and the Good Guys.

I was living in a WASP town and going to WASP debutante parties—not so much assimilated, perhaps, as completely and thoroughly *mingled*—but at the same time I also had these righteous great-uncles forty miles away on 47th Street named Yudl and Velvl. To these gentle souls, worldly diamond dealer brothers of my grandparents from Belgium, we were Connecticut outlaws. They didn't care how many celebrities and professionals we showcased, to them we were rabble rousers, we were Christmas carolers, we were that most unforgivable goyim thing: glitzy. Once or twice these great-uncles would show up at one of the parties we'd invite them to, a wedding, say, or a graduation. They didn't drive, it was out of the question, but every so often they took the New Haven Railroad and the somber expression on their faces when they emerged at the Darien station, hot and dusty, said what they thought. They thought: this was the Wild West. They thought they had taken the stagecoach and here they were in Dodge City. The suburban split-levels and cardboard palaces of Darien and Rowayton were Red River Gulch to them. Where were the sidewalks? Where was Lord & Taylor? When they got to the house they stood there stiff and sober in their gray flannel pants, fidgeting the diamonds in their pockets, and they would look out from the foyer at the balloons filling the bathrooms and the heiress barking on the floor and the news anchor giving me a noogie behind the bar because I had put tonic in his Scotch instead of soda, and my great-uncles would think, *For this we escaped Hitler's Europe?*

Or we would drive them to a barbecue at the beach. We would pick them up at the station in their pin stripes and ties and they'd sit in the back, leaving the passenger seat empty, as if they were riding in a cab. It wasn't rudeness—they just didn't know suburban car etiquette, that you fill up the front first. We'd drive them to the beach and it would be like out of Tolstoy, the urban dwellers coming by locomotive from St. Petersburg to visit country cousins in their provincial dacha, getting bundled in muffs and wraps to travel miles in a sleigh over snow-covered barrens. We would plunk them on the sand and they would look on in horror as we played touch football with the hot dog rolls between the picnic tables. Disdaining the *shmutz* beneath their soles, staking their claim to the beach blanket and not venturing off it except to make an occasional foray to the snack bar, they would tramp delicately across the wasteland in their leather sandals (*barefoot?* go naked in front of strangers?!) to order a Sanka and produce blank stares from the high school help who knew how to process orders only for Creamsicles and frozen Milky Ways. An impasse. There at the snack bar the Cossacks would stand staring at the Jews with their shirttails tucked inside their baggy bathing suits, their black socks pulled halfway up their hairless celery-white calves, and the Jews would stare back at the Cossacks with their necks sunburned leather-red around their dirty T-shirts, and eventually the first camp might loosen up enough to chuck them a Coors, and the second camp might let their hair down enough to *sip* the Coors, while munching on a roasted shrimp or a lobster tail with two fingers only, the other three fingers remaining kosher in the air, figuring perhaps that they were already transgressing by finding themselves so deeply among the goyim, a little two-finger transgression wouldn't hurt . . .

And yet they were my conscience. Yudl and Velvl would look at me mingling with my fisherman's punch and know me for what I was. Reading me with one glance, they would know the awful truth, that I was infected with a malignancy of self-loathing. The look from my righteous New York relatives told me what I already knew, that deep down I was neither one nor the other, neither a wild Connecticut kid with no blood history of persecution, nor a New York Jew with a sense of sobriety that wouldn't allow me to frolic. After the party would be over and the news anchor would be poured into the back of his Mercedes to go home, I would collapse on my bed with the whirlies only to realize that he had puked in my wastebasket. That's when it would stink to me, all that glitz, his celebrity puke mixed in with the furtive cigarette ashes I had deposited there; I would know it all for the shameful emptiness it was, and I would be sickeningly aware that I had nothing whatever in my teenage life to hold on to. There was a hole right in the center, a gaping lack where there should have been bedrock. Writhing nauseated on my bed, peering up at my bookshelves upon which my bar mitzvah books entitled *Views of the Holy Land* were overlaid with *Playboy* magazines, I would try to cling to the image of my parents, my family, some center that I could grab hold of. But there was no center there. In my center there was a desperate mingling of too many conflicted selves instead of any true sense of self—a frantic fraternizing instead of a deep and systematic knowing who I was. I was rooting around for social acceptance instead of driving my roots deep. What roots? I had no roots, no code, no key to understanding myself. I was indecipherable to myself, not able to sound out the words of my life, as unpronounceable as the vowel-less Hebrew words I'd struggled with as a boy. What was I? I had no cont*xt. I had no c*re.

Mericans

SANDRA CISNEROS

We're waiting for the awful grandmother who is inside dropping pesos into *la ofrenda* box before the altar to La Divina Providencia. Lighting votive candles and genuflecting. Blessing herself and kissing her thumb. Running a crystal rosary between her fingers. Mumbling, mumbling mumbling.

There are so many prayers and promises and thanks-be-to-God to be given in the name of the husband and the sons and the only daughter who never attend mass. It doesn't matter: Like La Virgen de Guadalupe, the awful grandmother intercedes on their behalf. For the grandfather who hasn't believed in anything since the first PRI elections. For my father, El Periquín, so skinny he needs his sleep. For Auntie Light-Skin, who only a few hours before was breakfasting on brain and goat tacos after dancing all night in the pink zone. For Uncle Fat-Face, the blackest of the black sheep—*Always remember your Uncle Fat-Face in your prayers*. And Uncle Baby—*You go for me, Mama—God listens to you*.

The awful grandmother has been gone a long time. She disappeared behind the heavy leather outer curtain and the dusty velvet inner. We must stay near the church entrance. We must not wander over to the balloon and punch-ball vendors. We cannot spend our allowance on fried cookies or Familia Burrón comic books or those clear cone-shaped suckers that make everything look like a rainbow when you look through them. We cannot run off and have our picture taken on the wooden ponies. We must not climb the steps up the hill behind the church and chase each other through the cemetery. We have promised to stay right where the awful grandmother left us until she returns.

There are those walking to church on their knees. Some with fat rags tied around their legs and others with pillows, one to kneel on and one to flop ahead. There are women with black shawls crossing and uncrossing themselves. There are armies of penitents carrying banners and flowered arches while musicians play tinny trumpets and tinny drums.

La Virgen de Guadalupe is waiting inside behind a plate of thick glass. There's also a gold crucifix bent crooked as a mesquite tree when someone once threw a bomb. La Virgen de Guadalupe on the main altar because she's a big miracle, the crooked crucifix on a side altar because that's a little miracle.

But we're outside in the sun. My big brother Junior hunkered against the wall with his eyes shut. My little brother Keeks running around in circles.

Maybe and most probably my little brother is imagining he's a flying feather dancer, like the ones we saw swinging high up from a pole on the Virgin's birthday. I want to be a flying feather dancer too, but when he circles past me he shouts, "I'm a B-fifty-two bomber, you're a German," and shoots me with an invisible machine gun. I'd rather play flying feather dancers, but if I tell my brother this, he might not play with me at all.

"*Girl.* We can't play with a *girl.*" *Girl.* It's my brothers' favorite insult now instead of "sissy." "You *girl,*" they yell at each other. "You throw that ball like a *girl.*"

I've already made up my mind to be a German when Keeks swoops past again, this time yelling, "I'm Flash Gordon. You're Ming the Merciless and the Mud People." I don't mind being Ming the Merciless, but I don't like being the Mud People. Something wants to come out of the corners of my eyes, but I don't let it. Crying is what *girls* do.

I leave Keeks running around in circles—"I'm the Lone Ranger, you're Tonto." I leave Junior squatting on his ankles and go look for the awful grandmother.

Why do churches smell like the inside of an ear? Like incense and the dark and candles in blue glass? And why does holy water smell of tears? The awful grandmother makes me kneel and fold my hands. The ceiling high and everyone's prayers bumping up there like balloons.

If I stare at the eyes of the saints long enough, they move and wink at me, which makes me a sort of saint too. When I get tired of winking saints, I count the awful grandmother's mustache hairs while she prays for Uncle Old, sick from the worm, and Auntie Cuca, suffering from a life of troubles that left half her face crooked and the other half sad.

There must be a long, long list of relatives who haven't gone to church. The awful grandmother knits the names of the dead and the living into one long prayer fringed with the grandchildren born in that barbaric country with its barbarian ways.

I put my weight on one knee, then the other, and when they both grow fat as a mattress of pins, I slap them each awake. *Micaela, you may wait outside with Alfredito and Enrique.* The awful grandmother says it all in Spanish, which I understand when I'm paying attention. "What?" I say, though it's neither proper nor polite. "What?" which the awful grandmother hears as *"¿Güat?"* But she only gives me a look and shoves me toward the door.

After all that dust and dark, the light from the plaza makes me squinch my eyes like if I just came out of the movies. My brother Keeks is drawing squiggly lines on the concrete with a wedge of glass and the heel of his shoe. My brother Junior squatting against the entrance, talking to a lady and man.

They're not from here. Ladies don't come to church dressed in pants. And everybody knows men aren't supposed to wear shorts.

"*¿Quieres chicle?*" the lady asks in a Spanish too big for her mouth.

"*Gracias.*" The lady gives him a whole handful of gum for free, little cellophane cubes of Chiclets, cinnamon and aqua and the white ones that don't taste like anything but are good for pretend buck teeth.

"*Por favor,*" says the lady. "*¿Un foto?*" pointing to her camera.

"*Sí.*"

She's so busy taking Junior's picture, she doesn't notice me and Keeks.

"Hey, Michele, Keeks. You guys want gum?"

"But you speak English!"

"Yeah," my brother says, "we're Mericans."

We're Mericans, we're Mericans, and inside the awful grandmother prays.

Negotiating

What Means Switch

GISH JEN

There we are, nice Chinese family—father, mother, two born-here girls. Where should we live next? My parents slide the question back and forth like a cup of ginseng neither one wants to drink. Until finally it comes to them, what they really want is a milkshake (chocolate) and to go with it a house in Scarsdale. What else? The broker tries to hint: the neighborhood, she says. Moneyed. Many delis. Meaning rich and Jewish. But someone has sent my parents a list of the top ten schools nationwide (based on the opinion of selected educators and others) and so *many-deli* or not we nestle into a Dutch colonial on the Bronx River Parkway. The road's windy where we are, very charming; drivers miss their turns, plough up our flower beds, then want to use our telephone. "Of course," my mom tells them, like it's no big deal, we can replant. We're the type to adjust. You know—the lady drivers weep, my mom gets out the Kleenex for them. We're a bit down the hill from the private plane set, in other words. Only in our dreams do our jacket zippers jam, what with all the lift tickets we have stapled to them, Killington on top of Sugarbush on top of Stowe, and we don't even know where the Virgin Islands are—although certain of us do know that virgins are like priests and nuns, which there were a lot more of in Yonkers, where we just moved from, than there are here.

This is my first understanding of class. In our old neighborhood everybody knew everything about virgins and nonvirgins, not to say the technicalities of staying in between. Or almost everybody, I should say; in Yonkers I was the laugh-along type. Here I'm an expert.

"You mean the man . . . ?" Pigtailed Barbara Gugelstein spits a mouthful of Coke back into her can. "That is *so* gross!"

Pretty soon I'm getting popular for a new girl, the only problem is Danielle Meyers, who wears blue mascara and has gone steady with two boys. "How do *you* know," she starts to ask, proceeding to edify us all with how she French-kissed one boyfriend and just regular-kissed another. ("Because, you know, he had braces.") We hear about his rubber bands, how once one popped right into her mouth. I begin to realize I need to find somebody to kiss too. But how?

Luckily, I just about then happen to tell Barbara Gugelstein I know karate. I don't know why I tell her this. My sister Callie's the liar in the family; ask anybody. I'm the one who doesn't see why we should have to hold our heads up. But for some reason I tell Barbara Gugelstein I can make my hands like steel by thinking hard. "I'm not supposed to tell anyone," I say.

The way she backs away, blinking, I could be the burning bush.

"I can't do bricks," I say—a bit of expectation management. "But I can do your arm if you want." I set my hand in chop position.

"Uhh, it's okay," she says. "I know you can, I saw it on TV last night."

That's when I recall that I too saw it on TV last night—in fact, at her house. I rush on to tell her I know how to get pregnant with tea.

"With *tea*?"

"That's how they do it in China."

She agrees that China is an ancient and great civilization that ought to be known for more than spaghetti and gunpowder. I tell her I know Chinese. *"Be-yeh fa-foon,"* I say. *"Shee-veh. Ji nu."* Meaning, "Stop acting crazy. Rice gruel. Soy sauce." She's impressed. At lunch the next day, Danielle Meyers and Amy Weinstein and Barbara's crush, Andy Kaplan, are all impressed too. Scarsdale is a liberal town, not like Yonkers, where the Whitman Road Gang used to throw crabapple mash at my sister Callie and me and tell us it would make our eyes stick shut. Here we're like permanent exchange students. In another ten years, there'll be so many Orientals we'll turn into Asians; a Japanese grocery will buy out that one deli too many. But for now, the mid-sixties, what with civil rights on TV, we're not so much accepted as embraced. Especially by the Jewish part of town—which, it turns out, is not all of town at all. That's just an idea people have, Callie says, and lots of them could take us or leave us same as the Christians, who are nice too; I shouldn't generalize. So let me not generalize except to say that pretty soon I've been to so many bar and bas mitzvahs, I can almost say myself whether the kid chants like an angel or like a train conductor, maybe they could use him on the commuter line. At seder I know to forget the bricks, get a good pile of that mortar. Also I know what is schmaltz. I know that I am a goy. This is not why people like me, though. People like me because I do not need to use deodorant, as I demonstrate in the locker room before and after gym. Also, I can explain to them, for example, what is tofu (*der-voo,* we say at home). Their mothers invite me to taste-test their Chinese cooking.

"Very authentic." I try to be reassuring. After all, they're nice people, I like them. "De-lish." I have seconds. On the question of what we eat, though, I have to admit, "Well, no, it's different than that." I have thirds. "What my mom makes is home style, it's not in the cookbooks."

Not in the cookbooks! Everyone's jealous. Meanwhile, the big deal at home is when we have turkey pot pie. My sister

Callie's the one introduced them—Mrs. Wilder's, they come in this green-and-brown box—and when we have them, we both get suddenly interested in helping out in the kitchen. You know, we stand in front of the oven and help them bake. Twenty-five minutes. She and I have a deal, though, to keep it secret from school, as everybody else thinks they're gross. We think they're a big improvement over authentic Chinese home cooking. Oxtail soup—now that's gross. Stir-fried beef with tomatoes. One day I say, "You know, Ma, I have never seen a stir-fried tomato in any Chinese restaurant we have ever been in, ever."

"In China," she says, real lofty, "we consider tomatoes are a delicacy."

"Ma," I say. "Tomatoes are *Italian*."

"No respect for elders." She wags her finger at me, but I can tell it's just to try and shame me into believing her. "I'm tell you, tomatoes *invented* in China."

"*Ma.*"

"Is true. Like noodles. Invented in China."

"That's not what they said in *school*."

"In *China*," my mother counters, "we also eat tomatoes un-cooked, like apple. And in summertime we slice them, and put some sugar on top."

"Are you sure?"

My mom says of course she's sure, and in the end I give in, even though she once told me that China was such a long time ago, a lot of things she can hardly remember. She said sometimes she has trouble remembering her characters, that sometimes she'll be writing a letter, just writing along, and all of sudden she won't be sure if she should put four dots or three.

"So what do you do then?"

"Oh, I just make a little sloppy."

"You mean you *fudge*?"

She laughed then, but another time, when she was showing me how to write my name, and I said, just kidding, "Are you sure that's the right number of dots now?" she was hurt.

"I mean, of course you know," I said. "I mean, *oy*."

Meanwhile, what *I* know is that in the eighth grade, what people want to hear does not include how Chinese people eat sliced tomatoes with sugar on top. For a gross fact, it just isn't gross enough. On the other hand, the fact that somewhere in China somebody eats or has eaten or once ate living monkey brains—now that's conversation.

"They have these special tables," I say, "kind of like a giant collar. With a hole in the middle, for the monkey's neck. They put the monkey in the collar, and then they cut off the top of its head."

"Whadda they use for cutting?"

I think. "Scalpels."

"*Scalpels?*" says Andy Kaplan.

"Kaplan, don't be dense," Barbara Gugelstein says. "The Chinese *invented* scalpels."

Once a friend said to me, You know, everybody is valued for something. She explained how some people resented being valued for their looks; others resented being valued for their money. Wasn't it still better to be beautiful and rich than ugly and poor, though? You should be just glad, she said, that you have something people value. It's like having a special talent, like being good at ice-skating, or opera singing. She said, You could probably make a career out of it.

Here's the irony: I am.

Anyway, I am ad-libbing my way through eighth grade, as I've described. Until one bloomy spring day, I come in late to homeroom, and to my chagrin discover there's a new kid in class.

Chinese.

So what should I do, pretend to have to go to the girls'

room, like Barbara Gugelstein the day Andy Kaplan took his ID back? I sit down; I am so cool I remind myself of Paul Newman. First thing I realize, though, is that no one looking at me is thinking of Paul Newman. The notes fly:

"*I* think he's cute."

"Who?" I write back. (I am still at an age, understand, when I believe a person can be saved by aplomb.)

"I don't think he talks English too good. Writes it either."

"Who?"

"They might have to put him behind a grade, so don't worry."

"He has a crush on you already, you could tell as soon as you walked in, he turned kind of orangish."

I hope I'm not turning orangish as I deal with my mail, I could use a secretary. The second round starts:

"What do you mean who? Don't be weird. Didn't you *see* him??? Straight back over your right shoulder!!!!"

I have to look; what else can I do? I think of certain tips I learned in Girl Scouts about poise. I cross my ankles. I hold a pen in my hand. I sit up as though I have a crown on my head. I swivel my head slowly, repeating to myself, *I* could be Miss America.

"Miss Mona Chang."

Horror raises its hoary head.

"Notes, please."

Mrs. Mandeville's policy is to read all notes aloud.

I try to consider what Miss America would do, and see myself, back straight, knees together, crying. Some inspiration. Cool Hand Luke, on the other hand, would, quick, eat the evidence. And why not? I should yawn as I stand up, and boom, the notes are gone. All that's left is to explain that it's an old Chinese reflex.

I shuffle up to the front of the room.

"One minute, please," Mrs. Mandeville says.

I wait, noticing how large and plastic her mouth is.

She unfolds a piece of paper.

And I, Miss Mona Chang, who got almost straight A's her whole life except in math and conduct, am about to start crying in front of everyone.

I am delivered out of hot Egypt by the bell. General pandemonium. Mrs. Mandeville still has her hand clamped on my shoulder, though. And the next thing I know, I'm holding the new boy's schedule. He's standing next to me like a big blank piece of paper. "This is Sherman," Mrs. Mandeville says.

"Hello," I say.

"Non how a," I say.

I'm glad Barbara Gugelstein isn't there to see my Chinese in action.

"Ji nu," I say. *"Shee-oeh."*

Later I find out that his mother asked if there were any other Orientals in our grade. She had him put in my class on purpose. For now, though, he looks at me as though I'm much stranger than anything else he's seen so far. Is this because he understands I'm saying "soy sauce rice gruel" to him or because he doesn't?

"Sher-man," he says finally.

I look at his schedule card. Sherman Matsumoto. What kind of name is that for a nice Chinese boy?

(Later on, people ask me how I can tell Chinese from Japanese. I shrug. You just kind of know, I say. *Oy!*)

Sherman's got the sort of looks I think of as pretty-boy. Monsignor-black hair (not monk-brown like mine), bouncy. Crayola eyebrows, one with a round bald spot in the middle of it, like a golf hole. I don't know how anybody can think of him as orangish; his skin looks white to me, with pink triangles hanging down the front of his cheeks like flags. Kind of delicate-looking, but the only truly uncool thing about him is that his spiral notebook has a picture of a kitty cat on it. A big white fluffy one, with a blue ribbon above each perky little ear. I get much opportunity to view this, as all the poor kid understands about life in junior high school is that he should follow me everywhere. It's embarrassing. On the other hand, he's obviously even more miserable than I am, so I try not to say anything. Give him a chance to adjust. We communicate by sign language, and by drawing pictures, which he's better at than I am; he puts in every last detail, even if it takes forever. I try to be patient.

A week of this. Finally I enlighten him. "You should get a new notebook."

His cheeks turn a shade of pink you mostly only see in hyacinths.

"Notebook." I point to his. I show him mine, which is psychedelic, with big purple and yellow stick-on flowers. I try to explain he should have one like this, only without the flowers. He nods enigmatically, and the next day brings me a notebook just like his, except that this cat sports pink bows instead of blue.

"Pret-ty," he says. "You."

He speaks English! I'm dumbfounded. Has he spoken it all this time? I consider: Pretty. You. What does that mean? Plus actually, he's said *plit-ty*, much as my parents would; I'm assuming he means pretty, but maybe he means pity. Pity. You.

"Jeez," I say finally.

"You are wel-come," he says.

I decorate the back of the notebook with stick-on flowers, and hold it so that these show when I walk through the halls.

In class I mostly keep my book open. After all, the kid's so new; I think I really ought to have a heart. And for a livelong day nobody notices.

Then Barbara Gugelstein sidles up. "Matching notebooks, huh?"

I'm speechless.

"First comes love, then comes marriage, and then come chappies in a baby carriage."

"Barbara!"

"Get it?" she says. "Chinese Japs."

"Bar-*bra*," I say to get even.

"Just make sure he doesn't give you any *tea*," she says.

Are Sherman and I in love? Three days later, I hazard that we are. My thinking proceeds this way: I think he's cute, and I think he thinks I'm cute. On the other hand, we don't kiss and we don't exactly have fantastic conversations. Our talks *are* getting better, though. We started out, "This is a book." "Book." "This is a chair." "Chair." Advancing to, "What is this?" "This is a book." Now, for fun, he tests me.

"What is this?" he says.

"This is a book," I say, as if I'm the one who has to learn how to talk.

He claps. "Good!"

Meanwhile, people ask me all about him, I could be his press agent.

"No, he doesn't eat raw fish."

"No, his father wasn't a kamikaze pilot."

"No, he can't do karate."

"Are you sure?" somebody asks.

Indeed he doesn't know karate, but judo he does. I am hurt I'm not the one to find this out; the guys know from gym class. They line up to be flipped, he flips them all onto the floor, and after that he doesn't eat lunch at the girls' table with me anymore. I'm more or less glad. Meaning, when he was there, I never knew what to say. Now that he's gone, though, I seem to be stuck at the "This is a chair" level of conversation. Ancient Chinese eating habits have lost their cachet; all I get are more and more questions about me and Sherman. "I dunno," I'm saying all the time. *Are* we going out? We do stuff, it's true. For example, I take him to the department stores, explain to him who shops in Alexander's, who shops in Saks. I tell him my family's the type that shops in Alexander's. He says he's sorry. In Saks he gets lost; either that, or else I'm the lost one. (It's true I find him calmly waiting at the front door, hands behind his back, like a guard.) I take him to the candy store. I take him to the bagel store. Sherman is crazy about bagels. I explain to him that Lender's is gross, he should get his bagels from the bagel store. He says thank you.

"Are you going steady?" people want to know.

How can we go steady when he doesn't have an ID bracelet? On the other hand, he brings me more presents than I think any girl's ever gotten before. Oranges. Flowers. A little bag of bagels. But what do they mean? Do they mean thank you, I enjoyed our trip; do they mean I like you; do they mean I decided I liked the Lender's better even if they are gross, you can have these? Sometimes I think he's acting on his mother's instructions. Also I know at least a couple of the presents were supposed to go to our teachers. He told me that once and turned red. I figured it still might mean something that he didn't throw them out.

More and more now, we joke. Like, instead of "I'm thinking," he always says, "I'm sinking," which we both think is so funny, that all either one of us has to do is pretend to be drowning and the other one cracks up. And he tells me things—for example, that there are electric lights everywhere in Tokyo now.

"You mean you didn't have them before?"

"Everywhere now!" He's amazed too. "Since Olympics!"

"Olympics?"

"Nineteen sixty," he says proudly, and as proof, hums for me the Olympic theme song. "You know?"

"Sure," I say, and hum with him happily. We could be a picture on a UNICEF poster. The only problem is that I don't really understand what the Olympics have to do with the modernization of Japan, any more than I get this other story he tells me, about that hole in his left eyebrow, which is from some time his father accidentally hit him with a lit cigarette. When Sherman was a baby. His father was drunk, having been out carousing; his mother was very mad but didn't say anything, just cleaned the whole house. Then his father was so ashamed he bowed to ask her forgiveness.

"Your mother cleaned the house?"

Sherman nods solemnly.

"And your father *bowed*?" I find this more astounding than anything I ever thought to make up. "That is so weird." I tell him.

"Weird," he agrees. "This I no forget, forever. *Father* bow to *mother!*"

We shake our heads.

As for the things he asks me, they're not topics I ever discussed before. Do I like it here? Of course I like it here, I was born here, I say. Am I Jewish? Jewish! I laugh. *Oy!* Am I American? "Sure I'm American," I say. "Everybody who's born here is American, and also some people who convert from what they were before. You could become American." But he says no, he could never. "Sure you could," I say. "You only have to learn some rules and speeches."

"But I Japanese," he says.

"You could become American anyway," I say. "Like I *could* become Jewish, if I wanted to. I'd just have to switch, that's all."

"But you Catholic," he says.

I think maybe he doesn't get what means switch.

I introduce him to Mrs. Wilder's turkey pot pies. "Gross?" he asks. I say they are, but we like them anyway. "Don't tell anybody." He promises. We bake them, eat them. While we're eating, he's drawing me pictures.

"This American," he says, and he draws something that looks like John Wayne. "This Jewish," he says, and draws something that looks like the Wicked Witch of the West, only male.

"I don't think so," I say.

He's undeterred. "This Japanese," he says, and draws a fair rendition of himself. "This Chinese," he says, and draws what looks to be another fair rendition of himself.

"How can you tell them apart?"

"This way," he says, and he puts the picture of the Chinese so that it is looking at the pictures of the American and the Jew. The Japanese faces the wall. Then he draws another picture, of a Japanese flag, so that the Japanese has that to contemplate. "Chinese lost in department store," he says. "Japanese know how go." For fun, he then takes the Japanese flag and fastens it to the refrigerator door with magnets. "In school, in ceremony, we this way," he explains, and bows to the picture.

When my mother comes in, her face is so red that with the white wall behind her she looks a bit like the Japanese flag herself. Yet I get the feeling I better not say so. First she doesn't move. Then she snatches the flag off the refrigerator, so fast the magnets go flying. Two of them land on the stove. She crumples up the paper. She hisses at Sherman, *"This is the U.S. of A., do you hear me!"*

Sherman hears her.

"You call your mother right now, tell her come pick you up."

He understands perfectly. *I,* on the other hand, am stymied. How can two people who don't really speak English understand each other better than I can understand them? "But Ma," I say.

"Don't *Ma* me," she says.

Later on she explains that World War II was in China, too. "Hitler," I say. "Nazis. Volkswagens." I know the Japanese were on the wrong side, because they bombed Pearl Harbor. My mother explains about before that. The Napkin Massacre. "*Nan*-king," she corrects me.

"Are you sure?" I say. "In school, they said the war was about putting the Jews in ovens."

"Also about ovens."

"About both?"

"Both."

"That's not what they said in school."

"Just forget about school."

Forget about school? "I thought we moved here for the schools."

"We moved here," she says, "for your education."

Sometimes I have no idea what she's talking about.

"I like Sherman," I say after a while.

"He's nice boy," she agrees.

Meaning what? I would ask, except that my dad's just come home, which means it's time to start talking about whether we should build a brick wall across the front of the lawn. Recently a car made it almost into our living room, which was so scary, the driver fainted and an ambulance had to come. "We should have discussion," my dad said after that. And so for about a week, every night we do.

"Are you just friends, or more than just friends?" Barbara Gugelstein is giving me the cross-ex.

"Maybe," I say.

"Come on," she says, "I told you *everything* about me and Andy."

I actually *am* trying to tell Barbara everything about Sherman, but everything turns out to be nothing. Meaning, I can't locate the conversation in what I have to say. Sherman and I go places, we talk, one time my mother threw him out of the house because of World War II.

"I think we're just friends," I say.

"You think or you're sure?"

Now that I do less of the talking at lunch, I notice more what other people talk about—cheerleading, who likes who, this place in White Plains to get earrings. On none of these topics am I an expert. Of course, I'm still friends with Barbara Gugelstein, but I notice Danielle Meyers has spun away to other groups.

Barbara's analysis goes this way: To be popular, you have to have big boobs, a note from your mother that lets you use her Lord and Taylor credit card, and a boyfriend. On the other hand, what's so wrong with being unpopular? "We'll get them in the end," she says. It's what her dad tells her. "Like they'll turn out too dumb to do their own investing, and then they'll get killed in fees and then they'll have to move to towns where the schools stink. And my dad should know," she winds up. "He's a broker."

"I guess," I say.

But the next thing I know, I have a true crush on Sherman Matsumoto. *Mister* Judo, the guys call him now, with real respect; and the more they call him that, the more I don't care that he carries a notebook with a cat on it.

I sigh. "Sherman."

"I thought you were just friends," says Barbara Gugelstein.

"We were," I say mysteriously. This, I've noticed, is how Danielle Meyers talks; everything's secret, she only lets out so much, it's like she didn't grow up with everybody telling her she had to share.

And here's the funny thing: The more I intimate that Sherman and I are more than just friends, the more it seems we actually are. It's the old imagination giving reality a nudge. When I start to blush, he starts to blush; we reach a point where we can hardly talk at all.

"Well, there's first base with tongue, and first base without," I tell Barbara Gugelstein.

In fact, Sherman and I have brushed shoulders, which was equivalent to first base I was sure, maybe even second. I felt as though I'd turned into one huge shoulder; that's all I was, one huge shoulder. We not only didn't talk, we didn't breathe. But how can I tell Barbara Gugelstein that? So instead I say, "Well, there's second base and second base."

Danielle Meyers is my friend again. She says, "I know exactly what you mean," just to make Barbara Gugelstein feel bad.

"Like *what* do I mean?" I say.

Danielle Meyers can't answer.

"You know what I think?" I tell Barbara the next day. "I think Danielle's giving us a line."

Barbara pulls thoughtfully on one of her pigtails.

If Sherman Matsumoto is never going to give me an ID to wear, he should at least get up the nerve to hold my hand. I don't think he sees this. I think of the story he told me about his parents, and in a synaptic firestorm realize we don't see the same thing at all.

So one day, when we happen to brush shoulders again, I don't move away. He doesn't move away either. There we are. Like a pair of bleachers, pushed together but not quite matched up. After a while, I have to breathe, I can't help it. I

breathe in such a way that our elbows start to touch too. We
are in a crowd, waiting for a bus. I crane my neck to look at
the sign that says where the bus is going; now our wrists are
touching. Then it happens: He links his pinky around mine.

Is that holding hands? Later, in bed, I wonder all night.
One finger, and not even the biggest one.

Sherman is leaving in a month. Already! I think, well, I suppose he will leave and we'll never even kiss. I guess that's all
right. Just then I've resigned myself to it, though, we hold
hands, all five fingers. Once when we are at the bagel shop,
then again in my parents' kitchen. Then, when we are at the
playground, he kisses the back of my hand.

He does it again not too long after that, in White Plains.

I invest in a bottle of mouthwash.

Instead of moving on, though, he kisses the back of my
hand again. And again. I try raising my hand, hoping he'll
make the jump from my hand to my cheek. It's like trying to
wheedle an inchworm out the window. You know, *This way,
this way.*

All over the world, people have their own cultures. That's
what we learned in social studies.

If we never kiss, I'm not going to take it personally.

It is the end of the school year. We've had parties. We've
turned in our textbooks. Hooray! Outside the asphalt already
steams if you spit on it. Sherman isn't leaving for another
couple of days, though, and he comes to visit every morning,
staying until the afternoon, when Callie comes home from
her big-deal job as a bank teller. We drink Kool-Aid in the
backyard and hold hands until they are sweaty and make
smacking noises coming apart. He tells me how busy his par-

ents are, getting ready for the move. His mother, particularly, is very tired. Mostly we are mournful.

The very last day we hold hands and do not let go. Our palms fill up with water like a blister. We do not care. We talk more than usual. How much airmail is to Japan, that kind of thing. Then suddenly he asks, will I marry him?

I'm only thirteen.

But when old? Sixteen?

If you come back to get me.

I come. Or you can come to Japan, be Japanese.

How can I be Japanese?

Like you become American. Switch.

He kisses me on the cheek, again and again and again.

His mother calls to say she's coming to get him. I cry. I tell him how I've saved every present he's ever given me—the ruler, the pencils, the bags from the bagels, all the flower petals. I even have the orange peels from the oranges.

All?

I put them in a jar.

I'd show him, except that we're not allowed to go upstairs to my room. Anyway, something about the orange peels seems to choke him up too. *Mister* Judo, but I've gotten him in a soft spot. We are going together to the bathroom to get some toilet paper to wipe our eyes when poor tired Mrs. Matsumoto, driving a shiny new station wagon, skids up onto our lawn.

"Very sorry!"

We race outside.

"Very sorry!"

Mrs. Matsumoto is so short that about all we can see of her is a green cotton sun hat, with a big brim. It's tied on. The brim is trembling.

I hope my mom's not going to start yelling about World War II.

"Is all right, no trouble," she says, materializing on the steps behind me and Sherman. She's propped the screen door wide open; when I turn I see she's waving. "No trouble, no trouble!".

"No trouble, no trouble!" I echo, twirling a few times with relief.

Mrs. Matsumoto keeps apologizing; my mom keeps insisting she shouldn't feel bad, it was only some grass and a small tree. Crossing the lawn, she insists Mrs. Matsumoto get out of the car, even though it means trampling some lilies of the valley. She insists that Mrs. Matsumoto come in for a cup of tea. Then she will not talk about anything unless Mrs. Matsumoto sits down, and unless she lets my mom prepare her a small snack. The coming in and the tea and the sitting down are settled pretty quickly, but they negotiate ferociously over the small snack, which Mrs. Matsumoto will not eat unless she can call Mr. Matsumoto. She makes the mistake of linking Mr. Matsumoto with a reparation of some sort, which my mom will not hear of.

"Please!"

"No no no no."

Back and forth it goes: "No no no no." "No no no no." "No no no no." What kind of conversation is that? I look at Sherman, who shrugs. Finally Mr. Matsumoto calls on his own, wondering where his wife is. He comes over in a taxi. He's a heavy-browed businessman, friendly but brisk—not at all a type you could imagine bowing to a lady with a taste for tie-on sunhats. My mom invites him in as if it's an idea she just this moment thought of. And would he maybe have some tea and a small snack?

Sherman and I sneak back outside for another farewell, by the side of the house, behind the forsythia bushes. We hold hands. He kisses me on the cheek again, and then—just when I think he's finally going to kiss me on the lips—he kisses me on the neck.

Is this first base?

He does it more. Up and down, up and down. First it tickles, and then it doesn't. He has his eyes closed. I close my eyes too. He's hugging me. Up and down. Then down.

He's at my collarbone.

Still at my collarbone. Now his hand's on my ribs. So much for first base. More ribs. The idea of second base would probably make me nervous if he weren't on his way back to Japan and if I really thought we were going to get there. As it is, though, I'm not in much danger of wrecking my life on the shoals of passion; his unmoving hand feels more like a growth than a boyfriend. He has his whole face pressed to my neck skin so I can't tell his mouth from his nose. I think he may be licking me.

From indoors, a burst of adult laughter. My eyelids flutter. I start to try and wiggle such that his hand will maybe budge upward.

Do I mean for my top blouse button to come accidentally undone?

He clenches his jaw, and when he opens his eyes, they're fixed on that button like it's a gnat that's been bothering him for far too long. He mutters in Japanese. If later in life he were to describe this as a pivotal moment in his youth, I would not be surprised. Holding the material as far from my body as possible, he buttons the button. Somehow we've landed up too close to the bushes.

What to tell Barbara Gugelstein? She says, "Tell me what were his last words. He must have said something last."

"I don't want to talk about it."

"Maybe he said Good-bye?" she suggests. "Sayonara?" She means well.

"I don't want to talk about it."

"Aw, come on, I told you everything about . . ."

I say, "Because it's private, excuse me."

She stops, squints at me as though at a far-off face she's trying to make out. Then she nods and very lightly places her hand on my forearm.

The forsythia seemed to be stabbing us in the eyes. Sherman said, more or less, *You will need to study how to switch.*

And I said, *I think you should switch. The way you do everything is weird.*

And he said, *You just want to tell everything to your friends. You just want to have boyfriend to become popular.*

Then he flipped me. Two swift moves, and I went sprawling through the air, a flailing confusion of soft human parts such as had no idea where the ground was.

It is the fall, and I am in high school, and still he hasn't written, so finally I write him.

I still have all your gifts, I write. *I don't talk so much as I used to. Although I am not exactly a mouse either. I don't care about being popular anymore. I swear. Are you happy to be back in Japan? I know I ruined everything. I was just trying to be entertaining. I miss you with all my heart, and hope I didn't ruin everything.*

He writes back, *You will never be Japanese.*

I throw all the orange peels out that day. Some of them, it turns out, were moldy anyway. I tell my mother I want to move to Chinatown.

"Chinatown!" she says.

I don't know why I suggested it.

"What's the matter?" she says. "Still boy-crazy? That Sherman?"

"No."

"Too much homework?"

I don't answer.

"Forget about school."

Later she tells me if I don't like school, I don't have to go every day. Some days I can stay home.

"Stay home?" In Yonkers, Callie and I used to stay home all the time, but that was because the schools there were *waste of time*.

"No good for a girl be too smart anyway."

For a long time I think about Sherman. But after a while I don't think about him so much as I just keep seeing myself flipped onto the ground, lying there shocked as the Matsumotos get ready to leave. My head has hit a rock; my brain aches as though it's been shoved to some new place in my skull. Otherwise I am okay. I see the forsythia, all those whippy branches, and can't believe how many leaves there are on a bush—every one green and perky and durably itself. And past them, real sky. I try to remember about why the sky's blue, even though this one's gone the kind of indescribable gray you associate with the insides of old shoes. I smell grass. Probably I have grass stains all over my back. I hear my mother calling through the back door, "Mon-a! Everyone leaving now," and "Not coming to say good-bye?" I hear Mr. and Mrs. Matsumoto bowing as they leave—or at least I hear the embarrassment in my mother's voice as they bow. I hear their car start. I hear Mrs. Matsumoto directing Mr. Matsumoto how to back off the lawn so as not to rip any more of it up. I feel the back of my head for blood—just a little. I hear their chug-chug grow fainter and fainter, until it has faded into the whuzz-whuzz of all the other cars. I hear my mom singing, "*Mon*-a! *Mon*-a!" until my dad comes home. Doors open and shut. I see myself standing up, brushing myself off so I'll have less explaining to do if she comes out to look for me. Grass stains—just like I thought. I see myself walking around the house, going over to have a look at our churned-up yard. It looks pretty sad, two big brown tracks, right through the irises and the lilies of the valley, and that was a new dogwood we'd just planted. Lying there like that. I hear myself thinking about my father, having to go dig it up all over again. Adjusting. I think how we probably ought to put up that brick wall. And sure enough, when I go inside, no one's thinking about me, or that little bit of blood at the back of my head, or the grass stains. That's what they're talking about—that wall. Again. My mom doesn't think it'll do any good, but my dad thinks we should give it a try. Should we or shouldn't we? How high? How thick? What will the neighbors say? I plop myself down on a hard chair. And all I can think is, we are the complete only family that has to worry about this. If I could, I'd switch everything to be different. But since I can't, I might as well sit here at the table for a while, discussing what I know how to discuss. I nod and listen to the rest.

Myrna and Me

LAURA BOSS

Myrna and I never really liked each other even though we were best friends. We really didn't have much choice or so we (or maybe even more important our mothers) thought in that typically Main Street quiet town of the 1950s. We were Jewish, and there were only three Jewish girls in the eighth grade at School Number Eleven. The other Jewish girl was so "square" that she had no interest in boys (our main interest), still enjoyed playing after school with her younger brother, still dressed the way we had dressed in sixth grade wearing Mary Janes to school, and to our horror still wearing an undershirt rather than a bra as we did even if it were the double A size, the smallest size made. To Myrna and me, a bra was a symbol (whether we needed it or not) that we had left childhood and were teenagers interested in guys—even if it were just talking about them. I had tried to get the other girl interested in talking boys and clothes, but she still liked playing tag after school and jumping rope with the younger kids on her block.

Ironically, it was this interest in boys that seemed to rule out deep friendships with girls who were not Jewish. It wasn't that we were ignored or that overtly rude remarks were made to us by girls who were not Jewish. But somehow through the years, it was understood that we would only marry Jewish men and that meant, so we were not tempted, only dating Jewish guys. I understood this when I heard the shocked whispering in my grandmother's apartment about some friend's daughter who had married a handsome *shaygets,* or non-Jew. My own grandfather when I was four had told me that "if you marry a Jewish boy, I'll give you a thousand dollars as a wedding gift." Then he had signed a paper promising me this, and I still had it in a box with pen pal letters, my diary, ancient birthday cards, and my year-end report cards.

Since Myrna was the rabbi's daughter, she obviously understood this invisible code of dating and marriage. With her doe eyes, her angled face with its high cheekbones, and her slimness that most people called skinny, Myrna was often told she looked like Audrey Hepburn. I, with my dark hair and thick eyebrows, was often told I looked like Elizabeth Taylor. This did not mean too much since any even slightly attractive blond female in those days was told she looked like Grace Kelly.

Myrna and I both knew that we could never get into Rainbow Girls though we both secretly yearned to wear the pastel gowns during initiation. No Jewish girl had ever been invited to pledge. On Saturdays, Myrna and I would go to the movies. She couldn't carry any money because it was the Sabbath, but she had a free pass given to her father as a courtesy. Afterwards, we would go to Cohen's for chocolate ice cream sodas. I always had to pay for hers since it was a sin for her to carry money on Saturday. On Sunday she would pay me back the money, always with a sanctimonious smile on her face. Everyone knew she was smart. Everyone knew she was the rabbi's daughter. I knew something was wrong.

Once when we went to an eighth grade party given by a girl who wasn't Jewish, Myrna told her mother I ate ham. Her mother told my mother (something Myrna probably knew would happen), and her mother added it was wrong of me even though I was always allowed to have any food when I was out visiting.

Still, Myrna and I would spend our playground time and after-school time together talking about which boys were the cutest and Myrna sometimes talking about how she was smarter than Doris Nicoletti, who was a math wiz and Myrna's only real competition for valedictorian.

One Wednesday I walked home from school alone and my face stung from the words "dirty Jew" sneered at me by one of the worst students in my grade. I couldn't help but wonder if others thought what he said but just didn't say it, though I tried at fourteen to rationalize. Later, someone told me that that sneering boy had a crush on me, which led to my feeling I'd never be able to figure out guys.

Finally, toward the end of eighth grade, one of the Jewish guys, Richard Gold, told me he "liked me" and wanted to go steady with me—which meant walking me home from school, taking me to the movies on Sunday afternoon, and walking me home from services Friday night—and unsaid, a closed-mouth kiss those nights. He gave me a silver bracelet with "Love, Richie" on the back. I was thrilled. The second Friday night when he was about to walk me home from services, Myrna said she would walk home with us. When we got to my house, she said it was too late and too dark for her to walk home by herself so Richie would have to walk her home (which was almost where we started out from since she lived directly across from the synagogue). Even in my innocence, I sensed something unfair and raged internally, though I said nothing as I watched Richie and her walk away from me, her body slightly leaning toward his.

It was then I stopped being her best friend though she never understood why. And though I was still often an outsider at school (and still could not get into Rainbow Girls), somehow I only became friends with girls I really liked even if we came from different worlds.

Dinner with Father

BRUCE A. JACOBS

The Father has the biggest head I have ever seen.

It is a crag of a head, a bulkhead of a head, a dumpster or a freight container held in impossible and confident balance atop a pale reed of a neck. It is a soft boulder, taut with blue-veined off-white skin. The bare pate juts like a cliff from his thin fringe of white hair. Just beneath it is a skull crammed to kingdom come, I am told, with brains.

The Father's I.Q. is, or was, as my friend, his daughter, somewhat sarcastically puts it, the equivalent of that of ten ordinary men. He retired from tenure at Princeton. He has spent his life telling smart people what to think. He himself, however, does not think; he knows. He sizes up intellectual mass in a room at a blink, as one appraises the mood of a cocktail party or surveys the sleek chairs and lamps of a fashionable apartment. He lives for intelligence. Reason is his proboscis. I imagine his frontal lobe as an infinitely compacted amalgam of intelligent gray worms, squirming in continually new patterns with inborn collective genius. He is a B-grade horror-film prosthetic creature of avenging superiority, a mutant tyrannosaur with gleaming claws sheathed by liver-spotted skin, a great lizard with an ego, an autocrat risen from the swamp to the top of the food chain. He is a boss of ecosystems, an arbiter of natural order, a dictator of dinner conversation, a designer of the universe seated in a padded chair with armrests at the head of the table.

He is rich. It is his wife's money, inherited from her parents. Her picture appears in the newspaper for donating one million dollars to charity. Members of her family give one another furniture and paintings for their birthdays. The Father's good fortune in having married money is not mere luck. It is entitlement. He works. He worked ideas day and night for forty years. He has worked all of his life at social propriety. In retirement, he works at predicting snowstorms in his children's home cities, and at sending packages to them with optimal efficiency. When the packages do not arrive on schedule, he works at tracing them, telephoning dispatchers to verify times and routes of delivery. He works at letting his two sons know that they do not know the meaning of work. He works at reminding his daughter that although she works hard, having established her own horse training and breeding farm, she does not work intelligently. She wants to work and write her poems, which have won numerous awards, and ride her horse in the woods, and have time to ask herself questions. The Father knows: she indulges fantasy. She does not know what is valuable. She has recently been published in a prestigious anthology, which lies, unnoticed, on the counter during dinner.

As we sit surrounding a hillock of rare prime rib, the telephone rings. The daughter winces. The Father sits up straight. He asks who will answer it. No one will answer it, replies the daughter. We work all day on this farm, she says; dinner is sacrosanct. He snorts over his plate. What if a horse has been struck by a car? What if a client has an emergency? The Father believes in answering telephones. Phones carry information. Information is vital to work. If information is lost or delayed, work does not get done. The sorts of people who ignore telephones to savor good food or good conversation do not value work. They are, ultimately, lazy. They shirk duty and are not entitled to wealth. They work from nine to five, following orders from people who know the importance of answering telephones. They have trouble paying their bills. Such people, including most blacks, like me, are his inferiors. Or else, like his daughter, they are women.

The telephone continues to ring. The Father stares at his daughter. She does not move. I chime in to support her. The farm telephone has voice mail, I tell him. Anything gained by the small chance of catching an emergency within those thirty minutes, I say, is more than offset by the added stress of being ruled by the telephone. The Father interrupts me. That sounds very pretty, he says, talking over my voice as if I am radio music, but it does not change the facts. A person must answer the telephone. The phone rings again, then stops, leaving a silence.

Conversation resumes, shifting to what the Father and the Mother will do tomorrow, on the second day of their visit. They could tour the farm, meet horses and clients. They could go for a pleasant drive in the country. They could take their grandchildren to the mall. The Mother speaks up. She hates malls. Malls are hell. It is promptly decided. Tomorrow afternoon, they will let the kids drag them through hell. I put down my fork. I tell the Father and his wife that they should do what they like. This is their vacation. The children will survive. Why don't the two of them simply enjoy themselves? He aims his bald bulkhead at me. You, my friend, have a lot to learn, he says impatiently; life is not simple. I return the Father's gaze and suggest that perhaps things are simpler than he thinks. But I have forgotten: there are no thoughts. Only knowledge. Around me, silverware clinks loudly enough to shatter china. The Father's would-be son-in-law, alert to the dangers of flying glass, makes a joke. The Father turns to him and laughs, slaps the table. He likes what he sees of himself in his daughter's suitor: a young man who knows how to work, a man who comes straight from the barns to dinner, a man who would have leaped from the table to answer the telephone had the daughter not stopped him.

The daughter announces dessert. But, the Father protests, there is a task at hand: a dozen boxes of heirloom china, and a rack of the Mother's old clothes, must be brought into the house from their car. The family agrees. We will wait for dessert. The son-in-law suggests a plan. We will drape the dresses and coats over an upstairs banister, then place the boxes of china in front of the cabinet where they are to be stored. The Father slaps the table, grins at the son-in-law, and declares loudly that logic always prevails.

Dessert is served on small, gold-leafed square plates freshly unpacked by the Father. While apple and cherry pies and ice cream make a circuit around the table, the Father stands, unpacking more china. He stacks gold-edged cups and saucers, twenty or more, atop the avocado-green antique cabinet. He places plates, bowls, platters, enough for an officers' banquet, upon the thick wooden shelves. Ice cream melts on his rectangular dessert plate. I cannot stop looking at the hard angles of his body: the abutment of his alabaster forehead, the steam shovel of his jaw, the stooped hinging of his back and long legs. I see his wild-eyed worship of work, his deafening grinding of gears, furiously clearing hillsides of forests and tearing trenches through mountains. I see the squirming gray workings, the clever worms, turning in his great oblong skull, calculating the yield of prairies and rivers. I see him at the first Thanksgiving, accepting gifts of fur and pumpkin and corn, an ill-clad, starving settler who would soon forget how his own science had failed him. I see him making soundly considered decisions: bison are limitless, wolves are an enemy, beef is a core nutrient, straight lines are natural. I see my wizened black great-grandparents shaking their heads on their porches about the way that white people think, the way that white people act, the things that white people believe.

And then I see more. I see a man with dark skin father a son. I see this Father work three jobs at a time, admonish all others as soft and lazy, build an all-consuming business that his son will learn to hate. I see this dark Father take quiet walks in the woods and then return to his family with a chain saw. I see him pile women and children like timber, carve a home by the whim of his measure. I see him plant a large foot in his eight-year-old son's ass because the boy could not mop a basement floor fast enough. I see this Father running for messages, running for deals, running for City Council, running for some kind of glint of respect in the gray eyes of white Fathers, running for rabbits named Sparky on a quarter-mile oval track, running to outpace the squeezed rush of his own metered blood until science gives way and the brain bleeds on itself, the movie monster collapsing on a city skyline in a cloudburst of red. I see this Father's son wander amid sirens and fire hoses and splashing pink water, proof in the flesh of a life's work well done.

I sit at my friend's table, chew slice after slice of sweet apple pie while I watch the Father stack china. I watch him work his long limbs over small boxes as ice cream pools on his plate, and the fine shells of china strike one another like bells. I bend over my plate with a ringing in my ears, a high, thin pulse in my skull, and I ask myself, why doesn't somebody answer that phone, and why does my fork have the weight of ten men?

Brandy Cake

BEENA KAMLANI

Preeti rounded the corner jauntily, her Walkman earphones on full blast. She was wearing white jeans and an oversized pink T-shirt. Her hair was drawn back in a ponytail, and she had her sneakers and bright-green scrunch socks on. She felt good, for the first time in weeks. The guidance counselor at school had been really helpful. "It's unlikely that you could be pregnant if you've only done it once. You've probably not had your period because of tension at home. But get it checked to make sure." She had smiled reassuringly. Preeti thought of the home pregnancy test kit in her knapsack. She'd check as soon as she got home. Please let Mom be out, she prayed.

But as she drew closer to home, she felt a sense of panic fill her. What if she *was* pregnant? What would she do? Where could she go? What luck that Papa was away in California for a physicians' conference. Things would be bad enough just having Mom to deal with. She glanced quickly at Chuck's house. His beat-up car was outside the garage. God, he was home. She didn't want to see him, didn't want him to see her. She sidled around the bushes in the backyard. She'd go in through the kitchen door.

Once inside the house, she rushed upstairs, dropping her things on the stairs as she headed toward the bathroom. Mom had been cleaning, she saw. The bathroom was pristine, sparkling. She reread the instructions that came with the package, then went through each step over again, her heart thumping loudly. Easy, easy, she said to herself. It might turn out wrong if I'm so worked up.

When the liquid showed up a dark pink, she thought she was going to faint. It can't be, it can't be. I must have done something wrong. She read through the instructions wildly, looking for her mistake. But she had done everything exactly as the instructions had said. She looked out of the bathroom window. Chuck was lying on the grass, his dog, chewing something, beside him. Preeti wanted to call out to him, but the words got stuck in her throat. Something about his attitude, sprawled carelessly across the grass like that, with no sense of the world around him, told her that she had been foolish. He wouldn't want to have anything to do with her now. But a little voice inside said. You don't know for sure. He's the father. He might want to help. He owes you that.

"Chuck," she called down. "Please come here."

"Preeti! What are you doing back so early? What's wrong? Look, I'm expecting a call. I'll be up a little later, okay?"

"Chuck, please come up here now," Preeti said urgently.

He looked up at her, then shrugged and walked toward the house. Preeti went into her bedroom and sat down in a chair. She could hear Chuck's heavy footsteps on the landing stairs. Help, help, help, she cried soundlessly. I can't go through with this.

"Okay, baby, what's up?" Chuck came in and lay down on her bed, propping his head against the pillows. "You've been missing me, is that it? Why are you sitting so far away? Come here, you sexy thing." He stretched himself out comfortably, patting the space next to him. "Come on. You know, you kids at school are hotter than most of the girls I date at college. You don't have as many hang-ups. You want to experience it all." Preeti watched him as he undid the top button of his jeans. So that's what he thought she wanted. More sex. He was humming the tune to "Layla." "Layla, you got me on my knees, Layla . . . ," he sang softly.

Preeti took a deep breath. "Chuck, I didn't call you up here because I wanted to do it." She watched her words register, saw him look a little less secure. "I called you here because I'm pregnant."

She saw the blood drain from his face, his eyes begin to look shifty, evasive. "The old, old trick, huh? Preeti, are you gonna tell me that I'm the father?"

"You are," Preeti said quietly. "There's been nobody else."

"You're crazy. I can't be the father. I had a condom on."

"That's what you said then. I'm not sure—like, you said you did but I don't know."

"And anyway, we only did it once. Virgins can't get pregnant the first time they do it. Everyone knows that. And it's only been six weeks or so. How can you be so damn sure?"

"I am sure," Preeti said, pulling him off the bed with her hands. "Look, see for yourself." She pulled him into the bathroom, where the pink blot still showed bleakly on the test kit.

"Look, Preeti, I'm really sorry for you. It's rough for a fifteen-year-old to be pregnant. But I can't be the one who got you pregnant. Shit, for all I know, with a face and a body like yours, you've got all the guys in your class dating you. Specially now that you know what it's all about."

"Chuck, I haven't been with anyone else. I've only done it once, like with you. I don't know how this happened, but I know you're the father of this baby growing inside me. And I really don't know what to do. My folks will kill me, that's for sure."

"Yeah, that's for sure." Chuck was beginning to look worried. "Of course, you'll get an abortion."

"I guess," Preeti said. "But I'll need their permission and then they'll find out."

"Look, they're going to find out anyway. There's morning sickness and stuff like that. Dead giveaways."

"You know quite a lot about all this stuff," Preeti said.

"Well, yeah, my cousin got pregnant when she was in high school."

"What did she do?"

"She got an abortion. There's nothing else you can do. You're still a kid, Preeti. You don't want a baby messing things up."

"It's easy for you to say. You just fuck people and say to hell with what happens after that. I wish I hadn't believed you when you said you had a condom on."

"Hey, baby, you would have done it anyway. Remember that rainy afternoon? You were so hot."

Yes, she remembered. She remembered going over to Chuck's to listen to some music one afternoon when her last-period teacher was sick and the class had been sent home. At first, they had simply drunk a couple of beers and laughed a lot in the backyard. Then it had started raining and he had taken her up to his room. "You're so special, baby," he kept saying as he kissed her, his hands already underneath her clothes, exploring, setting off fires, strange new sensations. She had loved the feel of him, what his hands were doing to her body. So this is what it's like, she thought. But the feeling grew, intensified, and then, only when he was in her, exclaiming "My God, it's true, you really are," that she realized guiltily what was happening, too late to change her mind. And she didn't want to change it. How could something that felt so neat be wrong?

Now, of course, it seemed different. Threatening. His hot breath all over her body, his hands rough on her skin, bruising all the tender places. She remembered not knowing what to think. Was it really fun?

"Anyway, what are you going to do?"

"You mean, what are *we* going to do?" Preeti asked, thinking: To hell with it, he made the moves. He took me up to his bedroom, he undressed me, he showed me how. It's my fault for letting him, but he's as much to blame for what's happened to me as I am.

"Preeti, look, it isn't such a big deal. I think it's your crazy parents that have you shit scared of everything. Look, I'll tell you what. I'll ask my cousin where she went for her abortion. She'll know how to deal with this. I know she didn't tell her folks. I'll find out, okay?"

It wasn't enough, but it was something. Preeti tried to look placated, just to get him out of her house. She wanted to be alone now to think things through before her mother got home.

"Chuck, please leave now. I want to be alone."

"Oh sure, baby. Now don't worry. Everything's going to be just fine. I'll call tonight, okay?" He had become his usual assured self, jaunty, cocksure. Making his way out of her room as fast as his legs could carry him.

Preeti began panicking as soon as she heard the door shut. It was such a mess. How would she tell them? Was there some way she could avoid telling them? No—without money and with nowhere to go, she couldn't hope to make it on her own. She'd have to tell them.

Preeti lay on her bed, pressing her stomach savagely, trying to stop the sickening, fluttery sensation inside. Then she got up and walked across the landing to her parents' bedroom. She pushed the door open and stood there, unnerved by the stillness, seeing the room's uncomplicated character as if for the first time: the white candlewick bedcover, the unadorned white walls, the clock on Sudhir's bedside table loudly ticking the minutes away, her baby photo in a heart-shaped frame on Mira's bedside table, the prayer table with its garlanded idols, the strong smell of sandalwood incense in the air. She sat on Mira's side of the bed, then looked through a pile of mail on the table. A letter from Madhu, an invitation to a birthday party, a thank-you note from someone. She looked away, her attention caught by Mira's leather slippers lying overturned by the foot of the bed. She must have been in a hurry to get somewhere. Probably Sheela Shilpa's. That's where all her mother's friends gathered every other afternoon to gossip and kill time. She could see them now, talking enthusiastically over tea and samosas about their children's achievements at school, their career goals and college choices, their latest acquisitions, their in-laws, their long-term plans for remodeling their houses. Preeti remembered those long, tedious afternoons with a sense of horror. Until school had claimed her afternoons, she had been dragged to every one of those get-togethers. No swimming lessons or baseball practice for her: just Sheela Shilpa's hot and spicy teas. The women talked about the future, always the future—what they could do, how things would be. As if arranging the future was any way of controlling the present. Something so unexpected could happen, suddenly and without warning, that you would have to fight just to survive. Like Janet, who in two years had gone from being a middle-class suburban kid to the life of a prostitute in the streets of New York City. Pregnancy. Then drugs. Then being kicked out of her home by her dad. Like me, Preeti thought. Yes, for her, too, and for her parents, life would change its course, no longer the safe, predictable road they had known.

She wanted to cry, but she laughed instead. A desperate, mirthless laugh that broke the calm silence like a clap of thunder. She laughed and laughed, each hysterical outburst a powerful thrust against her parents' world.

"Yes, now you mustn't panic," Mira said to her caller. "Listen to me, I know all about these things. You must go into your kitchen immediately and heat some red chillies. . . . Don't you know what red chillies are? . . . You must go to an Indian grocery store in your area and ask them for red chillies. Yes, the Koreans will also have it. Go there as soon as you can. . . . No, I'm not a witch. But I know about things like this because in my country we have them also. . . . I'm from India. Yes, there are all kinds of wicked people who cast evil eyes on other people. You have witches here, but in my country there are all kinds of people who believe in different things—they are sometimes astrologers and sometimes cult leaders and sometimes just evil people. Some of them live out in the villages and join the dacoits. . . . Dacoits are thugs. They waylay innocent people and take their belongings. Sometimes, they can even murder people. You have to guard yourself against people like that. . . . Yes, then you must heat the chillies. No, no, not in oil. Just in a pan. Yes. . . . Then you must take some rock salt. . . . No, you can get it in your supermarket. Then you must take the name of your God and throw the chillies and the salt together over your shoulder three times."

Then, incredulously, "How can you not have a God? You must have been born something. . . . Oh, if you're Catholic, then you must take the name of Jesus Christ, I think. Yes, I have many gods—their names are Rama, Krishna, Vishnu, Lakshmi, Siva, Parvati—there are many of them. But you should go to your priest and ask him for a blessing. . . . You're welcome. Don't be scared. God will help you."

Mira hung up, feeling quite pleased with herself. Here was something she understood well—the world of gods and demons, spirits and superstitions. Vicky, who was on the same shift, was looking at her oddly.

"What was that all about? Sounded bizarre."

"Oh, this poor man thinks there are some witches who are putting an evil eye on him."

"Oh Christ, not that nut! You didn't take him seriously, Mira?"

"What do you mean? These things are very serious."

"He just calls in for shock value. This is great, though. He probably wasn't expecting to be taken seriously. Perhaps now that he has, he won't bother us again. But all that stuff about chillies and salt—you were joking, weren't you?" She laughed. "You're really something else, Mira," and without waiting for Mira's answer, she picked up the phone to answer another call.

Mira reflected quietly while waiting for her next caller. Why did Vicky refuse to take this kind of call seriously? Maybe because they didn't have any living myths and legends in their culture. In her world, gods came in human as well as animal forms. Loyalty and intelligence brought forth the image of Hanuman, the monkey god. Wealth and prosperity and wisdom conjured up the image of Ganesh, the elephant god. And whenever you had an unexpected stroke of good luck, you knew deep inside that the goddess Lakshmi was pleased with you. And evil Ravana had many incarnations, mostly human. What was myth, what reality? For Mira, the one was part and parcel of the other.

Most of the calls she received dealt with relationships—between spouses, siblings, parents and children, lovers. She was intimidated by the male callers, unused to being in any kind of position of authority in her relationships with men. And the women were all so different from her, demanding, strident, defensive. What could she say to a woman who was contemplating divorce because her husband refused to give up his two beers a day and she hated the smell? Or to the one who threatened to walk out on her husband because he hadn't washed the dishes for a week? She would try to remember the things she had learned in the training sessions. But they didn't come naturally. She was constantly in awe of how these women treated the men in their lives. Sudhir would think she had lost her mind if she so much as suggested that he do the dishes even once.

The phone rang again. Mira rushed to pick it up.

"Emergency counseling," she said. "Yes, I am a mother. How can I help you?"

The voice at the other end was weary, exhausted, desperate. "I think my daughter's pregnant," the woman said. "And she's only sixteen. I don't know what to do. Her father will kill both her and me."

Mira paused. "How do you know?" she said.

"Because a mother knows. The girl's been throwing up every day for the past week. Her face looks so thin and pale, she reminds me of a waif. I don't know how to tell her I know, that I want to help. That we can talk."

Mira felt herself stiffening, as one does when one's instincts have already registered what the mind has not—or cannot—yet.

"What will you do?" Mira asked, sensing there was little advice she could give the woman. How could she advise someone on her own worst nightmare?

"I don't know. What would you do?"

"I don't know. It's a big problem. I haven't really thought about it before."

"Is your child a girl, a teenager?"

"Yes, she's fifteen." Mira paused. "And like your daughter she's been throwing up every day and looks like a refugee. I don't think it's pregnancy that is making her do that. I think she's bulimic. You know how these teenagers think—they all want to look like sticks because that's what the magazines tell them they must look like."

"Yes, I agree. But bulimia is different. They usually want to get sick late at night, when nobody's listening. The morning would be an odd time to force yourself to get sick. They have to go to school, after all. And she isn't eating all that much."

"That's true. Preeti's the same."

"Maybe your daughter's pregnant too?" the woman suggested.

"No, no. She can't be. She knows better than that. She isn't experienced. I watch her very closely. I don't think anything like that could be the matter in Preeti's case."

"But if she is, what would you do?"

"I would rather die," Mira said. Then, remembering she was supposed to be helpful, she added, "No, I wouldn't say anything until she chooses to tell me. Then . . ."

"Yes?"

"Then I would try to understand, I think. But I know I would feel terrible and I wouldn't know what to do."

"Would you suggest abortion?" the woman asked.

"No, she's too young for that. But she's still in school. How can she have a child?"

"This is exactly my problem too. We're Catholics, and abortion doesn't sit very well with our religion, know what I mean? So I can't really suggest it. But I can't let her have the child. Her life would be ruined."

"Yes, we're Indians. . . . No, from India. And in our culture, girls are supposed to be chaste until they get married. You go straight from your parents' house to your husband's. And if there's anything like this in your background, somehow they'll find out—I mean, the prospective in-laws. I don't know how, but they know everything."

The woman laughed. "That's just like us Catholics. With us, too, everybody seems to know everything. And her father is so devout, he'll probably whip her or something. I don't know what's going to happen. Don't you think it's difficult being a mother? When things go right, the fathers take the credit. When things go wrong, the mother's to blame."

"It's the same with us. My husband would probably turn into a block of stone, stop acknowledging her as his daughter. He would start treating her as a diseased thing. And it would be all my fault. I couldn't bear it."

Mira could hardly believe it. Here she was, talking to an

American mother as though they were friends. It had never happened before. She savored this for a minute. It was because the woman couldn't see her, couldn't see her dressed as she was, her foreignness. They were two disembodied voices, really talking to each other.

Mira forgot her counselor's role. "What shall I do if she is pregnant?" she asked.

"Well, you've got to protect her from her father, don't you think?"

"Yes, but how will we live? Things will never be normal again."

"Not normal, just different, I think. I've always wanted a closer relationship with my daughter. I don't think we've ever really understood each other. I come from such a strait-laced background. Things are different now. You have to try and understand their point of view."

"But how will one explain to all the others?"

"You don't really have to, if you're strong enough. The only explaining you really have to do is to yourself."

"You know, this is funny," Mira said. "You called me for advice and I'm taking it from you instead."

"That's because we're both lost, both unsure of how to cope. We can learn from each other, we can take comfort in each other."

"Yes," Mira said. "My name is Mira, and I'm here every Tuesday from ten in the morning to four in the afternoon. You can always reach me here."

"And I'm Helen. I'm so glad we talked. I hope things go well with your daughter. I'll call you again next Tuesday."

"That will be very nice. And good luck with your daughter." Mira put the phone down and immediately started worrying. How rational, how manageable it had all seemed while she was discussing it with Helen. Yet if Preeti really was pregnant . . . could that be it? The reason for the mood swings, the early-morning sickness?

It was three-thirty. "Vicky," Mira said. "I have to leave. I don't know—my daughter. Do you think you can manage on your own till the next shift?"

"Sure, Mira. Go ahead. Is something wrong?"

"I don't know. I'm going to find out."

Mira opened the front door quietly and entered the house. There was a strong smell of alcohol in the air. In the living room, the liquor cabinet door was wide open and a bottle of brandy stood at the front, its cork barely pushed in. It had been an unopened bottle; now it was only half full.

She put her bag down on the sofa and slid out of her sneakers. Then she walked up the stairs to Preeti's room. As she passed the bathroom, she heard muffled sounds of crying, followed by deep retching. Mira prayed it was the alcohol.

"Preeti, are you all right? Please open the door."

"Oh hell, oh hell," Preeti cursed. "Can't you just go away?"

"No, I can't," Mira said. "I have to come in."

There was silence. Mira pushed the door open and went in. Preeti was sitting on the floor, her eyes red and bloated with crying. On the floor next to her was a paper cup that looked as though it still held some brandy. The bathroom smelled of vomit and alcohol.

Mira walked up to Preeti and wordlessly wiped her face clean with a wet towel. Then she pulled her off the floor and led her into her room. Preeti didn't protest. She seemed to be in a daze. As they left the bathroom, Mira saw the easily recognizable torn packaging for the pregnancy kit. She had used the same brand herself a few years before, when she thought she was pregnant. It confirmed her worst fears. She knew now, even without asking the question, that her daughter was pregnant.

❦

Preeti worried that her mother might suspect, Mira worried that her daughter might think she knew. Mira wanted it to come from Preeti. She couldn't even begin to deal with the problem without Preeti's participation. So she kept silent, tormented deep within as she listened to Preeti being sick in the bathroom in the mornings, watched her pull herself together stoically to get dressed for school, carried on outwardly as if nothing were the matter. When Sudhir called from California, she tried to sound as normal as possible, asked questions about the hotel and the conference as though they were of prime importance to her, and even discussed their weekend engagements with neighboring Indian friends. If he seemed nonplussed by her mindless chatter on a long-distance call, he didn't show it. She must have convinced him that everything was fine at home, Mira thought, because he hadn't called again last night. So much the better; in her own territory, she was much more in control of things. She would handle Sudhir when the need arose.

The evening before Sudhir's return, Mira went into her room to pray. The atmosphere had been so tense these last few days, Preeti saying nothing, just going up to her room and listening to music or chatting at length to her friends on the telephone. Mira had asked her once or twice, "Preeti, are you all right?" trying to initiate a conversation, but the girl would just say, "Yes, Ma," and disappear into her room. This evening, Mira resolved to give up trying. Leave it to God. Pray. Then clean the house. Do anything rather than sit in the kitchen, waiting for Preeti's footsteps on the stairs. To this end, she was assembling her prayer things and had switched on a tape of devotional hymns. As the little diya flames danced before her eyes and the smell of incense filled the bedroom, Mira began praying earnestly. She was so deep in prayer that she didn't hear her bedroom door being opened. Preeti entered the room and lay down on Mira's bed, watching her mother seated cross-legged on the floor, praying silently.

When Mira turned around and saw her daughter waiting for her, she knew that the time had come and quickly prayed that she would know what to say and how to get through this. Whatever happened, she could not lose her daughter. But Preeti made it easy. She came across to her mother and sat down next to her, her bow-shaped lips quivering, then burst into tears. Mira hugged her tight, saying softly, "Preeti, I know something's wrong. Please let me help you. I love you so much, I would do anything for you. You know that. Why can't you tell me?"

Preeti was crying so hard she could not speak. Eventually, the tears subsided, and it came out bit by bit: the pressure at school to be part of the "in" crowd, the feeling that if you were inexperienced at fifteen, it was because none of the guys considered you worth their while; the guilt, the sense of shame now that she was pregnant—Mira winced at that, there was a finality about its coming from Preeti that made it harder to bear—since smart people never got pregnant, only dumb people got themselves into that situation, the way her friends were avoiding her now, the intense fear of what Sudhir would do to her, the fear that she'd wrecked her life forever. Preeti had been living with a nightmare, Mira realized. If her child had not already been an out-and-out ABCD, the cruel acronym India-born Indians used for American-Born Confused Desis ("Desi" was a colloquial term for Indians), she was certainly on her way to becoming one now. India would reject her now as surely as she had previously rejected India. So much for Mira's dreams of taking Preeti back to India as often as she could so that she would meet an Indian boy and settle down there. No one would have her over there now. She would be tainted by scandal; teenage pregnancies were unheard of among the professional Indian classes. And unwed mothers represented a social disease of the West.

It seemed to Mira as she smoothed her daughter's hair, just as she used to when Preeti had been a child, that the girl really had nowhere to go. America would never wholeheartedly embrace her now—she had broken an unwritten code, violated a social taboo. An American child might eventually win back social acceptance, but for her child, not ostensibly "American" in the way her friends were, social acceptance had been difficult in the first place. Now it would be impossible. She was an outcast from two societies, belonging to both but welcome in neither.

Mira hugged her daughter tightly, remembering the story of Sita's abduction by the demon Ravana. When Rama finally won his wife's freedom by fighting the demon, he rejected her as she walked toward him, citing Hindu religious principles which declared that a woman who has spent time in a male stranger's house can never be accepted by her husband again; the woman is guilty of misconduct until proved innocent. Rama subjected his wife to a trial by fire, insisting that she literally walk through a blazing fire to prove her innocence in front of huge crowds of people. Sita emerged unscathed. Mira's daughter would not.

Mira felt herself enter a place where none of the values she had grown up with were there to guide her. This situation would, in fact, require her to suspend, if only temporarily, her ideas of right and wrong, blame and innocence, shame and pride, in order to save her daughter from being permanently scarred. And then could one ever be the same again? Having discarded, even temporarily, the values that had been her prop and her stay throughout her time in America, could she go back, as though nothing had ever happened? How would this change her? Would she, too, become an outcast?

Preeti had stopped crying, and Mira asked gently, "Preeti, can you tell me who the father is?"

Preeti burst out crying again. "I can't, I can't. Please don't ask me. It's not important."

Mira then asked, "But does he know?"

"Yes, but he can't help." Then it wasn't important to know who the father was, Mira agreed. It was better not to know.

Mira put Preeti to bed, tucking her in carefully. She watched her as she cuddled her ragged teddy bear, like a child, Mira thought. Just like a child, with that frightened expression on her face. How could she not protect her—this was her child. Gone was that hardened expression of a few weeks earlier— that jaunty, devil-may-care attitude she had adopted toward her parents and her grandmother. All Mira could see now was fear, need, and helplessness. It broke her heart. Why was her daughter being taken to task so young, so unprepared for life's trials?

She went downstairs and switched on the television, want-ing to be distracted. But Sudhir's face kept flitting into her consciousness. For the first time in her married life, she had begun to feel the difference in their ages. Sudhir was ap-proaching sixty, she forty-two. A man of his generation would not know how to handle a situation like this—he would feel it as a deep personal insult. She would have to face him tomorrow evening and she felt sick at the thought. He would condemn, he would blame, he would drag them both through hell with his wrath. Sudhir seldom lost his temper, but when he did, it was cruel and damaging. Mira rested her head on the back of the sofa and shut her eyes, praying for oblivion.

Preeti was so pale the next morning, Mira promptly took her back to her bed and stuck a thermometer in her mouth. A hundred and two degrees, it read. Mira gave her some aspirin, brought her some lentil soup for lunch, and watched her carefully as she became almost delirious. "When is Papa coming home? He'll kill me, Ma. Where will I go? Will you come with me? Janet's parents threw her out when she got pregnant. I wish I knew where she was, because the same thing's going to happen to me. . . ." Mira just listened, knowing that nothing she said would really make a difference.

She herself had spent a sleepless night worrying about how they would all get through the next evening. She would have to tell Sudhir as soon as possible. He was Preeti's father; he had the right to know that his daughter was in trouble. And he might understand. After all, he was a doctor. Doctors knew that accidents happened sometimes. They dealt routinely with unwanted, unplanned pregnancies. He might even know exactly what to do. So she got through the day, trying to rationalize her worries away.

Still, when she heard the car crunching the gravel in the driveway, she got up from the sofa nervously, her voice threatening to desert her, terrified at the thought of telling him anything about Preeti. It had begun raining earlier in the evening and she could hear the thick rain, like her thumping heart, drumming on the car.

"Mira!" he called as soon as he entered. "Mira!"

"Yes, yes, I'm here." She rushed out of the drawing room. "Shh, Preeti's not well. The flu, I think. I've given her an aspirin and put her to bed. She's sleeping."

"Why she refuses to have that vaccine every year, I don't know. Surely it's better than coming down with it so often. Anyway, how are you?" He gave Mira a surprised look. She was wearing fresh lipstick and had put her hair up. He kissed her, then started toward the staircase.

"Let me unpack this right away. I'm sure the suit's crushed anyway, but I'll take it out now."

Mira followed him up the stairs.

"You don't have to come. Why don't you relax downstairs. I'll be down soon."

"No, I'll sit with you while you unpack."

It was good to have him back, Mira thought. She wasn't alone. Sudhir would help her through this. She watched his strong back as he hung up his clothes.

"How was the conference?" Mira asked.

"All right. The usual stuff. It was good to see some of those guys I went to school with. Brennan was there—remember him, when we lived in Ohio?"

"Yes."

"And Lipset. He sent his regards. Lost his wife last year."

"Oh, I'm sorry for him. She was young."

"Yes, poor chap. How have things been over here?"

"Okay. Asha Gupta called. She wants us to come early tomorrow—she's making bhajjias and tea. Then we'll hear the singers and then have dinner."

"Sounds too long for me. I want to plant some bulbs. Haven't done any gardening for months and it's already July."

"You can come later. But I'll have to go earlier, I think. You know how the women are supposed to help with everything. And I want to see how she makes those bhajjias. That woman is really terrible. She takes our recipes, yet when we ask her for hers, she leaves out some really important steps, I think. Mine never turn out like hers, and I don't know why."

"Mira, this is the fifth time in the past week I've heard about those damn bhajjias. Even on the phone from L.A. Look, I don't care if you never make another bhajjia in your life. I just don't want to hear another word about them. I'm more concerned about Preeti. How's she been, besides the flu? Any problems?"

"No," Mira said.

Sudhir wasn't convinced. Mira was usually much more reassuring. "Come on, let's go downstairs and have a drink."

On her way down, Mira remembered the brandy bottle. Had she replaced the cork properly? She couldn't recollect.

"Mira, this is strange," Sudhir was saying. "I bought a new bottle of brandy last week just before I left. It was unopened. Now it's only half full. What's going on?"

"Oh, that." Mira laughed nervously. "Shirin Mehta gave me her recipe for her brandy cake. You remember how delicious it was—we had it at her house last Christmas. You must remember; you really liked it."

"Yes," Sudhir was staring at her. "But how much brandy would a cake need? Half a bottle?"

"I tried three times, Sudhir. You know I can't bake cakes. It just kept coming out badly. So I made it again and again till it came out right."

"I hope you saved me a piece."

"No. Some of the ladies came for tea the other evening, and it was finished. Don't worry; now that I know how to do it, I'll make it again soon."

Sudhir poured himself a brandy. "What do you want to drink?"

"Nothing."

He stretched himself out on the sofa next to her. "Sorry for shouting about the brandy, but you know with a teenager around the house, one just has to be very careful."

"Come on, Sudhir, Preeti isn't alcoholic at least."

"No, not yet, but you never know." He yawned. "It's good to be back home. We should eat soon. I'm getting hungry."

"Yes. I'll get the dinner."

"No, not just yet. Let's talk for a little while first."

"Sudhir," Mira said, "Preeti told me such a sad story today. I really don't know how these parents can treat their children as though they belonged to someone else and were not of their own flesh and blood."

"What is it?"

"Oh, you know her friend Janet? She got pregnant last month and her father just threw her out of the house."

"Well, she was stupid to get pregnant. I can't believe these teenagers. They have counselors and everything at their schools, which is a lot more than you and I had. They're constantly being warned against these things. In our time, do you remember anyone talking to you about anything like this? People didn't talk about it, so it was easier to get into trouble. You didn't know what the consequences would be. Now they know everything, and if they're still so stupid, then they deserve it."

"Sudhir, I'm surprised at you. Being a father yourself and from a culture like ours, where your children are your life . . . I don't know how you can be so heartless."

"Mira, I didn't mean us. I was looking at their culture and their feelings about their children. I was seeing it in context."

"But what if it were us? I mean, it's not so impossible, with the way teenagers are these days—"

"But it isn't us, is it, so why should we worry about it? I don't have the time to sit around hypothesizing about problems that don't really exist. Come on, let's get dinner on the table."

It was after dinner. Sudhir was about to turn on the television, when Mira stopped him, saying, "Forget the news for one day. I want to talk to you."

Sudhir looked irritated. "All right, what is it?"

"You know that girl Janet?"

"Oh God, this bloody Janet again. Mira, I don't have the patience for this."

"All right, I'll tell you what the matter is, and I hope you're going to be helpful and not start raving, as you usually do when there's a problem with your daughter. Preeti is pregnant."

His expression changed from incredulity to horror as he took in her words.

"I know you're not joking. You wouldn't joke about something like this. How could this happen, Mira? How, under your wonderful, caring supervision of your child?"

Mira kept silent, knowing now that the anger would come, just as she had feared it would.

"I see it now—the half empty bottle of brandy, the useless talk about bhajjias and brandy cake. You have been lying to me, lying to save your child—who should be thrown out of this house, just like that whoring Janet. Does she even know who the father of this bastard is? The bloody tart—what was she trying to do with her heavily made-up face and her skin-tight clothes, if not to get laid and make monkeys of her parents. You only have yourself to blame." He raged at Mira. " 'Sudhir, please increase her curfew.' 'Sudhir, please let her go out for one evening. What can happen in one evening?' " he mimicked her. "Now you know what can happen in one evening, and I hope you're happy."

He ignored Mira's silent tears and marched up the stairs. "All right, Preeti," he called. "Come on out here and show your face. You must be so proud of what you have done. Shaming your parents just to get your own bloody back on us for trying to protect you." He walked into Preeti's room, saw her looking at him with naked fear in her eyes, and yanked her off the bed. "Come on downstairs. Flu, hahn? We'll see what kind of flu this is."

He dragged her down the stairs and brought her into the living room. She stood there shivering in her nightie. A little girl was what Mira saw. A frightened little girl.

"Leave her alone," Mira shouted at Sudhir. "Get out of here and leave her alone."

Sudhir laughed mirthlessly. "Me—get out? You"—he took hold of Preeti's hair and walked her toward the door— "you, you shameless tart, you get out," he snarled at her.

Mira walked up to Preeti and put her arms around her. "Be very careful of what you say at this moment, Sudhir," she articulated slowly and clearly. "You may live to regret it. Preeti needs me more than you do right now. If Preeti goes, I go with her. So choose your words carefully."

Sudhir looked at the two of them, then turned abruptly and walked out of the room. Mira could hear him noisily beating around the wooden hangers in the coat closet in the hall as he looked for an umbrella. In a few moments, he had left the house, banging the door behind him.

Preeti began crying, silently at first, then heaving great sobs, weeping from the pit of her stomach.

"It's all right now, Preeti," Mira said. "He knows now. It'll be much easier. Trust me."

Preeti finally let herself be taken up to bed. She fell asleep almost immediately, with Mira by her side. Soon Mira went to her bedroom. She tossed sleeplessly as she wondered what tomorrow might bring.

It was about three in the morning when Mira was wakened by the sound of deep sobbing. She put her dressing gown on and crept down the stairs. About halfway down, she bent her head to look into the kitchen. Sudhir was sitting at the dining table, the bottle of brandy in front of him. It was almost empty, Mira could see from where she was. His head was in his hands. Mira could not confront him; it would make tomorrow all that harder to deal with. So she walked back up to her room and tried to sleep through the wrenching cries that broke the night silence of her house.

Drowning Kittens

ENID DAME

Let me take you with me on a visit to Indiana, a place I've never seen. It is 1924, a muddy spring day on the edge of a small town. The sun is weak, lemony. The house needs a paint job. That angry man, my grandfather, is angry once more: this time at Dinah, the family cat. Three weeks ago, while he was away at a Gentlemen's Apparel Buyers Convention in Chicago, Dinah gave birth to four nondescript kittens on the floor of the spare-room closet. My grandfather has just discovered them this morning. He is furious. He had not even realized Dinah was pregnant.

My grandfather had other plans for this cat, a real Persian, a placid aristocrat with large feet, tufts of hair in her ears, and guileless blue eyes. He'd gotten her by a fluke, when a customer defaulted on a payment. Unlike his wife and children, my grandfather hates cats, which he associates with fleas and mice. But Dinah was a special case, a matter of business. He'd intended to mate her, when she came of age, with another Persian, owned by another customer. He'd sell the kittens and make, maybe, a fortune.

Everything was arranged. Dinah went into her first heat; the male cat, Sultan, arrived in splendor, in a special carrier. He was tremendous, twice as large as Dinah, with one green eye, one blue eye, and an aggrieved expression on his pushed-in face. My grandmother had disliked him instantly. She was pleased when Dinah rejected his advances, giving him a sharp rap just below his hairy right ear. She drew blood, and

Sultan sulked in a corner. My grandfather felt himself dis-
graced. He kicked the sofa leg. "Don't be silly, Jake," my
grandmother said. Her long braid had fallen down again; she
tossed it back, airily. "Maybe he isn't her type."

She was right. Two days later, Sultan dismissed, Dinah ran
outside and got herself pregnant by a striped, marauding tom
with one ear missing. Right now, she is suckling his disgrace-
ful kittens in a carboard box. My grandfather is beside himself. Once again, nothing has worked out. "That *putz!*" he
curses in his mother's language. "That *nafka!*" He decides he
will drown the bastard litter. That will be his project for this
Saturday. He announces his intention loudly, kicks the back
door for emphasis, and storms down to the garage.

During this uproar, my grandmother lies low in her
kitchen, busying herself with saucepans and stove lids. She is
adept at becoming invisible when necessary. This is a talent,
like making dresses without patterns or cakes that never fall.
It's a skill I often wish I'd inherited along with her name. She
was Renée; I'm Rita (and in Yiddish, we're both Riyka). In
some sense—according to Jewish myth if not Jewish law—
I *am* my grandmother; carrying her name, I'm her represen-
tative in my own place and time. This mythic commission
sometimes awes me: How can I be a person I've never met?
Occasionally I wonder: If the choice had been up to me,
would I have chosen her name?

My mother, if she were living, would say, "What's the
fuss? A name's a name." My mother Annie—that seething
little girl in a sailor dress. On this Saturday, she is furious at
her furious father. She follows him at a careful distance as he
kicks and mutters the length of the lawn. His temper is famous: it rips phones out of walls, smashes platefuls of noodles, beats children. Her anger is inside. It rocks and wallops
there like a hidden ocean, or soup on a too-high flame. It is a
powerful fuel; it scares Annie at times. She doesn't dare let it

out. It might blow up the house, the town, the state of Indiana. It might hurl them all, shattered and bleeding, into outer space.

Annie is especially enraged at that elusive lady, her mother. Why doesn't Mama try to stop her husband from committing a crime? How can she be an accomplice to murder? Besides, Mama loves cats, feeds strays at the back steps. That's how the unsavory tom got there in the first place. You might say it's really Mama's fault. Furthermore (Annie piles up each point in her legalistic, ten-year-old mind), a *mother* should stand up for another mother, no matter what. Annie has very decided ideas about what people should and should not do. In this, she resembles her father. Like him, she is always being disappointed.

The other children, David and Ruth, sit on the back steps, in tears. Ruth, at seven, can't imagine that force, her father's anger, changing direction or being stopped. She accepts it as she accepts the house they live in, or the weather. David is three. He does not really understand what is happening. He cries because Ruth, his favorite person, is upset; it is an act of companionship rather than grief. Unfortunately, it catches his father's attention. "Stop that racket, David Rabinowitz, or I'll *give* you something to cry about!" Jake hurls the threat offhandedly over his shoulder.

Reaching the garage, Jake pauses. He has threatened to drown the kittens. As a threat, it had sounded masterful. But now he must work out the details. He has heard of people drowning unwanted kittens, but has never done so himself. It is an activity he classifies as "country," like knowing how to milk a cow or read the sky. He has always regarded such knowledge—his neighbors' knowledge—with a mixture of admiration and contempt.

My grandfather is not a native Indianan. He is not even, literally, an American by birth. He pushed himself out of his mother's body unexpectedly one heaving night as her ship shoved its way across the water on the most difficult lap of her journey from Lithuania to Pittsburgh. A traveling midwife, luckily, was there to cut the cord.

His anger may have begun there, on the overheated ship, and taken root more firmly later in the tangled, Yiddish-speaking Pittsburg slums. My mother always claimed it was a gift from *his* mother, who as a girl in Vilna was nicknamed "Vildeh Chaya"—wild animal. No one in the family questioned it; it was simply *there,* a given, one knot in the fabric of family legend. It lives on, years after his death, in my mother's stories (now my stories), in my dislike of people with loud voices.

To my grandmother, Renée Lowenthal, Jake's Pittsburgh must have seemed far away as Lithuania. After all, her father William owned a dry goods store in Indianapolis. Mama told me many anecdotes about him and his large family. They were, of course, "assimilated" Jews. Yet, in my mother's recollections, they come off as exotic, out of place in the sedate Middle West. Even their attempts to be ordinary turn into excesses. Great-grandmother's best set of dishes, for instance, was *pink* crystal with a rose-colored cream pitcher and sugar bowl. Birthdays were extravaganzas, with fireworks on the lawn and gifts of precious jewels. Josephine, Renée's oldest sister, was the beauty and musician of the family. She played the violin in a long gown while Dickie, her pet canary, perched on the bow. (For years, this vision charmed me. Then I wondered if Dickie's singing interfered with Aunt Josie's playing. Mama laughed and said she hoped so, she could never stand violin music anyway. "Screech, screech, too sappy for me.")

In 1913, Mama said, the family store was very successful. That's why Great-grandpapa asked Renée to help out on Saturdays. Renée was seventeen, bored, engaged to a distant cousin, a lawyer. She was marking time, waiting for school to be over. She hated her public high school: the girls shrieked and giggled and the boys told dirty jokes. The year before, she had attended a Catholic girls' school, which she'd liked better. The nuns excused her from Religion.

Of course, Renée was working at the store when she met Jake. I've often tried to picture that meeting. What would a dry goods store look like in Indiana in 1913? Would it be large and pompous like a department store, or small and intimate, like a five-and-ten? Would Renée sit behind a counter on a high stool, her braid coiled tightly in a businesslike knot? That's how I imagine her, my teenaged grandmother, a trifle self-conscious, self-important, aware of looking good in this new role. Secretly, of course, she hopes no customer will intrude upon her thoughts.

At her back rise roller after roller of soft cloths, langorously waiting for the tape measure, the shears. It's a bazaar, a picnic of colors, textures, possibilities. Even their names give pleasure at this distance: calico, cambric, polished cotton, watered silk, satin, sateen, velvet, velveteen, lawn. Not that Renée would find them particularly wonderful. She would prefer the novel she surreptitiously pulls from her pocket. As she begins to read, she plays dreamily with the hairs working loose from her braid.

And now Jake Rabinowitz enters her department with his samples of shoelaces and socks. (He is in the wrong place; men's furnishings are downstairs.) He is handsome; my mother insists he was handsome then. He had a dark, confident moustache, he was twenty-five, a salesman, a man of the world. He had no trouble persuading Renée to marry him. They eloped that night, after the store closed.

"What did he say to her, Mama?" I often wondered.

"I don't know. What does a man say? He probably told her she was pretty, or something like that."

But she wasn't pretty. I've seen many pictures of her. At seventeen, at twenty-eight, at thirty-five, she looks much the same: a pleasant, vague-faced woman with light hair caught in a thick, frizzy braid. Later, she turned tired, sour, sick. She died at forty, of cancer.

Married, she had to discover Jake's anger, his bafflement, his habit of chasing fire trucks. He liked to watch things burn. No one in his family thought this odd. They nicknamed him "Klingele"—fire bell. In one Indiana town, he served on the Volunteer Fire Brigade. Usually, though, he was a free-lance fire buff.

One night, my mother remembered, Jake took her with him to watch a grocery store burn to the ground. His hand gripping hers was hot, sweating, heavy. As the flames grew large and the walls caved in, he squeezed her fingers. Her hand hurt, but she could not protest. His air of quiet, crushing reverence alarmed her more than his usual outbreaks of temper. Later, he said. "That was a good one." When Annie told her mother the next morning, Renée smiled her vague smile and flipped back her braid. "Papa can be silly sometimes," she said.

Was she sorry she married him? On that day of Jake's discovery, was she regretting her impulse—her decision? What *was* she thinking of? If she's at all like me, her namesake, her thoughts are probably wispy, scattered, ungraspable. I can see her staring out her kitchen window, fumbling for something in her apron pocket. She has forgotten exactly what she is looking for. In any case, the pocket is empty.

At some point, she decides she can't remain invisible much longer. After all, she hears her husband bellowing in the garage, she sees two of her children incoherent with tears and the third judging her severely. Upstairs, her cat is passionately nursing a disreputable brood. Perhaps Renée thinks: Who are all these creatures, and what is their relationship to me? Perhaps she is appalled by all these forces she somehow, at seventeen, set in motion.

Now Jake emerges from the garage, dragging a large washtub. He shoves it under the garden pump, and works the handle furiously. The old pump wheezes. The water, when it arrives, is rusty.

My ten-year-old mother watches from the edge of an imaginary circle. If she moves no closer, she will be safe. Finally, the tub is filled. Jake yanks it across the yard, sloshing water as he goes. Annie has a sudden, terrible thought: he will demand her help, he will make her his accomplice. He will force her to carry the doomed kittens down from the spare room. If she refuses, he will aim the hose of his anger in her direction. He likes to complicate his furies. Annie retreats to the house.

Climbing the back-porch steps, Annie thinks hard. She decides to confront her mother. Purposefully, she bangs the door open. Renée is still standing at the window. Her light-brown eyes have darkened, her light-brown hairs are spilling everywhere. She touches her throat, smooths out her apron, which is made of lace-trimmed, rose-sprigged lawn, cut down from an old dress. Renée hates to wear anything ugly.

"Mama, you've got to do something! This is getting serious. Papa's going to murder the kittens."

"Don't worry, maybe he won't." Renée pushes back a strand of hair. "You know how Papa is. Something might happen."

Annie is infuriated. She wants to stamp her feet, or scream, or tear her mother's teacups off their hooks. "What do you mean? What can happen? *Nothing* will happen if we don't do something!"

"Oh, you never know." Renée starts to untie her apron, smiling her slow smile. "Sometimes things work themselves out. Honey, are those grass stains on your socks?"

"*Mama!* Don't you understand? It's serious!"

At this moment, Jake explodes into the house. Ignoring his wife and daughter, he pounds up the stairs. When he returns, his arms are full of kittens. Dinah follows him, mewing.

"Don't let that *nafka* out!" he warns, slamming the screen door.

Annie and Renée rush after him. Joined by Ruth and David, they trail behind him down to the washtub, a small, silent parade. At the tub, Jake sets the kittens in a row, like toy soldiers. Dinah's children are soft and gray, fluffy as dust balls. Their eyes are dark-blue slits. Interrupted in the act of nursing, they squeal and suck at the air.

"Really, Jakie." Renée touches her husband's arm, lightly. "I think . . . do you have to? Can't we . . . I mean, Dinah is an unusual cat. Her kittens will be unusual too. I mean, we could find homes for them."

"Yes, we could!" Annie's voice escapes her, higher and louder than she'd intended. "I'll ask the kids at school. I'll *make* Charlie Krantz take one!"

"Please, Jake, they're so pretty. Everyone will want one. Their tails are going to be beautiful, like Dinah's, like plumes."

A tactical error! Annie recognizes it at once. It's a mistake to remind her father of the full-blooded Persians he—Dinah—might have had. Annie glares at her mother. Sometimes Annie thinks she is the only nonstupid person in the world.

"Pretty? These things? They look like rats!" Jake shakes off Renée's fingers. "*I'll* give you pretty!" He picks up a kitten. He holds it a second, then drops it into the tub. Then he picks up and drops in the others, one by one, just like Renée adds matzoh balls to her chicken soup.

The family leans forward. At least, that's how I picture them, a comic-book family, leaning forward in concert, a collective gasp locked in its throat.

But the kittens do not sink to the bottom of the washtub. Instead, all four strike out, shakily but surely, for its sides. They are determined swimmers.

Jake is astounded, impressed. Unexplained energies at work never fail to win him over.

"*Gottenyu,*" he breathes. "These are not ordinary cats. You were right, Renée. These are talented cats. Already they know how to swim."

Wet, sputtering, furious, the kittens try to climb out of the tub. One makes it; he falls headfirst onto the damp, receptive earth. Annie and Renée gently remove the others. They are shivering. They gravitate toward each other on the grass, a puddle of squeaks. Annie runs to liberate Dinah. The mother cat seizes each soaked kitten in turn and firmly scrubs it down with her tongue.

"Maybe we can sell them all to a circus!" Jake is excited.

"Yes, dear, maybe," Renée agrees.

Annie looks stonily at her father. She has remembered that cats can swim. They hate water, but they can, if they have to, travel through it. In order to drown them, you must put them in a sack weighted down with a rock. Her mother knows this too. Why did she pretend to be dumb? It occurs to Annie, in a sharp but imprecise way, that her mother may have counted on events unfolding exactly as they did. If so, Annie is angry. How can her mother take such chances with the great, stupid, dangerous forces? Annie decides to stay mad at both parents. She will never forget their behavior. She will never let either one off the hook.

Still, the kittens are safe. Renée and Annie will join forces to find them good homes. Dinah will live to conceive many litters, with mates of her own choosing. She will outlive both David and Renée. She will be buried under a rosebush in Cincinnati by Ruth, a young mother in 1940. Ann will not attend the funeral. She will be too busy driving from Pennsylvania to New York to second a strike vote.

ↂ

Last year, I decided to marry. Ann was still alive then, working part-time on the staff of a clerical union. She didn't approve of *my* prospective union—"I thought people just lived together nowadays!"—but she showed up the day before the ceremony with three presents. First, officially, was a ten-speed blender, "for the house." The other two were just for me. One was a savings account, in my name, for $2,000. "Don't tell *him*," she counseled. "Every woman needs a little money of her own." The other was less useful: a white Persian kitten with round, copper-colored eyes. With him came a shopping bag filled with a sack of kitty litter, a litter box, a metal comb, a plastic dish, and four cans of tuna.

"I see you came prepared," I said.

"Sure, prepared. Preparation, that's me!" My mother seemed pleased by my comment. We made dinner in my apartment, fed the new cat. Then she gave me another gift: the story of the attempted drowning. She told it rapidly, her back turned to me, while she boiled water and unfolded coffee filters.

"Mama, why didn't you ever tell me this one before?"

"I don't know. I haven't thought about it in years. Maybe because you're getting married."

"But Aaron isn't like Grandpa. We're old friends. We've known each other for ages."

Mama didn't reply. Instead, she watched the coffee as it dripped to the bottom of the pot. Then, gripping the handle firmly, she poured it into mugs, added milk, and turned to me, a mug in each hand. Her face, under the short, gray, efficiently cut hair, was unwrinkled as ever, but her eyes were tired. I realized she would soon be seventy.

"Preparation," she said dreamily. "That's what I keep telling these little office girls, but they don't listen. They don't want to hear."

She held out the mugs as if she wanted to offer them to the women she spoke of, young women unsure how to enter their own futures.

Gently, I took the mugs from her hands, set one down at my place, one at hers. "Here, Mama, we'd better drink it before it gets cold."

Mama slowly lowered herself into the chair and tasted the coffee.

"You know what? This isn't bad," she pronounced. She smiled at me. I smiled back, absurdly grateful. Usually, Mama hates my coffee. Of course, this was really her coffee.

"Not bad at all, Rivka," Mama continued. "Why don't you make us another cup?"

Portrait of the Lone Survivor

I used to throw snowballs at this girl who lived by my Grandmother's house. I came out in my army surplus parka & cap with ear flaps & waited for her, stomping my feet sometimes while I stood behind the bush. If the dog barked, I dirt-clodded him. While I waited sometimes I wrapped a rock in the snowball. Then sometimes the woman across the street would call my Grandmother & tell her I was after Azalea again. Grandma yanked the hood of my parka & shut me in the pantry. When she slept I crawled thru the window that tried to let light into her dark kitchen with its water pump on the sink & the swaying ceiling. I guess it was all her boys that slept upstairs. Herbert & Henry & my father, Roose, all jumping up & down & wrestling each other to the floor & falling out of bed & dive-bombing from the chest of drawers. She cried sometimes & didn't know what came over me after all she'd done. She sat at the north window in her house with her white cat Georgia & waited for the mailman who never brought her anything. I buttoned the cap with ear flaps & dug in the snow with my stick. I thought of the places I would go. Anywhere but there. Then suddenly Whamm there was Azalea & WHAMM * I hit her. The pink angora hat & her mittens flying!! I sat in the pantry with my finger in the boysenberry jam, Grandma's canning jars lined up on the shelves like snowballs.

I try. I am trying. I was trying. I will try. I shall in the meantime try. I sometimes have tried. I shall still by that time be trying.

My father gets me in the afternoon. We stop at Varnell's &
he jokes with Henry & his friends. I see the dent in the door
of his pickup. On the road, he barely makes a curve. The
brush jumps above the impact of a rock on the windshield *
then the long crack across the glass. On the way to the rodeo,
Roose passes a long row of cars. *ogi:do:da*. He laughs in his
Cherokee language when I scream.

I hope when Paw-naw comes, she crashes & the relish she
makes spills on the road, little bits of glass in tires & feet. I
hope Paw-naw falls out of bed & the planets wobble in orbit.
I hope I get sick & Georgia, the cat, gets in a fight, her ears
hanging like flaps on an old pilot's helmet. I hope Cousin
Flunella's spleen swells again & pouches like the weak place
in Grandma's tire. I hope Henry's infection keeps him home.
All the sweat & vomit & violent fever-dreams, shoes that were
all polished shit-on. I hope the house burns down. I'm going
to stare into the blueberry eye of the neighbor's half-blind
dog. I hope Paw-naw limps when she gets old & gets Alz-
heimer's disease. I hope the Christmas tree falls over this year
& the turkey, cranberry jelly & Grandma's pickles rot before
we eat them. I hope someone breaks into Henry's house again
while he's gone. His car in the yard. I hope someone siphons
out the gas.

She calls my name in class & my heart pumps my throat. I
feel Roose pound me under the covers. I feel the heat race
thru my hands. My head whacks an ax chopping a totem
pole. She calls my name in class & her voice is a rock wham-
ming my head. I feel chained to the backyard like the dog I
pass on the way to school. Then Roose's pickup races at me &
I stand in the road watching the headlights swallow me until
the fierce roar passes. She calls my name in class & I am a
pulsing star. A flag flapping on its pole above the schoolyard.
I try to hide behind the desk but she stands over me. I feel the
whack of Grandma's stick. The choke-collar on the dog. She
is the bear in my nightmares whose teeth drip with saliva at

my flesh. She tears bone & sinew, shredding vocal cords until I can't talk.

I see Roose in front of the liquor store. He asks a man for money. I think I will get a grocery cart from Dabner's & push it down the alley. I'll rattle thru trash cans for bottles with a ½ swallow of gin or whiskey, sleep on the park bench & stumble on the curb when I cross the street. I'll slobber as we talk about the visions of the Grandfathers, their bravery on the Trail to the New Territory. I will tell him how Grandma survives. We'll spit & urinate on the town square of Tahlequah, Oklahoma. We'll dry out gladly in the jail.

ogi:do:da / galv:la?di / he:hi / galv:ghw(o)di:yu / ge:se:sdi / winiga: / hl(i)sda / hada:n(v)dhesgv:i / e:lohi / galv:la?di / tsiniga:hl(i)sdi:ha / o:gahl(i)sda:y(v)di / dago:dagwisvi:i / sgiyane:hlvsge:sdi / itsv:sganv:tshelv:i / sgi:yago:li:gi / tsideo:tsido:li:gi / dogi:sganv:tshe:hi / a:le / dhle:sdi / udale:na:sdi:yi / widi:sgiya:dhinv:sdanv:gi / tsatse:li:yehno / tsa:hlini:gidi / ge:sv:i / a:le / etsalv:ghw:(o)di:yu / nigo:hilv:i / na:shigwo / winiga:hl(i)sda. Our Father / above / who dwellest / honored / be / thy name. / Let happen / what thou wilt / on earth / above / as does happen. / Our food / day by day / bestow upon us. / In that we have transgressed against thee / pity us / as we pity / those who transgress against us. / & / do not / place of straying / lead us into. / For thine is / thou strong / the being / & / thou honored / forever. This / let be.

Roose thrashes under the strap that holds him. The medicine men nail a cow-skull over his bed. They burn cedar & chant. I would pack if I could go with him. Unzip my skin from my bones. Wear my powwow buckskin. Leave thru the crack in the ceiling where the soul passes. Roose stops breathing. I stand to my feet & he starts again. That's how it will be. He'll stomp out the back door, leaving the screen to bang. It's not a great journey to the stars. I see the blueness of his feet & fingers. Part of him is gone already. His eyes closed, sometimes he calls her name as if waiting for the lift in the hotel lobby she had just taken. Sometimes he thrashes again as though still war-dancing in the rodeo arena.

I sit in the grasses at his grave. I name this day Holy. I walk back to the house thru the cockleburs that tear my legs. I will remember *ogi:do:da*. Who creates unless he has a vacuum to fill? A white crayon on white paper. A snowfleck in the sky. Who thinks of justice unless he knows injustice? Georgia sits on my lap under a corner of the white shawl. Her owl-eye looks from the window at birds in the wisteria. I think what we do matters. I tell her this & her ear flicks the shawl-edge. I stroke her old fur. She holds her paw over my knee. If the house were burning, yes, I'd take the back of her neck in my teeth & climb thru the pantry window.

Holy Toledo

JOSEPH GEHA

Looking for the charm against the Evil Eye, Nadia stretched up on the footstool—a tomboy in her dungarees—and searched the shelves of the bathroom cabinet one by one. The charm was a tiny object, no larger than a rosary bead, and it was forever getting lost. But despite the clutter of this house (her grandmother threw nothing away) it was forever turning up again, too.

Sitti, her grandmother, had had the amulet ever since the old country when she herself was a child. A Lazerine monk claimed he'd found it lying amid the rubble of an ancient excavation and, hoping to gain some favor, he brought it directly to Sitti's uncle, the district magistrate. When the monk was gone—the favor granted or not, Sitti never said—her uncle simply looked down at the charm in his hand and shrugged. After all, what was this thing to him? Nothing more than a drop of porcelain painted to look like a miniature eyeball. And so the amulet was forgotten, mislaid until after his death when it turned up again among his things. No one claimed it, so Sitti decided to keep the charm for herself. Attaching it to a stiff golden thread, she'd had the amulet ever since, over the years misplacing it, yet always finding it again somewhere.

But not here. Here on the top shelf there were only razors, old women's salves, and jars of black ointments meant to be kept out of a child's reach. Nadia stepped down from the footstool and carried it back into the front room.

"Achhh. . . ."

The long, familiar moan floated down the hallway from the kitchen; Sitti must be searching there now. And Mikhail was still in the front room where Nadia had left him, still doing nothing to help.

"Mikhi," she said, "it wasn't in the bathroom either."

"It doesn't matter," he said. Crossing his legs on the sofa, her brother spoke without turning to look at her.

"Then it has to be in the cellar. Me and Sitti, we looked everyplace else." Mikhail said nothing. "I bet I know where in the cellar, too." She waited for him to ask where. He didn't. "How much you want to bet," she went on anyway, "that it's in one of those boxes Uncle Eddie took down there last spring?"

Still her brother said nothing. He would not even look at her.

"Mikhi? You wouldn't just sit there if Uncle Eddie was here. He'll give you the belt again for not helping."

At that, Mikhi turned his gaze, slowly, the wide brown eyes of their father. "You telling?"

"No, not *me*." She wanted very much for him to believe this, but even as she spoke she realized that her voice was too solemn, unnatural in its earnestness. "I meant *Sitti*."

"Don't make me laugh." He was her little brother by two years, yet it seemed always as if he were the older one. Nadia was the one who giggled and could keep no secrets.

With another loud moan, Sitti left the kitchen and went into the dining room directly next to them. They remained motionless, silent in the ticking stillness of the front room lest she hear them and be reminded of their presence in her house: maybe if she forgot that someone was here to listen she would stop groaning that way—achh—every time she bent over, every time she pulled open a drawer or leaned back her head against the dizziness.

"Achhh. . . ."

(It hadn't been long after breakfast—maybe she was still drinking her coffee—when the pain and the groaning began. "What's wrong, Sitti?" Mikhi kept asking her over and over, but she wouldn't answer. Later, as the noon heat grew unbearable to her, she undressed, put on a nightgown, and braided her hair up off her neck.)

Sitti was a short woman, her broad hips spreading the nightgown as she bent low to pull and shove at the buffet drawers. Nadia almost smiled, watching her through the archway; the nightgown was white, and except for the three iron braids sticking out, her grandmother looked from behind like a little fat altar boy.

"Achhh. . . ."

Her groans were getting louder, and a hint of worry flickered across Mikhi's eyes. Then, just as quickly, he brightened, curling himself into a hollow of the sofa and tucking the souvenir cushions one under each arm so that their tasseled corners met beneath his chin like a silver beard. He grunted twice, as if to hold his sister's attention, then he made a face at her—an old man wagging a toothless mouth—and she had to turn away to keep from laughing out loud.

"Achhh. . . ." It was Arabic, but Nadia knew it meant nothing, wasn't even a word so much as the sound of effort and pain.

The drawers were crammed full of all sorts of odds and ends, and Sitti would be busy there a long time. That was her way: looking for one thing, she had to stop and muse over every other thing she came across. She could throw nothing away.

The satin pillows looked smooth and cool against Mikhi's hands. The American pillows, Sitti called them. Uncle Eddie had brought them home for her from the navy. The blue one had on its decorated side the figures of anchors and stars, the red one a poem stitched in silver thread. When he came home to stay, Uncle Eddie read the poem aloud to Sitti, showing her how the first letter of each line spelled the word *Mother.* The women said that Sitti was lucky to have at least one son who cared so much for his mother. What they meant, of course, was that the children's father did not care so much because he left. Especially since Papa was the elder son and it was his duty to stay. More than that, the custom still held, even here in America: a widower with children is expected to either remarry or else return to his mother's house. Papa did neither. Instead, he remained in his own house after the funeral. For almost five years until, one hot July morning, he dressed Mikhi and Nadia in their Sunday clothes and brought them to Sitti's house, all their things packed in grocery bags. And after that he simply went away.

Nadia watched a moment more as her brother's fingers brushed lightly over the stitching, tracing stars and letters, then she stood up. "I'm going to look in Sitti's room again."

Mikhi looked up from the cushions. The charm wasn't in Sitti's room, they both knew that; the bedrooms had been searched twice already, and all she was doing now was simply trying to put off having to go down to the cellar alone. Mikhi's wry, sidelong glance mocked her.

She crossed in front of him, ignoring the face he once more made at her, lipping his teeth that way to get her laughing. She was only eleven, and a girl given to giggling, but she wasn't a fool. Mikhi was up to something, all day just sitting there and doing nothing to help. There was going to be trouble—once more Uncle Eddie would have his snakeskin belt out and flashing—and she would be a part of it. She'd have to be. Mikhi was younger than her, yet she had always followed his lead, even into trouble.

"Mikhi?" she paused in the doorway. "I don't want to go down there alone." Nadia kept her eyes downward on a curled edge of the rug. Sitti was dying, or said she was, and she needed the amulet to ease the pain of her dying. At least it might quiet her. "Will you come with me when I go?"

Again he didn't answer. Nadia stomped angrily into the hall—her dungarees, bought large so she'd grow into them, slap-slapping at her ankles—and pushed open the bedroom door.

Sitti's room was papered with dark flowers. The walls, like everything else in that house, were cluttered. Holy pictures hung in uneven diamond patterns above the bed, and there were photographs everywhere, dark-framed pictures of Sitti when she was young, of Jiddo—Nadia's grandfather—rimmed in black because he was dead, and of Papa and Uncle Eddie when they were little boys. None of them were smiling, not even little Papa, his big eyes staring blankly at her through the dusty glass.

The dresser top had been cleared at least twice that day, and there was nothing on it now but a small statue of the Virgin. Almost two years before, when Uncle Eddie was still in the navy and it looked like he might be sent to Korea, Sitti had taped a folded dollar bill to the statue's base. Like a prayer, almost.

(". . . Great to be back," Uncle Eddie had kept saying after his discharge. "Great to be back."

"What was it like?" visitors would ask.

"We never did go overseas, unless you count once to Panama. Mostly it was up and down the West Coast."

"And how was that?"

"Truth is, I was lost the whole time. Really. I never knew where I was. And when we put in it was even worse. I was always getting lost in the cities. You honestly don't know what homesick is until you've been out there."

Then Uncle Eddie would take his mother's hand in both of his. "Great to be back." He praised her cooking every single day of that first week home. "Great to be back," he said it even to himself, idly fingering one of the sofa doilies, then actually noticing it, as if discovering at his very fingertips yet one more familiar marker against the lostness from which he had returned. . . .)

The bedroom was warm, musty with the smell of sleep. Nadia opened a window, then knelt and put her face to the faint breeze. Except for the furniture and the pictures, this could have been her old bedroom at home. The two houses were almost identical, both built of glazed brick with tall, narrow windows and rooms that were dark even in daytime since they shared walls with the row houses on either side (and beneath those rooms the cellars, damp honeycombs of thick walls and uneven floors); both houses, too, were within that same general neighborhood of East Detroit, the Little Syria centered at Congress Street and Larned. Pressing her face to the window screen, she could see the dome of the Maronite Catholic Church and the onion-shaped twin steeples of the Greek Orthodox. Farther up Congress there were shops that sold woven artifacts and brass from the old country. They had food, too, things that couldn't be found anywhere else in Detroit; pressed apricots, goat cheese, sesame paste and pine nuts and briny olives. ("The food, that's what I missed most," Uncle Eddie said. "The Americans, they don't know how to eat.") And there were the *ahwa* shops too, where old men sat all day amid tobacco smoke and the bitter smell of Turkish coffee.

On Saturday mornings Americans came into the neighborhood to shop. Women, mostly; the merchants called them "Mum" (and behind their backs "College Mum," not so much because of the university nearby as for the way these women spoke English—everything in the nose). Nadia often used to sit outside just to watch the college mums pass. While most women dressed up in hat and gloves to go shopping, clutching a narrow black purse, the college mums seemed younger than that. They always had on something bright, like a scarf or a bandanna. The handbags slung carelessly from their shoulders were huge, made of woven rope or straw, and patterned with beads. Usually they wore no makeup, and with their hair pinned up or back there was always something boyish about their faces. A few even dressed in trousers, like men. And they were always excited about something, always smiling as they pointed out this or that to a companion who'd never been there before, exclaiming too loudly about the inlay work on a cedar music box or the smell of a foreign spice, and always asking "Oh, and what do you call *this?*" as if they'd never seen a barrel of olives before. The shopkeepers would smile back at them and say *olives* in Arabic, and the college mums loved that, chattering on and on as they spent their money. By early afternoon they would begin leaving—silly women—and always Nadia wished that she were one of them, returning with them into that huge strangeness, America, luring her despite the threat it seemed to hold of loss and vicious homesickness.

"Achhh. . . ."

The drawers of Sitti's dresser were sticking with the heat, and Nadia had to tug hard to open them. In a corner of the bottom drawer, tucked beneath the stockings and yellowed underwear, were several envelopes banded together. These contained photographs never pasted into the album books, among them the two or three remaining pictures of Nadia's mother. Since she was an American, the old people hardly ever mentioned her when they talked of the dead. Nadia barely remembered her at all, and she always envied Mikhi who, though younger, could state with the quiet assurance of a witness that their mother's eyes, which were so dark in the photographs, had been bright blue.

Cached also amid the underthings were broken rosaries, pages from Arabic prayerbooks, shreds of holy palms plaited years ago into the shapes of crosses and crowns of thorns. Although the younger people gave such things a kind of grudging respect (the whole time he was at sea Uncle Eddie wore the charm against the Evil Eye—the very one that was missing now—and he said he wasn't the only one on his ship with a lucky piece), it was usually just the old people who were careful not to point at certain stars, who never ate from a yellow dish or left a slipper upside down with its sole stepping on God's face. Once, Nadia told her uncle about how Mikhi had imitated the ritual that old people had of kissing a piece of bread that had fallen to the floor. It was so funny, she had to tell somebody; Mikhi popping his eyes in exaggerated horror as the bread fell, the reverence with which he picked it up and kissed it, finally working his mouth sideways and sucking passionately, the way people kissed in movies.

Uncle Eddie didn't laugh. Instead, he simply lit a cigarette. Nadia began to worry as she watched the smoke puff twice with each rapid double-drag. It was a busy, nervous way of smoking that Uncle Eddie had learned in the navy. Her uncle had always been quick to laugh at almost anything. But as the months passed after his return from the service, Eddie seemed to grow more serious, more easily irritated. Some said that it had started while he was still in the navy, just after he'd heard that Papa was gone.

The cigarette was still lit when Mikhi came in from playing outside. Uncle Eddie drew one last double-drag and tapped it out in a saucer. Then he removed his belt and called Mikhi into the kitchen. Nadia hadn't meant to tattle. She tried to show Mikhi this by the look on her face, but Mikhi saw only the belt as he backed slowly away from the kitchen door.

The narrow snakeskin belt was one of the first things that

Eddie had bought after the service. He was in San Diego and not yet out of uniform when he passed a shop window, and the gleam of its scales caught his eye.

"Achhh. . . ."

The moans were growing louder, and from the front room Nadia heard a sound like something thrown against the wall, something soft. She pushed the last drawer shut and went out to see.

The front door stood wide open, the screen door ajar. And Mikhi was gone. The cushion he'd thrown, the red one, lay across the room, wedged between the baseboard and an end table.

Nervous like Papa, he never could bear it the way she could. "She's old, Mikhi," she used to tell him. "Old people get sick, then they die. That's all.") And so to find the amulet, she would have to go down alone into the cellar. He had left that to her.

She lingered a moment, listening while the groans became soft again, as regular as the tiny pendulum swings of the mantel clock. Nadia was afraid to go down there alone, and Mikhi knew it, and here he'd gone off anyway and left it to her.

She ran the fingers of one hand through her hair, an absent gesture; then, suddenly aware of the gesture, she dropped her hand to her side. Another moment of that and the tears would have started for sure.

Her father had a way of combing his fingers through his hair when he was worried, the nervous habit of a nervous man. His gray hair stood out in whorls because of it. And on that day almost three years ago (even into adulthood she and her brother would remark the very date their father brought them to Sitti's house and left them there: Sunday, July the eighth, 1951) it seemed that every few seconds his hand would go up to his hair as they waited on the front stoop for Sitti to answer her door. They waited a long time, and when she did answer, how grim she was, how stone-faced, as she let them in. The bags they carried were heavy, even though Nadia herself had repacked them. (Papa had packed them first, confused from the start, unsure of what to take and what to throw out or leave behind.) He never came in after them but remained on the stoop as if still confused. There was a frightened sadness in the way he stood there, and his kiss was a good-bye.

Afterward, nobody spoke much of him except to repeat what was already known: that Mikhail Yakoub—married late in life (and to an American), a failure at any business he tried, finally a widower with children—was never a lucky man.

But then Mikhail Yakoub never respected luck as the others did, not even grudgingly. He preferred to be free of it. "Bad luck or good luck," Nadia remembered him saying, "to hell with them both." One time, he took her and Mikhi with him on an errand down Congress Street. While there, he stopped in at one of the *ahwa* shops to talk to a man. The coffeeshops did not admit females, not even little girls; she had to wait at the door while her father and brother went inside. The windows, like the doorway, were wide open, and flies buzzed everywhere among the tables. Old men sat drinking from tiny cups, all of them smoking cigars or water pipes. A group at a near table were playing cards. Suddenly, one of these men looked up as a shadow flitted past the lampshade dangling above him. Then they were all scrambling to their feet, crying out and cursing. A chair was overturned, and Nadia had to step aside to keep from getting trampled as the men jostled and elbowed one another out the door and onto the street. She heard her father before she saw him, his loud laugh booming above the confusion. Only after the three of them had woven their way through the small crowd did Mikhi, himself red-faced with laughter, pause long enough to explain it to her.

"What happened is, is a bird flew in the window."

"So?" she said.

"It's an omen," her father said.

"A bad one?"

"The worst. It means a death in the house. Holy Toledo," her father began laughing again, "I never saw a room clear out so fast."

Nadia chuckled a little, even though she didn't see anything funny, not at first. Holy Toledo was a city near Detroit, and Papa called out its name sometimes when things were funny. But after a moment, remembering how quickly the old men had moved, their baggy trousers flapping as they shuffled and pushed, she began to laugh in earnest.

"I almost hurt myself," Papa was saying, and the children hurried after him to hear, "when old Stamos the Greek tried to climb out a window. I had to grab him by the suspenders and hold him back."

And so her father never respected luck, himself luckless. After he went away, those people who mentioned Mikhail Yakoub at all spoke of him as if he were gone forever. But he wasn't dead—she and Mikhi had been able to wheedle that much out of them. He had simply disappeared from the neighborhood. And when the children pressed to know where he'd gone, some said "Boston," others "Chicago," but none of them was certain. Sitti answered them only by saying "America!" and fluttering fingers to temple in the Arabic gesture *tarit,* which meant *it has flown out.* Yet how could that which was sealed within the hard bone of the skull simply fly away? Nadia couldn't understand it, and so she clung to what was certain: he was gone, swallowed up somehow by the vast America beyond these streets, alive, forever luckless, and free. And in her imagination forever homesick, too, forever standing at a closed door somewhere, lost, running his fingers through his hair.

Still blinking against the tears—not much of a tomboy after all—she was startled to find the cellar stairs already lit. "Mikhi?" she called.

The stairwell before her was cool despite the day's heat, its walls seeping spiderwebs of black moisture.

"Mikhi?"

"Down here, Nadia. Come on down here." Her brother's voice was clapped instantly from behind by a thin, sharp echo.

"Did you find it?" she asked, leaning into the doorway. It was quiet for a moment, then she heard his voice again, thinned so by the echo that she thought of the sound of her own voice, as if from far away.

"Okay, Nadia?"

"Okay what?"

"Are you coming down?"

"Is it there? Did you look in the boxes?"

"Aww, Nadia!" The way he called her name, thin and sad from within that darkness, it was a plea. She hesitated, then descended quickly after it, the way medicine is swallowed quickly so as not to taste it.

"Where are you?" she called. The cellar gradually deepened into its maze of half-walls that baffled, then blocked altogether the faint stairwell light.

"In here."

She stepped cautiously along the uneven floor, following her brother's voice into a corner room. The only light was a smudged glow from the single high window. Mikhi sat beneath the window, legs dangling atop Sitti's old steamer trunk.

"Did you find it?"

"I didn't look." Mikhi's voice caught. "Aww, Nadia. It doesn't matter."

"But why didn't you just—" she stopped herself, realizing that Mikhi probably had come down here for her sake, because she was afraid and she'd asked him to come with her. And the strange thing was that she wasn't so scared anymore. At least not now. There she was in the deepest corner of the cellar; she almost laughed.

When she turned to Mikhi, his head was down, eyes on the trunk beneath him. Brass and black leather, one side of the trunk was crayoned with writing from forty years ago. Their father had once pointed out to them the different languages—Turkish, Arabic, French, and finally, in English, the yellow and blue admittance stamp of Ellis Island, New York.

"What is it, Mikhi? What's wrong?"

"She's not going to die," he said with sureness. Then, the sureness faltering: "Do you think she's going to die?"

"Yes."

"Honest?"

"She's old, Mikhi. Old people—"

"I don't care," he said quickly. "I'm going anyway."

"Where?"

For a moment there was silence—only the muffled sounds of Sitti's footsteps above them—before Mikhi sighed, "I don't know . . . out there. Away from here." Then he touched his hair with his fingertips.

"Don't do that," Nadia said, and he lowered his hand. "When are you going?"

"I don't know."

She nodded once, slowly, as if in solemn agreement, but it was relief that she felt. If he didn't know where and he didn't know when, then maybe he wouldn't really go. And then she wouldn't have to go either, because what would they do? Who would take care of them out there in America, a girl and her little brother?

"I mean it, Nadia."

But he didn't mean it, not really. Alone, Mikhi wouldn't know what to do. Not even what to take and what to leave behind. Especially that. He wouldn't know that any more than Papa had known it.

"Nadia, will you come with me?"

"Sure," she answered quickly, easily. After all, a boy can't just walk off the way a man does.

"It doesn't matter," Mikhi said, the disappointment in his voice showing her that she'd answered too quickly. "But at least you won't tell on me, will you?"

"I don't tattle. Not anymore."

Above them, Sitti was moving something heavy, dragging it across the floor. Her moans carried even to the cellar.

"You promise?"

He still didn't believe her. She began to promise, but just then the moans from upstairs were cut short by a brief cry of surprise as something, glass or china, shattered on the dining room floor. The two of them remained still for a moment of teetering imbalance that ended abruptly with a heavy, resounding thump. Mikhi leaped from the trunk and ran ahead of her up the stairs.

"Help to stand," Sitti said, hearing the sound of their feet. She had fallen to her knees, the side of her face leaning against an open drawer of the buffet. She must have been trying to shove the buffet away from the wall so she could search behind it.

"Sitti," Mikhi spoke quickly, "should I go find Uncle Eddie?"

"No," Sitti said, whispering, as if she had strength only for that. "Jus' help to stand." She held out one arm, and Mikhi took it.

"Ach!" she cried out at the force of his grip. Immediately, Mikhi released the hand.

"My heart," Sitti hugged herself, "my heart. Achhh. . . ."

"Is it a heart attack?" Mikhi's voice rose on the word *attack*, threatening to rise to a screech if she answered yes, but Sitti didn't answer. Instead, she braced her forearms against the buffet and slowly, but with less effort than Nadia had imagined it would take, raised herself to her feet.

"Did you find it, Sitti?" Nadia asked. She looked down at the shattered remains of what had been the china teapot. "Was it in the tea—"

Sitti closed her eyes as if to silence her. She stood that way for a few seconds, consulting some inner pain. Then the three braids that stuck out over the collar of her nightgown quivered a little, and she belched, a low weak sound.

"G'wan," she told them—they were staring at her— "G'wan, don't lookit me." She leaned against the buffet. "Achhh. . . ."

"What *is* it, Sitti?" Again Mikhi's voice rose, like a girl's.

"Nothing. G'wan."

"Can I get you something? What do you want us to *do?*"

"Nothing," she answered, but simply, even lightly, as if somehow pleased.

Mikhi looked to Nadia. His eyes were wide, near panic. Then he lowered his head and spoke. "You're not sick," he said.

There was utter silence, and Nadia was frightened by the sudden realization that she was about to laugh.

"You're not sick at all," Mikhi said once more, looking up now. He was actually smiling, although his eyes kept blinking as if somebody were shaking a fist in front of them. "You're all right. It's just gas. I know it is."

"You be shaddap!" Sitti growled. Then she cursed him in Arabic, *"Ibn menyouk!"*

Mikhi flinched, but stood firm. "You're not sick," he said again.

Sitti turned furiously to Nadia, as to a witness. Mikhi, too was looking at her now. Then, slowly, he shifted his gaze to Sitti, and her face collapsed in fear at the sight of him. She raised both hands to her eyes and began to cry out weakly, muttering like a child on the verge of tears.

"And that was when he give to me the Evil Eye, *ya djinu, ya ibn menyouk!* The girl here, she see it all!"

Uncle Eddie listened patiently while Sitti went on and on, slipping in and out of Arabic and rushing the words so rapidly together that the children—made to sit quietly at the kitchen table—could barely follow it. She paced back and forth behind Mikhi's chair, and Nadia watched her uncle smoke his cigarette with those nervous double-drags. Now and then, distractedly, he reached to his neck and touched the golden thread. The charm against the Evil Eye was suspended from it, a single porcelain gleam at the hair of his throat. Nadia had noticed it as soon as he walked in the house. She was sure Mikhi must have seen it. And Sitti too, as she hurried to the door, grasping Eddie's sleeve with both hands before he was hardly inside. Uncle Eddie didn't even try to hide it. All he did was shrug—a son cowed by the suddenness of his mother's fury—and call her and Mikhi into the kitchen. Then Sitti started all over again from the beginning: Mikhi had been tormenting her all day. Worse yet, she was sick to dying, and the boy gave her the Evil Eye—wasn't that so, Nadia?

She squirmed in her chair, answering neither yes nor no. She was innocent, but for the first time uneasy in the tattletale pleasure of such innocence; after all, Mikhi was right. Here their grandmother stood, alive, hands working as she spoke, and her voice strong. She wasn't sick at all. Mikhi knew that. She wasn't going to die.

"Isn't that so, Nadia? Speak up, girl," Sitti paused only a second before again launching into an angry jabber of Arabic.

And the charm, all the good luck of it hanging there at Eddie's throat the whole time they were searching, seemed forgotten; its luck granted or not—both Sitti and Uncle Eddie were acting now as if it never mattered in the first place. And Mikhi had known that too.

Her brother was watching her. She could feel the heat of his stare, and she turned to him. *No matter what you answer,* his look told her, *I'm still going to catch it.* Then he turned away. *So save yourself,* his turning away said, and she was free.

"Well, Nadia?"

Uncle Eddie put out his cigarette. Then he reached down and rested one hand on the buckle of the snake skin belt, waiting.

"Sitti isn't sick," she found herself saying, and so calmly that her own voice sounded strange to her. "And all Mikhi did, he just looked at her, that's all. It wasn't the Evil Eye."

"Ach!" Sitti was furious, betrayed.

And so, after Mikhi got the belt, Nadia would be next. She knew that. But already, calmly, she was beginning to think about what it would be like for them afterward. It would not be easy; even so, she felt a wordless yet certain anticipation: the two of them luckless, free in Boston and Chicago and Holy Toledo, the rest of their lives lost in the American homesickness. What should they take with them?

Next to her, Mikhi released a nervous sound, almost a laugh.

Then it was over, her brother's voice cut off in the suck of breath as Uncle Eddie reached out to grasp him by the arm. The belt flashed, and Mikhi shrieked with each sharp flick and slap, again and again and again.

Nadia would be next. Calmly, she closed her eyes and tried to imagine America, how it will be, and what they should take with them when they go.

Carlton Fredericks and My Mother

MARIA MAZZIOTTI GILLAN

On the counter the battered black radio hummed with advice
to the housewife, the dieter, the car owner, the consumer, the
bargain hunter, the average American. Carlton Fredericks
proclaimed that vitamins could cure anything. Bernard
Meltzer warned of stingy insurance companies waiting to
cheat their customers. Joan Hamburg tipped single women
on the best places to meet men. They alternately bellowed
and soothed as their disgruntled or dissatisfied callers
pleaded, fumed, and ranted, their duets complementing the
clanking pots and sizzling garlic perpetually boiling and
browning on my mother's stove. My mother always listened
to the radio in the kitchen while she worked, her small
hands, efficient and quick, cleaning the counter, washing the
dishes, cutting vegetables. If she could, she would have listened all day to these radio voices—Carlton Fredericks and
his array of vitamins meant to cure everything from ham-
mertoes to cancer or Bernard Meltzer with his practical
advice on buying a home or saving money. The advice
competed in the kitchen with the popping sounds of frying
peppers and the whistling of the steam blowing out of the
spout of the tin espresso pot. As she performed her daily food
preparations, she was enveloped all the while in the comforting advice that for my mother had an almost olfactory
presence, an elusive aroma of Americanness. It was as if
Hamburg's or Fredericks's advice saturated her clothes with
the essence of that intangible something that made an Amer-

ican. Those voices crackling from their various AM frequencies comforted her, because through the democracy of radio, they treated her as American—something the rest of the world certainly never did.

Often, my mother acted as if those radio shows were lectures of a great professor and gave us oral reports on such topics as vitamin C as a cure for hair loss. She informed us of the dangers of the scheming con artist who might pretend to be a roofer who happened to be passing by your house and notice that the roof was severely damaged; he might then offer you a special "one-time-only" roof repair with only $200 down, payable immediately in cash, of course. She treated me to one of these minilectures every time I sat at the kitchen table to sip espresso or taste the meatballs before dinner. In a way, those radio shows were her university education, teaching her how to be more American or at least revealing to her the fears and foibles of a typical American. When she learned something from the radio, she seemed amazed as if something that had eluded her for many years was finally within her reach.

My mother was twenty-three when she came to America from San Mauro, a little Italian village in southern Italy where she attended school through the third grade, when public education ended. Even fifty years later, she talked about her days in school as exciting. Her voice took on a lilt when she described the classroom, the teacher, the books. She even recited poems she had memorized in first grade and still remembered the exact words the teacher used to describe them. She hung on to these memories because she desperately desired more knowledge.

Sometimes she seemed wistful when she told us stories about her past. Although she left the Old World behind, she had no intention of losing us too. She believed in keeping us all close to her. In a way, those radio shows allowed her to do that by giving her something to talk about she thought we'd understand. More important, she wanted to convince us that she, too, was learning to be an American. This language of radio seemed to provide her with the questions to ask that would open the door between us, the door that was slowly slamming shut, even while she tried to keep us safe in her warm kitchen.

Once on one of those radio programs she heard someone mention "petting." I was about eleven years old, and she asked, "So, what is petting?" I, who was still lost in a world of books, explained, "Why it's like when you touch a cat, you are petting the cat." To illustrate, I made smooth motions as if I were petting the cat's fur. My mother giggled and averted her eyes so I knew that the answer I had given her was not the one she was looking for. It was a couple of years before I realized what she wanted to know.

My mother was the hub of our lives. We all revolved around her. Yet as we grew older, it became harder and harder for her to give advice we didn't mock. I remember my brother teasing her. When we were in the car, he'd point to her head and say, "Hey Ma, what's that little bump on your shoulders?" Ignoring him, she'd sit in the front seat of the car, her head barely reaching the top of the seat back, her purse securely tucked under her arm, her hand clutching the door handle. All the while, her feet made jerking motions as if she could stop the car. Though she'd never driven, she would direct my father, "Too fast." Or "Watch out. Here comes car." My brother called her the "little general," teasing but also serious because she did, after all, want to keep her hands on our lives, kneading us into shape the way she kneaded bread in the big bowl.

She was fiercely protective of us. I was not even allowed to step off the front porch unless my older sister was with me. Mostly, my mother encouraged us to play Monopoly, dominoes, or checkers at a rickety table that we set up for that purpose on the stoop. The few times we were allowed to go anywhere, my mother paced and worried until we were home again.

I was surprised, therefore, when I told her I was applying to the University of Virginia and she didn't tell me that I couldn't go. Instead, her dresser quickly filled up with votive candles that formed a circle of flickering light around the Saint Anthony statue that already presided over her room. The candlewicks glowed ominously in the weeks before the letters from colleges were scheduled to arrive. I am not sure what I imagined the University of Virginia to be like, but I wanted to go there since I was positive that it was a world away from Paterson. I cringe now when I think of the picture of me I attached to the application, a picture in which I looked about as un-American as anybody could. Of course, since I had rarely been out of Paterson in my life, I don't think my mother would ever have really let me go. The matter was settled when I got a full four-year scholarship to the branch campus of a working-class university, a campus in Paterson a few blocks from the high school I had attended. Her prayers were answered; it didn't matter what other news the mail held. I would live at home, taking the bus at the corner of our street to the college.

My dreams of ivy-covered buildings receded as my fear about going to college consumed me. On the first day of class, I was terrified because I thought I'd never fit in. Those first weeks were exhilarating and terrifying. I joined everything I could and soon made more friends than I ever had. I even took twenty-one credits a semester because my scholarship paid for as many classes as I wanted to take. I guess I was my mother's daughter after all. I wanted to learn everything I could, hungry for the world outside the isolated Italian neighborhood and the sometimes overpowering atmosphere of my mother's fragrant kitchen. I threw myself into college life, made friends with other working-class kids, and enjoyed it all. Of course, each night I had to ride the bus home.

The world I was constructing for myself was so different from the world my mother had known. From the time she left school, she worked in the fields, cooked the family's meals, and helped her father in his grocery store. Her life followed the same routine until she married my father. He was an American by virtue of his birth certificate and his one year of life he spent in Philadelphia as a baby. As an adult, he went back to Philadelphia to work and returned to Italy when he decided to find a wife. The first time he saw my mother she was chasing the family pig up the mountain, her face rosy-cheeked, her body strong and sensual. He decided then and there to marry her.

Three months after she caught that reluctant pig, my mother found herself married and living in an Italian neighborhood in Paterson, New Jersey. Maybe she thought that America would be a place where she could break out of the constrictions most women faced when they married and lived the rest of their lives in San Mauro. I know she hoped to go to school, to pick up where she left off in Italy. Although my father went to night school to learn English, he insisted, "Women don't need to go to school." My mother cried for days, remembering how much she loved going to school. She knew she needed to learn English and night school was the only way she'd be able to find out about all the things she wanted earnestly to know. She pictured herself reading a book or memorizing poems in English as she had done in Italian. At the very least, she'd be able to read the signs in the grocery store and on the street. But all her pleading and tears would not change my father's mind. Consequently, she never did learn English correctly. She only knew the words my sister and I taught her and those phrases she learned from the radio.

Perhaps the voices of Meltzer, Hamburg, and Fredericks replaced the elders that my mother might have known in her village of San Mauro. Certainly, she accepted the radio hosts' advice as sage wisdom, wisdom she believed could improve my life as well. Daily she'd repeat the advice she'd heard, her mind serving up these tidbits on demand. "Oh, yes," she'd say. "Take vitamin C. Good for your hair," When we'd argue, I'd scold, "Ma, where did you hear that garbage?" She'd retreat, muttering, "Levermind, levermind," and go on believing what she chose, not even accepting that the word was "nevermind." She'd continue to say it as she heard it. Her mind appeared to be a jumble of information, much of it contradictory, picked up from her favorite radio show hosts— advice on love and dating, on how to raise children or where to find the perfect cashmere sweater.

The American world of the radio was so different from the daily Italian world she usually occupied. She worked in the Ferraro Coat Factory on River Street where all the women workers were Italian; while they sewed, they chattered all day in their own language. Then at night, after dinner, we visited our aunts and uncles and my parents' friends. Since Italian was the only language they knew, my mother did not get much practice in American conversation. Her spoken English remained limited even after she had lived in America for fifty years, though she understood a lot more words than she could say. We'd talk to each other in a mixture of Italian and English so blended together that I couldn't say where one language ended and the other began. My mother had trouble saying English words, the sounds too hard and clipped for her Italian tongue. She even called Bernard Meltzer "Bohnarulza," and it took awhile for me to figure out that she was referring to Meltzer, her favorite of all the gurus who kept her company through her days.

Despite her seeming deafness to our correction of her pronunciation, I know she was ashamed of her illiteracy. Once when I was in college, my father was driving us home from the Farmer's Market and she saw a store that said "Package Goods" in big letters across its window. "What is that?" she asked. "It says package goods, Ma," I answered. "We'll have to go there to buy material one day," she said, and I laughed. "Ma, package goods doesn't mean material. It's a liquor store!" "Oh," she said, turning her face away from mine, but not before I saw the shame that colored it.

Twenty-five years after I left home to get married, my daughter graduated from the kind of college I would like to have attended—ivy-covered buildings, brick paths, archways, towers. My mother sat with my daughter's huge yearbook with its brightly colored photographs in her lap. She gazed at the pictures of the beautiful, upper-class young men and women with their vitamin-enriched skin, their straight teeth, their shining hair. Seemingly amazed by the lavish photos spread before her, she kept saying, over and over, "Look how beautiful they are! Can you believe it? Look!" I understood that to my mother these young people represented a world she could not have imagined twenty years ago, a world of lush grass and gracious buildings where the sun seemed to shine only for these privileged people as it had never shone for her. She was amazed that her granddaughter, only two generations from San Mauro, could go to a place like this one and actually look as though she belonged. She rubbed her small hand across the faces in the glossy pages as though she had discovered something miraculous. She kept shaking her head, and proclaiming, "Oh, how beautiful!"

She turned suddenly to me then, and said, "Ah, I was so proud of you when you graduated from college. The first one in our family. I was so proud, I thought I'd burst." "But Ma," I stammered, "You never said anything. I didn't know." All this time I thought she was angry with me for choosing a different path, for leaving her behind. "Ah," she declared, "it wasn't for me to say. I'm your mother. I didn't want to bring bad luck on you."

She smoothed the yearbook one last time, and then she tied her apron tighter and automatically flipped on the radio. She half-listened to her secondhand information, pleased when she'd hear some tidbit she could share with us. How many hours of her life had she listened to those radio voices and followed the clues they offered to her, cut off as she was from the world of America, the world her children inhabited with such ease? "Ah," she said, "I love America. There's no place like it in the world," and smiled at us, her children and grandchildren, American to the bone.

Honey Boy

AFAA MICHAEL WEAVER

Honey Boy was our cousin. When we was growing up in Baltimore, me, Pigmeat, Jimmy Edward, and Honey Boy was all cousins, but Honey Boy could eat more hot dogs than all of us put together, no matter how much he had done already ate or how much his mama, our Aunt Lois, told him not to. Honey Boy was big and dark-skinned like his mama, and they had the same kind of hair that just fell down on their heads without no grease or nothing. They got their hair from Big Mama, our grandmama, and she was born down in that part of Virginia where there was some Cherokees because that's where white folk put the Cherokees after they chased them off the land what belonged to nobody. Anyway Big Mama told us her father was a Cherokee, and she showed us his picture. He looked like Big Mama a whole lot, and he had his hair spilling out of this hat. We all knew we was black, but that man, our Great-Grandpa Willy Little Bear, was what made Honey Boy and his mama's hair black and falling down.

Aunt Grace used to cook hot dogs for us in the summertime when we went swimming in Clifton Park swimming pool. She made them a special way. Aunt Grace was Jimmy Edward's mama, and he used to brag about how good her hot dogs was. One day me and Jimmy Edward got into a fight 'cause I said her hot dogs wasn't all that great. Shit, I had made some myself that was just as damn good, and we got to punching each other and tussling and rolling around and down the hill in front of Aunt Grace's house. We was always fighting each other 'cause we was growing up to be men. Our Uncle Richard told us he didn't want no sissies for no nephews. Uncle Richard used to walk everywhere he went, and he always carried two knives. He said one was to take your attention off the other. If you went for the first one, then you was a dead nigger 'cause he was gonna cut you for sure with the one you ain't figured on. Baltimore was a rough town in those days, back in the early sixties, but it's downright deadly now that I done got old. People from Baltimore can be so vicious that they kill you and follow your soul to wherever it goes so it can kick its ass, too, and the Good Lord or Satan had better just get the hell out the way.

Aunt Grace's hot dogs was good, truth be told. She put them in the oven with cheese and bacon on them and let them cook awhile, and then she stuck them on rolls and let the rolls get a little brown, but she waited until we came in from the swimming pool before she did the rolls. The houses we lived in there in Baltimore was like castles to us. The kitchens was in the basement part with a back room like a club room, some of them with paneling. Aunt Grace would look out the windows of her kitchen, peeping through the curtains to see if we was coming, and once she saw us dragging down the street with our wet towels and swimming trunks, trying to pop each other with our towels, she would throw them hot dogs on those rolls so they would be just right when we got in from Clifton Park swimming pool, where all the black boys went to go swimming and feel the girls underwater. Honey Boy was always the first to get his hot dogs 'cause he was the oldest and biggest, and we all knew he could kick all our asses at one time. Honey Boy was our hero, our stone, sure 'nough hero. He could eat twenty-two hot dogs.

Pigmeat was Honey Boy's brother, and he tried to outdo

Honey Boy. One day when we came back from the pool, Pig-meat tried his best to eat twenty-two hot dogs. Aunt Grace was cooking them as fast as we could put them down. She kept the refrigerator loaded with hot dogs and frozen french fries, and she could cook and talk on the phone at the same time. With the receiver on her shoulder, she lined those hot dogs with bacon and cheese, while Pigmeat and Honey Boy put them down. Me and Jimmy Edward just had five each and sat over in the corner by the television 'cause we knew somebody's gut was gonna bust wide open. Damn if Pigmeat didn't get up and try to make it for the bathroom, but he slumped down against the wall, holding his stomach and cry-ing. Aunt Grace started laughing and tried to push another hot dog in his mouth.

Aunt Lois came in a few minutes later from the market, and Pigmeat was rolling around.

"Boy, why are you always cutting the fool?"

"Ma," Pigmeat cried, "I was just trying to keep up with Honey Boy. He always showing off."

"Honey Boy near 'bout a man. You can't outdo him, and you can't outdo me. Can you?"

"No ma'am."

Aunt Lois was three hundred fifty pounds if she was any-thing, and that day she sat on Pigmeat. He thought he was gonna die. We thought he was gonna die. Aunt Lois had made herself the angel of death and come down on Pigmeat in a serious way. He was like a bug, squirming and wiggling under her. At first he thought it was a joke, but then she wouldn't move. She was like a granite statue sitting right on his back, posed there like a African queen sitting on her short throne, except this throne was about to crumple like a doll-house chair does when you mash it with your finger. Pigmeat wailed and wailed and said he couldn't breathe.

"Mama, I'm gonna die!"

"Lois, maybe you oughta let the boy go," Aunt Grace said half chuckling.

"I pushed his little behind into the world, and I'll push it out," Aunt Lois said, as she looked down at Pigmeat, whose tears were thick and flowing.

"Please, Ma, please," he said.

Honey Boy interceded. "Mama, I'll make sure he don't eat himself sick no more. I'll watch him."

Aunt Lois was tired anyway, so she told me and Jimmy Edward to help her up, and we got ahold of her arms and pulled until we got her to her feet. Pigmeat was so embarrassed he got up and went in the backyard and ran out into the alley and disappeared until it got dark. Honey Boy had to go look for him. They came back together, with Honey Boy holding his arm around Pigmeat's shoulders. Pigmeat loved his big brother, and he really wanted to be like him. Maybe he just wanted to have Honey Boy's place, the place of being a young lord in the neighborhood, somebody the girls all liked, somebody even the serious hoodlums gave respect to 'cause we wasn't no hoodlums. We could fight and all, but we wasn't no tough-time criminals. The criminals was all around us, but so was the girls, every girl from smooth, downtown brown Wanda to long-legged redbone Marsha, with everything in between, and most of them went to Clifton Park swimming pool in the summertime, with us right behind them. We used to hear our mamas say men and boys was dogs because of the way a bunch of boy dogs follow a girl dog around. Well, we was a pack of serious hounds, even though we didn't know a clitoris from a vulva and would have gone into shock if the girl got an orgasm.

We knew one word—pussy. We thought that was the name of all that a girl had up there. It was just one place, a place we tried desperately to get to once we started growing the things that make you look like a man, even though you a long way from it, a long way. Honey Boy was the oldest, and he got to that famous place between a girl's legs long before we did.

It was Janice. She was a pretty girl. The reason we all knew it was 'cause she and Honey Boy did it in Aunt Lois's house while wasn't no grownups there, and me and Pigmeat and Jimmy Edwards sneaked in and got quiet and listened at the bedroom door. They was on Aunt Lois's bed, and it had a hole in the middle 'cause Aunt Lois was so big. Janice kept saying she was falling in the hole. We didn't know what hole they was talking about. Was there some part of the pussy that a woman could fall into herself? Was Honey Boy gonna fall into the hole? Was falling in the hole a way of saying she couldn't keep up with Honey Boy? That had to be it. She couldn't keep up with Honey Boy 'cause he was our hero. Then we heard her scream real loud, and Honey Boy grunted. Did she kill him, we wondered as we crouched outside the closed door, but then they spoke.

"Honey," Janice sang, "I love you."

"I love you, too," Honey Boy said.

We got away without them hearing us, and we didn't dare ever tell Honey Boy that we heard him. We was wondering if things was gonna change because of this love business. We didn't trust that love.

Honey Boy stayed with us. We still went to Clifton Park swimming pool, and he was still our warrior hero. That never changed, although he and Janice sat out on the steps many a summer night and up until it was too cold. But in the summer, we was still at the pool. Clifton Park was all black and mighty, mighty tough. There was some dudes in there that had rocks for fists, monster masks for faces, and daggers for hearts. Walking up Sinclair Lane from the Goetze meat-packing plant, we could see the dark mass in the water splashing and carrying on, a thick web of black skin like ours cooling out in the hot summer heat. It made me think of Africa, although I had never been to Africa and had only seen the foolish way white folk made us look in Tarzan movies. But here we were, walking down Sinclair Lane with our little change in our pockets, little folding knives we bought from the hardware store and hid from our mothers, our towels wrapped up with clean underwear on the inside because everybody's mama in Baltimore told you to have clean underwear in case something happened. We didn't know what they was talking about. We didn't know a whole bunch of people could lose their minds at one time. We didn't really understand the television news where police dogs were chewing up black people. We knew hate, but we didn't understand nothing about how hate was a whole big world to itself, with all kinds of hate, even the hate that have you hating your own black self.

At Clifton Park, Honey Boy protected us. You got into the swimming pool by going into this stone pavilion that sorta looked like the Greek and Roman buildings we studied in school, no windows or nothing, just these high stone pillars all around so you could see in any direction by just standing in one spot. We went in there and went down the stairs to pay our money and get into the pool. It wasn't but a little bit of money, thirty-five cents or something. Things was cheap back then. Thirty cents could buy you a pack of smokes. We paid our way and went into the locker room, where you put your stuff in a basket and give it to this man, and he gave you a tag on a rubber bracelet that you put on your leg. That way you didn't lose your clothes and knife and stuff. You had to run through the cold shower to clean yourself off before you got into the pool, and Honey Boy always told us to go on ahead 'cause the locker room was where the serious hoodlums hung out and tried to take stuff from you while you was undressing.

One day we was undressing and these two stocky-looking boys came over to us. They was short, but they was like four feet thick. Honey Boy ignored them, as they eased on over to us.

"Who you muthas think you are," they asked.

Honey Boy looked at me and Pigmeat and Jimmy Edward and said, "Y'all go on and get in the water."

Pigmeat said, "I got your back, Honey."

Honey shouted at us, and it almost scared me 'cause his voice was getting so deep, deeper than ours, and I was scared, scared for Honey Boy.

The short, thick sonofabitches said, "These your children? What you do, your mother? She black and ugly like you?"

It must have been faster than the speed of sound that Honey Boy hit that one what was talking, and he hit him three times in what was so short a time we hardly saw it. We did see blood gushing from the boy's face. Honey Boy hollered to us, "Y'all go on and get in the pool. Go on!"

The man what used to take the baskets and give us those rubber bracelets told Honey Boy and those short dudes to cut it out, but the other short dude jumped on Honey Boy like a cat. Honey Boy wrestled him off, and started backhanding the boy across the locker room, while the other one got up and ran.

"Didn't I tell y'all to get in the pool," Honey Boy screamed at us.

We ran through the cold shower, splashed through the wading pool, and then hauled ass into the water. Pretty soon we was in the five foot deep section, our heads just above the water. Honey Boy wasn't long after us. He came striding out from the locker room, looking jet black like he was with his thin, curly hair falling down all over his head from the shower. The girls turned around and started giggling and fidgeting 'cause a lot of them liked Honey Boy. He even made the lifeguards jealous 'cause they thought they had all the women, but Honey Boy could swim just as good as they could. He went over to the deep water and got on the low diving board and dived into the water. When Honey Boy was in the air and heading for the water, he looked like one of those black panthers in Africa, so dark and shiny he made you think you could see yourself just by looking into him. Girls used to ask me and Pigmeat and Jimmy Edward if we was with Honey Boy, and we would say he was our partner. Honey Boy was our king, and we was his young lords. That was the truth of us being cousins and all.

The Clifton Park swimming pool wasn't as clean as it used to be. When we was real little, the water was clear and even tasted clean if a little bit got in your mouth. But something happened. A different group of children moved in, and the ones that was going there all the time started acting different over the years so that by the time we was teenagers, by the time Honey Boy was with Janice, things got real dirty at Clifton Park. Janice used to go with us once in a while, but Honey Boy told her to stay home. People pissed in the pool all the time. One day I was swimming, and my hand caught onto something like stringy cloth it seemed. I pulled my hand up, and there was a Kotex on it. People wasn't taking the cold shower no more. They was just getting in the pool with mean looks on their faces. Girls started fighting right there on the side of the pool. It was like some kind of fever had taken over the black folk around East Baltimore. They were getting short on patience and long on anger, and they took it out on everything. It was the time after they killed Malcolm X and before they killed Martin Luther King, and I guess the children what changed Clifton Park came out of what I called The Purple Funk, a disease that made people want to tear up everything all around them, and a disease that made people who had what they wanted, mostly white folk, as tight and protective of their shit as Pigmeat used to be when he had a plate of ham and candied sweets and biscuits. If you got too close to him, he would growl. Seemed like everybody was growling. The Purple Funk killed Malcolm X.

Honey Boy decided we should go on down to Patterson Park, the white pool. Some other friends of ours had been down there. They said it was clean, nothing in the water. Some of our friends was talking about how pretty the white girls was, but that didn't faze Honey Boy. He was in love with Janice, but me and Pigmeat and Jimmy Edward wanted to see these blondes, brunettes, and redheads in skimpy bathing suits. We was curious and ready to go when Honey Boy first said something about it, but it seemed like he wasn't really sure about going where things was supposed to be clean just 'cause they was white. One night we went on up to the garage where Uncle Richard and some of our other uncles used to work on cars. Uncle Richard was sitting there sipping on some bourbon. He gave us a little taste as we was getting to be men. Uncle Richard loved all of us, but he was really proud of Honey 'cause he saw himself in Honey Boy. Uncle Richard was born and raised in Baltimore, and he was in the gangs back in the time of World War II when gangs ruled Baltimore. Uncle Richard killed two men, and he didn't do one day of time. Honey Boy stood up there on the hill and looked over to where the Clifton Park swimming pool was and heaved a big sigh in his chest. He was eighteen years old.

Honey looked over to where black folk gathered in the pool and hollered and laughed, and he said, "You got to fight to stay black, and you got to fight 'cause you is black. I wonder why."

Uncle Richard said, "Being black is being more full of life. You like a bottle of good wine that's old and dark as blood. You make people jealous."

Janice and Honey Boy was spending more time together. She was eighteen, too, and was heading off to Morgan State College. It was just over on the other side of Lake Montebello, a short ride from where we lived, but she and Honey acted like she was going to St. Louis or somewhere. We used to tease Honey and tell him he had the St. Louis blues, like the movie we saw at the Hippodrome movie house on Pennsylvania Avenue.

"You afraid Janice gonna run off with some jive ass from St. Louis, and I bet she will," Pigmeat taunted him.

I added, "You know, Honey, I heard my mama say it's a poor rabbit that ain't got but one hole to run to."

Jimmy Edward just laughed and said, "Y'all crazy."

We saw Honey pick up some rocks, and we all got in the wind cause we knew Honey could throw a rock like Satchel Paige could throw a fastball, and we ran in three different directions so he couldn't hit us all with the same rock. He had done that once before, or at least he said it was the same rock. I know all three of us was hurting at the same time, right upside our heads.

The first day we went to Patterson Park swimming pool Uncle Richard dropped us off 'cause he didn't have to work that day. I think he took the day off so he could ride us down there. When we was going through the white neighborhood, women was out there with cans of Comet and Ajax, scrubbing them white steps, and every now and then one of them looked at Uncle Richard's car, a '64 Impala Super Sport that he had fixed up with a stereo he could flick on with one button. He didn't have the stereo on that day. He was listening and watching.

Honey Boy was sitting up in the front seat, his head almost touching the roof of the car. He was taller than Uncle Richard and bigger than any of us. Honey Boy's muscles had got like a statue, and he didn't lift weights or nothing. He just grew and filled out so he was like a body builder. He sat up there real quiet, going with the rhythm of the car as it went over the little bumps in the street, looking like a hunk of dark chocolate that God carved with a giant pocket knife and then made it hot enough to move but not melt with that hair like his mama and his great-grandpa Willy Little Bear just lifting up and bouncing on his head. Didn't none of us say nothing. We didn't talk like we did on the way to Clifton Park. We sat in the car like marines being taken inside enemy territory, and it was enemy territory 'cause we wasn't wanted in there.

Uncle Richard let us out, and it was a long walk from the car to the pool, going across the grass of the park next to a softball field. The park looked better than Clifton Park, with its statue and Eastern Avenue off in the distance. It looked like they took better care of it, like they had more space. There was white folk all around us, and some of them looked at us, and some of them ignored us. Fathers was out with little boys playing catch. Mothers was out with their little children in strollers, some of them letting the little babies try to walk, standing them up and then pretending to leave them. We walked to the pool house, with our towels and clean underwear tucked under our arms, wondering what it was going to be like to be in the pool with white people, to be wearing just trunks around white girls with that long hair, now that we all was getting hard-ons sometimes for no reason at all, just 'cause our dicks took a notion to rise, wondering if we could handle the big Polish boys everybody told us ruled Patterson Park swimming pool. We thought all white people down here was Polish. We didn't know nothing about Irish, or German, or Italian, except that white people had different colors of hair, like their heads was they flags.

Honey Boy didn't have to fight in the locker room. Everything was copacetic. We walked through the cold shower and into the pool together, but we noticed that the smell and the feel was different. We were used to the body odor of black folk at Clifton Park, a kind of funk that reminded you of ham and greens or Aunt Grace's hot dogs. Here was something different, like a kind of spicy butter. It wasn't like it was really bad or nothing. It was just so different it shocked us, made us pick up our noses and sniff and breathe deep, while we stood in the cold shower a few moments longer than we would have at Clifton Park, as if the cold water was gonna put a shield around us. Honey Boy stood under the shower looking like black ice. We walked out to the pool, and right away we knew we was the only black folk out there. The white people were so thick that the water looked white, like one wave that was flashing in a crazy river.

Pigmeat said the girls had real pretty legs, and they did it seemed. At first we studied the girls, looking at the ones who sat on the side to keep from getting their hair wet. Jimmy Edwards couldn't see much without his glasses, but he said after the hair they was just regular faces. Me and Pigmeat asked him how did he know since he couldn't see. Pigmeat liked them white girls, but I was afraid of them. I was shy with girls anyway, but I wasn't afraid to be crazy about a black girl. There was some big gray fear between me and these white girls. Honey Boy didn't study them long 'cause he was watching them white boys, and some of them was big just like we heard. They was bigger than Honey, but Honey stood out like a tree blooming black in the midst of dogwoods, and we was the bushes that kept him company. Honey Boy had told us before we came down here that white girls had the same thing black girls had. The difference was black girls was made for us. Once Honey figured something out and came to a conclusion, that was all there was to it, nothing more to be said. He told us to swim. We eased into the water, and before long we had a lane to ourselves. One or two white folk smiled at us, but we didn't know where those smiles came from.

We didn't stay as long as we would have stayed at Clifton Park, even though this white pool was cleaner. We walked home in a tight bunch, looking at the white faces looking at us, most of them pretending to ignore us, but we knew they couldn't ignore the only black thing moving through them. We got back to Aunt Grace's and ate our hot dogs, but Honey Boy didn't eat but five that day. He stood up and looked out the kitchen window in the direction of Clifton Park and said, "We goin' back where black folk swim."

We did for a few weeks, but some other black folk started to go to Patterson Park pretty regular. There was even rumors of fights starting when some boy got a feel on a white girl. Some of these black folk was girls, the fighting kind from down on Biddle Street near Gay Street. They carried knives and razors like the boys, and I even heard a few of them had guns. One day I saw them walking back from Clifton Park, and I knew they was from The Purple Funk. They was mean 'cause they was angry about everything, and being angry had got to be the way it s'posed to be for them. Being angry gave them a high. Fighting gave them more joy than laying down and letting a boy push himself into them. Still all these folk had respect for Honey Boy.

We went back to Patterson Park. On one real hot and sticky day in that same summer, we walked down there. Uncle Richard was working, and Aunt Grace figured it was okay since so many black folk was going down there, although women think different than men. Uncle Richard said it was never gonna be alright, something was always gonna turn up and tighten in somebody's stomach when black folk rolled into white folk's territory like a wave taking over a town built near a beach. White folk get a warning that a storm is coming, but God is the somebody what sends it, and they can't do much except tighten up everything and make sure they know how to swim. Swim is all they can do when we roll in, or fight.

We got into the water, and there was bunches of black kids, colored children Aunt Grace called us all. The white kids was different now. The girls sat on the side kind of pouting, and combing their hair and talking. It made me wonder why they came to the pool just to do that, and I guess they wondered the same thing. Pigmeat was staring at them, and he talked about how pretty they was with all that long hair, some of it the color of gold. Honey Boy slapped him, playing kinda but still a slap, and Pigmeat started crying. Me and Jimmy Edward looked at each other real funny 'cause we didn't never see Pigmeat act like that, and we just figured it had to be 'cause Pigmeat felt like he had done been embarrassed by his big brother in front of all these white girls, and the children from The Purple Funk, who was all about respect.

That slap Honey Boy gave Pigmeat musta had something in it 'cause pretty soon there was commotion bursting out here and there. Some boy pushed some girl in the water by sticking his hand in her face. A girl slapped another girl. Some boy pulled down the panties on a girl's bikini. It was all colored children doing this stuff to other colored children, and white kids doing it to other white kids. One brunette grabbed a blonde by her hair and pulled her off the bench. Honey Boy laughed at that, and then the shit broke loose.

One of The Purple Funk girls pulled a white girl's bikini top off and slapped her into the water. Her hand looked like it had dynamite in it when it hit the white girl's face 'cause her long brown hair went swinging around her head, as she fell kinda limp like into the water. We used to talk about slapping each other dead, but that was the first time I had seen a girl slap somebody like that, and the whole pool froze. The big Polish boys unfolded their arms from the corners they was standing in like they was the police. The lifeguards started blowing their whistles, and we all started shivering. Sometimes you could be in those pools real long and a cloud came over and chilled you and made it feel like the temperature just dropped. Sometimes the temperature did drop. These chills made you feel like the water on you was ice. This time it felt like we was in the North Pole, in between floating icebergs, and God was gonna chop up things with an ice pick. He did.

Honey Boy got us together in a bunch and said, "Let's get back up the way. Let's go home."

Honey never ran from nothing, but we didn't disagree with him. The white people in the park stopped and started looking. Then a few of them started running 'cause they could see there was fights all over the pool. The Polish boys had hell on their hands. One of them was on the ground with about five or six black kids all over him, stomping his ass. They wasn't used to stomping. That's something we did to each other. Stomping was the most humiliating thing you could do to somebody, and usually when you stomped somebody, it was all over. That was it. Folk walked away and left you to pick up your pride if you could find it, but the white folk just saw it as another step. On the news, they used the word *escalating,* like when they was talking about the war that was going on in Vietnam at the time. We got our clothes, and left the pool house. While we was walking, we saw white folk lined up on the sidewalk looking mean and angry, one line of them, and as we got closer we heard the word.

"Niggers!"

We got behind Honey Boy and bunched up close together, walking on each other's tennis shoes. We was all wearing white, high-top Converse shoes, and we had just polished them the night before.

"Get your black asses up there where you belong," one of them shouted out as we walked through.

"Dirty, stinking niggers! Don't bring your black asses down here no more, you monkeys!"

Honey Boy didn't have to tell us to be quiet 'cause we knew we had six good blocks to go before we got to the train trestle where the train going back and forth to New York crossed and divided Blacktown from Whitetown in East Baltimore. Honey Boy did speak once we were through the thick of the crowd.

"Y'all go on in front of me, and when you see the train trestle, y'all start running. Hear?"

We was too scared to hear, but we moved in front of Honey. Rocks started landing in front of us, and we walked faster. We just thought Honey was walking, too. Rocks turned into glass bottles, and Pigmeat got cut on his leg kinda bad. The blood was squirting out in long streams. We heard Honey tell us to keep on, and we saw the train trestle, but it was hard to hear Honey. Before we started to run, we turned around, and Honey was fighting three grown white men. He picked up one and threw him into the marble steps, and he took one of the others' head and banged it into a car fender. We started to call after him, but we heard a car horn blowing on our side of the train trestle. It was Uncle Richard driving down. He told us to get on up the street.

There was all kinds of noise, screaming and crashing and popping, but Uncle Richard went roaring down the street in his Impala and made a fishtail turn in the street. Honey jumped in, while white folks banged on the trunk, and Uncle Richard drove Honey on under where the New York train separated Blacktown from Whitetown. Janice, Aunt Grace, and Aunt Lois was there wrapping up Pigmeat's leg, and Honey opened the car door. He looked funny, like the color was leaving him, making him ashy.

"Baby, are you alright?" Janice eased over to the door, as she tried to see about Honey.

Honey Boy stood up like I never seen a man stand up, real straight, like he was gonna fly, and he smiled at his mama.

He walked over to Janice, just a smiling, and then he sunk to his knees real hard and breathed a deep sigh. The noise of his knees scared us way inside our bones. What we could touch of Honey was still there, but our warrior king was gone. Janice screamed, and she bent down and held him real tight. Aunt Lois and Aunt Grace wailed. Pigmeat shook all over. Me and Jimmy Edward got sick. There was a hole in Honey Boy that his spirit flew out of, a hole in his back. We put Honey Boy's body in the car and rushed to the hospital, all the time knowing it wasn't no need. That evening Uncle Richard drove back to a hard-to-see section of that train trestle and pumped his forty-five into the enemy territory, into its houses, wherever he thought there was life to take for the life what was taken from us.

Nowadays Patterson Park ain't no big thing. Black folk live in what was once Whitetown. Times change, I guess. But I ain't sure people really change all that much. Stuff is in their hearts what don't go nowhere, although folk claim they done changed.

Pigmeat stays on the move, driving a tractor trailer. We hardly see him much.

Me and Jimmy Edward got little piece a jobs delivering, but mostly we just stay up here at the garage where Uncle Richard hung out until he died. We keep the tough ways of East Baltimore in mind 'cause The Purple Funk is still alive, calling itself *gangstas,* carrying all kinds of guns, and most white folks ain't changed a bit. Anyway, I keep a forty-four magnum and two forty-fives hanging up inside the garage door in holsters, along with a automatic shotgun.

We all starting to ache in places our mamas and papas talked about. Me and Jimmy Edward got the gout and high blood. We getting old. Something gotta take you outta here, I guess, something gotta close your eyes. We just hope it's natural.

Bridging

This Is What It Means to Say Phoenix, Arizona

SHERMAN ALEXIE

Just after Victor lost his job at the BIA, he also found out that his father had died of a heart attack in Phoenix, Arizona. Victor hadn't seen his father in a few years, only talked to him on the telephone once or twice, but there still was a genetic pain, which was soon to be pain as real and immediate as a broken bone.

Victor didn't have any money. Who does have money on a reservation, except the cigarette and fireworks salespeople? His father had a savings account waiting to be claimed, but Victor needed to find a way to get to Phoenix. Victor's mother was just as poor as he was, and the rest of his family didn't have any use at all for him. So Victor called the Tribal Council.

"Listen," Victor said. "My father just died. I need some money to get to Phoenix to make arrangements."

"Now, Victor," the council said. "You know we're having a difficult time financially."

"But I thought the council had special funds set aside for stuff like this."

"Now, Victor, we do have some money available for the proper return of tribal members' bodies. But I don't think we have enough to bring your father all the way back from Phoenix."

"Well," Victor said. "It ain't going to cost all that much. He had to be cremated. Things were kind of ugly. He died of a heart attack in his trailer and nobody found him for a week. It was really hot, too. You get the picture."

"Now, Victor, we're sorry for your loss and the circumstances. But we can really only afford to give you one hundred dollars."

"That's not even enough for a plane ticket."

"Well, you might consider driving down to Phoenix."

"I don't have a car. Besides, I was going to drive my father's pickup back up here."

"Now, Victor," the council said. "We're sure there is somebody who could drive you to Phoenix. Or is there somebody who could lend you the rest of the money?"

"You know there ain't nobody around with that kind of money."

"Well, we're sorry, Victor, but that's the best we can do."

Victor accepted the Tribal Council's offer. What else could he do? So he signed the proper papers, picked up his check, and walked over to the Trading Post to cash it.

While Victor stood in line, he watched Thomas Builds-the-Fire standing near the magazine rack, talking to himself. Like he always did. Thomas was a storyteller that nobody wanted to listen to. That's like being a dentist in a town where everybody has false teeth.

Victor and Thomas Builds-the-Fire were the same age, had grown up and played in the dirt together. Ever since Victor could remember, it was Thomas who always had something to say.

Once, when they were seven years old, when Victor's father still lived with the family, Thomas closed his eyes and told Victor this story: "Your father's heart is weak. He is afraid of his own family. He is afraid of you. Late at night he sits in the dark. Watches the television until there's nothing but that white noise. Sometimes he feels like he wants to buy a motorcycle and ride away. He wants to run and hide. He doesn't want to be found."

Thomas Builds-the-Fire had known that Victor's father was going to leave, knew it before anyone. Now Victor stood in the Trading Post with a one-hundred-dollar check in his hand, wondering if Thomas knew that Victor's father was dead, if he knew what was going to happen next.

Just then Thomas looked at Victor, smiled, and walked over to him.

"Victor, I'm sorry about your father," Thomas said.

"How did you know about it?" Victor asked.

"I heard it on the wind. I heard it from the birds. I felt it in the sunlight. Also, your mother was just in here crying."

"Oh," Victor said and looked around the Trading Post. All the other Indians stared, surprised that Victor was even talking to Thomas. Nobody talked to Thomas anymore because he told the same damn stories over and over again. Victor was embarrassed, but he thought that Thomas might be able to help him. Victor felt a sudden need for tradition.

"I can lend you the money you need," Thomas said suddenly. "But you have to take me with you."

"I can't take your money," Victor said. "I mean, I haven't hardly talked to you in years. We're not really friends anymore."

"I didn't say we were friends. I said you had to take me with you."

"Let me think about it."

Victor went home with his one hundred dollars and sat at the kitchen table. He held his head in his hands and thought about Thomas Builds-the-Fire, remembered little details, tears and scars, the bicycle they shared for a summer, so many stories.

Thomas Builds-the-Fire sat on the bicycle, waited in Victor's yard. He was ten years old and skinny. His hair was dirty because it was the Fourth of July.

"Victor," Thomas yelled. "Hurry up. We're going to miss the fireworks."

After a few minutes, Victor ran out of his house, jumped the porch railing, and landed gracefully on the sidewalk.

"And the judges award him a 9.95, the highest score of the summer," Thomas said, clapped, laughed.

"That was perfect, cousin," Victor said. "And it's my turn to ride the bike."

Thomas gave up the bike and they headed for the fairgrounds. It was nearly dark and the fireworks were about to start.

"You know," Thomas said. "It's strange how us Indians celebrate the Fourth of July. It ain't like it was *our* independence everybody was fighting for."

"You think about things too much," Victor said. "It's just supposed to be fun. Maybe Junior will be there."

"Which Junior? Everybody on this reservation is named Junior."

And they both laughed.

The fireworks were small, hardly more than a few bottle rockets and a fountain. But it was enough for two Indian boys. Years later, they would need much more.

Afterwards, sitting in the dark, fighting off mosquitoes, Victor turned to Thomas Builds-the-Fire.

"Hey," Victor said. "Tell me a story."

Thomas closed his eyes and told this story: "There were these two Indian boys who wanted to be warriors. But it was too late to be warriors in the old way. All the horses were gone. So the two Indian boys stole a car and drove to the city. They parked the stolen car in front of the police station and then hitchhiked back home to the reservation. When they got back, all their friends cheered and their parents' eyes shone with pride. *You were very brave,* everybody said to the two Indian boys. *Very brave.*"

"Ya-hey," Victor said. "That's a good one. I wish I could be a warrior."

"Me, too," Thomas said.

They went home together in the dark, Thomas on the bike now, Victor on foot. They walked through shadows and light from streetlamps.

"We've come a long ways," Thomas said. "We have outdoor lighting."

"All I need is the stars," Victor said. "And besides, you still think about things too much."

They separated then, each headed for home, both laughing all the way.

Victor sat at his kitchen table. He counted his one hundred dollars again and again. He knew he needed more to make it to Phoenix and back. He knew he needed Thomas Builds-the-Fire. So he put his money in his wallet and opened the front door to find Thomas on the porch.

"Ya-hey, Victor," Thomas said. "I knew you'd call me."

Thomas walked into the living room and sat down on Victor's favorite chair.

"I've got some money saved up," Thomas said. "It's enough to get us down there, but you have to get us back."

"I've got this hundred dollars," Victor said. "And my dad had a savings account I'm going to claim."

"How much in your dad's account?"

"Enough. A few hundred."

"Sounds good. When we leaving?"

When they were fifteen and had long since stopped being friends, Victor and Thomas got into a fistfight. That is, Victor was really drunk and beat Thomas up for no reason at all.

All the other Indian boys stood around and watched it happen. Junior was there and so were Lester, Seymour, and a lot of others. The beating might have gone on until Thomas was dead if Norma Many Horses hadn't come along and stopped it.

"Hey, you boys," Norma yelled and jumped out of her car. "Leave him alone."

If it had been someone else, even another man, the Indian boys would've just ignored the warnings. But Norma was a warrior. She was powerful. She could have picked up any two of the boys and smashed their skulls together. But worse than that, she would have dragged them all over to some tipi and made them listen to some elder tell a dusty old story.

The Indian boys scattered, and Norma walked over to Thomas and picked him up.

"Hey, little man, are you okay?" she asked.

Thomas gave her a thumbs up.

"Why they always picking on you?"

Thomas shook his head, closed his eyes, but no stories came to him, no words or music. He just wanted to go home, to lie in his bed and let his dreams tell his stories for him.

Thomas Builds-the-Fire and Victor sat next to each other in the airplane, coach section. A tiny white woman had the window seat. She was busy twisting her body into pretzels. She was flexible.

"I have to ask," Thomas said, and Victor closed his eyes in embarrassment.

"Don't," Victor said.

"Excuse me, miss," Thomas asked. "Are you a gymnast or something?"

"There's no something about it," she said. "I was first alternate on the 1980 Olympic team."

"Really?" Thomas asked.

"Really."

"I mean, you used to be a world-class athlete?" Thomas asked.

"My husband still thinks I am."

Thomas Builds-the-Fire smiled. She was a mental gymnast, too. She pulled her leg straight up against her body so that she could've kissed her kneecap.

"I wish I could do that," Thomas said.

Victor was ready to jump out of the plane. Thomas, that crazy Indian storyteller with ratty old braids and broken teeth, was flirting with a beautiful Olympic gymnast. Nobody back home on the reservation would ever believe it.

"Well," the gymnast said. "It's easy. Try it."

Thomas grabbed at his leg and tried to pull it up into the same position as the gymnast. He couldn't even come close, which made Victor and the gymnast laugh.

"Hey," she asked. "You two are Indian, right?"

"Full-blood," Victor said.

"Not me," Thomas said. "I'm half magician on my mother's side and half clown on my father's."

They all laughed.

"What are your names?" she asked.

"Victor and Thomas."

"Mine is Cathy. Pleased to meet you all."

The three of them talked for the duration of the flight. Cathy the gymnast complained about the government, how they screwed the 1980 Olympic team by boycotting.

"Sounds like you all got a lot in common with Indians," Thomas said.

Nobody laughed.

After the plane landed in Phoenix and they had all found their way to the terminal, Cathy the gymnast smiled and waved good-bye.

"She was really nice," Thomas said.

"Yeah, but everybody talks to everybody on airplanes," Victor said. "It's too bad we can't always be that way."

"You always used to tell me I think too much," Thomas said. "Now it sounds like you do."

"Maybe I caught it from you."

"Yeah."

Thomas and Victor rode in a taxi to the trailer where Victor's father died.

"Listen," Victor said as they stopped in front of the trailer. "I never told you I was sorry for beating you up that time."

"Oh, it was nothing. We were just kids and you were drunk."

"Yeah, but I'm still sorry."

"That's all right."

Victor paid for the taxi and the two of them stood in the hot Phoenix summer. They could smell the trailer.

"This ain't going to be nice," Victor said. "You don't have to go in."

"You're going to need help."

Victor walked to the front door and opened it. The stink rolled out and made them both gag. Victor's father had lain in that trailer for a week in hundred-degree temperatures before anyone found him. And the only reason anyone found him was because of the smell. They needed dental records to identify him. That's exactly what the coroner said. They needed dental records.

"Oh, man," Victor said. "I don't know if I can do this."

"Well, then don't."

"But there might be something valuable in there."

"I thought his money was in the bank."

"It is. I was talking about pictures and letters and stuff like that."

"Oh," Thomas said as he held his breath and followed Victor into the trailer.

When Victor was twelve, he stepped into an underground wasp nest. His foot was caught in the hole, and no matter how hard he struggled, Victor couldn't pull free. He might have died there, stung a thousand times, if Thomas Builds-the-Fire had not come by.

"Run," Thomas yelled and pulled Victor's foot from the hole. They ran then, hard as they ever had, faster than Billy Mills, faster than Jim Thorpe, faster than the wasps could fly.

Victor and Thomas ran until they couldn't breathe, ran until it was cold and dark outside, ran until they were lost and it took hours to find their way home. All the way back, Victor counted his stings.

"Seven," Victor said. "My lucky number."

Victor didn't find much to keep in the trailer. Only a photo album and a stereo. Everything else had that smell stuck in it or was useless anyway.

"I guess this is all," Victor said. "It ain't much."

"Better than nothing," Thomas said.

"Yeah, and I do have the pickup."

"Yeah," Thomas said. "It's in good shape."

"Dad was good about that stuff."

"Yeah, I remember your dad."

"Really?" Victor asked. "What do you remember?"

Thomas Builds-the-Fire closed his eyes and told this story: "I remember when I had this dream that told me to go to Spokane, to stand by the Falls in the middle of the city and wait for a sign. I knew I had to go there but I didn't have a car. Didn't have a license. I was only thirteen. So I walked all the way, took me all day, and I finally made it to the Falls. I stood there for an hour waiting. Then your dad came walking up. *What the hell are you doing here?* he asked me. I said, *Waiting for a vision.* Then your father said, *All you're going to get here is mugged.* So he drove me over to Denny's, bought me dinner, and then drove me home to the reservation. For a long time I was mad because I thought my dreams had lied to me. But they didn't. Your dad was my vision. *Take care of each other* is what my dreams were saying. *Take care of each other.*"

Victor was quiet for a long time. He searched his mind for memories of his father, found the good ones, found a few bad ones, added it all up, and smiled.

"My father never told me about finding you in Spokane," Victor said.

"He said he wouldn't tell anybody. Didn't want me to get in trouble. But he said I had to watch out for you as part of the deal."

"Really?"

"Really. Your father said you would need the help. He was right."

"That's why you came down here with me, isn't it?" Victor asked.

"I came because of your father."

Victor and Thomas climbed into the pickup, drove over to the bank, and claimed the three hundred dollars in the savings account.

Thomas Builds-the-Fire could fly.

Once, he jumped off the roof of the tribal school and flapped his arms like a crazy eagle. And he flew. For a second, he hovered, suspended above all the other Indian boys who were too smart or too scared to jump.

"He's flying," Junior yelled, and Seymour was busy looking for the trick wires or mirrors. But it was real. As real as the dirt when Thomas lost altitude and crashed to the ground.

He broke his arm in two places.

"He broke his wing," Victor chanted, and the other Indian boys joined in, made it a tribal song.

"He broke his wing, he broke his wing, he broke his wing," all the Indian boys chanted as they ran off, flapping their wings, wishing they could fly, too. They hated Thomas for his courage, his brief moment as a bird. Everybody has dreams about flying. Thomas flew.

One of his dreams came true for just a second, just enough to make it real.

Victor's father, his ashes, fit in one wooden box with enough left over to fill a cardboard box.

"He always was a big man," Thomas said.

Victor carried part of his father and Thomas carried the rest out to the pickup. They set him down carefully behind the seats, put a cowboy hat on the wooden box and a Dodgers cap on the cardboard box. That's the way it was supposed to be.

"Ready to head back home," Victor asked.

"It's going to be a long drive."

"Yeah, take a couple days, maybe."

"We can take turns," Thomas said.

"Okay," Victor said, but they didn't take turns. Victor drove for sixteen hours straight north, made it halfway up Nevada toward home before he finally pulled over.

"Hey, Thomas," Victor said. "You got to drive for a while."

"Okay."

Thomas Builds-the-Fire slid behind the wheel and started off down the road. All through Nevada, Thomas and Victor had been amazed at the lack of animal life, at the absence of water, of movement.

"Where is everything?" Victor had asked more than once.

Now when Thomas was finally driving they saw the first animal, maybe the only animal in Nevada. It was a long-eared jackrabbit.

"Look," Victor yelled. "It's alive."

Thomas and Victor were busy congratulating themselves on their discovery when the jackrabbit darted out into the road and under the wheels of the pickup.

"Stop the goddamn car," Victor yelled, and Thomas did stop, backed the pickup to the dead jackrabbit.

"Oh, man, he's dead," Victor said as he looked at the squashed animal.

"Really dead."

"The only thing alive in this whole state and we just killed it."

"I don't know," Thomas said. "I think it was suicide."

Victor looked around the desert, sniffed the air, felt the emptiness and loneliness, and nodded his head.

"Yeah," Victor said. "It had to be suicide."

"I can't believe this," Thomas said. "You drive for a thousand miles and there ain't even any bugs smashed on the windshield. I drive for ten seconds and kill the only living thing in Nevada."

"Yeah," Victor said. "Maybe I should drive."

"Maybe you should."

Thomas Builds-the-Fire walked through the corridors of the tribal school by himself. Nobody wanted to be anywhere near him because of all those stories. Story after story.

Thomas closed his eyes and this story came to him: "We are all given one thing by which our lives are measured, one determination. Mine are the stories which can change or not change the world. It doesn't matter which as long as I continue to tell the stories. My father, he died on Okinawa in World War II, died fighting for this country, which had tried to kill him for years. My mother, she died giving birth to me, died while I was still inside her. She pushed me out into the world with her last breath. I have no brothers or sisters. I have only my stories which came to me before I even had the words to speak. I learned a thousand stories before I took my first thousand steps. They are all I have. It's all I can do."

Thomas Builds-the-Fire told his stories to all those who would stop and listen. He kept telling them long after people had stopped listening.

Victor and Thomas made it back to the reservation just as the sun was rising. It was the beginning of a new day on earth, but the same old shit on the reservation.

"Good morning," Thomas said.

"Good morning."

The tribe was waking up, ready for work, eating breakfast, reading the newspaper, just like everybody else does. Willene LeBret was out in her garden wearing a bathrobe. She waved when Thomas and Victor drove by.

"Crazy Indians made it," she said to herself and went back to her roses.

Victor stopped the pickup in front of Thomas Builds-the-Fire's HUD house. They both yawned, stretched a little, shook dust from their bodies.

"I'm tired," Victor said.

"Of everything," Thomas added.

They both searched for words to end the journey. Victor

needed to thank Thomas for his help, for the money, and make the promise to pay it all back.

"Don't worry about the money," Thomas said. "It don't make any difference anyhow."

"Probably not, enit?"

"Nope."

Victor knew that Thomas would remain the crazy story teller who talked to dogs and cars, who listened to the wind and pine trees. Victor knew that he couldn't really be friends with Thomas, even after all that had happened. It was cruel but it was real. As real as the ashes, as Victor's father, sitting behind the seats.

"I know how it is," Thomas said. "I know you ain't going to treat me any better than you did before. I know your friends would give you too much shit about it."

Victor was ashamed of himself. Whatever happened to the tribal ties, the sense of community? The only real thing he shared with anybody was a bottle and broken dreams. He owed Thomas something, anything.

"Listen," Victor said and handed Thomas the cardboard box which contained half of his father. "I want you to have this."

Thomas took the ashes and smiled, closed his eyes, and told this story: "I'm going to travel to Spokane Falls one last time and toss these ashes into the water. And your father will rise like a salmon, leap over the bridge, over me, and find his way home. It will be beautiful. His teeth will shine like silver, like a rainbow. He will rise, Victor, he will rise."

Victor smiled.

"I was planning on doing the same thing with my half," Victor said. "But I didn't imagine my father looking anything like a salmon. I thought it'd be like cleaning the attic or something. Like letting things go after they've stopped having any use."

"Nothing stops, cousin," Thomas said. "Nothing stops."

Thomas Builds-the-Fire got out of the pickup and walked up his driveway. Victor started the pickup and began the drive home.

"Wait," Thomas yelled suddenly from his porch. "I just got to ask one favor."

Victor stopped the pickup, leaned out the window, and shouted back. "What do you want?"

"Just one time when I'm telling a story somewhere, why don't you stop and listen?" Thomas asked.

"Just once?"

"Just once."

Victor waved his arms to let Thomas know that the deal was good. It was a fair trade, and that was all Victor had ever wanted from his whole life. So Victor drove his father's pickup toward home while Thomas went into his house, closed the door behind him, and heard a new story come to him in the silence afterwards.

from *Mama's Girl*

VERONICA CHAMBERS

Ten years before Air Jordans, I learned to fly. It's like the way brothers pimp-walk to a basketball hoop with a pumped-up ball and throw a few shots, hitting each one effortlessly. Like a car idling before a drag race, there is an invitation, perhaps even a threat, in the way their sneakers soft-shoe the pavement and the ball rolls around in their hands.

As double-dutch girls, we had our own prance. Three of us and a couple of ropes. It had to be at least three girls—two to turn, one to jump. We knew the corners where you could start a good game. Like guys going up for a layup, we started turning nice and slow. Before jumping in, we would rock back and forth, rocking our knees in order to propel ourselves forward; rocking our hips just to show how cute we were. It wasn't a question of whether we'd make it in, we'd conquered that years before. The challenge was to prove how long we could jump. The tricks we would do—pop-ups, mambo, around the world—were just for show, just to work the other girls' nerves. The real feat was longevity. So when we picked the corner where we were going to double-dutch, we came with ropes and patience.

There is a space between the concrete and heaven where the air is sweeter and your heart beats faster. You drop down and then you jump up again and you do it over and over until the rope catches on your foot or your mother calls you home. You keep your arms to your sides, out of the way, so they don't get tangled in the rope. Your legs feel powerful and heavy as they beat the ground. When you mambo back and forth, it's like dancing. When you do around the world, it's like a ballet dancer's pirouette. In the rope, if you're good enough, you can do anything and be anything you want.

> *Beverly Road go swinging,*
> *Beverly Road go swing-ing,*
> *Beverly Road go swinging,*
> *Beverly Road go swing-ing.*

On my side of the street is where we jumped rope because Drena, who lived by me, had the best rope, and like cattle, we followed the rope. The best kind of jumping rope was telephone wire because it was light, yet sturdy, and it hit the sidewalk with a steady rhythm—tat tat tat. The telephone wire that connected your phone to the jack was not long enough. The only way to get telephone rope was from someone who worked for the telephone company. Drena's uncle was a telephone repairman so she always had rope.

The worst kind of rope was the kind you bought in the store—cloth ropes with red plastic handles that came in plastic packages with pictures of little blond girls on them. First of all, they were too short. It would take two or three to make one side of a good double-dutch rope. Second, the ropes were too soft for serious jumping (which only made sense because everybody knew that white girls were no kind of competition when it came to jumping rope). But in a clutch, you could run a soft rope under a hose and get it good and wet to make it heavier. The only problem was keeping it wet.

> *Miss Mary Mack-Mack-Mack,*
> *All dressed in black-black-black,*
> *With silver buttons-buttons-buttons*
> *All down her back-back-back.*

We would split into teams. Only two positions: jumper and turner. You had to be good at both. No captain, just Shannon with her big mouth and Lisa, who really couldn't jump, but talked a lot of junk. With two people turning and one person jumping and everybody else sitting around, waiting for their turn, it wasn't hard to start a fight.

"Pick your feet up! *Pick your feet up!*"

"I hear you."

"Well then, act like it."

"You just mind your business, okay?"

Sometimes when I was jumping, I would catch someone on my team yanking the rope so she could call a time-out. Usually, it was Drena because it was her rope and she thought that meant she didn't have to play fair.

"Uh-huh. Start over. Jeanine is turning double-handed," Drena would say. To us, double-handed was something like being crippled or blind. When a double-handed person turned, the ropes would hit against each other, spiraling in lopsided arcs. It not only messed up our jumping, it looked ugly, shaky, and uneven. A good double-dutch rope looked like a wire eggbeater in motion.

"It's okay. It's fine," I would say.

Drena wouldn't be swayed. "Veronica, don't try to cover up. Everybody on the block knows Jeanine is double-handed."

"I am not," Jeanine would mumble.

If there wasn't someone to take Jeanine's place, Drena would wrap up the rope and declare the game over. Then we'd go back to her house and watch TV. Drena was the only girl on the block to have her own room, plus a canopy bed, a dressing table, a TV, and a stereo. Staring blanky at *Gilligan's Island,* I would ask Drena, "Why'd you mess up the game? You know Jeanine is not double-handed."

She would roll her eyes. "I'm so sick of those girls. I was

just trying to get us out of there." But other times, she would stick to her story and refuse to budge. "You *know* that girl is double-handed. Shut up and pass the Munchos."

> *Ooh, she thinks she's bad.*
> *Baby, I know I'm bad.*
> *Ooh, she thinks she's cool.*
> *Cool enough to steal your dude.*

We'd meet at about three-thirty, after we'd changed from our school clothes into our play clothes. Then we'd jump until the parents started coming home. Most of our parents worked nine to five in Manhattan and it took them about an hour to get home. We knew it was coming up on six o'clock when we saw the first grown-up in business clothes walking down the hill from the Utica Avenue bus stop.

Sometimes a grown-up woman, dressed in the stockings and sneakers that all our mothers wore for the long commute home, would jump in—handbag and all—just to show us what she could do. She usually couldn't jump for very long. These women had no intention of sweating their straightened hair into kinkiness anyway. But we always gave them props for being able to get down. Secretly, I loved the way they clutched their chests, as if bras were useless in double-dutch, and the way their bosoms rose and fell in the up-and-down rhythm of the rope. I longed for the day I would jump double-dutch and have something round and soft to hang on to.

Around this time, I would start looking out for my mother. I could usually spot her from two blocks away. In the spring, she wore her tan raincoat. In the fall, she wore the same raincoat with the liner buttoned underneath. I knew the purses she carried and the way she walked. If I hadn't made up my bed or if I was jumping in my good school clothes, I could usually dash into the house before she got there and do what I was supposed to do. If I was not in trouble, I'd try to make my turn last long enough so that my mother could see me jump.

"Wait, Mom, watch me jump!" I would say. Even though I knew she'd say no.

"I've got to start dinner," she'd say. "And I've seen you jump before."

"But I've learned a new trick!" I'd try not to sound like a baby in front of my friends.

But she wouldn't even turn around. She'd be carrying a plastic shopping bag that held her work shoes and the *Daily News*.

"Some other time," she'd say, closing the gate behind her.

There's so much I can do. So much stuff she doesn't know. But it's always some other time with her.

Here is what I wish she knew: There is a space between the two ropes where nothing is better than being a black girl. The helix encircles you and protects you and there you are strong. I wish she'd let me show her. I could teach her how it feels.

from *Recollections of My Life as a Woman*

DIANE DI PRIMA

It was at my grandmother's side, in that scrubbed and waxed apartment, that I received my first communications about the specialness and the relative uselessness of men, in this case my grandfather. There was no doubt that he was the excitement of our days, the fire and light of our lives, and that one of his most endearing qualities was that we had no idea what he was going to do next. But it was the women, and there were many of them, who attended on all the practical aspects of life. In the view that Antoinette Mallozzi transmitted, there was nothing wrong or strange about this. We women had the babies, after all, and it was enormously more interesting to us than to any man to know that there would be food on the table.

Not that I wish in any way to denigrate my grandfather: he worked enormously hard for his family—*but he would at any time throw everything over for an ideal.* There were many stories of his quitting an otherwise okay job to protest some injustice to a fellow worker. At which point he would arrive home with the fellow worker and his entire family, at the very least for dinner. Often they stayed for weeks. My grandmother would set the table for that many more, and if a solution was not rapidly forthcoming, she and the six girls would take in crochet beadwork to keep cash coming in until my grandfather found another, less unjust employer.

Now, this sort of thing was not still going on when I was little—by then my grandfather was no longer working for others as a custom tailor—but the stories and the memory of it were in the air. My grandfather was regarded somewhat as the family treasure: a powerful and erratic kind of lightning generator, a kind of Tesla experiment we for some reason kept in the house.

It was clear to me that he was as good as it got. My father, a sullen man with a smoldering temper, was easily as demanding as Grandpa, but did not bring these endearing qualities of excitement and idealism, this demand for something more than we already had or knew, into our lives. It was like tending a furnace in which the fire had gone out.

Antoinette was always busy, but there was a way in which she communicated the basic all-rightness of things. I loved to watch her hands. As I think about it now, I realize that as a little person, I was not separated from the old: the sight and feel of soft, dry, wrinkled skin was associated with the sight and feel of love. Of those who had the time to listen, to tell a story. I learned to love the smells and feel of old flesh— I loved to put my round child's cheek up against her wrinkled one.

Her hands always smelled of garlic and onions, beeswax and lemons, and a thousand herbs. There was that sense of cleanness and the good smells of the world. A sense of the things that went on. In the turbulent 1930s into which I was born, my grandmother taught me that the things of woman go on: that they are the very basis and ground of human life. Babies are born and raised, the food is cooked. The world is cleaned and mended and kept in order. Kept sane. That one could live with dignity and joy even in poverty. That even tragedy and shock and loss require this basis of loving attendance.

And that men were peripheral to all this. They were dear, they brought excitement, they sought to bring change. Printed newspapers, made speeches, tried to bring that taste

of sanity and order into the larger world. But they were fragile somehow. In their excitement they would forget to watch
the clock and turn the oven off. I grew up thinking them a
luxury. . . .

My grandfather and I had our secrets—as when we listened
to Italian opera together. Opera was forbidden Domenico because he had a bad heart—and so moved was he by the vicis-
situdes and sorrows of Verdi's heroes and heroines that the
doctor felt it to be a danger. We would slip away together to
listen—I was three or four—and he would explain all the
events extraordinaire that filled that world. All that madness
seemed as natural as anything else to my young mind. The
madness in the air around me, I felt, was no different.

We would share forbidden cups of espresso, heavily sweet-
ened. Drops of the substance, like an elixir of life, were
slipped into my small mouth on a tiny silver spoon, while
the eggshell china with its blue-and-gold border gleamed iri-
descent in the lamplight. I remember that his hand shook
slightly. It was the world of the child—full of struggles larger
than life, huge shadows cast by the lamp, circumventing the
grown-ups. It was a world of enchantment, and passion.

But then, he told me stories. Terrifying stories, fables
whose morals seemed to point to the horror of social custom,
of emulation. Or he read me Dante, or we would practice my
bit of Italian together. Italian which was forbidden me in my
parents' house, and which I quickly forgot when we were finally separated. Italy was a part of that world of enchantment. Domenico would describe the olive groves of the
south, till I saw them blowing silver-green in the wind.
When I was seven he promised to take me there "after the
war," but he died before the war was over. I grew up nostal-
gic for a land I'd never seen. . . .

∞

I stood beside him as he sat at his desk. He only half-looked'
at me as he spoke. This was unusual; in the story times I always sat on his lap. Sat in a bentwood chair, sometimes *facing
the wall* together as if to shut out distractions. A Zen auster-
ity. Or were there only certain corners we could go to for
these exchanges, where the grown-ups would not see us and
swoop down—"Leave the child alone. . . . Come on, Diane,
your mother (or whoever) wants you. . . . Pop is a little crazy"
(an aside, an undertone). If Pop was crazy, I well knew by
then that I was crazy with him. They were too late, with
their attempts to save me for themselves. The conspiracy between us ran too deep.

I stood beside him at his desk, and his eyes were not on
me. Only, I could feel the stuff of his shirtsleeve against my
cheek, the smell of bluing, of starch. He said, "Someday you
are going to go out at night and look at the stars and you will
wonder how they got there. Then you'll study like I studied,
and you'll suffer like I suffered, and *in the end you'll find nothing.*" I was not very old but I didn't flinch at that "nothing."
Only I knew with my full child's certitude that it wasn't
true. Or anyway the despair that accompanied the word had
no truth, however much he felt it. I had no words to argue,
only the desire to comfort. I may have put my hand on his
starched shirtsleeve.

I was being recruited, initiated, and I knew it. With my
full consent, entering a world larger than life. I knew there
was no turning back, and in fact, yearned only to go forward.
To go forward, with him, into the darkness. The struggle for
Truth. Only, for me, the darkness held no despair. *Not nothing, Grandpa.* It was someone other than a child who longed
to say that.

Not nothing, Grandpa. It was a promise, a vow. I, Diane,

age four or five, would make meaning in the world. Make meaning for him, for myself. The dark was luminous, of that I was certain. That much I *knew*.

With that exchange we achieved the full status of lovers. Without further touch or words, we shaped the prototype, the pattern for all my deepest loves to come. Always this despair, this hope, this luminous dark. The conspiracy between us was complete.

Red Velvet Dress

NAOMI SHIHAB NYE

The other people who lived on Lena's street were: Beverly, who was fifteen, who combed and combed Lena's glistening hair from the time she was little, as the afternoon light fell in smooth waves across the grass and curbs and softened the shadow of the postman with his cracked leather bag. Margaret, whose mother lived in a wheelchair in the back room of their house. She didn't roll to the front room very often, but once she did, and told Lena she wasn't bitter about her life, a secret that Lena carried with her like a fine pearl button. Annie, who ate a wide lasagna noodle boiled without anything on it. Norma, who was plump and pale as a Sunday bun in a basket alongside the German smorgasbord down by the railroad tracks. Peter, who pressed his face into the metal rungs of the fence, calling out in a thin voice, "Lena, Lena! Can you play?" The floating lady in the house with no paint. They could see her float by her upstairs windows late at night when they drove home from being somewhere out in the world. The Robitailles from Quebec with seven children and steaming blueberry pies. They wore French beneath their English like an undershirt.

Then there stood the many houses of no-names-known-to-us people which Lena and her brother and friends passed as they walked up the hill to school and down the hill home. The crooked-drainpipes house and the house of yellow shutters and the house with three broken station wagons and men sticking out from under them and the house with the crazy dog that bit Lena under the eye once and had to be taken to the dog pound for observation. They were people who could have been Lena's friends too, but were not because of the mystery of streets and blocks and knowing only some people while others belong to the quiet backdrop of trees.

Nobody had too much money. Almost everybody saved things. Lena's mother saved the little boxes strawberries came in and used them to hold her bills and spools of thread. Norma's mother saved the scraps of yarn from all the sweaters she knitted, then knitted a tiny striped sweater for their dachshund. The Canadians saved paper advertisements and let their children draw and paint on the backs of them. Only Annie's mother threw away the last little mound of mashed potato. Only Annie's mother did not darn Annie's socks. But it was nothing to do with money, more with style. Most people had a saving style in those days and nobody locked their cars when they got out of them. There wouldn't have been much to steal but an ashtray anyway.

Lena never thought twice about answering the front door if somebody knocked. It might be one of her friends or it might be a fireman selling tickets to the fish fry. Once it was a man complimenting the radiant rows of red tulips bordering their front yard. He seemed very dramatic. He stretched his arms out wide toward the sidewalk and driveway and said, "These are the most beautiful tulips in St. Louis! These are the most beautiful tulips in the whole world!" Lena's mother came out of the kitchen with her spoon to see who was making such a racket. They said thank you and he went away. Later they thought they should have given him a bouquet of them, at least, but they weren't in the habit of picking the tulips. They just left them alone and their petals slipped down the same way as old loose socks.

Once Lena dreamed two gypsies came to the front door and tried to drag her off with them. The man gypsy had a silk suit and a top hat like Abraham Lincoln and the woman gypsy had a chicken in her purse. She woke up in a sweat and went to stand beside her mother's bed until her mother, startled, sat upright. "What's going on?"

"I had a bad dream," Lena said. She was eleven already and felt a little foolish to get scared from a dream. She did not want to say someone was trying to steal her.

"What about?"

"About—the unknown."

Her mother said sleepily, "Every bad dream is about the unknown. Probably every good dream too. You want me to crawl over or you want to go back to your own room?" Lena's father was snoring his snipping-scissors snore. Lena said, "I'll go back." Now the shadows casting their bony fingers across the top of the wall in her room seemed to point at her. Ha, ha, ha.

So the next afternoon before dinner when a loud knocking came at the front door as she was deep inside a book on her bed, she didn't run to answer. Her little brother did. She could hear the big door creaking open and him saying, "Who?" Then a long pause. She could hear mumbling.

She peeked around the corner. Two children she had never seen before stood there awkwardly. The taller one, a girl, said, "Is anybody else home?" and Lena stepped forward.

"May I help you?" she spoke like the lady in the ticket booth at the theater on Saturday afternoons.

The girl said, "We heard . . . well, we wondered . . ." and stopped.

Behind her, the floating lady was floating home with a basket full of groceries to hold her down to earth. She ate mushroom soup and marshmallows. She ate meringue and puffy muffins.

"You wondered what?" Lena asked.

"If we could see the Arab."

Another floating moment. In this long space Beverly next door would be pulling three long hairs out of her pink plastic comb. Annie would bounce a rubber ball up against the side of her house and feel the hard ping of it back into her hands.

"What Arab?"

"The one we heard lived here."

Lena looked around her living room. Piano, blue painting of candles, a lamp. Her mother was in the kitchen peeling apples for applesauce. Her father was in the backyard pitching twigs and dried leaves into a barrel and burning them. He thought it might be illegal, but was taking a chance.

"We don't have one," Lena said, and the girl and boy looked disappointed.

"Oh, but we heard . . ."

Lena closed the door as quietly as she could without saying good-bye. There was a small clicking sound instead of the usual swoosh. Her brother was looking at her. She went outside and sat on the back step next to the broom. She stared at her father in his white undershirt and square blue jeans. He was standing back from the spiraling smoke. He was tipping his head to one side as if he were hypnotized.

Oh, she knew where he had come from all right. She knew he came from Jerusalem, Palestine, the Holy Land, the land of Jesus, the land of camels and donkeys and olive trees, the land of her grandmother whom she had never seen. She knew the stories of Joha, the wise fool, which their father told them every night before they went to bed, and she knew about the pilgrims walking from the Old City to Bethlehem. When her father was a boy, he asked his mother if he could walk with the pilgrims, even though his family was Muslim, not Christian. "My mother said yes. She said, Be polite."

Lena had never been to her father's old home yet, but she was going, someday, one big day when the horizon opened up.

But he wasn't An Arab, the way that girl had said it. He was Daddy. He was Aziz to his friends and their mother. He was a funny tipped laugh and a red-and-white headdress folded up in his bottom dresser drawer. He was worried too, about money, same as everybody was. He didn't want Lena to do things she would regret. Should she tell him what those children asked for and what she said?

In the next neighborhood over from their neighborhood lived the Collins boys and the Parker boys that Lena knew from their jobs together working on the berry-picking farm and the Emerson girls who spent every Saturday morning at the library like Lena did and sometimes they all traded favorite books and the big grandmother with the high hair that Lena's mother stared at once in the grocery checkout line. "I should have been her," she whispered to Lena, which Lena found very strange. How could anybody be anyone else? But Lena would never go to their houses and ask to see the Africans.

Because once you knew Billy Collins, you knew about his lizard collection and his turquoise stone that he kept in a pouch inside an egg carton with old pennies worth ten dollars each and the rusted key he dug out of the ground one day while they were plucking the berries. You knew his voice and shirts. You did not think A Group of Different People, when you were thinking of friends.

Maybe the Robitailles weren't even like any other French-Canadians at all. Maybe Annie's grandfather who snapped his suspenders and brought them a fancy cold dessert called Tiramisu which he carried on ice cubes in his green car was just himself more than An Italian. In those days not many people talked about being half-and-half, but years later Lena would know it was one of the richest kinds of milk.

So her father burned the dry leaves and a bat flew over him. Lena called out, "Bat! Daddy! Look, it's not a bird!" and he looked up. *"Ahlan wa sahlan,"* he called out, which meant "Welcome" in his own first language of Arabic, and she laughed as the bat dipped and rose in graceful arcs. He did not say, Get away. He did not say, I wish you were something else. He said "Welcome" and the bat seemed to understand by circling close above his head.

Then she took a deep breath and called out to him. "Daddy, some children came to the door. They wanted to see the Arab and I said we didn't have one. I never saw them on this street before. I never saw them at school either. But they might be from school. Are you mad at me?"

And her father came and sat beside her and took her hand in his own hand.

He sat between her and the broom and the night.

Inside the kitchen window her mother was reaching for a stack of four white plates with sheaves of golden wheat bowing around their edges. Her brother was turning the bathroom faucet off and on so the whole house shook a little bit.

Her father said, "The world asks us all a lot of questions, doesn't it," and stared off into a strip of pink sky.

Then there was a long slow calling of a dog from out in the field beyond the houses.

Then there was the clatter-bang muffler sound of Peter's father turning into his driveway next door.

Lena thought his feelings might be hurt. She said, "I'm sorry," and her daddy laughed so loudly he startled her. He stood up again and waved his hands in the air.

"You could have said Yes, but you were also right in saying No! All the questions have more than one good answer, don't you think?"

Lena felt gloomy. "That's not what they tell us at school."

"I could have put on my headdress for them! You could have pretended I didn't speak English. Maybe they'll come back and we can make them happy."

Lena's brother stepped outside, banging the green screen door of their back porch, and pitched his ball high into the air. He said, "Daddy, catch?" And their daddy was catching. He had stepped off against the nearly dark sky, so Lena could see him from a distance again and he could have been anybody from any place in the world. Without the long shafts of light from the windows of their house, they wouldn't have been able to see the ball very well by now.

A few days later a package arrived from the old country for Lena. Inside it was a red velvet dress, sewn by her grandmother and aunts in the village overseas, stitched with figures of children playing and two angels and birds and interlocking vines, all in different bright colors. At first Lena's mother said it would be a dress-up dress, but Lena didn't dress up that much and it seemed a shame just to let it hang in the closet. So Lena wore it to school. Her mother tied the long velvet ribbons in the back at the waist. She said, "Look at you! You look so elegant I almost don't recognize you!"

At school her girlfriends took deep breaths over her dress. They rubbed the velvet between their fingers. "Where did you get this?" they whispered.

Lena said, "It is my Arab dress from my Arab relatives far across the sea."

Some people said, "We never knew you were an Arab!" and she said, "Oh yes." But she was also thinking about the German words inside the dreams of her grandparents on her mother's side—they had told her they still had dreams in German even though they hadn't really spoken the language since they were children—and all the people on her block. What other country did Margaret's mother in the wheelchair belong to? The country of long quiet hours. The country of Slow and Ramps and Wait Till Everybody Else Comes Home. But Lena had also heard her singing.

The only problem about the red velvet dress was Lena

wanted to wear it every day. It felt so smooth, and comforting. It fit just perfectly around the neck. Not tight, not pulling. All her other dresses and blouses and skirts seemed shabby beside it. Down the street, Norma asked her mother if she could make her a blue velvet dress. She didn't want to copy Lena, but if Lena wouldn't mind . . .

Something had changed. Now Lena thought about her faraway relatives more. She imagined what her world would look like to them. What would they think of the art wagon at school and the tornado drills when everybody rushed down to the school basement to crouch on the floor and cover their heads with their arms? She wondered if her cousins would be able to climb the rope in PE. Now she thought of their faraway fingers pulling threads through velvet *for her,* thinking of her, and what that meant. It meant they were connected, just as she felt connected to all the people on her block and her friends lining their lunch sacks up beside her own. Now when she pledged allegiance, it was secretly to everywhere.

Grandpa's "Chicaudies"

FRED L. GARDAPHÉ

The sun sits screened by a layer of gray clouds. It looks
like the thumbprint of one who had been rubbing his thumb
in the yellow pollen of the dandelion flower. The air is thick
with the humidity of late spring. Even with the windows
rolled down, the inside of the car is heavy with moist air.
"The sky is sweating," thinks Frankie, who sits in the back-
seat of his mother's station wagon. In the front seat, next to
his mother, sits Grandpa. It is early Saturday morning.
Frankie wants to be home in bed, waiting to wake for the
late-morning ball game that he plays when there is no school,
but today Grandpa has summoned him to pick "chicaudies,"
the dirty, bitter greens that he hates to eat. Everyone, it
seems, but Grandpa knows they're not really *cicoria,* but dan-
delions, yet the old man insists on calling them "chicaudies."

Grandpa is wearing his baggy work pants and a coat that
is the color of today's sky. Squeezed over his head is a gray
wool cap, the kind the newsboys wear in the old movies. The
car turns off the busy street and slows as it reaches the open
field in the forest preserves. As far as Frankie's eyes can see
the field is flooded with yellow dandelion flowers. Even
Frankie knows that it is too late to pick the weeds; once
they've flowered, the greens have beome tough and bitter and
only the old people will eat them.

At Grandpa's command the car stops and Frankie grabs
five empty potato sacks and slides across the seat, out of the
car. Angela leans to kiss her father. He tells her they will be

finished before sunset. Frankie stretches and yawns. His eyes wander and he wonders how much of the yellow will be gone by the time his mother rescues him. Over the treetops he can see the Ferris wheel of Kiddieland. It is motionless. Grandpa grunts as he lifts himself out of the car. He softly shuts the door and Angela has to lean over and pull it closed. The white wagon pulls away leaving the two alone in the vacant field. The horn beeps and Frankie follows it until he can see only its blue roof moving into the stream of early morning shopping-center traffic.

By now Grandpa is standing in the high grass and looks like a tramp searching for a cigarette butt. Frankie sighs; the connection to his world is gone. Now he must follow the old man into the Old World. He pulls the brim of his blue baseball cap down and heads toward Grandpa. Frankie's world will return only when the station wagon returns, only after all five sacks have been stuffed full of chicaudies.

Without taking off his coat Grandpa bends down and pulls a leaf up to his mouth. He bites it in half and chews it slowly. He nods and turns to say, "Franco! Whoa-aye! Franco! Ova 'ere we start." Frankie drags the sacks behind him and jogs to where Grandpa is bent down. Grandpa takes a sack, hooks it over the middle button of his coat, reaches into his pocket, and grabs the small curved knife that is always in his pocket. With the knife in his right hand he poises it above his left hand which has made a fist around the leaves of one flower. Without looking, he slices the bunch just under the base of his hand, tosses the severed leaves into the sack, and reaches for the next plant. Frankie watches until the old man twists his neck and as though in pain calls out, "Whoa-aye! Doan you know how to pick the chicaudies?"

Frankie responds by pulling out his pocket knife, then imitating his grandfather. He loops a sack over his belt buckle. They work face to face a few feet apart. For every bunch that

Frankie picks the old man picks four. Soon Grandpa is a good distance away, working rhythmically, sliding sidestep from plant to plant. After an hour Frankie's back aches and he thinks only of the many hours he had yet to spend in this field. He stops to watch Grandpa.

The old man is still bent, head even with his broad backside. Occasionally he pulls a bunch to his mouth. His tobacco-stained teeth part to make way for the muddy greens that he quickly stuffs into his mouth. He tastes the weeds to tell his next direction. Now sweating, he rubs his muddied wrist against his dripping forehead as though his wrist was a matchstick and his forehead the striking surface.

The friction leaves a red impression on his already sunburned skin. Under the cap, behind the sweatband, head causes hair to itch and itch causes eyes to wince. Soon his hands stop picking and with knife yet in hand he pulls back the woolen cap. Out pours more sweat in thin streams. The silvered hair is matted with oily sweat. He runs his fingers through the thick hair, scratching vigorously with his fingernails. He replaces the cap; all the while his eyes have not left the field he works in. Sweat puddles the ridge where his glasses usually rest. It is a thick sweat that deposits grime deep into the honey-colored glasses that ride the tip of his nose, like a loose saddle on a cantering horse. The glasses' frames wedge red rims into the sunburned cheeks and the old man's eyes puff with moisture that seeps from irritated tear ducts. He takes out a handkerchief and rubs it across his face, his glasses still on. He returns to work, not noticing that Frankie has stopped and is watching him from more than ten yards away. As Grandpa retakes his straddling stance Frankie returns to his picking.

Hours pass. The old man still wears his thick jacket. The sky remains unchanged, still sweating into the air of late morning.

Grandpa never stops and his pace leaves Frankie far behind. He is now just over the side of a small hill. Only his cap is visible, bobbing into and then peeking over the tips of golden grass. Frankie looks up and sees only the gray cap. He hurries to catch up. He can't move as quickly as Grandpa can in this bent position. He crouches and hops plant to plant, like a throb as though it was a bat that repeatedly bounces against his spine. A cold sweat pours. Patience battles pain, pride wages war with passivity. To shorten the distance between him and the General he skips yards of plants, squishing the unpicked flowers underfoot so that Grandpa won't see that he's missed them. He hears Grandpa wheezing as he sucks in air with emphysematic lungs. He returns to picking only when he feels he is within Grandpa's sight. He cuts, throws, digs, cuts, and throws the leaves into his sack. The half-full sack slows him down. "Francino, bring me a nudder sacco. Whoa-aye Francino, hurr' up!" Frankie hobbles to Grandpa and the exchange is made without eye contact. "Grandpa is so serious. He doesn't talk. He stops swinging his knife only to chew more chicaudies. That's okay though. What could we talk about anyway? He embarrasses me. Hope no one sees me here, like some beggar." And he remembers the time that his friend Pickles tried to chase Grandpa from left field.

The guys were standing around home plate when Frankie arrived.

"What's up, guys. I thought I'd be late. Thought my grandfather would never finish that lawn."

"We got to play left field out."

"Why?"

"Some old Moustache Pete is out there picking weeds. He chased Pickles out with a knife."

He looked out to left field to see Grandpa. He couldn't believe it. There he was picking chicaudies right when they were trying to play ball. Frankie agreed that they should play left field out. Just then Grandpa moved to center. Pickles screamed, "Look. We can't play center field out now. Hey, old man! Get the hell out of there." Grandpa looked up and shook his knife at them.

"Let's go play on the school grounds," Frankie suggested, and they left before anyone could recognize that it was Grandpa. "Why can't he be like Grandpa Benet? Work on a lawn or something."

Grandpa needs Frankie only for the feeling of working with someone in the fields. He's strong enough to carry the full sacks without slowing his pace. He knows there is some reason that he can't do this without Frankie. Working with Frankie reminds him of working in the fields with his brothers and father. For hours they used to work without speaking words. The sounds of their work spoke to each other, keeping them company. There's water, wine, bread, and cheese in his large pockets. Frankie's thirsty and he knows that Grandpa won't stop to eat until three bags are filled.

As Grandpa works sweat rolls into his mouth. Frankie wants to ask him for water. "How could he not be thirsty? Could it be that he drinks his sweat?" Finally Grandpa waves him over. "We eat now." He pulls his coat off, revealing a white short-sleeved shirt that is soaked through with perspiration. The shirt has become transparent and his undershirt can be seen through it. The exchange of bread and cheese is silent. Grandpa sips his wine and Frankie, his water. The melody of the turning carousel breaks the silence and Frankie lifts his eyes to the turning Ferris wheel. A roller coaster takes a dip, a sharp turn, and a chorus of screams echoes in the forest. Grandpa eats with his eyes closed.

The crust is dry but the bread is moist in the middle as it has soaked out the moisture of the cheese. The cheese crumbles in his mouth. The water is warm. Frankie chews rapidly and swallows hard. Grandpa pulls a few leaves from where he sits and stuffs them into the sandwich. He finishes and lights up a Pall Mall. The smoke spirals blue against the gray sky. Grandpa coughs and when he can't stop, he stubs the cigarette out against his shoe and slips the butt into his shirt pocket. Then he is back picking chicaudies. He leaves his coat and the water and wine bottles next to his grandson, who is still chewing. Grandpa moves to the other side of the hill, down to a small valley, and leaves Frankie alone on the crest, next to the three filled bags.

Frankie stretches out on Grandpa's coat and soon falls asleep, blanketed by the windless, humid air. Even in his sleep he picks chicaudies. It is a shallow sleep and the smell of the grass near his nose leads him to think he is not asleep, but awake, picking chicaudies. Now as he works he is completely refreshed and feels heat only on his forehead. He picks the last two bags by himself as Grandpa sits watching, applauding, commending his labor in perfect English. He raises his hand to pull his cap lower. The motion startles him awake and he sees Grandpa straddled over him, knife in his right hand, his left hand tugging the brim of his baseball cap. All Grandpa has to do is to swing that knife down to cut off the hat's brim, just like it was a chicaudie. Frankie is frightened by the knife and the hand on his hat, but then the hand tilts the brim back and Grandpa smiles, teeth yellowed with bits of dandelion greens sticking in between the front teeth.

"Whoa-aye Franco, you fall asleep. What's the matter? You tire. C'mon boy wake yourself up. We gotta more to go. C'mon you poor boy."

Grandpa grabs Frankie's left cheek in between his thumb and forefinger, twisting the chunk of skin firmly. Frankie jumps up, rubbing his cheek. He grabs the water, the coat, the sacks, and follows Grandpa down the side of the hill. There is still one bag left to fill.

Thanksgiving in a Monsoonless Land

ROSHNI RUSTOMJI

The last conversation I had with my dying mother, Dinaz Mehta, was in a hospital room in South San Francisco. Outside the closed window, the morning was heavy with fog. The wind would not begin to whip through the hospital parking lot until later in the day.

"Kamal," my mother demanded from her bed. "Are you a *convinced* American? A practicing citizen of the U.S.A.?"

The question startled me. I had been preparing to answer my mother's demand, repeated daily for the last seventeen days, that she be taken back to Bombay. My mother had had a headache for seventeen days which the doctors refused to attribute to the cancer. To the deadly growth surprising the very marrow of her being. Mother had agreed with her doctors. Her headache had nothing to do with the cancer. It was merely her familiar childhood reaction to the pre-monsoon season. The headache which kept pace with the suffocating heat and the heavy clouds pushing down upon the land. The waiting for the rains as the ceiling fans and the flies circled around without much enthusiasm. And then the rains. The relief from the headache. And once again the pain, the heat, the brief, sharp brightness before the next lightning and thunder, and then once again the rains.

My mother had of course experienced neither her premonsoon headache nor the monsoons in the past fifty-odd years which she had spent rooting herself into an unfamiliar land, living her life on the continent of North America. She assured me, her doctors, and her nurses that her headache would disappear the minute the rains came down on her ancestral home on Malabar Hill in Bombay. But she would not be in Bombay. She would be in South San Francisco. She complained that she was not happy about spending eternity with her pre-monsoon headache. All because she had died in a monsoonless land.

I found my mother's surprising question about citizenship rather unfair. Especially since it came on the day I had decided that I would offer to take her home to India. To die without a headache. But instead of unrelenting headaches, heavy monsoons, rain-drenched fragrant earth, and eternity, she had asked about being an American. She was insistent.

"Really, Kamal, dear, tell me! Are you a practicing, convinced American?"

And in that hospital room while my mother was dreaming of the monsoon heat and rains, I remembered the Thanksgiving celebration nearly thirty-five years earlier. I had been exactly twelve years and one month old.

We were living in Oakland, California, that year. In a one-bedroom apartment with cracks in two of the five windows and a perpetually leaking toilet. Five weeks before that Thanksgiving, a disturbing amount of the paint on our kitchen ceiling had peeled off and dropped into the lentils mother had left to cook, uncovered, on the stove. She had to throw away the lentils. My mother hated to waste any food, throw away anything she thought might be useful. To someone, anyone. Sometime. Someplace. As a good Zoroastrian, she would beg Ahura Mazda's forgiveness any time she was forced to throw out any food. She prayed even when she had to tear off the slimy, wilted edges of old lettuce. As she was throwing out the lentils with the flakes of paint floating on the top, she told me, "Kamal, your Grandfather Tehmurasp would have laughed and said to me, 'Use your imagination,

Dinaz! Think of the plain rice without any of the lentil daal that you will have to eat as the best mutton palau you have ever tasted!' "

But I refused to accept the plain rice as any kind of palau. I had eaten palau very few times in my life. I doused my plate of plain white rice with soy sauce and ate it with the chopsticks our landlady, Mary Crawford, had given me one Christmas. When mother looked somewhat perplexed, I raised my glass of milk and said, "In honor of my Chinese great-great-grandmother, whose name we do not know."

Later that evening, a couple I didn't know, Philip and Ginny Johnson, telephoned us. Although my mother had not heard from either Philip or Ginny for at least ten years, she invited them for the forthcoming Thanksgiving meal.

When I demanded to know why strangers were being invited to what my mother usually referred to as the "Two for Turkey and Turkey for Two, Turkey for You and Turkey for Me" celebration, she said, "Because of your late and wonderful Grandfather Tehmurasp. Because he considered the Johnsons as his friends. They used to visit our home on Malabar Hill to look at all the books on Parsis that your grandfather had. Even one by a Peruvian. In Spanish. Your grandfather met them the year your father and I got engaged and joined the group that made bombs to throw out the British, and the police found out and we were sent off to America by your grandparents. Instead of to jail by the police."

On that Thanksgiving day, when I was twelve years and one month old, mother was hot and frustrated. The turkey had somehow managed to expand monstrously in the process of cooking. It was impossible to baste it while it was in the small oven. She had to pull out the heavy roaster every twenty-five minutes, balance it on the stove top cluttered with the pots and pans she had used to fry the vegetables for the sweet-sour-hot Parsi wedding stew and cook the sweet-sour-hot shrimp, baste the miraculously swollen turkey, and then bend down to push it back into the oven.

Philip Johnson walked into the apartment with a package of papadums, a jar of pickled mango achaar, and the news that Ginny could not come because she had to go to Massachusetts. "A family emergency. Sorry we didn't call. Lost your number. But to make up, here's genuine papadums and authentic mango achaar from our last trip to India."

I wanted to say, "We had to disconnect our phone three days ago," but was stopped by the expression on Philip's face. He was staring at my mother while she was in the process of carefully putting the turkey into the oven after her final bout of basting it. Philip was frowning.

"What, Dinaz Mehta! What is this? A turkey! Have you forgotten to cook Parsi food? I came here for pukka, real Parsi food. And what do I see? A turkey! What do you think you are? An American!"

I wondered if I should say, "But she has also made Parsi stew and Parsi shrimp." I said, "But it is Thanksgiving."

Mother shut the oven door, uncrouched herself, and said, "You are damned right I am an American!"

Later that night, I asked her how one could dam right. Right wasn't water. She hadn't bothered with explanations. "You can use the word when you understand it."

To Philip she had said, "I have lived here for over eighteen years. I have borne my one and only child here. I have buried my husband here. Here in America. Only five years and three months after we came here. Buried him while I was seven months' pregnant. My husband, my Ashok, shot by a drunken idiot who wanted to clean America out. Get rid of all us heathen Asians. Shot because the man was insulted by my husband's accent! My husband is buried somewhere in New York. Oh yes. Don't worry yourself. I am an American.

I breathe here. I speak here. I sing here. I laugh and cry here. I have left parts of my body all over this place. Nail clipping and hair trimmings across the country. My uterus in North Carolina. Both ovaries in Milwaukee. Wisdom teeth in Los Angeles and rotted teeth right here in Oakland. I have eaten the food of this land and made friends with the people of this land. And I have worked here. I have given my hands to this land. Look. Look at these hands!" And she had waved her hands stained with the turkey basting and smelling of onions, garlic, green chilies, cilantro, vinegar, and shrimp right in front of Philip's face. The man had retreated into a petulant silence.

"I have cut cloth. Yards and yards and yards and yards of cloth. I have sewn garments. Skirts. Frocks. Blouses. Embroidered tablecloths and altar cloths and God knows what other cloths. Look. Do you see my fingers? Always swollen and cut all over. Scratched. I have nightmares. At least two every night. Those sewing machines in those small rooms with those bare bulbs burning around the clock and the tired, tired, tired, tired women. Women ordered to work quickly. All the time. Told to shut up and work.

"And," my mother continued her one-sided argument with Philip, "I have always paid my taxes. My enemies are here. My friends are here. My only family, my daughter, is here. God and the beautiful, Asho Farohars, our guardian angels, are of course everywhere. You are damned right I am an American. And I am an Indian. Who are you to tell me that I can't love two places? No one, no one can cut boundaries into my heart! Do you want this authentic American turkey? It will most probably taste quite good with the authentic Indian achaar. Better than with cranberry sauce."

It was a very short Thanksgiving dinner. Mother had not served the stew or the shrimp. That Thanksgiving was memorable because of the glorious leftovers we ate for many weeks following that "Turkey for Four or Maybe Three" celebration. I was sure that my mother, our landlady Mary Crawford, who liked rich, hot food, and I were the only people in the whole world who had eaten turkey dhaan-saak for eight days straight. The rice fried with cinnamon and brown sugar, covered with the thick, spicy daal made with lentils and filled with potatoes, carrots, pumpkin, and roasted turkey cut into chunky pieces. It was on the second day of the turkey dhaan-saak feasting that I discovered that soy sauce isn't really called for with this particular Parsi specialty.

And now, my mother was dying in South San Francisco and asking me about "American." Since I didn't know quite what to say, I asked, "Mamma, do you want me to take you back to Bombay? It is not the monsoon season there but you could make believe and maybe your headache will go away. I will ask your doctor and I am sure . . ."

"No," she said. "Just bury me here. Your father is a part of this earth now. It will be my gift to this land . . . swollen fingers, failed eyesight, and all. After all, I have eaten the food from this land and breathed the air here for most of my life. But remember. No coffin. I want to disintegrate quickly. Maybe my bones and flesh and blood will wipe out the blood spilled all over here. So much blood!"

I told her that she sounded like a martyr. "That early Bombay convent-school training is beginning to show in your old age."

"Martyr-tamatyr! Just because you are a hot-shot architect, you think you know about dead, decaying bodies and the earth. And the worms. Now, those worms . . . they do bother me, Kamal, dear. And don't forget that it was, after all, Mother Hilda at the convent who forced me to learn how to sew and embroider. And that is what put food on our table for many years!

"And," she continued, "remember to track down our old

landlady Mrs. Mary Crawford, and get back our Chinese silk sari, the Parsi gaaro, from her."

"Mamma, you gave it to her. Remember? For our rent."

"And because she had always lusted after that sari and because we liked her. She was a good woman. Of course I remember. I am not losing my mind, I am only dying. We gave her that sari and a shawl in exchange for a month's rent and money to buy those Louisa May Alcott books. And you didn't even have the decency to cry when Beth died! I cried. All you said was, 'Thank God. She's dead. At last!' Pay Mary Crawford, build her a house if you want to, but get back that gaaro. Let her keep the shawl. The gaaro is important. You know that it is the only thing we have from your Chinese great-great-grandmother. My mother's grandmother. It was given to me before I left India by my cousin who had inherited the sari. To keep me safe in America. She told me that the Chinese lady, our great-grandmother, embroidered that sari herself. All those hand-embroidered white spider patterns all over the sari. She embroidered it specially for the wife and the daughter and the granddaughter and so on and so forth of the one child, the eldest son, she and your great-great-grandfather who never returned home, sent back to India from Malaysia. Back to his Parsi family in India. He stayed there, in Malaysia, with his wife and his other children. And died there."

"Mamma, let Mrs. Crawford keep the gaaro."

"Listen to me, Kamal. Get it back and then decide what you want to do with it. Your ancestress sent it to the land she would never see. With the son she never saw again. As long as you have it, you will be blessed. You will remember Asia. You will remember the men and women who stayed and the ones who traveled away. I always meant to get it back." And she closed her eyes, turned her back to me, and fell asleep.

I was still sitting beside her when she woke up a few hours

later. The wind had blown away the fog but it was still chilly.

"Open the window, Kamal. I want to look at the air! It smells just like the earth in the garden on Malabar Hill. When the rains begin to fall. I want to look at the air."

"Mamma, one can't look at the air!"

But my mother was dead and the only things she had asked me to do were to bury her without a coffin and to get back the maroon sari, the gaaro, with the spider pattern embroidered in white silk. One spider in each square inch of the six yards.

Instead of leaving her body to the mercy of worms, I decided to cremate my mother. And in honor of her Thanksgiving litany of what part of her body she had left in which parts of the United States of America, I decided that my mother's final gift to the land would be best given by scattering her ashes across the continent instead of interring her in one, limited burial space.

And so I traveled across the United States, leaving small amounts of my mother's ashes in various places. I began by surreptitiously placing the fine ash mixed with tiny gray-and-white crystals under a tree root which had pushed through the earth in the Golden Gate Park. I then dropped some of the contents of what I called my "mother bag" into Lake Michigan in Chicago, some in the Mississippi, in Wisconsin, and some on a mountain trail behind a souvenir shop along the Blue Ridge Parkway. Remembering my mother's fascination with witches, I set afloat some of the ashes onto the Atlantic from Salem. When my travels took me to New Mexico, I scattered ashes in a ravine on a mountain road between Santa Fe and Taos. A silent, watchful raven and a very old man with a straw hat watched me. The man took off his hat and bowed to me. The raven flew off, diving after the ashes, as they drifted down the ravine.

My general route across the United States was pre-selected by my search for Mary Crawford.

Mary Crawford had apparently been on a quest. She had left her two-story home on Santiago Avenue in San Francisco. Abandoning the foam from the Pacific Ocean which constantly blew across two blocks and settled in front of her house, she had gone to Chicago, Illinois, then Boston, Massachusetts, then Charlottesville, Virginia, then Taos, New Mexico, and then to San Antonio, Texas. Mary Crawford had begun her quest in the company of the followers of a lady with electric spiritual teachings, great charisma, and a genuine urge to help people overcome their ennui and despair. The lady called herself Divine Sister Magda and sometimes Mataji Dolores.

I lost track of Mary Crawford for a short time in Texas. When I called Divine Sister Magda's office in Chicago from my motel in Texas, the office computer informed me that Mary Crawford had extended her quest into Mexico. She had become interested in healing and healers and had decided to find a true *curandera*. The secretary at the office told me that according to her informants on the Internet, Mary Crawford was in Oaxaca. Oaxaca was currently the targeted place for those in search of authentic *curanderas*.

So, I found myself in Oaxaca. In front of a house on the fringes of the cobblestoned Colonia Jalatlaco. A crazy-looking mobile made of newspaper piñatas was hanging from a pole on the sidewalk in front of the entrance gate and a small statue of Nuestra Señora de La Soledad, the Virgin of Oaxaca, guarded the entrance to the yard.

An old woman, no more than five feet tall, with two gray braids tied together with Day-Glo pink yarn, an apron with a bright red embroidered flower over her polyester blue dress, and a pair of steel-rimmed round spectacles firmly anchored onto her nose answered my knock. She identified herself as

Señora Florencia Nunez, at the foreign lady's service, and informed me that yes, Señora Mary Crawford had lived in this house but unfortunately, the señora had died three months ago. She had died in the house. Her body had been sent off to San Diego, to her son, in an airplane. She had died peacefully.

The house, Señora Nunez told me, did not belong to Señora Mary. "And please call me Florencia. Any friend of Señora Mary is a friend of mine." The house belonged to Señora Florencia's nephew, Rogelio. He was an artist. A few months before Mary Crawford's arrival, he had retreated, first to the mountains of Oaxaca and then to Peru, in pursuit of his art and to look for UFOs.

Mary Crawford had rented two rooms in the house and Señora Florencia had been her cook and Spanish teacher. And in the end, her nurse. And what could she, asked Señora Florencia, do for the señorita who had arrived at her door during today's dull, hot siesta hours? But first the señorita should get out of the heat and come into the house. Yes, the piñatas were her nephew Rogelio's work. He had left them there, together with the Virgin, to guard his aunt and their home.

As I crossed the yard with flowers growing on vines, flowers growing in clay pots, flowers growing in tin cans, two sleeping parrots and the sweet smell of jasmines, I wondered if my mother's garden on Malabar Hill had resembled this yard. Sitting in the small room with bright pictures of the Virgin in her many incarnations, a faded picture of Pope John cut out from a magazine, flowers made from newspapers stuck into black pottery vases, and a large television, I asked Señora Florencia if she knew anything about a long piece of heavy silk embroidered cloth which might have been in Señora Mary's possession.

I tried to explain what a sari was and the importance of this particular sari, grateful that my mother had insisted that

I take Spanish in high school and the first two years of college. "I have taught you Gujarati, Kamal. But when I am dead, you may have very little chance to speak it. And if you continue to speak only English, you might decide to believe like the rest of the people around you that English is either the only language spoken on this earth or that it is the only language worth knowing. Learn Spanish. Maybe one day we can go to Peru. I want to see if a person from Peru would really be interested in writing about Parsis! As I told you, your Grandfather Tehmurasp had a book on Parsis which he insisted was written by a scholar from Peru."

To my complete bewilderment, Señora Florencia answered my question about the sari, a long piece of embroidered silk, with, "¿Conoce usted la China Poblana?"

I knew of "La China Poblana" only as a Mexican-Indian restaurant which used to be in Berkeley, on San Pablo Avenue. Mother and I had frequented it until it closed down. The owners-cooks-servers were a Mexican woman from Puebla and an Indian man from Goa.

But no, Señora Florencia wasn't speaking of any restaurant. She was speaking of the original China Poblana: Mirrha, a princess, who had been stolen from India by Spanish pirates, taken to the Philippines and then to China, as they put together their cargo of spices and silks and ivory and sandalwood for New Spain. Mirrha had arrived with the cargo from Asia to the coast of what was to be named Mexico. In 1621, Señora Florencia seemed sure about the date of arrival as well as the fact that the young girl, who had eventually ended up as a slave in Puebla de los Angeles, had been baptized, somewhere along the way, with the name Catarina de San Juan. Mirrha's once scintillating, sequined, silk embroidered skirts and shawls from India had reputedly influenced the clothes worn by the China Poblanas. The dashing, glamorous young women of Puebla. Señora Florencia wasn't too sure about the clothes part. She had read in one of the biographies about Mirrha that her abductors had brought her to New Spain disguised in boy's clothing, in order to protect her virginity. Chastity and beauty for the highest bidder.

Señora Florencia assured me that she often dreamed of Catarina de San Juan. In all her manifestations. As a young girl slave, as the woman who had refused to consummate her marriage to another slave, as a widow, as a visionary.

I listened to Señora Florencia's account of the girl abducted from India and wondered if my Chinese great-great-grandmother's gaaro was in this house or in San Diego or in San Francisco. I found myself telling my hostess about my mother. My mother's headache, her longing to feel the monsoon rain in her garden on Malabar Hill, her request that I find the sari and of her death. Señora Florencia looked at me for four long minutes. It was neither a rude nor a disturbing stare. She got up from the couch and gestured me to follow her into the room behind the kitchen. It contained two long tables, a bed, and a chest. The rose vine in the garden had climbed across the room's single window. Señora Florencia led me to one of the tables, which was covered with jars and bottles filled with dried leaves, twigs, seeds, and roots. Each container had a piece of paper wrapped around it with a thick rubber band. The name and uses of an herb or a healing plant was written in beautiful, straight script in jet black ink on each piece of paper. She picked up a jar labeled TÉ MALABAR and poured some of the contents into a small plastic bag. "Scatter these herbs on your mother's grave. It will help to cure her homesickness."

I told her that there was no grave. I described my ash-scattering, continent-spanning expedition. I went to the living room and returned with my "mother bag." The old woman nodded, plunged her hand into the bag, pulled out the plastic Ziploc bag I had been using for my mother's ashes, and emptied the ashes into a small clay bowl. She then added the *té* Malabar to the ashes and carried the bowl to the other table in the room. There were candles, flowers, and a beautifully framed picture of the Virgin of Guadalupe on the table. A bowl carved from a gourd, painted in reds, oranges, pinks, greens, and blues and filled with rose petals stood in front of the picture. As Señora Florencia lit a fat pink candle that was stuck into a small brass candlestick, I leaned forward and grabbed the corner of the cloth that covered the table.

"This is what you are looking for?" Señora Florencia didn't seem surprised.

It had been a very long time since I had seen the maroon silk, threadbare and delicate, the white "spiders" carefully embroidered across the length and width of the sari.

Señora Florencia said, "I sent Señora Mary's belongings to her son in San Diego. But I kept this. She herself had spread it on this table as the altar cloth but I knew it was not hers. There is no feel, no touch of Señora Mary on this cloth. But if you touch it . . ." She unclenched my hand, freeing the sari corner, and pushed it across the silk. "No, no. Do not become tense. There is nothing to fear. Close your eyes and be strong. Touch this silk. Don't you see her? A woman. She has the face of the Chinese women in my Rogelio's book with pictures from China. She is working on this cloth. She has tears in her eyes. I do not know why."

"Because one son will be sent away, never to see her again."

"¿China está cerca de la India, no?"

I shook my head. No, I told her. China isn't all that close to India. And I began to cry. For the loss of my mother, for my own ignorance of the land my mother had been forced to leave.

"This cloth," Señora Florencia was saying, "it is so full of life! But I must tell you, Señorita Kamal, I am sorry, but a piece is missing!"

I knew all about that missing piece. The sari had a piece missing from it even before it was given to Mary Crawford. Even before mother and I had moved to California. The sari was cut in Wisconsin. It happened when my kindergarten teacher in Milwaukee, Miss Betty Paul, had arranged a spring pageant called "Costumes of Many Lands." The note I had brought home one March afternoon read,

Dear Mrs. Mehta,
The children in Kamal's class are putting on a fashion show, "Costumes of Many Lands," next Friday after-noon. Please dress Kamal in the costume of an Indian princess.
   It will teach her friends about her country. Thank you.

"I get to carry a bow and arrow! And wear moccasins! Real ones with beads and all!" I was thrilled.

My mother was appalled. Her lecture for the next fifteen minutes was garbled between explaining about Indian "like me, like your father, like our families, like the Indian part of you," and the first people of the Americas, "as usual, mis-named, mistreated by these conquerors." Her outrage at the word "costume" was part of the tirade.

Costume-fostume! Indian princess! What does she think we are? Some kind of actors? Circus performers? We wear clothes just like everybody else. Not costumes. I will make you a jbabloo, a special Parsi dress for my special little Parsi girl in America. You are not too old or too big yet for a jhabloo."

But, according to mother, a real jhabloo needed a Chinese embroidered silk cloth and so she had taken her scissors to the gaaro and cut off three-fourths of a yard. She had sewn the short straight sleeveless dress and crocheted a white silk cap for my tight black curls within two days.

"Don't worry," I said to Señora Florencia. "I know about the missing piece. My mother cut it out to make me a dress. When I was about six years old."

"Yes, but I too cut a piece from this material. For Rogelio. He never wraps up his neck or covers his head when he goes out in the cold. He is always catching a cold. So I took a piece of this cloth because he said he liked it. I gave him a piece of this cloth to wrap around his neck. I will try and get it back for you and sew it on again but as I told you, the last I heard from him he was going to Peru. And he always gives away everything."

Señora Florencia didn't look overly upset or apologetic about the missing piece from the sari. The scarf was most probably now in the possession of an alien who had made contact with Rogelio on Macchu Picchu.

"I never answered my mother's last question. About being an American."

"Rogelio says that even people from other stars come and live here. All over. In the North and Mexico and Guatemala and Chile and Cuba and everywhere. I asked him if they were angels and he said, 'Why would angels want to live here?' I told him that he knows nothing. Even if he reads all the time and sleeps only three hours a day. This earth, she is good to live on. Here. And in your mother's country. The place where your ancestress, la China, lived. Where you live. I see all these places on the television. Help me to clear this table. The candles and the Virgencita are from my mother's house. I will fold up this cloth and then you can take it back with you."

I looked at the sari being used as an altar cloth. The maroon silk and the stylized spiders looked comfortably, quietly at home on that table.

"Señora Florencia," I said. "I already have a piece of this sari in the dress my mother made. Another piece is most probably in Peru. Let's just keep what's left of this sari here. In Oaxaca. When you dream of la China Poblana, Mirrha-Catarina, maybe you will also dream of the rain falling on my mother's garden and of my Chinese great-great-grandmother, whose name I don't know. And maybe one day I will come back and visit you for a longer time. And sit in your garden."

"Yes," said Señora Florencia. "You are right. This is a good place for this cloth to rest for some time. With an old woman, in her old woman's house, with an old woman's herbs and flowers and dreams. All the way from China to India to Mexico!"

To Change in a Good Way

SIMON J. ORTIZ

Bill and Ida lived in the mobile home park west of Milan. They'd come out with Kerr-McGee when the company first started sinking shafts at Ambrosia Lake. That would be in '58 or '59. He was an electrician's helper and Ida was a housewife, though for a while she worked over at that 24-hour Catch-All store. But mostly she liked to be around home, the trailer park, and tried to plant a little garden on the little patch of clay land that came with the mobile home.

She missed Oklahoma like Bill did too. He always said they were going to just stay long enough to get a down payment, save enough, for some acreage in eastern Oklahoma around Eufala.

That's what he told Pete, the Laguna man he came to be friends with at Section 17. Pete worked as a lift operator, taking men into and out of the mine, and once in a while they worked the same shift and rode carpool together.

You're lucky you got some land, Pete, Bill would say.

It's not much but it's some land, Pete would agree.

He and Mary, his wife, had a small garden which they'd plant in the spring. Chili, couple rows of sweet corn, squash, beans, even had lettuce, cucumbers, and radishes, onions. They irrigated from the small stream, the Rio de San Jose, which runs through Acoma and Laguna land. Ida just had the clay red ground which she had planted that first spring they'd spent in New Mexico with lettuce and radishes and corn, but the only thing that ever really came up was the corn

and it was kind of stunted and wilty looking. She watered
the little patch from the little green plastic hose hooked up to
the town water system that started running dry about mid-
June.

One Saturday, Pete and Mary and Bill and Ida were all
shopping at the same time at the Sturgis Food Mart in Milan,
and the women became friends too. They all went over to the
mobile home park and sat around and drank Pepsis and
talked. Ida and Bill didn't have any kids but Mary and Pete
had three.

They're at home, staying out of trouble I hope, Mary said.

Bill had a younger brother nicknamed Slick. He had a
photo of him sitting on the TV stand shelf. Bill was proud of
his little brother. He passed the photo to Pete and Mary. Slick
was in the Army.

In Vietnam, Bill said. I worry about him some but at least
he's learned a trade. He's Spec-4 in Signal. Slick's been kind
of wild, so I know about trouble.

Ida took Mary outside to show her her garden. It's kind a
hard trying to grow anything here, Ida said, different from
Oklahoma.

I think you need something in it, Ida, to break up the
packed clay, Mary said. Maybe some sheep stuff. I'll tell Pete
to bring you some.

The next weekend Pete brought some sheep stuff and
spread it around the wilty plants. Work it around and into
the ground, he said, but it'll be till next year that it will be
better. He brought another pickup load later on.

Ida and Bill went down to Laguna too, to the reservation,
and they met Pete and Mary's kids. Ida admired their small
garden. Slick was visiting on leave and he came with them.
He had re-upped, had a brand new Spec-5 patch on his
shoulder, and he had bought a motorcycle. He was on his
way to another tour.

I wish he hadn't done that, Bill said. Folks at home are worried too. Good thing your boys aren't old enough.

In the yard, the kids, including Slick, were playing catch with a softball. He wasn't much older than Pete and Mary's oldest. Slick had bright and playful eyes, handsome, and Bill was right to be proud of his kid brother.

I'm gonna make sure that young jack-off goes to college after the damn Army, Bill said.

After that, they'd visit each other. Ida would come help Mary with her garden. A couple times, the kids went to stay with Ida when Bill worked graveyard or swing because she didn't like to be alone. The kids liked that too, staying in town or what there was of it at the edge of Milan at the mobile home amid others sitting on the hard clay ground. The clay had come around to being workable with the sheep stuff in it. Ida planted radishes and lettuce and carrots and corn, even tomatoes and chili, and she was so proud of her growing plants that summer.

One afternoon, up at Section 17, Bill got a message from the foreman to call Ida. They were underground replacing wire and he had to take the lift up. He called from the pay phone outside the mine office.

Pete held the lift for him and when he came back Bill said, I gotta get my lunch pail and go home.

Something wrong, Bill? Pete asked. You okay?

Yeah, Bill said, something happened to Slick. The folks called from Claremore.

Hope it's not serious, Pete said.

On the way home after shift, Pete stopped at Bill and Ida's. Ida answered the door and showed him in. Bill was sitting on the couch. He had a fifth of Heaven Hill halfway empty.

Pete, Bill said, Slick's gone. No more Slick. Got killed by stepping on a mine, an American mine—isn't that the shits, Pete? Dammit, Pete, just look at that kid.

He pointed at the photo on the TV stand.

Pete didn't say anything at first and then he said, *Aamoo o dyumuu.* And he put his arm around Bill's shoulders.

Bill poured him some Heaven Hill and Ida told him they were leaving for Claremore the next morning as soon as they could pack and the bank opened.

Should get there by evening, she said. And then Pete left.

When Pete got home, he told Mary what had happened.

Tomorrow morning on your way to work, drop me off there. I want to see Ida, Mary said.

You can go ahead and drive me to work and take the truck, Pete said.

That night they sat at the kitchen table with the kids and tied feathers and scraped cedar sticks and closed them in a cornhusk with cotton, beads, and tobacco. The next morning, Mary and Pete went by the mobile home park. Bill and Ida were loading the last of their luggage into their car.

After greetings and solaces, Mary said, We brought you some things. She gave Ida a loaf of Laguna bread. For your lunch, she said, and Ida put it in the ice chest.

Pete took a white corn ear and the cornhusk bundle out of a paper bag he carried, and he showed them to Bill. He said, This is just a corn, Bill, Indian corn. The people call it Kasheshi. Just a dried ear of corn. You can take it with you, or you can keep it here. You can plant it. It's to know that life will keep on, your life will keep on. Just like Slick will be planted again. He'll be like that, like seed planted, like corn seed, the Indian corn. But you and Ida, your life will grow on.

Pete put the corn ear back into the bag and then he held out the husk bundle. He said, I guess I don't remember some of what is done, Bill. Indian words, songs for it, what it all is, even how this is made just a certain way, but I know that it is important to do this. You take this too but you don't keep it.

It's just for Slick, for his travel from this life among us to another place of being. You and Ida are not Indian, but it doesn't make any difference. It's for all of us, this kind of way, with corn and this, Bill. You take these sticks and feathers and you put them somewhere you think you should, someplace important that you think might be good, maybe to change life in a good way, that you think Slick would be helping us with.

You take it now, Pete said, and I know it may not sound easy to do but don't worry yourself too much. Slick is okay now, he'll be helping us, and you'll be fine too.

Pete put the paper bag in Bill's hand, and they all shook hands and hugged and Mary drove Pete on to Section 17.

After they left, Bill went inside their trailer home and took out the corn. He looked at it for a while, thinking, Just corn, just Indian corn, just your life to go on, Ida and you. And then he put the corn by the photo, by Slick on the TV stand. And then he wondered about the husk bundle. He couldn't figure it out. He couldn't figure it out. He'd grown up in Claremore all his life, Indians living all around him, folks and some schoolteachers said so, Cherokees in the Ozark hills, Creeks over to Muskogee, but Mary and Pete were the first Indians he'd ever known.

He held the bundle in his hand, thinking, and then he decided not to take it to Oklahoma and put it in the cupboard. They locked up their mobile home and left.

Bill and Ida returned to Milan a week later. Most of the folks had been at the funeral and everything had gone alright. The folks were upset a whole lot but there wasn't much else to do except comfort them. Some of the other folks said that someone had to make the sacrifice for freedom of democracy and all that and that's what Slick had died of, for. He's done his duty for America, look at how much the past folks had to put up with, living a hard life, fighting off Indians to build homes on new land so we could live the way we are right now, advanced and safe from peril like the Tuls' *Tribune* said the other day Sunday, that's what Slick died for, just like past folks.

That's what a couple relatives had advised and Bill tried to say what was bothering him, that the mine that Slick had stepped on was American and that the fact he was in a dangerous place was because he was in an army that was American, and it didn't seem to be the same thing as what they were saying about past folks fighting Indians for democracy and it didn't seem right somehow.

But nobody really heard him; they just asked him about his job with Kerr-McGee, told him the company had built itself another building in Tulsa, Kerr's gonna screw those folks in New Mexico just like he has folks here being Senator. Ida and Bill visited for a while, comforted his folks for a while, and then they left for Milan.

By the time, they got back to their mobile home, Bill knew what he was going to do with the bundle of sticks and feathers. He'd been thinking about it all the way on I-40 from Oklahoma City, running it through his mind, what Slick had died of. Well, because of the bomb, stepping on the wrong place, being in a dangerous place, but something else. The reason was something else and though he wasn't completely sure about it yet he felt he was beginning to know. And he knew what he was going to do with the bundle in the cupboard.

The next morning, he put it in his lunch pail and went to work, reporting to the mine office first. He changed into his work clothes and put on his yellow slicker because they were going down that morning and he was glad for that for once. He took that paper bag out of his pail and put it in his overall pocket. After they went down he said he was going to go and check some cable and he made his way to the far end of a drift that had been mined out. He stopped and put the bundle down behind a slab of rock.

He didn't know what to do next and then he thought of what Pete had said. Say something about it.

Well, Bill thought, Slick, you was a good boy, kind of wild, but good. I got this here Indian thing, feathers and sticks, and at home, at home we got the corn by your picture, and Pete and Mary said to do this because it's important even if we're Okies and not Indians who do this. It's for your travel they said and to help us with our life here from where you are at now and they said to maybe change things in a good way for a good life and God knows us Okies always wanted that. Well, I'm gonna leave this here by the rock. Pete said he didn't know exactly all the right Indian things to do anymore but somehow I believe they're more righter than we've ever been led to believe. And now I'm trying too.

So you help us now, Slick. We need it, all the help we can get, even if it's just so much as holding up the roof of this mine that the damn company don't put enough timbers and bolts in, Bill said. And then he stepped back and left.

When Bill got home that evening, he told Ida what he had done, and she said, Next spring I'm gonna plant that Indian corn and Slick, if he's gonna help hold up the roof of Section 17, better be able to help with breaking up that clay dirt too.

Bill smiled and chuckled at Ida's remark. Nodding his head, he agreed.

The Moths

HELENA MARÍA VIRAMONTES

I was fourteen years old when Abuelita requested my help.
And it seemed only fair. Abuelita had pulled me through the
rages of scarlet fever by placing, removing, and replacing
potato slices on my temples; she had seen me through several
whippings, an arm broken by a dare jump off Tío Enrique's
toolshed, puberty, and my first lie. Really, I told Amá, it was
only fair.

Not that I was her favorite granddaughter or anything
special. I wasn't even pretty or nice like my older sisters and I
just couldn't do the girl things they could do. My hands were
too big to handle the fineries of crocheting or embroidery and
I always pricked my fingers or knotted my colored threads
time and time again while my sisters laughed and called me
Bull Hands with their cute waterlike voices. So I began keeping a piece of jagged brick in my sock to bash my sisters or
anyone who called me Bull Hands. Once, while we all sat in
the bedroom, I hit Teresa on the forehead, right above her
eyebrow, and she ran to Amá with her mouth open, her hand
over her eye while blood seeped between her fingers. I was
used to the whippings by then.

I wasn't respectful either. I even went so far as to doubt the
power of Abuelita's slices, the slices she said absorbed my
fever. "You're still alive, aren't you?" Abuelita snapped back,
her pasty gray eye beaming at me and burning holes in my
suspicions. Regretful that I had let secret questions drop out
of my mouth, I couldn't look into her eyes. My hands began

to fan out, grow like a liar's nose until they hung by my side like low weights. Abuelita made a balm out of dried moth wings and Vicks and rubbed my hands, shaped them back to size, and it was the strangest feeling. Like bones melting. Like sun shining through the darkness of your eyelids. I didn't mind helping Abuelita after that, so Amá would always send me over to her.

In the early afternoon Amá would push her hair back, hand me my sweater and shoes, and tell me to go to Mama Luna's. This was to avoid another fight and another whipping, I knew. I would deliver one last direct shot on Marisela's arm and jump out of our house, the slam of the screen door burying her cries of anger, and I'd gladly go help Abuelita plant her wild lilies or jasmine or heliotrope or cilantro or hierbabuena in red Hills Brothers coffee cans. Abuelita would wait for me at the top step of her porch, holding a hammer and nail and empty coffee cans. And although we hardly spoke, hardly looked at each other as we worked over root transplants, I always felt her gray eye on me. It made me feel, in a strange sort of way, safe and guarded and not alone. Like God was supposed to make you feel.

On Abuelita's porch, I would puncture holes in the bottom of the coffee cans with a nail and a precise hit of a hammer. This completed, my job was to fill them with red clay mud from beneath her rosebushes, packing it softly, then making a perfect hole, four fingers round, to nest a sprouting avocado pit, or the spidery sweet potatoes that Abuelita rooted in mayonnaise jars with toothpicks and daily water, or prickly chayotes that produced vines that twisted and wound all over her porch pillars, crawling to the roof, up and over the roof, and down the other side, making her small brick house look like it was cradled within the vines that grew pear-shaped squashes ready for the pick, ready to be steamed with onions and cheese and butter. The roots would burst out of the rusted coffee cans and search for a place to connect. I would then feed the seedlings with water.

But this was a different kind of help, Amá said, because Abuelita was dying. Looking into her gray eye, then into her brown one, the doctor said it was just a matter of days. And so it seemed only fair that these hands she had melted and formed found use in rubbing her caving body with alcohol and marijuana, rubbing her arms and legs, turning her face to the window so that she could watch the bird-of-paradise blooming or smell the scent of clove in the air. I toweled her face frequently and held her hand for hours. Her gray wiry hair hung over the mattress. For as long as I could remember, she'd kept her long hair in braids. Her mouth was vacant, and when she slept her eyelids never closed all the way. Up close, you could see her gray eye beaming out the window, staring hard as if to remember everything. I never kissed her. I left the window open when I went to the market.

Across the street from Jay's Market there was a chapel. I never knew its denomination, but I went in just the same to search for candles. There were none, so I sat down on one of the pews. After I cleaned my fingernails, I looked up at the high ceiling. I had forgotten the vastness of these places, the coolness of the marble pillars and the frozen statues with blank eyes. I was alone. I knew why I had never returned.

That was one of Apá's biggest complaints. He would pound his hands on the table, rocking the sugar dish or spilling a cup of coffee, and scream that if I didn't go to mass every Sunday to save my goddamn sinning soul, then I had no reason to go out of the house, period. *Punto final.* He would grab my arm and dig his nails into me to make sure I understood the importance of catechism. Did he make himself clear? Then he strategically directed his anger at Amá for her lousy ways of bringing up daughters, being disrespectful and unbelieving, and my older sisters would pull me aside and tell me if I didn't get to mass right this minute, they were all going to kick the holy shit out of me. Why am I so selfish? Can't you see what it's doing to Amá, you idiot? So I would wash my feet and stuff them in my black Easter shoes that shone with Vaseline, grab a missal and veil, and wave good-bye to Amá.

I would walk slowly down Lorena to First to Evergreen, counting the cracks on the cement. On Evergreen I would turn left and walk to Abuelita's. I liked her porch because it was shielded by the vines of the chayotes and I could get a good look at the people and car traffic on Evergreen without them knowing. I would jump up the porch steps, knock on the screen door as I wiped my feet, and call, Abuelita? *Mi* Abuelita? As I opened the door and stuck my head in, I would catch the gagging scent of toasting chile on the *placa.* When I entered the *sala,* she would greet me from the kitchen, wringing her hands in her apron. I'd sit at the corner of the table to keep from being in her way. The chiles made my eyes water. Am I crying? No, Mama Luna, I'm sure not crying. I don't like going to mass, but my eyes watered any-way, the tears dropping on the tablecloth like candle wax. Abuelita lifted the burnt chiles from the fire and sprinkled water on them until the skins began to separate. Placing them in front of me, she turned to check the menudo. I peeled the skins off and put the flimsy, limp-looking green and yellow chiles in the *molcajete* and began to crush and crush and twist and crush the heart out of the tomato, the clove of garlic, the stupid chiles that made me cry, crushed them until they turned into liquid under my bull hand. With a wooden spoon, I scraped hard to destroy the guilt, and my tears were gone. I put the bowl of chile next to a vase filled with freshly cut roses. Abuelita touched my hand and pointed to the bowl of menudo that steamed in front of me. I spooned some chile into the menudo and rolled a corn tortilla thin with the palms of my hands. As I ate, a fine Sunday breeze entered the kitchen and a rose petal calmly feathered down to the table.

I left the chapel without blessing myself and walked to Jay's. Most of the time Jay didn't have much of anything. The tomatoes were always soft and the cans of Campbell soup had rust spots on them. There was dust on the tops of cereal boxes. I picked up what I needed: rubbing alcohol, five cans of chicken broth, a big bottle of Pine-Sol. At first Jay got mad because I thought I had forgotten the money. But it was there all the time, in my back pocket.

When I returned from the market, I heard Amá crying in Abuelita's kitchen. She looked up at me with puffy eyes. I placed the bags of groceries on the table and began putting the cans of soup away. Amá sobbed quietly. I never kissed her. After a while, I patted her on the back for comfort. Finally: *"¿Y mi Amá?"* she asked in a whisper, then choked again and cried into her apron.

Abuelita fell off the bed twice yesterday, I said, knowing that I shouldn't have said it and wondering why I wanted to say it because it only made Amá cry harder. I guess I became angry and just so tired of the quarrels and beatings and unanswered prayers and my hands just there hanging helplessly by my side. Amá looked at me again, confused, angry, and her eyes were filled with sorrow. I went outside and sat on the porch swing and watched the people pass. I sat there until she left. I dozed off repeating the words to myself like rosary prayers: when do you stop giving when do you start giving when do you . . . and when my hands fell from my lap, I awoke to catch them. The sun was setting, an orange glow, and I knew Abuelita was hungry.

There comes a time when the sun is defiant. Just about the time when moods change, inevitable seasons of a day, transitions from one color to another, that hour or minute or second when the sun is finally defeated, finally sinks into the realization that it cannot, with all its power to heal or burn, exist forever, there comes an illumination where the sun and earth meet, a final burst of burning red-orange fury reminding us that although endings are inevitable, they are necessary for rebirths, and when that time came, just when I switched on the light in the kitchen to open Abuelita's can of soup, it was probably then that she died.

The room smelled of Pine-Sol and vomit, and Abuelita had defecated the remains of her cancerous stomach. She had turned to the window and tried to speak, but her mouth remained open and speechless. I heard you, Abuelita, I said, stroking her cheek, I heard you. I opened the windows of the house and let the soup simmer and overboil on the stove. I turned the stove off and poured the soup down the sink. From the cabinet I got a tin basin, filled it with lukewarm water, and carried it carefully to the room. I went to the linen closet and took out some modest bleached-white towels. With the sacredness of a priest preparing his vestments, I unfolded the towels one by one on my shoulders. I removed the sheets and blankets from her bed and peeled off her thick flannel nightgown. I toweled her puzzled face, stretching out the wrinkles, removing the coils of her neck, toweled her shoulders and breasts. Then I changed the water. I returned to towel the creases of her stretch-marked stomach, her sporadic vaginal hairs, and her sagging thighs. I removed the lint from between her toes and noticed a mapped birthmark on the fold of her buttock. The scars on her back, which were as thin as the lifelines on the palms of her hands, made me realize how little I really knew of Abuelita. I covered her with a thin blanket and went into the bathroom. I washed my hands, turned on the tub faucets, and watched the water pour into the tub with vitality and steam. When it was full, I turned off the water and undressed. Then, I went to get Abuelita.

She was not as heavy as I thought, and when I carried her in my arms, her body fell into a V, and yet my legs were tired, shaky, and I felt as if the distance between the bedroom and bathroom was miles and years away. Amá, where are you?

I stepped into the bathtub, one leg first, then the other. I bent my knees to descend into the water, slowly, so I wouldn't scald her skin. There, there, Abuelita, I said, cradling her, smoothing her as we descended, I heard you. Her hair fell back and spread across the water like eagle's wings. The water in the tub overflowed and poured onto the tile of the floor. Then the moths came. Small, gray ones that came from her soul and out through her mouth fluttering to light, circling the single dull light bulb of the bathroom. Dying is lonely and I wanted to go to where the moths were, stay with her and plant chayotes whose vines would crawl up her fingers and into the clouds; I wanted to rest my head on her chest with her stroking my hair, telling me about the moths that lay within the soul and slowly eat the spirit up; I wanted to return to the waters of the womb with her so that we would never be alone again. I wanted. I wanted my Amá. I removed a few strands of hair from Abuelita's face and held her small light head within the hollow of my neck. The bathroom was filled with moths, and for the first time in a long time I cried, rocking us, crying for her, for me, for Amá, the sobs emerging from the depths of anguish, the misery of feeling half born, sobbing until finally the sobs rippled into circles and circles of sadness and relief. There, there, I said to Abuelita, rocking us gently, there, there.

Talking to the Dead

SYLVIA A. WATANABE

We spoke of her in whispers as Aunty Talking to the Dead,
the half-Hawaiian kahuna lady. But whenever there was a
death in the village, she was the first to be sent for—the priest
came second. For it was she who understood the wholeness
of things—the significance of directions and colors. Prayers
to appease the hungry ghosts. Elixirs for grief. Most times,
she'd be out on her front porch, already waiting—her boy,
Clinton, standing behind with her basket of spells—when
the messenger arrived. People said she could smell a death
from clear on the other side of the island, even as the dying
person breathed his last. And if she fixed her eyes on you and
named a day, you were already as good as six feet under.

I went to work as her apprentice when I was eighteen.
That was in '48—the year Clinton graduated from mortician
school on the G.I. Bill. It was the talk for weeks—how he returned to open the Paradise Mortuary in the very heart of the
village and brought the scientific spirit of free enterprise to
the doorstep of the hereafter. I remember the advertisements
for the Grand Opening—promising to modernize the funeral trade with Lifelike Artistic Techniques and Stringent
Standards of Sanitation. The old woman, who had waited
out the war for her son's return, stoically took his defection in
stride and began looking for someone else to help out with
her business.

At the time, I didn't have many prospects—more schooling didn't interest me, and my mother's attempts at marrying

me off inevitably failed when I stood to shake hands with a prospective bridegroom and ended up towering a foot above him. "It's bad enough she has the face of a horse," I heard one of them complain.

My mother dressed me in navy blue, on the theory that dark colors make everything look smaller: "Yuri, sit down," she'd hiss, tugging at my skirt as the decisive moment approached. I'd nod, sip my tea, smile through the introductions and small talk, till the time came for sealing the bargain with handshakes all around. Then, nothing on earth could keep me from getting to my feet. The go-between finally suggested that I consider taking up a trade. "After all, marriage isn't for everyone," she said. My mother said that that was a fact which remained to be proven, but meanwhile, it wouldn't hurt if I took in sewing or learned to cut hair. I made up my mind to apprentice myself to Aunty Talking to the Dead.

The old woman's house was on the hill behind the village, just off the road to Chicken Fight Camp. She lived in an old plantation worker's bungalow with peeling green and white paint and a large, well-tended garden out front—mostly of flowering bushes and strong-smelling herbs.

"Aren't you a big one," a voice behind me said.

I started, then turned. It was the first time I had ever seen the old woman up close.

"Hello, uh, Mrs., Mrs., Dead," I stammered.

She was little—way under five feet—and wrinkled, and everything about her seemed the same color—her skin, her lips, her dress—everything just a slightly different shade of the same brown-gray, except her hair, which was absolutely white, and her tiny eyes, which glinted like metal. For a minute, those eyes looked me up and down.

"Here," she said finally, thrusting an empty rice sack into my hands. "For collecting salt." And she started down the road to the beach.

In the next few months, we walked every inch of the hills and beaches around the village.

"This is *a'ali'i* to bring sleep—it must be dried in the shade on a hot day." Aunty was always three steps ahead, chanting, while I struggled behind, laden with strips of bark and leafy twigs, my head buzzing with names.

"This is *awa* for every kind of grief, and *uhaloa* with the deep roots—if you are like that, death cannot easily take you." Her voice came from the stones, the trees, and the earth.

"This is where you gather salt to preserve a corpse," I hear her still. "This is where you cut to insert the salt." Her words have marked the places on my body, one by one.

That whole first year, not a single day passed when I didn't think of quitting. I tried to figure out a way of moving back home without making it seem like I was admitting anything.

"You know what people are saying, don't you?" my mother said, lifting the lid of the bamboo steamer and setting a tray of freshly steamed meat buns on the already crowded table before me. It was one of my few visits home since my apprenticeship—though I'd never been more than a couple of miles away—and she had stayed up the whole night before, cooking. She'd prepared a canned ham with yellow sweet potatoes, wing beans with pork, sweet and sour mustard cabbage, fresh raw yellow-fin, pickled eggplant, and rice with red beans. I had not seen so much food since the night she'd tried to persuade her younger brother, my Uncle Mongoose, not to volunteer for the army. He'd gone anyway, and on the last day of training, just before he was shipped to Italy, he shot himself in the head when he was cleaning his gun. "I always knew that boy would come to no good," was all Mama said when she heard the news.

"What do you mean you can't eat another bite," she fussed now. "Look at you, nothing but a bag of bones."

I allowed myself to be persuaded to another helping, though I'd lost my appetite.

The truth was, there didn't seem to be much of a future in my apprenticeship. In eleven and a half months, I had memorized most of the minor rituals of mourning and learned to identify a couple of dozen herbs and all their medicinal uses, but I had not seen—much less gotten to practice on—a single honest-to-goodness corpse.

"People live longer these days," Aunty claimed.

But I knew it was because everyone—even from villages across the bay—had begun taking their business to the Paradise Mortuary. The single event which had established Clinton's monopoly once and for all had been the untimely death of old Mrs. Pomadour, the plantation owner's mother-in-law, who'd choked on a fishbone during a fundraising luncheon of the Famine Relief Society. Clinton had been chosen to be in charge of the funeral. He'd taken to wearing three-piece suits—even during the humid Kona season—as a symbol of his new respectability, and had recently been nominated as a Republican candidate to run for the village council.

"So, what are people saying, Mama?" I asked, finally pushing my plate away.

This was the cue she had been waiting for. "They're saying that That Woman has gotten herself a new donkey"; she paused dramatically.

I began remembering things about being in my mother's house. The navy blue dresses. The humiliating weekly tea ceremony lessons at the Buddhist Temple.

"Give up this foolishness," she wheedled. "Mrs. Koyama tells me the Barber Shop Lady is looking for help."

"I think I'll stay right where I am," I said.

My mother drew herself up. "Here, have another meat bun," she said, jabbing one through the center with her serving fork and lifting it onto my plate.

A few weeks later, Aunty and I were called just outside the village to perform a laying-out. It was early afternoon when Sheriff Kanoi came by to tell us that the body of Mustard Hayashi, the eldest of the Hayashi boys, had just been pulled from an irrigation ditch by a team of field workers. He had apparently fallen in the night before, stone drunk, on his way home from Hula Rose's Dance Emporium.

I began hurrying around, assembling Aunty's tools and bottles of potions, and checking that everything was in working order, but the old woman didn't turn a hair; she just sat calmly rocking back and forth and puffing on her skinny, long-stemmed pipe.

"Yuri, you stop that rattling around back there!" she snapped, then turned to the sheriff. "My son Clinton could probably handle this. Why don't you ask him?"

Sheriff Kanoi hesitated. "This looks like a tough case that's going to need some real expertise."

"Mmmm." The old woman stopped rocking. "It's true, it was a bad death," she mused.

"Very bad," the sheriff agreed.

"The spirit is going to require some talking to."

"Besides, the family asked special for you," he said.

No doubt because they didn't have any other choice, I thought. That morning, I'd run into Chinky Malloy, the assistant mortician at the Paradise, so I happened to know that Clinton was at a morticians' conference in the city and wouldn't be back for several days. But I didn't say a word.

ැ⃝ත

Mustard's remains had been laid out on a green Formica table in the kitchen. It was the only room in the house with a door that faced north. Aunty claimed that you should always choose a north-facing room for a laying-out so the spirit could find its way home to the land of the dead without getting lost.

Mustard's mother was leaning over his corpse, wailing, and her husband stood behind her, looking white-faced, and absently patting her on the back. The tiny kitchen was jammed with sobbing, nose-blowing relatives and neighbors. The air was thick with the smells of grief—perspiration, ladies' cologne, last night's cooking, and the faintest whiff of putrefying flesh. Aunty gripped me by the wrist and pushed her way to the front. The air pressed close—like someone's hot, wet breath on my face. My head reeled, and the room broke apart into dots of color. From far away I heard somebody say, "It's Aunty Talking to the Dead."

"Make room, make room," another voice called.

I looked down at Mustard, lying on the table in front of me—his eyes half open in that swollen, purple face. The smell was much stronger close up, and there were flies everywhere.

"We're going to have to get rid of some of this bloat," Aunty said, thrusting a metal object into my hand.

People were leaving the room.

She went around to the other side of the table. "I'll start here," she said. "You work over there. Do just like I told you."

I nodded. This was the long-awaited moment. My moment. But it was already the beginning of the end. My knees buckled and everything went dark.

Aunty performed the laying-out alone and never mentioned the episode again. But it was the talk of the village for weeks—how Yuri Shimabukuro, assistant to Aunty Talking to the Dead, passed out under the Hayashis' kitchen table and had to be tended by the grief-stricken mother of the dead boy.

My mother took to catching the bus to the plantation store three villages away whenever she needed to stock up on necessaries. "You're my daughter—how could I *not* be on your side?" was the way she put it, but the air buzzed with her unspoken recriminations. And whenever I went into the village, I was aware of the sly laughter behind my back, and Chinky Malloy smirking at me from behind the shutters of the Paradise Mortuary.

"She's giving the business a bad name," Clinton said, carefully removing his jacket and draping it across the back of the rickety wooden chair. He dusted the seat, looked at his hand with distaste before wiping it off on his handkerchief, then drew up the legs of his trousers, and sat.

Aunty picked up her pipe from the smoking tray next to her rocker and filled the tiny brass bowl from a pouch of Bull Durham. "I'm glad you found time to drop by," she said. "You still going out with that skinny white girl?"

"You mean Marsha?" Clinton sounded defensive. "Sure, I see her sometimes. But I didn't come here to talk about that." He glanced over at where I was sitting on the sofa. "You think we could have some privacy?"

Aunty lit her pipe and puffed. "There's nobody here but us. . . . Yuri's my right hand. Couldn't do without her."

"The Hayashis probably have their own opinion about that."

Aunty waved her hand in dismissal. "There's no pleasing some people. Yuri's just young; she'll learn." She reached over and patted me on the knee, then looked him straight in the face. "Like we all did."

Clinton turned red. "Damn it, Mama! You're making yourself a laughingstock!" His voice became soft, persuasive.

"Look, you've worked hard all your life, but now, I've got my business—it'll be a while before I'm really on my feet—but you don't have to do this," he gestured around the room. "I'll help you out. You'll see. I'm only thinking about you."

"About the election to village council, you mean!" I burst out.

Aunty was unperturbed. "You considering going into politics, son?"

"Mama, wake up!" Clinton hollered, like he'd wanted to all along. "The old spirits have had it. We're part of progress now, and the world is going to roll right over us and keep on rolling, unless we get out there and grab our share."

His words rained down like stones, shattering the air around us.

For a long time after he left, Aunty sat in her rocking chair next to the window, rocking and smoking, without saying a word, just rocking and smoking, as the afternoon shadows flickered beneath the trees and turned to night.

Then, she began to sing—quietly, at first, but very sure. She sang the naming chants and the healing chants. She sang the stones, and trees, and stars back into their rightful places. Louder and louder she sang—making whole what had been broken.

Everything changed for me after Clinton's visit. I stopped going into the village and began spending all my time with Aunty Talking to the Dead. I followed her everywhere, carried her loads without complaint, memorized remedies and mixed potions. I wanted to know what *she* knew; I wanted to make what had happened at the Hayashis' go away. Not just in other people's minds. Not just because I'd become a laughingstock, like Clinton said. But because I knew that I *had* to redeem myself for that one thing, or my moment—the single instant of glory for which I had lived my entire life—would be snatched beyond my reach forever.

Meanwhile, there were other layings-out. The kitemaker who hanged himself. The crippled boy from Chicken Fight Camp. The Vagrant. The Blindman. The Blindman's dog.

"Do like I told you," Aunty would say before each one. Then, "Give it time," when it was done.

But it was like living the same nightmare over and over—just one look at a body and I was done for. For twenty-five years, people in the village joked about my "indisposition." Last year, when my mother died, her funeral was held at the Paradise Mortuary. I stood outside on the cement walk for a long time, but never made it through the door. Little by little, I had given up hope that my moment would ever arrive.

Then, one week ago, Aunty caught a chill after spending all morning out in the rain, gathering *awa* from the garden. The chill developed into a fever, and for the first time since I'd known her, she took to her bed. I nursed her with the remedies she'd taught me—sweat baths, eucalyptus steam, tea made from *ko'oko'olau*—but the fever worsened. Her breathing became labored, and she grew weaker. My few hours of sleep were filled with bad dreams. In desperation, aware of my betrayal, I finally walked to a house up the road and telephoned for an ambulance.

"I'm sorry, Aunty," I kept saying, as the flashing red light swept across the porch. The attendants had her on a stretcher and were carrying her out the front door.

She reached up and grasped my arm, her grip still strong. "You'll do okay, Yuri," the old woman whispered hoarsely, and squeezed. "Clinton used to get so scared, he messed his pants." She chuckled, then began to cough. One of the attendants put an oxygen mask over her face. "Hush," he said. "There'll be plenty of time for talking later."

ୠଡ଼

The day of Aunty's wake, workmen were repaving the front walk and had blocked off the main entrance to the Paradise Mortuary. They had dug up the old concrete tiles and carted them away. They'd left a mound of gravel on the grass, stacked some bags of concrete next to it, and covered them with black tarps. There was an empty wheelbarrow parked on the other side of the gravel mound. The entire front lawn was roped off and a sign put up which said, "Please use the back entrance. We are making improvements in Paradise. The Management."

My stomach was beginning to play tricks, and I was feeling a little dizzy. The old panic was mingled with an uneasiness which had not left me ever since I had decided to call the ambulance. I kept thinking maybe I shouldn't have called it since she had gone and died anyway. Or maybe I should have called it sooner. I almost turned back, but I thought of what Aunty had told me about Clinton and pressed ahead. Numbly, I followed the two women in front of me through the garden along the side of the building, around to the back.

"So, old Aunty Talking to the Dead has finally passed on," one of them, whom I recognized as the Dancing School Teacher, said. She was with Pearlie Mukai, an old classmate of mine from high school. Pearlie had gone years ago to live in the city, but still returned to the village to visit her mother.

I was having difficulty seeing—it was getting dark, and my head was spinning so.

"How old do you suppose she was?" Pearlie asked.

"Gosh, even when we were kids it seemed like she was at least a hundred."

" 'The Undead,' my brother used to call her."

Pearlie laughed. "When we misbehaved," the Dancing School Teacher said, "my mother used to threaten to send us to Aunty Talking to the Dead. She'd be giving us the licking of our lives and hollering, 'This is gonna seem like nothing, then!' "

Aunty had been laid out in one of the rooms along the side of the house. The heavy, wine-colored drapes had been drawn across the windows, and all the wall lamps turned very low, so it was darker in the room than it had been outside.

Pearlie and the Dancing School Teacher moved off into the front row. I headed for the back.

There were about thirty of us at the wake, mostly from the old days—those who had grown up on stories about Aunty, or who remembered her from before the Paradise Mortuary.

People were getting up and filing past the casket. For a moment, I felt faint again, but I remembered about Clinton (how self-assured and prosperous he looked standing at the door, accepting condolences!), and I got into line. The Dancing School Teacher and Pearlie slipped in front of me.

I drew nearer and nearer to the casket. I hugged my sweater close. The room was air-conditioned and smelled of floor disinfectant and roses. Soft music came from speakers mounted on the walls.

Now there were just four people ahead. Now three. I looked down on the floor, and I thought I would faint.

Then Pearlie Mukai shrieked, "Her eyes!"

People behind me began to murmur.

"What, whose eyes?" the Dancing School Teacher demanded.

Pearlie pointed to the body in the casket.

The Dancing School Teacher peered down and cried, "My God, they're open!"

My heart turned to ice.

"What?" voices behind me were asking. "What about her eyes?"

"She said they're open," someone said.

"Aunty Talking to the Dead's eyes are open," someone else said.

Now Clinton was hurrying over.

"That's because she's not dead," still another voice put in.

Clinton looked into the coffin, and his face turned white. He turned quickly around again, and waved to his assistants across the room.

"I've heard about cases like this," someone was saying. "It's because she's looking for someone."

"I've heard that, too! The old woman is trying to tell us something."

I was the only one there who knew. Aunty was talking to *me*. I clasped my hands together, hard, but they wouldn't stop shaking.

People began leaving the line. Others pressed in, trying to get a better look at the body, but a couple of Clinton's assistants had stationed themselves in front of the coffin, preventing anyone from getting too close. They had shut the lid, and Chinky Malloy was directing people out of the room.

"I'd like to take this opportunity to thank you all for coming here this evening," Clinton was saying. "I hope you will join us at the reception down the hall."

While everyone was eating, I stole back into the parlor and quietly—ever so quietly—went up to the casket, lifted the lid, and looked in.

At first, I thought they had switched bodies on me and exchanged Aunty for some powdered and painted old grandmother, all pink and white, in a pink dress, and clutching a white rose to her chest. But the pennies had fallen from her eyes—and there they were. Open. Aunty's eyes staring up at me.

Then I knew. In that instant, I stopped trembling. This

was *it:* my moment had arrived. Aunty Talking to the Dead had come awake to bear me witness.

I walked through the deserted front rooms of the mortuary and out the front door. It was night. I got the wheelbarrow, loaded it with one of the tarps covering the bags of cement, and wheeled it back to the room where Aunty was. It squeaked terribly, and I stopped often to make sure no one had heard me. From the back of the building came the clink of glassware and the buzz of voices. I had to work quickly—people would be leaving soon.

But this was the hardest part. Small as she was, it was very hard to lift her out of the coffin. She was horribly heavy, and unyielding as a bag of cement. It seemed like hours, but I finally got her out and wrapped her in the tarp. I loaded her in the tray of the wheelbarrow—most of her, anyway; there was nothing I could do about her feet sticking out the front end. Then, I wheeled her through the silent rooms of the mortuary, down the front lawn, across the village square, and up the road, home.

Now, in the dark, the old woman is singing.

I have washed her with my own hands and worked the salt into the hollows of her body. I have dressed her in white and laid her in flowers.

Aunty, here are the beads you like to wear. Your favorite cakes. A quilt to keep away the chill. Here is *noui* for the heart and *awa* for every kind of grief.

Down the road a dog howls, and the sound of hammering echoes through the still air. "Looks like a burying tomorrow," the sleepers murmur, turning in their warm beds.

I bind the sandals to her feet and put the torch to the pyre.

The sky turns to light. The smoke climbs. Her ashes scatter, filling the wind.

And she sings, she sings, she sings.

Contributors ↝

Sherman Alexie is a Spokane/Coeur d'Alene from Wellpinit, Washington. He is the author of two novels, *Indian Killer* and *Reservation Blues*. He adapted his story collection *The Lone Ranger and Tonto Fistfight in Heaven* into the 1998 Miramax film *Smoke Signals*. He is at work on *The Bones of Al Capone*, a novel.

Laura Boss is founder and editor of *LIPS*. She was a first-place winner of the Poetry Society of America's Gordon Barber Award and a finalist for the Alice Fay di Castagnola Award. Her books include the Alta Award–winning *On the Edge of the Hudson* and *Reports from the Front*.

Mary Bucci Bush is an associate professor of creative writing at California State University Los Angeles. Her stories have appeared in *Ploughshares, Story*, and *Missouri Review*. William Morrow & Co. published her story collection, *A Place of Light*, in 1990.

Bebe Moore Campbell is the best-selling author of *Singing in the Comeback Choir, Brothers and Sisters*, and *Your Blues Ain't Like Mine*, which won the NAACP Image Award for fiction. Her memoir is entitled *Sweet Summer: Growing Up With and Without My Dad*.

Nash Candelaria is the author of a collection of short stories, *The Day the Cisco Kid Shot John Wayne*. He won an American Book Award for his novel *Not by the Sword*. His other novels include *Memories of the Alhambra* and *Inheritance of Strangers*.

Veronica Chambers, the author of *Mama's Girl*, is a former editor at *The New York Times Magazine* and *Premiere*. Currently she is a contributing editor at *Glamour*. She is coauthor with John Singleton of the film *Poetic Justice*.

Frank Chin is the author of two plays, *Chickencoop Chinaman* and *The Year of the Dragon*. He has also written a book of short stories, *The Chinaman Pacific & Frisco R. R. Co.* and two novels, *Donald Duk* and *Gunga-Din Highway*.

Sandra Cisneros was born in 1954 in Chicago. In 1985, her first work of fiction, *The House on Mango Street*, was awarded the Before Columbus Foundation American Book Award. Her other books include *Woman Hollering Creek and Other Stories* and *My Wicked Wicked Ways*, poems.

Judith Ortiz Cofer was born in Puerto Rico and grew up in Paterson, New Jersey. Her books include *The Latin Deli: Prose & Poetry, The Line of the Sun* (a novel), and several volumes of poetry. Her collection of personal essays is entitled *Silent Dancing: A Partial Remembrance of a Puerto Rican Childhood*.

Enid Dame's fiction has appeared in *Confrontation, Fiction,* and *Sing Heavenly Muse!*, among other journals. She received a grant from the Puffin Foundation in 1997 to work on a novel. She is coeditor of *Home Planet News*.

Diane di Prima was born in Brooklyn, New York. An important writer of the Beat movement, she has lived in California for the past thirty years. She is the author of thirty-four books of poetry and prose. Her memoir, *Recollections of My Life as a Woman,* is forthcoming from Viking.

E. L. Doctorow was born in the Bronx during the Depression and now lives in a suburbs of New York City. He is the author of a collection of stories, *Lives of the Poets,* and several novels, including *The Book of Daniel, Ragtime*, and *World's Fair.*

Louise Erdrich was born in Minnesota and is of German-American and Chippewa descent. She has written two collections of poetry, *Jacklight* and *Baptism of Desire.* Her first novel, *Love Medicine*, won the National Book Critics Circle Award. Her other novels include *The Bingo Palace* and *Tracks*.

Fred L. Gardaphé is the author of *Moustache Pete Is Dead!* and *Dagoes Read: Tradition and the Italian/American Writer,* and the editor of *Italian-American Ways.* His critical study *Italian Signs, American Streets: The Evolution of Italian American Narrative* was published in Duke University's *New Americanists* series in 1996.

Joseph Geha is the author of *Through and Through: Toledo Stories* and has been awarded the Pushcart Prize. His fiction appears widely in literary publications and was selected for inclusion in the Permanent Collection, Arab American Archive, of the Smithsonian Institution. He teaches at Iowa State University.

Maria Mazziotti Gillan, born in Paterson, New Jersey, is director of the Poetry Center, Passaic County Community College, and editor of *Paterson Literary Review.* Her seven poetry books include *Things My Mother Said, Where I Come From: Selected Poems*, and *The Weather of Old Seasons.* She is at work on a memoir, *My Mother's Stoop.*

Diane Glancy was born in Kansas City, Missouri, to German-English and Cherokee parents. She is an associate professor of English at Macalester College in St. Paul, Minnesota, and the author of several volumes of poetry and prose. Her historical novel about the 1838 Trail of Tears, *Pushing the Bear*, was published in 1996.

Bruce A. Jacobs's first book of poems, *Speaking Through My Skin*, won the 1996 Naomi Long Madgett Poetry Award. His poems and prose have appeared in *African American Review* and *American Writing*. His nonfiction book, *Race Manners*, was published in 1999.

Gish Jen is the author of two novels, *Mona in the Promised Land* and *Typical American*. Her work has appeared in the *Atlantic Monthly*, *The New Yorker*, and *Best American Short Stories*, in 1998 and 1995.

Beena Kamlani works as an editor at a New York publishing house. She won a fiction grant from the Connecticut Commission on the Arts for her novel *Carry-On Luggage*, excerpts of which appear in this anthology and in *Identity Lessons: Contemporary Writing About Learning to Be American*. She is at work on *Desertion*, a new novel.

Tiffany Midge is an enrolled member of the Standing Rock Sioux. She is the author of *Outlaws, Renegades and Saints: Diary of a Mixed-Up Halfbreed*, the winner of the Diane Decorah Memorial Poetry Award.

Toni Morrison was born Chloe Anthony Wofford during the Depression in Lorain, Ohio. Her 1987 novel, *Beloved*, was awarded the Pulitzer Prize and in 1998 was adapted into a film. Her other novels include *Paradise, Song of Solomon, Sula*, and *The Bluest Eye*. She won the Nobel Prize for Literature in 1993.

Kathryn Nocerino is a poet, short story writer, and critic whose work has appeared in the United States and England. Her books of poetry include *Wax Lips* and *Death of the Plankton Bar & Grill*.

Naomi Shihab Nye was born in St. Louis of a Palestinian father and an American mother. Her poetry collections include *Yellow Glove* and *Hugging the Jukebox*, winner of the National Poetry Series Award. She is the coeditor of *I Feel a Little Jumpy Around You: A Book of Her Poems and His Poems Collected in Pairs*.

Simon J. Ortiz is the author of several volumes of poetry and *Fightin': New & Collected Stories*. He wrote the narrative for *Surviving Columbus*, a PBS documentary about the Pueblo people. He was born in 1941 at the Indian Hospital in Albuquerque, New Mexico, and raised in McCartys, a small village of Acoma Pueblo.

Darryl Pinckney is the author of *High Cotton*, winner of the *Los Angeles Times* Book Prize for Fiction. His work has appeared in *Granta* and the *New York Review of Books*.

Daniel Asa Rose is the O. Henry prize–winning author of *Flipping For It* (a novel) and *Small Family with Rooster* (stories). His essays, stories, reviews, and travel and humor pieces have appeared in *The New Yorker, Esquire,* and *Vanity Fair*, among others. He is working on *Hiding Places*, a memoir forthcoming from Simon & Schuster.

Liz Rosenberg is the author of two books of poetry, *The Fire Music* and *Children of Paradise*, and a novel. She has published more than a dozen picture books for children, and edited two anthologies of poetry for young readers, *The Invisible Ladder* and *Earth-Shattering Poems*. She teaches at State University of New York at Binghamton.

Roshni Rustomji has lived, studied, and worked in India, Pakistan, Lebanon, the United States, and Mexico. She is the coeditor of *Blood into Ink: South Asian and Middle Eastern Women Write War* and the editor of *Living in America: Poetry and Fiction by South Asian American Writers*.

Lynne Sharon Schwartz is the author of two story collections and a nonfiction book, *Ruined by Reading: A Life in Books*. Her five novels include *The Fatigue Artist, Disturbances in the Field*, and *Leaving Brooklyn*. She lives in New York City.

Gary Soto was born and raised in Fresno, California. He is a prizewinning poet and essayist as well as a children's book author and producer of short films for Spanish-speaking children. His 1990 collection, *Baseball in April and Other Stories*, was named as the American Library Association's Best Book for Young Adults.

Amy Tan was born in Oakland, California, in 1952, two and a half years after her parents immigrated to the United States. She is the author of *The Kitchen God's Wife* and *The Joy Luck Club*, which was a finalist for the National Book Award and the National Book Critics Circle Award, and which was made into a film in 1993.

Helena María Viramontes was born in East Los Angeles in 1954 to a family of eleven. She is the author of *The Moths and Other Stories*. She lives and teaches in Irvine, California, and is the coordinator of the Los Angeles Latino Writers Association.

Sylvia A. Watanabe was born in Hawaii on the island of Maui. She is the author of a collection of stories, *Talking to the Dead*, and coeditor with Carol Bruchac of *Home to Stay: An Anthology of Asian American Women's Fiction*. Her work has appeared in numerous journals and anthologies.

Afaa Michael Weaver (formerly Michael S. Weaver) worked for fifteen years as a blue-collar factory worker in his native Baltimore, Maryland. His sixth book of poetry is *Talisman* and his new play is *Candy Lips & Hallelujah*. The recipient of a 1998 Pew fellowship for his poetry, he holds an endowed chair at Simmons College.

Index ✐